Richard Stuart Wood, a retired civil
servant, was born at Monken Hadley in
Hertfordshire, but has lived for more than
thirty years in the West Country, the last
twenty of them in Cornwall.

A lifelong country-lover and active
participant in a wide variety of sports, he
now divides his time between writing
historical novels, painting in water
colours, playing golf, and walking the
Cornish coastal footpath.

The Riding Officer

Richard Stuart Wood

BANTAM BOOKS
TORONTO · NEW YORK · LONDON · SYDNEY · AUCKLAND

THE RIDING OFFICER

A BANTAM BOOK 0 553 17285 9

First publication in Great Britain

PRINTING HISTORY
Bantam edition published 1987

This book is set in 10/11 pt Baskerville
by Colset Private Limited, Singapore.

Bantam Books are published by Transworld Publishers Ltd.,
61–63 Uxbridge Road, Ealing, London W5 5SA, in Australia
by Transworld Publishers (Australia) Pty. Ltd., 15–23 Helles
Avenue, Moorebank, NSW 2170, and in New Zealand by
Transworld Publishers (N.Z.) Ltd., Cnr. Moselle and
Waipareira Avenues, Henderson, Auckland.

Made and printed in Great Britain by
Cox & Wyman Ltd., Reading, Berks.

To my loving wife, Margaret, without whose support and forbearance this book could not have been written

Acknowledgements

I would like to record my special thanks to; my very good friend and 'conseiller nautique', Commander John Pearson, with whom I have shared many amusing hours of relaxation on both land and sea;

also to my fellow Cornish writer, Jane Jackson, for her enthusiastic encouragement and help at all times;

and finally, to the Librarians at Falmouth Library who have cheerfully suffered my frequent requests for authentic background reading.

CHAPTER ONE

Free Trading

The weather was steadily worsening as *Percuel Rose* quietly nosed her way out of Roscoff harbour. To most sailors, the lowering clouds and the ominous whistle of wind in shrouds might have induced an uncomfortable flutter in the pit of the stomach. But to Amos Penberth, skipper and owner of the lugger, it was sweet music. By the time they reached the Cornish coast the weather, he hoped, would have become so foul that the Riding Officer and all his colleagues in the Preventive service would be safely tucked up in their beds – exactly where he wanted them. And on a night like this it was highly unlikely that a Revenue cruiser would be out patrolling the Cornish coastline. After all, even officers of the Crown were human beings – especially where warmth and comfort were concerned.

So, Amos Penberth felt he had little to worry about. For nearly ten years he had been making regular three or four-day 'fishing' trips over to Roscoff, and bringing back those little luxuries of life – a drop of brandy to keep out the winter cold, a fill of 'baccy for the old clay pipe, silks and laces to charm a lady's heart and, of course, the necessary wherewithal for making a steaming hot cup of tea. So far, apart from one or two narrow squeaks, his luck had held and he had never been caught.

It was also in his favour that the Collector of Customs at Falmouth was well-known to be sympathetic towards the gentlemen of the trade, and provided you were careful not to flaunt his authority too openly, he would normally leave you to get on with your business while he made token displays of getting on with his – just enough, that is, to keep his superiors in London reasonably satisfied. In that way he managed to hold on to his job – at the same time keeping his cellar well stocked.

Nevertheless, you couldn't be too sure. You had to have your wits about you all the time. Every now and again some member of Parliament would get up in the House of Commons and draw attention to the enormous loss of revenue arising from the smuggling of contrabrand. Out of the six hundred thousand gallons of brandy imported into the country, four hundred thousand gallons it was said had come in through the back door without so much as a penny piece of duty being paid on them. And every time that sort of statement was made, Collectors of Customs throughout the country would receive a disturbing prod from higher authority. The Falmouth Collector was no exception. He would immediately feel obliged to mount a special display of vigilance. Someone had to be caught – somehow.

So as Amos Penberth set course for the Helford estuary, and as he watched the murky outline of the Brittany coast dissolve into the distance, he was aware of the familiar sensation of excitement. It was always the same; every time he made a run.

The outward journey was different – relaxed, good-humoured; to everyone else they were just fishing. But once the goods were on board, whether it be finest white cognac in four-gallon tubs, or tobacco, tea, laces and silks, – once these highly dutiable goods were safely stowed and concealed from prying eyes, then the very timbers of the ship seemed invested with a new tension, a mounting excitement. The adventure was on.

It was not only the money – a successful run would yield at least a hundred per cent profit – it was the feeling of comradeship; the stimulating pulse-quickening anticipation of a dangerous undertaking successfully carried through together, and plumb under the noses of authority.

Unlike some, Amos Penberth had no real need to do it. His farm, Treworden, in the fertile strip between

Constantine and Mawnan provided all that he and his wife, Marianne, really needed. It had been his friendship with those Carter boys, John and Harry, that had done it. Smuggler princes, they had introduced him to the thrill of the chase – as when they had been surprised by a Revenue cutter while making for the safety of Porthleah Cove – escaping only after a nerve-tingling chase by slipping through the narrow channel between the Enys rocks and the entrance to Bessie Bussow's cove. Ever since that hazardous, exciting first experience of a run, Amos Penberth had been converted.

And Bessie Bussow! How could he help laughing at the memory! She who kept *The Kiddleywink* at the top of the cliff above the cove. It was there they had hidden the precious cargo, down in the cellar, while the Revenue officers fruitlessly searched the Carter family's house and outbuildings.

No, it could not be said that the Penberths were in need of money; they had enough for just the two of them. But Marianne, although she seldom expressed her mind on the subject, regarded her husband's smuggling activities with very mixed feelings. True, smuggling provided simple folk with a few of life's little luxuries which they couldn't otherwise afford – a nice cup of tea at a reasonable price, a bit of lace to trim a pretty dress – but it wasn't really right. If the Government said it wasn't right, then it couldn't be right, and she was all for keeping on the right side of the law. After all, she would say to herself, 'this new preacher man from up-country, John Wesley his name is – the one that's been stirring them up so frantic with his sermons over there in the pit at Gwennap – well, he's come out strongly against this yer smuggling, so they say, and they reckon he's undoubtedly a man of God. So, it can't be right – now, can it?' And she would convince herself even further by recollecting that there were a lot of very disreputable people engaged in smuggling – even though the Vicar at Breage for one was very upset if he didn't find 'a little something' behind the vestry door after there'd been a successful run.

It was difficult to know what to think, really. But she

wished Amos would give it up, all the same. It was a dangerous occupation at the best of times, even more so now that the soldiers from Exeter had been given instructions to assist the Preventive whenever needed. And it was very important that nothing should happen to Amos – especially now that their first baby was expected in three week's time.

Wisely, Marianne kept her thoughts to herself. She knew all too well they weren't the views of the majority. While most people welcomed the 'gentlemen' with open arms, and in the strictest of secrecy, of course, there were just a few of the older ones who said it was 'Devil's money', and that no good could ever come of it. In her heart of hearts, Marianne Penberth was one of them.

Above everything, Amos loved the sea. Born and brought up on his father's smallholding at Perranuthnoe, his carefree childhood had provided matchless outlets for a roving spirit. From Cudden Point to the far side of Marazion he knew and loved every inch of the rugged seaboard. It was there he had first become friendly with the Carter boys of Porthleah Cove – the 'Cove boys', as they were known, forever playing at soldiers, with John, the eldest brother, always insisting on being 'the King of Prussia', the military idol of the moment. It was from the Carters of Porthleah – or Prussia Cove, as it came to be called that Amos learnt the art of seamanship, the knowledge of tides, winds and currents, and it was they who introduced him to the palpitating, dare-devil excitement of 'the trade'.

And he learned something else from them, as well; honesty and fair dealing in matters of business, coupled with a deep respect for the sea, and the Almightly who made it. And something of Harry Carter's fanatical dislike of swearing on board had rubbed off on Amos Penberth.

It was for this very reason that the conversation of Zephaniah Curnow, crewman at the helm of *Percuel Rose*, was noticeably free from the usual nautical obscenities, as he now addressed Amos.

'Wind be fresh'nin' a bit, I reckon, skipper,' he observed, leaning his thin, wiry frame against the tiller, to

10

keep the lugger on course. 'Us'll be makin' a fast crossin', I wouldn't wonder. Faster than us expected.'

'No matter,' Amos assured him, 'They'll be ready for us whenever we make landfall. I've seen to that.'

Zephaniah grunted agreement, spitting a large gob of reeking, sodden tobacco into the swirling wake of the lugger. The persistent drizzle ran down the rutted lines of his young but much weathered face like a confluence of moorland streams. He peered into the gathering gloom.

'So long as it ted'n they pesky Preventives that be waitin' for we,' he growled, threateningly. But his eyes twinkled as he said it. The very thought of a confrontation with officers of His Majesty's Preventive Service – those goddamned enemies of all decent society – added spice to the night's undertaking. Even so, he would really much prefer them not to interfere, especially on a filthy night like this.

Amos tried to sound cheerful. 'Oh, they'll not be out in this stew, for certain. But even if they are, Tom and the lads'll have the blaze going in good time on Rosemullion.'

Zeph Curnow grinned appreciatively. The skipper was right, of course. Old Tom Pengelly, the gamekeeper up at Treviades, had been acting as spotsman for many years. He knew every cove and inlet from Pendennis right up to Gweek, and no one could make a better blaze than he if things suddenly turned sour.

Yes, he was a good old boy, was Tom – one of the old uns, Amos reflected. You could trust him. And that was important at any time in matters of business. But it had become even more so after the government had brought in that iniquitous Act of 1736 under which any man engaged in smuggling could claim a reward of £50 for every one of his comrades he betrayed to the authorities.

'Ted'n right, though,' Zeph remarked, seeming to interpret Amos's thoughts. 'Ted'n right, this yer Judas money. 'Tis turnin' man agin man, neighbour agin neighbour. Ted'n right.' He shook his head vehemently. 'But old Tom, he'm different,' he went on. 'Why, he'd sooner be found

11

swingin' from a tree than give the game away to they damned Preventives.'

Amos grunted approval. 'And that's probably just where he *would* be found, if ever he were to be so foolish.'

But it wasn't the old uns, like Tom, that gave trouble, Amos reflected, it was the younger ones, growing up with very different ideas. Dangerous ideas, some of them; and it was all due to this Frenchy fellow – what did they call him, Rousseau, or something – always saying and writing things to undermine decent, civilised people. And a right proper no-good fellow he was, too; a real vagabond of a man, with a servant-girl for a mistress and half a dozen illegitimate children littering up the place, so they said. Might not have been so bad by itself – those Frenchies always were a bit peculiar, even if they did know how to make a drop of right good brandy – trouble was that every time our own young fellows made a carrying trip over to Roscoff or St. Malo they came back full of these god-damned revolutionary ideas. 'Jack's (or Jacques) as good as his Master', and all that dangerous rubbish. And coupled with this £50 award to informers – a mighty lot of money to a young fellow – well, you never could be sure.

Zephaniah Curnow was different, though; one of the old brigade was Zeph, though still quite a young man. Turn his hand to anything on the farm – ploughing, milking, hedging, shepherding – and never so much as a squeak of complaint out of him. And good though he was on the land, what Zeph relished most of all was the feel of a ship's planking under his feet – especially when a cargo of contraband was hidden beneath a false bottom. Like his master, he just enjoyed the thrill of it; and that extra guinea Amos gave him every time they made a successful run was more than welcome. Not that he wasn't content in his small cottage at Treworden. His wife, her face like a shining russet apple, always kept everything spotless, besides being ready at any time to help with the harvest or nurse a sickly lamb. But Zeph – he liked to be wherever the action was, especially when there was a whiff of danger.

12

And a surprisingly good seaman he was, too. Although born near the sea at St. Keverne, he'd never had time or opportunity in his youth to test his reactions to the water – always so busy trying to earn a crust on the land. But then he committed the unpardonable sin of 'marrying out of the parish', by choosing for his bride a girl from Manaccan, and they had moved across the Helford River to work for a Master with the salt of Mount's Bay in his veins and a fast-sailing lugger at Porth Navas. Then Zeph quickly discovered in himself the true Cornishman's love of the sea. In a very short time he had become an enthusiastic and competent helmsman. And because he was good with the other lads from the farm who made up the rest of the crew, he quickly established himself as a reliable first mate.

So it was Zeph who had been supervising the stowing of the cargo at Roscoff. No less than eighty four gallon tubs of finest French brandy were now roped together and slung inboard just below the gunwales – ready to be sunk off the Cornish coast if anything should go wrong. Providing all went well – and it nearly always had in the past – the carrying party of about forty men and some twenty ponies would be waiting, concealed from prying eyes by the trees below Mawnan church. After landing, the tubs which cost only £1 each at Roscoff, would be carried up the sloping pathway, past the church – dropping one off at the Vicarage, of course – and then along the lane leading to *The Red Lion Inn*. There they would be smuggled in through the low, cellar door at the back of the inn, to be sold to the eagerly waiting customers at £4 per tub.

'You managed to get a few kegs stowed away this time, then, Zeph,' Amos observed, joining the hunched figure at the tiller.

Zeph nodded, and pointed to the floor boards. 'Under they, Mester,' was all he needed to say.

These smaller kegs would be taken by reliable women 'messengers' – with the keg strapped under the smock, and giving rise to much ribald comment about the sudden increase in girth – and distributed among the special customers who, for the sake of strict privacy, were prepared to pay above the normal price.

'And you got hold of a bit of 'baccy and some fancy stuff as well, I see,' Amos added, glancing at the bill of sale which Zeph handed him.

'Aw, ais,' Zeph affirmed, 'twouldn' seem right to come without some o' they.' He wiped the end of his running nose with the back of his hand, impatiently flicking the contents over the side of the ship. 'And besides,' he added with a twinkle, 'us must always keep the ladies sweet.'

That was Zeph's favourite task – not only keeping the ladies sweet but using his inventiveness in concealing these smaller items of contraband in the most unlikely places; tobacco leaves intertwined with the ship's ropes, silks and laces inserted into hollowed-out sections of the masts. He took an impish delight in the thought of baffling the Revenue men.

'It be blawin' up a fair bit, Skipper, I reckon,' he said, raising his voice above the level of the wind, and glancing up at the scudding clouds. 'We'm in for a fair old blaw, shouldn't wonder.'

It was ten hours or more since they had cleared Roscoff, and during the night the weather had deteriorated unpleasantly – more so than Amos liked. The wind was now howling through the rigging, and all around them the sea, black and ominous, was being whipped up into mountainous, threatening waves. The lugger was being swept forward at a surging pace.

'Us'll have to shorten sail afore long, I reckon,' Zeph shouted above the roar. 'Even now, 'tis all I can do to hold her steady.'

Glancing astern at the menacing waves, Amos moved closer alongside Zeph and gripped the highly varnished tiller. The lugger was undoubtedly becoming difficult to steer; as the crest of each wave passed under her, the rudder was lifted almost clear of the water.

'You're right,' Amos shouted back, 'we'll reeve her down.'

He recognised, all too clearly, that to reeve her down in such a seaway would be no easy task. But it had to be done. Taking a turn of rope around him in case of accident, he gave the order, and Zeph and the rest of the crew immediately went for'ard to close reef the mainsail. That they succeeded in such hostile conditions was a credit to their seamanship, and Amos felt a glow of pride as he watched them battling against the lurching ship and the thrashing wind.

With less canvas, the ship settled down and steered more easily, but the following sea still looked dangerously steep, and a lot of rudder was necessary to keep her on a straight course.

During the night the rising wind had blown away any semblance of mist or drizzle, and the ship was now thrusting northwards with the wind astern and under a clear, starlit sky. A third-quarter moon shed a pale light on the turbulence around them, and each angry breaker bore a foaming, silvered crest as it came surging up under the stern. Far away, over the port bow, the dim outline of the Lizard peninsula could just be discerned jutting out into the English Channel. Otherwise, all was darkness and night.

Then, just when Amos was contemplating the warm prospect of climbing into bed beside Marianne to snatch a few hours sleep before commencing another day's work, he heard Zeph exclaim, exasperatedly;

'God's jellyfish!! Just look at that! Well, I'll be goddam, bloody-well bug. . . .' He hurriedly smothered the oath, remembering the rule about swearing on board.

'What is it, Zeph?'

'Over there,' Zeph bellowed back, pointing over the starboard bow. 'Right there – right on Rosemullion Head.'

He was right, of course. His keen eyesight had spotted the tiny speck of light, low down and seemingly coming right out of the water. Gradually it increased in size and brilliance until, after a little while, it had grown into a strong, steady and clearly visible light.

'Tis Tom's bonfire, all right, Mester,' Zeph shouted again, 'clear as winkin'.'

Amos recognised its significance; the traditional signal from shore party to incoming smuggling vessel that it was unsafe for the goods to be landed. The coast was *not* clear; something untoward was afoot. They were being 'Blazed Off'.

'Aw, 'tis one o' they Preventive bastards about some-where, I shouldn't wonder,' volunteered one of the crew.

'Yarse,' agreed another, 'it be that Ridin' Officer bugger, I 'spec.

Whatever the reason, they were unquestionably being warned not to come ashore. Indeed, Amos knew exactly where Tom Pengelly had prepared his blaze – on the hill running down towards Prisk Cove, and well tucked in below the headland so as not to be visible from Falmouth. Only a few days ago Tom had reported, with a prodigious wink, that he had been doing a bit of 'hedgin' an' cuttin', Maister,' out on Rosemullion Head, ready for a good old burn up, should it be necessary. The fact that it was illegal to light a bonfire anywhere along the coast after dark, and car-ried the possibility of a £100 fine, bothered Tom Pengelly not at all.

'Aw, naw,' he would laugh, 'ted'n no more than a widden of a risk. Well worth it for the sake o' a tub or two o' cousin jacky.'

Besides, in all the years he had been acting as spotsman for Cap'n Penberth, he'd only needed to light his bonfire once previously – when the Riding Officer had been seen entering the *Red Lion*, just before a run was to be made, and there hadn't been enough time for the barmaid to go to work on him.

For Amos, having enjoyed such a long sequence of almost unchallenged success, it was a bitter blow that, on what he had promised Marianne would be his very last run, they should be blazed off.

For the first time since the Carter boys had introduced him to the thrills of smuggling, Amos felt an uncomfortable sense of premonition.

That blaze out there on the headland could mean only

one of two things. Either the Riding Officer, whose every movement would have been closely monitored by Tom Pengelly and his assistants, had been seen in the district; or it meant that a Revenue cruiser was known to be out on the prowl somewhere in the wide sweep of Falmouth Bay. It might even be both.

'What d'you think, Zeph,' Amos asked, speaking low. 'Has someone fallen for the "Thirty pieces of silver"?'

'The Judas money? Could be,' Zeph nodded. ' 'Tis a powerful temptation for some. To cotch Cap'n Penberth on his final run. Could be.'

Whatever the reason for the blaze, its message was abundantly clear. It would be madness to land a cargo in the Helford area just now. Capture by the King's men meant not only the loss of a valuable cargo – the seizure of contraband always provided a much-needed reward for lowly paid Revenue officers – it also meant certain imprisonment for the ship's captain and crew.

'And I don't fancy a spell behind bars just now,' Amos grimaced. 'Not when the baby's due in a few weeks.'

'Aw, naw, Mester,' Zeph spat, 'We'm not lettin' they buggers cotch we! An' we'm not allowin' they stinkers to go cuttin' up *Percuel Rose*, nor neither.'

Zeph was right, of course. A ship taken with contraband on board would systematically be sawn up into three sections so that she could never be used for smuggling again. It was standard procedure – and to someone who loved boats as Amos did it was sacrilege.

But this was no time for such thoughts. A vital decision had to be made – and made quickly. Already the first streaks of dawn were piercing the eastern horizon, and with luck they could just reach the seclusion of Gillan Creek before daybreak. They could lie up there, looking for all the world as though they were just preparing for a fishing trip. Kegs under the floorboards, tobacco, silks and laces cleverly secreted by Zeph would be safe from any prying eyes on the creekside banks, but the tubs were a different matter. They could not so easily be hidden, and if they remained on board, slung along the bulwarks, there was a very serious risk that captain and crew might be caught redhanded. So the decision had to be made, and made quickly, whether to sink the tubs off the mouth of the Helford, or keep them on board, concealing them as much as possible until nightfall; and then run them up to Manaccan.

'What be aimin' to do 'bout they tubs, then, Skipper?' Zeph shouted through the howl of the wind. 'Best have un overboard now, I reckon. Us'll be able to creep un up tomorrow, or next day.'

Zeph sounded so confident; Amos felt less certain. It would be a nuisance to have to sink the tubs now, and then creep them up with the grapnels, later. Apart from the irritating delay, it would double the risks. Two landings would have to be made: first the kegs, silks, laces and tobacco, either tonight or tomorrow; then at some later date, and when the weather was right, the one gallon tubs, having hauled them up from the bottom of the sea and brought them ashore in an innocent-looking fishing boat. True, they were all ready, roped, weighted with stones, and attached to an anchor – but it would be far simpler to run the whole cargo in one operation.

Amos had just made up his mind to risk keeping the tubs on board when the youngest crewman's voice split the roar of the sea with an oath of astonishment.

'Hell's bloody creepers!' he exploded, temporarily forgetting Skipper's orders, 'Would ee ever bloody well believe un!'

'What is it, boy?' Amos shouted sternly, 'What's amiss?'

'There, Cap'n. Over there!' The boy was pointing over the starboard beam. 'And she'm headin' this way, Cap'n. Can ee not sight un, then?'

Amos strained his eyes in the direction indicated. He could see nothing – nothing but the ominous turmoil of the wind-whipped sea.

'What is she then, boy? What can you see?'

The lad cupped both hands around his face to keep out the stinging spindrift from his eyes. 'She'm a cutter, I reckon, Cap'n. One o' they Revenue buggers, looks like. And her's on to we, Cap'n. Her's on to we.'

The boy was right; uncomfortably accurate in his assumption. Within the next ten minutes, the sky lightened and the distance between the two craft had narrowed enough for Amos to rocognize the familiar outline of a Falmouth Revenue cruiser. Almost certainly she was at the South West end of a normal patrol across Falmouth Bay and the Helford River approaches, and she was keeping well off-shore because of the weather.

Despite what the lad had said, it seemed at first that the cruiser might not yet have spotted *Percuel Rose*, and Amos felt reasonably hopeful that the reserve suit of dark brown sails which he always set when on contraband business had made the lugger sufficiently invisible to enable them to slip into Gillan creek unobserved.

But this optimistic appraisal was quickly shattered when the boy shouted; 'She'm alterin' course, Cap'n. I telled ee she were on to we.'

There could be no room for doubt. The Revenue cruiser was clearly intent on intercepting the incoming lugger.

For Amos, the premonition of danger grew uncomfortably stronger. It solidified, and settled in the pit of his stomach. How ironic that this should be happening now, just when he had promised his wife to make this his very last participation in 'the trade'. After the birth of their much longed-for child, he would abandon all connection with smuggling; he would be content to settle down to being a good farmer. Just one more run – one more really successful and profitable trip across the Channel – and after that he would have nothing more to do with it.

And now, on the very verge of success, he had to go and pick up this accursed Revenue cruiser.

'What be aimin' to do, then, Skipper,' Zeph enquired, a note of anxiety creeping into his voice.

'Give 'em the slip,' Amos replied with a cheerfulness far removed from his innermost feelings. 'After all, what was *Percuel Rose* built for if it wasn't to outstrip any confounded

Revenue cruiser. We'll teach 'em a lesson,' he shouted above the wind. 'We'll just show 'em what the *Rose* can do. We'll make for Porthleah. The Carter boys'll see us right. And what's more, lads,' he went on, making sure the younger crewmen could hear, 'there'll be a right good welcome up at Bessie Bussow's *Kiddleywink*, and plenty of warming grog and grub to go with it.'

This assurance brought forth a welcoming cheer from the crew. Fortified by their infectious disregard for danger, Amos brought the lugger round on to a port tack and set course for the Lizard.

But he had left it late. In the murky light of that cold, unfriendly dawn the outline of the Revenue cruiser was becoming clearer, sharper, her grey-white sails giving her the eerie appearance of a phantom ship. Disturbingly, she seemed to be keeping pace with *Percuel Rose*.

'Tis the weight o' they tubs that be slawin' we down,' Zeph suggested. 'Us'd better have un over while us can, Mester.'

Amos hesitated, reluctant to let go the precious cargo. But it had to be now or never. The Revenue ship was clearly on course to intercept them somewhere off Porthoustock, and unless the lugger could make more headway, they were in danger of being trapped on the wrong side of the Manacles. Zeph was right; the tubs would have to go. They had been well buoyed; they could be crept up in a day or two's time.

In response to the Skipper's order, the tubs were strung out over the washstrakes, and after a few moments came Zeph's answering shout, 'Ready to let go tubs, Sir.'

'Right-ho, then. Let go tubs.'

Immediately the line of small casks began streaming astern, rapidly gobbled up by voracious waves before being dragged down to the sea bed by the heavy intersecting stones and finally held fast by the anchor. The crop had been well and truly sown.

With the tubs gone, and the ship once more trimmed for fast sailing, *Percuel Rose* began to pick up speed. Even so, she did not appear to be out-distancing the Revenue cutter quite so convincingly as Amos would have wished. He was being manoeuvred into a trap. The advancing cutter was effectively blocking his seaward escape. The murderous rocks off Manacle Point lay ahead on the starboard bow, and all the while the *Rose* was being driven closer and closer to the lee shore.

There was only one real chance of escape. Amos was already forming a plan. First, he must bamboozle the Revenue men into thinking the contraband goods were to be landed either at Porthallow or the secluded little shingle beach at Porthkerris. He must dangle before them the lucrative bait of a valuable seizure; he must lure them inshore as far as he possibly dare.

Then, at the very last moment, he would make a dash for the narrow channel between the Manacle rocks and Manacle Point. Although *Percuel Rose* had a fairly shallow draft for'ard, it was over 5 feet aft. Even at high water the risk was daunting; on a falling tide it was distinctly hazardous.

But it was the only real hope of giving the King's men the slip; the commander of one of Her Majesty's vessels would never dare follow *Percuel Rose* through the Manacles – especially in weather like this.

Once through the channel, Amos would go about and make for the open sea, giving himself enough sea room to clear Black Head and round the Lizard. From then on it would be a straight run down to Prussia Cove – and all the comforts of Bessie Bussow's *Kiddleywink*.

It was a bold plan – it had to be – and so far it appeared to be succeeding. The cutter was doing exactly what Amos wanted; it was closing in.

Having delayed for as long as he dared, Amos placed one hand on the Good Luck horseshoe affixed to the sternpost and then set the lugger, close-hauled, on a course fractionally inshore of the Manacle rocks. His beloved *Percuel Rose* responded superbly. Dipping and rising like a praying Muslim, and shuddering from stem to stern each time she was hit by the gigantic waves, she lunged forward on her precarious dash for freedom.

All around was foaming chaos. The full force of the Atlantic crashed against the unyielding granite of the Cornish coast. Each gigantic wave, having failed to demolish its objective, was sent back, reeling with cascading defiance, to joust with its oncoming successor. But still the *Rose* kept going – gamely holding her course. As they neared the Carn Dhu group of rocks, the most fearsome of the Manacle group, Amos braced himself against hearing the sound he most dreaded – the ghastly scrape, shudder and screech of the hull's timbers being torn by jagged, barnacled rock.

But it did not come – at least, not as he feared. Just once, when the stern dipped steeply in the trough of a vicious coamer, he felt an ominous judder along the tiller. Either the keelson or the rudder must have struck something. But it was only momentary; all he could do was to hope – and pray.

Then, at last, they were through the hazardous channel. The wicked Carn Dhu rocks were gradually slipping astern. The worst of the ordeal was over.

Amos held his course until well clear of Dean Point and while still well short of the rocks off Lowland Point, he decided to go about and head for the open sea.

'Ready about, lads,' he commanded, a note of joyous relief in his voice. Then, 'Lee – O,' as he put the held down hard a – lee.

But as he lowered the tiller handle – deliberately made loose-fitting fore and aft on the rudder head to facilitate clearance of the mizzen mast – and raised it again to pass over the washstrake on the starboard quarter, he felt the usual, tremendous pressure of water against rudder suddenly give way. Momentarily, he thought the tiller had been forced off the rudder head.

Then, in a flash, the full extent of the catastrophe struck him. The rudder arms had sheared; within seconds the whole blade had broken loose.

At the worse possible moment, the ship had gone out of control.

Immediately, Amos let fly main sheets, and using only

the mizzen sail, he tried desperately to keep the ship head to wind. The crew were already making frantic efforts to get out the oars to regain control, but before they had time to make any impact the once proud *Precuel Rose* lay like a stricken bird, her sails flapping uselessly, her hull now broadside on to the full fury of the pounding seas.

Amid the horrifying sounds of howling wind, scraping, screeching, splintering timbers – like the music of some demented orchestra let loose out of Hell – the beautiful *Rose* was picked up and smashed against the rocks off Manacle Point, flinging Amos and his crew into the merciless, seething turmoil around them.

Though each man fought ferociously for his life, only Zeph Curnow survived. Battered, bleeding, and knocked almost senseless by the thundering breakers, he was finally, miraculously, swept ashore onto the shingle of Godrevy Cove. It was among friends at St. Keverne that eventually he found succour.

It fell to him also to break the news to Amos's widow, Marianne Penberth.

Two days later, Marianne gave birth to her son. Born prematurely – brought on by the shock, so the Doctor said – he would never see his father. But even though a bit on the small side, he was a fine, healthy boy.

His name, his mother said, would be Ashley.

CHAPTER TWO

Tainted Proceeds

The senselessness of it all; that was what struck Marianne Penberth so strongly. He was a good man, was Amos; more important, he was *her* man; and nobody would ever be allowed to say anything against him. Not in her hearing, at any rate. But he really ought not to have put himself in that kind of danger. After all, it wasn't that they were in need of the money – even though she had to admit, in all honesty, that it was rather useful to have a little bit put by for emergencies. Like having a baby, for instance; and having to bring him up all on your own. Not that she expected to get anything from that last fatal run. Those kegs beneath the floorboards, like the beautiful *Percuel Rose* herself, would have been smashed to pieces on the Manacle rocks, and the silks, laces and tobacco would be hopelessly ruined by the salt water.

In fact, as Marianne cuddled in her arms the pink and white bundle that was her baby son, she hardly dared contemplate the future. True, the doctor who had brought her baby into the world, and who also happened to be her landlord, had shown every possible kindness and sympathy. But the fact remained that the rent was owing, and the farm hands had to be paid, somehow.

Zeph, as Marianne had expected, had shown his usual resilience. Within a few weeks he was back on the farm, scarred and shaken, but determined to act as though nothing exceptional had occurred. He had been devoted to Amos and had made up his mind that, come what may, he would stand staunchly beside his master's widow.

24

Ever since the time of the wreck, the weather had continued in ferocious mood. It constantly reminded him of that fearful dawn; it also prevented him from completing that little bit of unfinished business that was so much on his mind.

Then, one evening in early November, while Marianne was bathing her baby son in the circular, low-sided tin bath in front of the range, there was a discreet knock on the back door. It was Zeph, looking unusually spruce in a freshly laundered farm smock, and with a clean red-and-white spotted kerchief round his neck. His right hand was kept firmly behind his back.

'Evenin', Missus,' he began shyly, doffing his best Sunday hat awkwardly with his left hand. 'I hope I baint disturbin' ee.'

Marianne smiled her slow, friendly smile as she shook her head. 'Of course not, Zeph. You know you're always welcome.'

Zeph clattered across the stone-flagged kitchen floor and knelt reverently beside the tin bath. He gazed down at the fair-haired, frog-like figure as it wriggled and squirmed in the warm water. For a long time Zeph remained kneeling, a half smile of wonder and affection creasing his still young but weather-beaten face. His gnarled, work-roughened left hand hovered over the edge of the bath, as though it could hardly restrain itself from touching the baby's skin. Marianne smiled again as the hand went up, first to one eye and then the other, to dash away an involuntary tear. 'Poor little mite,' she heard Zeph mutter, 'poor little babe!' And then, almost inaudibly, he added, 'But he'll not suffer. I'll see to it.'

Slowly he rose to his feet and looked straight at Marianne. 'I've brought ee somethin', Missus,' he said quietly. 'Somethin' that may help ee out a bit.'

The solemn note in his voice alerted Marianne. 'What is it, then, Zeph?' She tried to see what was behind his back.

' 'Tis the proceeds, Missus. I was afraid un might have gone stinkibus, but they'm all right. Us got em all up, in the end.'

25

Marianne frowned – puzzled. 'Stinkibus? What are you talking about, Zeph. I don't quite understand.

' ''Stinkibus'', Missus. That's what us do call a tub o' brandy that's been too long in the sea. ''Stinkibus'', that's what we do call un. But they wasn't, and us was able to sell 'em. Made 'andzum provvitt, too, us did. Mester Amos, he bought un in 'Rusco' at £1 a tub, an' we do sell un at £4, as usual. So, us made a provvitt of three poun' a tub for ee.' He looked up from beneath his shaggy brows. 'An' yur it all ez – all of it in this yur bag.' He proudly produced a battered old leather pouch from behind his back, and placed it on the kitchen table. 'My figurin' edn too good, mind, but I reckon,' he scratched his ear, 'that eighty tubs at three pun' a time makes about two-forty pun'. Anyways, that's what's in the bag, thur, an us hopes tez all right.'

For a moment, Marianne was speechless. She stared at Zeph, incredulously. When breaking the news of the wreck to her he had clearly implied that the ship and all its cargo was a total loss. In any case, she knew enough about ''the trade'' to understand that the difference between the Roscoff price and the landed selling price was never entirely profit. The shore party deputed to carry the tubs up from the beach got ten shillings a night; the owners of the pack animals would have to be paid something for the loan of their beasts.

'But Zeph,' she said eventually, 'that can't be right. I thought you said everything was lost when the ship . . .' she clutched at her throat, and looked away from him, momentarily overcome with emotion, '. . . when the ship foundered,' she concluded, almost in a whisper. 'I thought you said everything was lost.'

'Well, I dedn think it right to tell ee just then, zee. I dedn know for certin that us'd be able to save they tubs. Mester gave the order for the ''crop to be sowed'', as we say, and so we did sink un some ways off Polnare, if ee knows where that's to. Well then,' he continued, warming to his subject, 'as ee must know, the weather's been that freakish ever since, that us didn't dare to go out an' creep un up, zee. But soon as it relented, Tom Pengelly and several of th'others an' me, us went out night afore last an' crep un up, zee.'

He was obviously enjoying the telling of his story, despite the tragic consequences of the original undertaking, and Marianne wisely allowed him to continue. The baby focussed his eyes on the craggy, wind-burnt features above him, and gurgled approval.

'Us brought un ashore in the pullin' boats,' Zeph went on, 'and when us got 'em up to the *Red Lion*, us all agreed among ourselves, like, that whatever we could make of the tubs would be for ee . . .' he glanced down at the squirming figure in the bath tub, and added '. . . and the bebby.'

Marianne studied Zeph's face. She had never before seen such softness and compassion in his features. He gazed lovingly at the wriggling baby, inviting him to grasp the craggy finger with which he gently prodded the little round tummy, and Marianne realised for the first time just how much it would have meant to Zeph to have had children of his own.

'Maybe the money'll come in handy for the bebby's eddication, later on, p'raps,' Zeph murmured. ' 'T' would be what Mester would have wanted, I fancy.'

Marianne thought for a moment. Zeph was right, of course; Amos would certainly have wished any son of his to be given a good education, and the £240 would probably be more than sufficient for that – especially if, in the meanwhile, it was carefully invested in land and stock. But it was tainted money; there could be no denying that. Smuggling was against the law, and any money obtained from it must be tainted – even though, as in this case, it had been obtained at such a terrible cost. At the same time, it would be utterly churlish to refuse to accept it, Marianne knew that. Watching Zeph's obvious devotion to his Master's baby son, and realising the sacrifices which had been made in order that she should have the money, she knew she must gratefully accept it.

Although it seemed ludicrous to be contemplating anything so high-minded and so remote as an 'education' for her tiny baby, Marianne said quietly, 'Very well, Zeph, I'll be pleased to do as you say. The money you and your helpers have so kindly given me shall be put to the boy's education when the time comes.'

Zeph nodded, approvingly. It pleased him to think of the Master's son 'gettin' a bit o' larnin' ' – although he had only a very hazy idea of what that would entail. Going away 'to college', he supposed; like the Doctor's son. And being able to talk on equal terms with the Vicar's family. That would be a really worthwhile achievement. Best of all would be if 'young master Ashley' could one day be seen cavorting with the Squire's daugthers up at Trevadne. That would really set the village talking! The idea began to grow on him.

'An' I could.teach un a bit 'bout varmin',' he muttered, almost inaudibly, 'Teach un to ride – an' to shoot – so's he'd be upalong o' the gentry.'

Marianne smiled. She could see that Zeph had it all planned. Already he was visualising for himself a supremely important role in the boy's upbringing.

'But I'll tell you one thing,' she announced firmly. 'There'll be no more smuggling. Do you understand that, Zeph?'

The memory of that last fatal expedition was still painfully fresh in Zeph's mind. He winced visibly, recollecting that it was not only the Master they had lost but those young farm lads that had gone with him, as well. The Penberths of Treworden were not the only family in the village suffering bereavement. And Zeph felt at least a measure of responsibility.

Beneath puckered brows, he looked up at his Mistress. 'I understand,' he said. 'There's to be no more o' that.'

Marianne studied him, thoughtfully. Was that hang-dog expression on his face quite genuine; did he realise fully that the one thing her mind was absolutely made up about was that she would never, never lose her precious baby – as she had lost her husband – in the pursuit of that devilish thing they called 'the trade'? Never!

She fixed him with a penetrating stare. Then she said slowly, pointedly: 'I want you, Zephaniah Curnow, to promise me that you will never, ever help or encourage my son to have anything watsoever to do with smuggling. Will you promise me that?'

For a moment Zeph hesitated. For a man who loved the sea and thrived on excitement, it was a hard condition she was imposing. But then, staring at the stone-flagged kitchen floor, and with ill-disguised reluctance, he finally nodded his head. 'Yus,' he conceded, 't'is only fair that I should grant ee thaat.'

CHAPTER THREE

Trevadne

The seasons came and went; the years rolled by and Zephaniah Curnow kept his word.

From the first, shattering days of her widowhood, Marianne had realised that she could not run the farm by herself. Although it was not a large holding, and despite the fact that she was a farmer's daughter, she did not feel she had sufficient knowledge or enthusiasm to do so. And yet, she must retain the tenancy; not only because she needed the income to support herself and her son, but because she wanted something to hand on to the boy when he was old enough – something firmly land-based which would keep him away from the sea. Doctor Cantley had been very good about the tenancy. He had great faith in her ability, he said; he would allow her to keep on the farm until the boy was of an age to decide whether or not he wished to be a farmer. And Sir Andrew Mackenzie, the new squire up at nearby Trevadne, had been very kind and sympathetic. Having only recently lost his wife from an obscure disease while out in the West Indies, he had been particularly understanding. He had helped Marianne with farming advice, and had allowed her the use of some of his own men.

But Marianne did not really like the outdoor life. She felt far more at home among the shining copper pots and pans in the kitchen, and beneath the well-cured hams hanging from the beams in the ceiling, than ever she did in the dung and straw of the cobwebbed cow house. And though she had always helped Amos at lambing time, and she knew she was good with the baby calves, she had sensibly decided that this was not enough. So she had made Zeph Curnow her farm manager.

And Zeph, in return, never lacked enthusiasm. With his quick, energetic movements he would stride out across the Treworden fields to bring the cows home for milking. And almost as soon as he was able to walk the young Ashley Penberth would be trotting contentedly at his side. Zeph would take the boy with him when he went 'out over' to see the sheep up at High Cross, and then, with the Welsh collie's white-tipped tail streaming in the wind like a ship's burgee, they would bring down the ewes to the home field for tupping or lambing. Sometimes, if the weather was right and the farm work not too demanding, they would go down to the Helford river to fish from the rocks below Calamansack.

Despite the age gap, they became inseparable companions. Zeph had always longed for a son of his own. His wife, Hannah, also yearned exceedingly. But, as like her biblical namesake, the Lord had shut up her womb and she did not conceive. For Hannah there were the children of the village, who found their way into her shining kitchen, drawn there by the irresistible baking smells which always seemed to be wafting out of it. She loved them all in her cosy, comfortable way.

For Zeph, there was Ashley. The fair haired, curly-headed child – born, as it were, with the echo of thunderous seas and splintering timbers forever ringing in his ears – was growing into a fine sturdy boy. He had no desire for any companion other than Zeph – because Zeph, as is so often the way with those who have been deprived of them, had a special way with children. Ashley would sit contentedly beside him, tucked into the shelter of the hedge, just watching the flock of long-wool sheep peacefully graze the Treworden meadows. Zeph would entertain him with anecdotes about foxes and badgers, rabbits and stoats, and teach him how to distinguish a bird not only by its feathers but by its call and its flight. The boy was enchanted; he scarcely ever left Zeph's side.

If, sometimes, Marianne wondered as she watched from the kitchen window while her stocky little son helped Zeph to clean out the cow shed, manfully wielding a pitchfork several sizes too big for him and slavishly imitating his mentor's every action – if sometimes Marianne wondered whether her son was too much in the company of her rough-hewn farm manager, she never showed it. True, deep in her heart she cherished ambitions for her only child far beyond the confines of Treworden. Nevertheless she was eternally grateful for all that Zeph was teaching the boy – so long as it did not include any trips to Roscoff!

On that score, she had no occasion to worry. Zeph was scrupulously keeping his promise. Never a word about smuggling – not within Ashley's hearing, at any rate. Not even when he took him out in the dinghy and taught him how to row. It was fishing they would be about, nothing more. Later on he would be teaching him how to sail, but they would never go beyond the mouth of the Helford. Not for a long time, anyway.

So Marianne had little to worry her in that direction. It was the boy's schooling that exercised her mind just at present; that 'eddication' for which Zeph and his confederates in crime had so unselfishly given up their share of the unlawfully gained £240.

It was while she was pondering the question of Ashley's future that she had a surprise visit from Sir Andrew MacKenzie.

No one in the village knew very much about Sir Andrew – but what they did know they liked. His craggy, red-whiskered features and his stocky build seem to confirm his Gaelic origins, but there was a lightness of touch and an exuberance of character which belied the accepted image of the dour Highland Scot. Like the Cornish he was proud of his ancestry. Although he seldom spoke of it unasked, he was nevertheless very willing to remind the interested listener that the MacKenzies were out in force with King James IV at the battle of Flodden, where the flower of the Scottish nobility was cut to shreds, and the MacKenzie chieftain narrowly escaped capture by the English. He would also remember proudly that the MacKenzies fought staunchly for Mary, Queen of Scots, at the battle of Langside, and then, warming to his subject, he would give a graphic description of how the MacKenzie clan chief was badly wounded at the battle of Glenshiel in 1719 before escaping to France where he remained, licking his wounds, until pardoned some seven years later.

It was this French influence on the family, Sir Andrew liked to think, which had given him such a strong partiality for the best French brandy. The discerning observer might also have concluded that it was this same influence which had introduced that special lightness of touch to his manner.

But the village only knew him as an energetic squire who was a good employer and dealt fairly with the local traders. It was known he had spent some time in the West Indies, and that he still had business interests there. Exactly what was the extent of those interests was not known. He had left his native Ross-shire because it was thought that the milder climate in Cornwall might improve his wife's health. She had just come through a difficult pregnancy with their second daughter, and when the extensive property known as Trevadne came into the market, Sir Andrew became its new owner.

Almost exactly a year after Marianne had lost her husband in the shipwreck off Manacle Point, Lady MacKenzie died. She and her two little daughters were accompanying Sir Andrew on a business trip to Trinidad when she was suddenly taken ill. She died within a few days, so they said, and Sir Andrew was left to bring up a ten-month old baby girl and her three-year old elder sister.

It was during the early part of his shattering bereavement that he came to know Marianne. They could understand, if not share, each other's sorrow; and if the difference in their social standing – he was the squire while she was only a tenant farmer's widow – at first precluded anything resembling a close friendship, there nevertheless grew between them a bond of increasing sympathy. He would drop in to see her after a day's hunting, warming himself in front of the kitchen range, and discussing anything and everything to do with the farming of Treworden. He felt strangely relaxed and at ease in that homely atmosphere – despite the resilience of the straight-backed, stiffly upright wooden arm chair with its much sat-upon, crumpled cushion which seemed only to increase a creeping numbness in the sitter's bottom. There was a timeless charm about that old kitchen, he thought; the blackened oak beams near the chimney, the ever-present circular pan on the Cornish range from which, in the morning, would be skimmed the day's offering of thick, yellow-crusted clotted cream; the solid, well-scrubbed kitchen table with its pile of crumpled clothes at one end smelling delightfully clean and fresh but waiting to be ironed and darned; the all-pervading smell of milk, straw and manure that persistently found its way in from the cowhouse. It was peaceful, it was unhurried. So different from his own surroundings at Trevadne.

And yet, he would not have it otherwise. Trevadne, with its tasteful elegance, reflected the elusive charm of his deceased wife. It was her creation, everything except the walls and roof. Even the gardens had been laid out to her design. She had seen the possibilities of what, otherwise, was a quite ordinary farm house overlooking the Helford river, and she had transformed it into an imposing squire's residence. It was exactly the kind of home he had always wanted – solid, four-square yet somehow hauntingly mysterious – and she had made it. When she was snatched from him, his immediate reaction was to reject any idea of ever returning to the home which she had so embracingly invested with her own personality. He could never forget her in those surroundings. Every corner must contain her shadow, her footstep must echo in each doorway, and throughout the house there would always linger the fragrance of her individuality. But after the first shock had worn off, he knew that he could never leave Trevadne. He would feel nearer to her there than anywhere else – and above all he wanted to be near her.

So, resolutely withstanding the temptation to wallow in his own misfortune, he picked himself up, physically and mentally, and sailed back to Cornwall. After all, he kept telling himself, he was still a comparatively young man, and somehow he must find a way of making a life of fulfilment, not only for himself but far more importantly for his two lovely little daughters. There was Jeannie, his beloved first-born; she with her dark, curly hair and her shining, mischievous eyes. In her colouring she most favoured her mother, but her impudence and love of devilment, he reflected, she must have acquired from the irrepressible MacKenzies of Highland temper.

Then there was the baby – Alethea. Her hair was the colour of ripening barley, straighter than Jeannie's and thinner, and her eyes seemed to reflect the mysteries of some far off sun-drenched rock pool. She was his special pet, perhaps; but he never would have admitted it.

How lucky he was to have found Bess Trethewy to look after them. Although boasting a Cornish name, she came from a Tavistock family, and she nannied the two little girls with that special brand of Dartmoor balm which can turn mountains into molehills and soothe away the very nastiest of bumps. Though nothing can completely replace a mother's love, Bess Trethewy surrounded her two charges with a warmth of affection and understanding which even a mother might had found difficult to excel.

But now that they were growing up – Jeannie was ten and Alethea was just seven – Sir Andrew had engaged Miss Agnes Proudfoot to be their governess and it was about this very subject that he had dropped in to see Marianne.

'Well, what are ye planning to do about your lad's education?' he asked, changing the subject from the depressing topic of the downward trend in cattle and sheep prices. 'I can't say I think overmuch of the local facilities. I wondered if ye'd like him to come over and share our Miss Proudfoot. After all, she might as well be teaching three of them instead of just my two.' And when he saw Marianne hesitate, he added rather gruffly. 'There'd be no question of fees or any nonsense like that. My girls would be delighted to have him, I'm sure.' He gave a short, embarrassed laugh. 'They'd soon be looking upon him as a little brother, I wouldn't wonder. Just what they need – especially Jeannie. She's a proper little madam. Needs someone to stand up to her, I fancy.'

'Well, I don't know, I'm sure,' Marianne dumurred. 'It's very kind of you, Sir Andrew, but I don't think the children even know each other, do they? Your two little girls might not like my Ashley. And then what?'

'In that case, my dear Mrs. Penberth,' Sir Andrew chortled, 'I think we'd just have to knock their heads together and put some sense into them!'

The following Monday morning Marianne was waving goodbye to her eight-year-old son as he set forth on his moorland pony, Tiger, to ride over to Trevadne for his first lesson with the MacKenzie girls. The ever faithful Zeph, mounted on one of the light farm horses, was at his side. Zeph would see the boy safely there, and then ride back to continue his normal day's work.

Ashley was not looking forward to this change in his carefree days on the farm with Zeph. When his mother had informed him of the new arrangement he had just looked at her with those large blue, expressive eyes of his and said, with all the boyish disgust he could muster, the one word, 'Girls!' Then he had run off across the yard to the barn where Zeph was paring the foot of a lame ewe.

Now, here he was, with a pencil and an exercise book in his saddle bag, setting off on the long road which his mother called 'getting him an education'. An education indeed! Whatever could a girl's governess teach that Zeph couldn't teach him far better – and with much more fun, too.

'You'm a bright lad,' Zeph was saying, as if in answer to his thoughts, 'Messus is right when she sez you need a good eddication. Things is goin' on around us all the time so fast that us has just go to be eddicated, see. Tedn no good pertendin' otherwise. So, you just be a good boy an' larn as much as ee can, see, and then – ' Zeph emphasised the point with a broad wink, 'and then you'll be fitted to do . . . well, to do all manner o' things, see.'

Ashley decided to keep his own council about that. In the meanwhile he accepted that he must bow to his mother's wishes, and as the imposing façade of Trevadne loomed ahead of them, he prepared himself for the ordeal of meeting his two school mates.

An imposing-looking flunkey opened the front door in response to Zeph's knock. He glanced haughtily at the rough-and-ready figure of the farm worker, and then peered down his long nose at the neatly dressed boy on the doorstep.

'This is Mester Ashley,' Zeph announced, thrusting forward almost menacingly, as though to protect the boy from this intimidating figure. 'Mester Amos' boy.'

The footman merely inclined his head. 'Come this way, Master Ashley, if you please.'

With a backward, nostalgic glance at Zeph, Ashley followed the footman into a large, panelled hall, and then along a broad passage towards a half-opened door at the end. The hall, Ashley noticed, was liberally decorated around the walls with the stuffed heads of animals killed in the chase, most of them red deer. The passage walls were hung with colourful sporting prints. The whole effect was impressive, and the young Ashley felt uncomfortably overawed by the time the footman swept aside the half-open door and announced, 'Master Ashley Penberth.'

The room which Sir Andrew had allocated for his daughter's education was his study. He had done this not because he was an exceptionally unselfish man but simply because, being essentially an outdoor person, he seldom used it himself. It was a pleasant room, lined from floor to ceiling with leather bound volumes, and had a long, highly polished oak refectory table running lengthwise down the middle of the room. Tall, leaded windows looked out on to the rose garden, and the whole room smelt engagingly of old leather.

At one end of the table sat Miss Proudfoot – neat, bespectacled and smiling. On either side of her were the two girls.

37

'Come along in then, Ashley,' Miss Proudfoot welcomed brightly. 'Don't be shy. First of all, come and be introduced. This is Jeannie. . . .' The girl with the lovely dark curls flashed him a smile remarkably provocative for a ten-year old. Ashley blushed. His skin began to tickle beneath his hair. He wanted to scratch it, but daren't. He bowed, gravely, as his mother had taught him – and he felt a fool.

'. . . and this is Alethea,' Miss Proudfoot concluded.

The small, fair-haired little girl quietly rose from her chair and slowly walked to where Ashley stood fumbling with his exercise book and pencil. She took hold of his hand, and led him round to her side of the table.

'You come with me, Ashley,' she invited, in a voice so soft that it seemed no more than the rustle of a feather. 'You shall sit on my side.'

As he sat down in the leather upholstered chair beside her, he shyly smiled his thanks. And as he did so he looked straight into her lovely clear blue eyes.

Instinctively he recognised a friend.

CHAPTER FOUR

To catch a falling leaf

For Ashley Penberth the days now drifted pleasantly by. Each morning he would ride over for lessons at Trevadne, and each morning he became increasingly aware of the ever-changing magic of the Helford river countryside. Often, especially during Spring and Summer, he would vary his route. Sometimes he would strike off across the fields at Trecombe and turn down the lane at Bosvarren where two enormous granite lions threatened to claw you to death if you entered the lawns at Bosvarrick. But mostly, particularly when the morning air was soft and languid, and when the early mist had risen from the river, he would slip down through the tall fir trees at Trewince, down to Port Navas, to look at the new boat which he and Zeph Curnow were building.

Then he would take a roundabout route to Trevadne through the mysterious glen at Polwheveral. There he would dismount, by the bridge, allowing Tiger to drink at the crystal clear, fast-flowing stream which cascaded and sparkled its way down to the river from Pixie's Hall above. While Tiger drank and then pulled at the succulent fresh green grass at the stream's edge, Ashley would play the familiar game of throwing twigs into the swirling waters and then rushing across to the other side of the bridge to watch them emerge. Reluctantly he would drag himself from this magic playground, and dawdle up through the woods towards Constantine. Then, at the top, he would give Tiger his head and they would go hell-for-leather all the way along the track to High Cross, eventually turning down into the stable yard at Trevadne with a noisy but satisfying clatter of hoofs. It would be lessons then for the rest of the day.

At first, it had been only until lunch time; the afternoon would be free for him to join Zeph at whatever farm task was in hand. But now that his voice was beginning to break and he was fast growing up, it had been decided that he must stay for the afternoon as well. Not that he minded much because it meant he could be longer with Alethea and Jeannie, subtly egging them on in the jokes they played on Miss Proudfoot. Poor Miss Proudfoot! She could never be sure that the removable seat of her chair had not been replaced by a soft, unresisting cushion. Every time she would fall into the trap. Down she would go, legs in the air, expostulating vehemently about the naughtiness of her charges. But, good-naturedly, she never complained to Sir Andrew. She loved 'her children', and she counted the pranks they played on her as expressions of their affection.

And Ashley had long since lost his place beside Alethea. Jeannie, in her positive way, had decided that because she was the elder sister Ashley must sit by her. Ashley might have protested were it not for the fact that by sitting opposite Alethea he was better able to enjoy the gentle beauty of her smile. Almost reluctantly he had to admit to himself that even though she *was* only a girl, he felt strangely affected by her presence.

With Jeannie it was quite different. She had discovered that he often dawdled beside the stream at Polwheveral bridge, and one peerless autumn morning he found her waiting for him there. She had ridden down on her pony and was sitting demurely on the end of a fallen tree, swinging her ribboned bonnet and staring soulfully into the tumbling water. She was wearing her prettiest day dress – a patterned linen with pale blue stripes and sprigs of red, brown and yellow. To Ashley she had never looked more alluring.

She pretended surprise when first she saw him. Her eyes were shining and flashing more provocatively than usual, and her breathing was rather deliberate. And when she took his hand and made him sit close beside her on the tree trunk, the mere touch of her flesh on his sent an unfamiliar, voluptuous thrill coursing through his body. They sat for several minutes talking and laughing, about nothing in particular, and then a rustle of breeze in the tree tops sent a shower of golden leaves spiralling earthwards.

'Come on!' she burst out, impetuously. 'Bet you can't catch a falling leaf!'

'Bet you I can, if you can,' he called, bounding after her as she twisted and turned, vainly trying to grasp an elusive leaf. 'What's so special about catching a falling leaf?'

'It's a superstition. It'll bring us good luck,' she called back over her shoulder, 'and everlasting happiness, as well. Come on!'

Together they rushed widly, hither and thither.

At last, simultaneously, they each snatched at, and miraculously grasped, the same quietly descending leaf. In the supreme effort they both fell, clutching their prize, into a shallow, moss-lined ditch.

They lay there, panting but triumphant, her sweet-smelling breath fanning his face. He was acutely aware of the closeness, warmth and gentle rhythm of her body. And when she drew his face towards hers, saying 'Seal it with a kiss,' and planted her soft, girlish lips firmly on his, he felt a tightening in his breeches, and his head began to swirl.

For a thirteen year-old boy it was alarming. Exciting, yes – but he felt no longer in control. His immediate response – like that of a scared woodland animal or bird – was flight. Wrenching himself away, he jumped on to Tiger's back, and with a 'Race you back to Trevadne!' he galloped up through the spinney in the direction of High Cross.

It may have been the way his elder daughter looked at Ashley thereafter – or it might have been the undoubted development of her figure – but Sir Andrew MacKenzie decided it was time to have another talk with Ashley's mother.

'The bairns are growing up fast, now, are they not?' he

began, a few days later. Comfortably sprawling himself on the chintz-covered sofa in the drawing room at Treworden, he went on – 'There'll not be much more knowledge they can gain from our Miss 'Pruddy', I'll wager.' He looked pointedly at Marianne from beneath his sandy-coloured eyebrows. 'Have ye any thoughts about a bit of proper schooling for young Ashley?'

'That's just what I was wanting to ask you about, Sir Andrew. As you know, I have a little money put by so as to be able to give him the best. . . .'

Sir Andrew chuckled. 'That means the local grammar school would hardly be good enough.' He gently groomed his ginger moustache with the forefinger and thumb of his right hand. 'And there's nothing much better at Truro or Penzance,' he continued, reflectively. 'In fact, there's really nothing of any standing nearer than John Blundell's at Tiverton.'

'Oh, but I wouldn't want him to be as far away from me as that,' Marianne protested. 'Why, that's right the other side of the Tamar, Sir Andrew. Right out of the county. Oh, I wouldn't want my Ashley to be educated out of Cornwall.'

Sir Andrew gave a wry smile. 'You Cornish are all the same. Anywhere beyond the Tamar is foreign territory, is it not?'

'And what about you Scots, might I ask? Bonnets over the Border, or whatever it is you say.'

Sir Andrew laughed.

'Well, I agree,' he went on, 'Tiverton is rather far away – even though the school does have a fine reputation. But I can understand that you'd like to have the boy nearer at hand – in case of illness, or anything like that.' He sat staring out of the window at the distant beauty of Nare Point and the mouth of the Helford. 'There is one other alternative you might like to consider,' he suggested eventually, 'and that's this new Lyttleton Granville foundation, near Launceston. A friend of mine, Edward Stewkeley, is one of the Governors. They call the place Lydford College.'

Perhaps too grand for a Cornish farmer's son, Marianne

thought. 'I should think that would be an expensive school, wouldn't it?' she countered.

Sir Andrew stroked the tip of his chin reflectively. 'No - o, I don't think so. Being quite a new venture, they daren't charge too much. The idea is to build up something on the lines of the really old establishments, like George Heriot's or Charterhouse, for instance - and they're keen to have boys from good class parents.' Sir Andrew grinned, contemptuously, 'Especially those with any sort of a title, "Young Eton", and all that sort of thing,' he snorted.

Eton, Charterhouse, George Heriot's - they all meant little or nothing to Marianne. But she did rather like the idea of her Ashley rubbing shoulders with some of the titled families. Like any other mother, she was ambitious for her son, and there could be no doubt about it, to have friends among the upper classes was a considerable advantage.

'I suppose it would mean him being away for quite a long time?' she enquired, sadly. 'Being a boarder, is that what they call it?'

'Oh yes, he'd have to be a boarder. Three terms a year, you understand. Good for a young lad to be away from his mother for a while. Makes a man of him.' Sir Andrew was at his heartiest. Marianne liked him least in that mood. But she supposed he was right about a boy not being tied to his mother's apron strings for too long. 'And the college,' Sir Andrew continued, 'Lydford College, it's called, is in a fine situation. Old country house, on the banks of the river - marvellous fishing.' His eyes gleamed, 'And not far from the heathland round St. Giles. Good hunting and shooting country.'

'And what about the headmaster?' Marianne asked. 'That's important isn't it?'

'Ah, now that should please you. As with the other prestigious schools and colleges, the headmaster is in Orders - a Reverend. Reverend Cyril Bernard Chaunter, by name and a Doctor of Divinity, no less. Recently appointed because - because, er . . . because they think he's a bit of a ladies' man and will charm a few more boys from their titled mothers. At least, that's what Stewkeley tells me. But it may only be a wee bit o' clishmaclaver. I've no doubt he'll be a good man at his job.'

While this momentous conversation was taking place, Ashley was blissfully unaware that his future was in the melting pot. He was climbing a tree with Alethea. For once they had given Jeannie the slip and were playing together, alone. Not that Alethea seemed to mind, one way or the other – she appeared to have no streak of jealousy eating her insides – but Ashley minded. He was delighted to have Alethea to himself. Too often, he was being made to feel inadequate by the much more forceful Jeannie. With Alethea, he could show off a bit, making her gasp as he swung dangerously from branch to branch; watching the admiration appear in her pretty eyes as he presented her with a rook's egg which he had brought down in his mouth from the topmost branch of the tree. In her soft voice she would gently scold him for being so brave, and then she would warn him that 'one day you'll fall and break your leg, or something awful. You shouldn't climb so high, Ashley.' And it made him feel big and brave and dashing.

He was feeling anything but big or dashing – and certainly not brave – as, in the darkening late afternoon of the following January, he stood in the courtyard at the back of Lydford College. Together with four other new boys he waited, supporting on its end his new leather trunk and wondering what he was supposed to do with it.

After a tearful goodbye at Treworden, he had been driven up by Sir Andrew's coachman who, with a cheerful 'Best o' luck, Master Ashley', had deposited him on this bleak and terrifying threshold to his new life. At that moment, above everything else, he wanted to drop the trunk and chase after the retreating coachman, pleading to be allowed to return home. In return for all he possessed he would willingly have changed places with Sir Andrew's servant – to be going back to the warmth and familiarity of the Trevadne household. But deep down, and remorselessly twisting his innards, was the inescapable feeling that those halcyon days

44

had gone forever. He had been sent to Lydford to become a man. And even in the depths of his misery, he recognised that his mother had done this to him because she honestly believed it was for his good.

Fortunately he was permitted to indulge in thoughts of self-pity for no more than a few moments before the staccato voice of a second-termer named Jordan pierced the evening gloom.

'Come on, then, you bunch of half-baked ninnies! What d'you think you're doing. Waiting for nanny to carry your trunk up to your bedroom, eh?'

Ashley found his voice first. 'We're not quite sure where to go,' he said stoutly.

'Oh, ho!' retorted Jordan, fixing Ashley with a venomous stare, 'so you're the cheeky one of the party, are you? Well, you can carry up my trunk first, and I'll show you the way.'

Jordan indicated a heavy-looking trunk standing on its end close to an open doorway.

'Come on, then, boy! Pick up that trunk, I said.' The tall, wiry figure of Jordan moved menacingly close to Ashley. 'Do as I say, boy. Pick up that trunk. You're not at home with 'Mother', you know,' he mimicked.

This last jeering shaft produced a nervous titter from the other new boys. In Ashley, the mention of 'Mother' – his own beloved mother – produced neither amusement nor sadness. It created in him a fierce determination not to be defeated by this hateful boy and, dashing away a tear of frustrated rage, he picked up the heavy trunk and staggered after the insolently slinking figure of Jordan.

To the accompaniment of such shouts as, 'On swine! Up those bloody steps, boy! Thought you were in for a nice soft life at Lydford did you? School for little gentlemen, eh? You'll soon find out. . . .' Ashley somehow managed to carry or drag the trunk up the spiral stone staircase leading to the dormitories. At the top, watching the procedure, stood an older boy, dressed much more flamboyantly than either Jordan or any of the new boys. He waited until the perspiring Ashley, now almost at the limit of his physical strength, allowed the trunk to fall with a thud on the floor.

'Whose trunk is that, Jordan?' demanded God's anointed.

'His, Bates,' Jordan replied, jerking his head in Ashley's direction. Slowly the imperious gaze transferred itself to the panting figure of Ashley.

'What's your name, boy?'

'Penberth, sir. Ashley Pen. . . .' He got no further. Before he could complete the surname, the almighty one turned on him, cheeks reddening with anger, and shouted, 'DON'T CALL ME "SIR".'

'I beg your pardon, si . . .' he stopped himself just in time. 'I beg your pardon,' Ashley concluded. Well, what was he to call him if he didn't know his name?

God's anointed, recognising the new boy's confusion, condescended to explain.

'My name is Bates. I'm Praefectus Major. I'm not a master. You only call masters 'sir'. Do you understand that, boy?'

'Yes, si . . .' There, he nearly did it again. But this senior boy looked so grown-up and important! 'Yes, Bates.' Ashley corrected himself, 'Thank you, Bates.'

The Praefectus Major permitted a half smile to flicker across his handsome features. He rather liked the look of this new boy. Good sturdy stock, he'd think. Might be a credit to the House, one day.

Then he slowly and deliberately turned his attention to Jordan. 'So that trunk belongs to Penberth here, does it?'

Jordan shuffled his feet, muttering.

'Then why,' went on Bates, 'does it have *your* initials so clearly painted on it?'

Jordan grinned foolishly, continuing to shuffle.

'Report to my lodge in five minutes time,' was all that Bates said to him. Then he turned to Ashley. 'And you, boy. Find Henderson G.W.W. and send him to my lodge.' He stalked off along the corridor.

Ashley had not the slightest idea who Henderson G.W.W. was – or, indeed, where he might be found – but chancing to meet another, older boy, rather less fearsome-looking than Jordan, he plucked up enough courage to enquire the whereabouts of the mysterious Henderson G.W.W. The boy whose name was Crookes and who was destined to follow his father into Holy Orders, took pity on the nervous Ashley and explained that Henderson G.W.W. was the senior Praefectus Minor, was fat and rather jolly, and might be found in the Library.

'And what's a lodge, please?' Ashley asked, tentatively.

'Another word for a study. You'll soon learn.' The flaxen-haired Crookes grinned encouragingly through his thick, pebble-glass spectacles. Ashley felt emboldened to ask, 'And could you please tell me where Bates' lodge is?'

But Crookes suddenly seemed to feel that his good nature was being imposed upon and his dignity as a fifth former impugned, so, averting his short-sighted gaze, he swept past the new boy, saying 'I'm afraid you'll have to find that out for yourself.'

When eventually Ashley found the elusive Henderson G.W.W., he was immensely relieved to see that he was, as Crookes had said, fat and jolly – and, more important by far – almost human. He even condescended to ask Ashley, on their way to the senior lodge, whereabouts his home was, and when Ashley replied that he lived near Falmouth, Henderson G.W.W. actually volunteered the information that he had a maiden aunt living at Penzance. It was a comforting thought, Ashley felt, that in this jungle of hostility a senior person such as Henderson G.W.W. should have anything so ordinary and so homely as a maiden aunt. For the very junior Penberth A. it was the first moment of relaxing tension since his arrival.

But the tension was all too quickly heightened once more when Ashley became aware of an intermittent 'Thwack!' reverberating along the corridor as he and Henderson G.W.W. approached the senior lodge. One! . . . thud, thud, thud, . . . Two! . . . thud, thud, thud, . . . Three! . . . The thudding footsteps shivered the floorboards of the corridor. Ashley felt his stomach turn over. Already, on the very first day of term, someone was being made to 'take his medicine'.

It was an unfortunate induction to the rigours of boarding school life; it was doubly unfortunate that as they approached the door of the lodge, a tall, gangling figure erupted into the corridor, flush-faced and ignominiously clutching the seat of his worsted shag breeches. It was Jordan. Punishment for being found a liar as well as a bully had been swift and painful. Worse still, he had actually been seen emerging from his chastisement. It was bad enough for a second-termer like Jordan to be caught blubbing by anyone; it was intolerable that it should have been witnessed by a new boy!

'Lighten our darkness we beseech Thee, O Lord. . . .'

The first day of the new term at Lydford College was drawing to a close. Cranbourne House had gathered in the Junior Common Room for House Prayers. Poker-faced A. St.J. Bates, Praefectus Major, Captain of cricket, Master of College Beagles – worried about his forthcoming Exhibitioner examination and flushed from recent flagellation exertions – droned monotonously on:- '. . . and by Thy great mercy defend us from all the perils and dangers of this night.'

What perils, what dangers? Already Ashley had endured a further encounter with a tender-seated, enraged Jordan. This time, in the Bog House. Having found his own way to that most essential geographical location, Ashley was just turning away from the urine trough when Jordan entered. Face to face once more with the new boy responsible for his recent summary punishment, Jordan had grabbed Ashley's arm, twisted it painfully and demanded a display of his victim's penis. Refusal to comply had merely brought forth an even more painful arm twist.

To someone with previous school experience – charity school or grammar school, perhaps – this type of molestation and demand might have seemed neither unusual nor particularly offensive – after all, since the beginning of time both men and animals have always exhibited a somewhat embarrassing interest in genitalia – but to a boy brought up almost exclusively in the genteel surroundings of Trevadne and the wholly feminine atmosphere of Miss Proudfoot and the two MacKenzie girls, it was an outrageous invasion of privacy. Until now, because everything was so new and strange, Ashley's natural instinct had been to endure unprotestingly every insult or indignity hurled in his direction. But suddenly it was all too much. A powerful, bruising back-kick on the shins made Jordan momentarily relax his grip. In a flash, Ashley was gone – fleeing down the corridor and into the Junior Common Room just as the House began to assemble for evening prayers. Although Jordan quickly followed, Ashely knew that for the time being at least there would be safety in numbers.

At the end of what Ashley would soon come to recognise as the nightly imprecation to 'Lighten our darkness we beseech Thee, O Lord,' the House barked its 'Amen' and the supercilious Bates, after nodding briefly to the assembled company, turned on his heel and left the room.

The crescendo of voices and shuffling of feet which followed Bate's departure was promptly quelled by a voice demanding, 'Wait for it. Wait for it!' A sardonic, heavily pock-marked face had appeared above the throng. Standing on a chair, and reading from a sheet of paper in his hand, Praefectus Minor Baring was assigning each boy to his respective dormitory.

'Dormitory No 1. Bowles, Craddock, Parker, Stevenson-Hamish, Wilson Major and Cartwright. Dormitory, Clock Tower – Henderson R.J., Howard-Wyke, de Travis Major and Minor, Vivyan and Ormonde. Dormitory, Mezzanine – Courtier, Davidson. . . .

Names, meaning nothing to Ashley, rolled on; one thing only mattered. Penberth had not been assigned to the same dormitory as Jordan. For the night hours at least, Ashley reflected, he would be free from the attentions of someone who, in the space of a single afternoon, had become an implacable enemy.

Shortly after ten o'clock that night, the vindictive-looking Baring came round the dormitories declaring 'Lights Out!', and it was in the ensuing darkness while trying to extract some warmth from the coarse blanket on his comfortless, unyielding bed that Ashley took stock of his circumstances. It had not been a good beginning. Here he was, miles away from home and apparently friendless in a completely strange world. Worse still, only a few doors down the corridor a revengeful Jordon would be waiting to renew hostilities in the morning.

As the night deepened, an intense longing for his home and his mother flooded over him. He pulled the blanket up round his head; angrily chewed the edges of his pillow, trying hard to stifle the sobs that increasingly racked his body. He must not cry. After all, he had been sent away to this expensive new boarding school to be made a man of – and this was anything but manly behaviour. But try as he would he could not erase from his mind the image of his mother – gentle, loving, deeply concerned for her only child – sitting at home in her warm kitchen but feeling utterly bereft. The recurring thought of her eventually proved too much. Despite every effort to control himself, each succeeding sob seemed to feed upon its predecessor until finally the crushing misery of his loneliness overwhelmed him. Tears flooded down his cheeks, his shallow pillow became a sodden, clammy bag of feathers, and the voice from the bed next to his, saying 'Oh, for God's sake, stop blubbing, boy!' merely added to his dejection.

In the end, it was sheer exhaustion that came as a friend and carried him off into sleep.

CHAPTER FIVE

To be made a man of

Sunday morning – the first Sunday at Lydford – dawned so crisply beautiful in its cloak of shimmering hoar frost that Ashley found it hard to believe he was now incarcerated within the confines of this gaunt, granite building. The air, when he first put his nose outside the large double doors beneath the tower, had that extra special, invigorating 'turn-of-the-year' tang. Had he been at home at Treworden, he would have been out early with Zeph to look over the sheep. Soon, the ewes would be dropping their lambs, the first of the new season, and the fields would resound with that ever-increasing crescendo of Spring music – the high-pitched bleating of hungry lambs answered by the deep-throated chuckle of their mothers.

But at Lydford, Sunday was quite different. For one thing, the first bell echoed along the dormitory corridors an hour later than on week-days – it was considered entirely appropriate that 'the sons of gentlemen' should be allowed a lie in on Sunday mornings; for another thing, instead of the usual offering of gruel for breakfast, the Lord's Day was marked by the spectacular metamorphosis of the water porridge into a milk porridge with the added luxury of a piece of bread and butter.

Morning Chapel – held in the picturesque medieval village church – was at ten o'clock; it would be over in time to allow the villagers to attend their own Matins service at the usual hour of 11 a.m. On the day after his arrival, Ashley had been tested for his singing potential by the saturnine, slightly mad-looking music master, and because he had a

51

good voice like most Cornishmen, he had been pitched straight into the choir. In the weeks and months ahead, he would find this an unexpected boon because the boys in the choir sat immediately in front of the intricately carved chair stalls invariably occupied by the masters. There could be no molestation – no ear flicking, hair pulling or heel kicking – by the bullies in the pew behind. For one glorious hour it was a sanctuary.

But on this particular Sunday, the first of the term, all the new boys were to have tea with the Headmaster – 'the H.M.' – in his study. It would be a chance, Ashley thought, to get to know – and perhaps more important, to be known by – the tall, remote and aesthetic-looking Doctor of Divinity, Dr Chaunter, who that very morning, and with an almost visible halo around his powdered wig, had preached such a warm, softly spoken sermon from the pulpit. He *must* be a nice, kindly man, Ashley thought; after a sermon like that, with the angels seemingly perched on his shoulders. He just *had* to be the sort of person in whom every frightened new boy could confide.

Promptly at four o'clock, the six new boys – D.W. Braund, A.J. Courtier, C.T.T. Ingleby-Maddox, J.C. Innes, S.W. Parker and A. Penberth – faces scrubbed to shining, hair plastered down with comb and water, waited nervously in the lobby outside the door of the almighty. Five minutes later that fearsome door was being opened by Dr Chaunter himself who sinuously motioned his perspiring new scholars to seat themselves in the gilded chairs around the blazing fire. The elegant furnishings of the Headmaster's study contrasted strongly with the bleak cheerlessness of the dormitories and the common rooms, and instead of engendering a warm sense of well-being, they merely served to increase the feeling of home-sickness.

Dr Chaunter, moving with a stealth that suggested the habitual wearing of soft slippers, took up his position in front of the fire. Hands behind back, spectacles at the end of his nose, he quizzically surveyed his charges from above the freshly laundered white band around his stringy neck. His

52

idea of putting new boys at their ease – and, at the same time, impressing them with his own authority – was to make them feel more home-sick then ever by asking each one where he came from and what his father did – despite being acquainted already with their background.

Peering through half-closed, colourless eyes at the diminutive figure perched on the very edge of a large, upright arm-chair, he purred encouragingly, 'Now, let me see, your name must be. . . .?'

'Courtier, sir,' squeaked the youngest and smallest member of the group.

'Ah yes. Courtier. Of course it is.' Dr Chaunter gazed at the boy as though seeing him through nothing clearer than a piece of mutton cloth. 'Well, Courtier, I hope you find that arm-chair large enough for you.'

Fortunately, the youthful audience recognised the remark as being intended as a joke – and tittered, hugely.

'Now don't tell me,' the Headmaster continued, always seeking to impress the boys with his phenomenal memory, 'your family comes from Gloucestershire, does it not . . . and your father is a high-ranking officer in the Royal Navy?'

Courtier blushed with pride. 'That's right, sir,' he piped. 'In fact, we live quite close to the cathedral.'

Dr Chaunter beamed. Savouring the words, he murmured almost inaudibly, 'Gloucestershire Courtiers. Very acceptable.' Then, turning to the thick-set boy with freckled face and flaming red hair, he continued 'And you must be. . .?'

The redhead waited, lips pursed into a cheeky smile, obstinately refusing to enlighten the Divine.

'What is your name, boy?' the Doctor snapped, the beatific smile suddenly assuming the sweetness of vinegar.

'Braund, sir,' freckle-face said, 'Dave Braund.'

Doctor Chaunter regarded the boy as though he were something fouling the pavement.

'*Dave* Braund,' he echoed, witheringly, 'You mean, I suppose, that your name is David Braund.'

' 's right, sir,' the boy agreed tartly, 'but at home they always call me Dave.'

The Doctor sniffed – averting his gaze to the most salubrious prospect of the parterre beyond his study windows.

He was about to resume his normal line of questioning, enquiring about the boy's home and background, when he remembered that the Braunds were brewers – somewhere in the South of England – *Braund's Prime Porter* – that was it. Brewing! of all disgusting occupations. The very smell of hops was revolting enough, but when one considered all the filth and vomit which so frequently besmirched a common ale house. . . . Well, the mere thought of having to consort with such 'canaille' was quite nauseating.

Almost imperceptibly he edged a little further from the brewer's son, but then he edged back again, reminding himself that he had been appointed to lift the whole tone of the school from the commonplace to the elite; to attract the sons of the wealthy and the celebrated. To achieve that end he must be prepared to accept boys from the lower strata of society, scholastic make-weights, to swell the numbers . . . He turned, hopefully, to Ashley.

'And who have we here?' he murmured, with that softness of timbre calculated to charm the most intractable of mothers. 'Someone from the healthy climate of rural England, perhaps?' Ashley's normal, ruddy complexion contrasted strongly with the limpid pallor of the Headmaster.

'Penberth, sir.' Ashley replied, succinctly. What true Cornishman ever gave away more information that he was obliged to!

'Ah, yes,' the Doctor mused; the boy's circumstances were vaguely distressing he seemed to remember. 'Penberth, yes.' Dr Chaunter very gently caressed his lower lip as he gazed out over the Elysian splendour of the new cricket field. 'How does the jingle run – 'Tre, Pol or Pen is the prefix of all good Cornishmen' – is that how it goes? You are a Cornishman, Penberth, are you not?'

Ashley proudly affirmed that 'yes' he was a Cornish boy. The Headmaster continued to regard him through half-closed eyes. 'Your father is a big landowner near Falmouth,' he went on, hopefully. 'Is that correct, Penberth?'

'No, sir. My father is dead. My mother is the tenant of a farm near the Helford river.'

The Headmaster winced – ever so slightly. Carefully brushing an imaginary speck of dust from his black lace-edged cuff he went on. 'Oh, I see. How unfortunate. A tenant farmer, did you say?' The note of disparagement was thinly disguised. 'How very interesting. . . .' His voice trailed away as he turned to the languid-looking boy lolling with a bored expression in the arm-chair next to Ashley.

'And you are. . . .?' Dr Chaunter enquired.

The boy made a token effort to uncurl himself. 'Ingleby-Maddox,' he drawled, before spreading himself in the chair once more. Momentarily, the Headmaster regarded the boy with transparent distaste. The insolent attitude! – the total absence of the appropriately respectful 'Sir' could not be tolerated! The Doctor's eyes narrowed venomously. The boy must be verbally chastised, forthwith. Dr Chaunter prepared to deliver himself of one of his most withering ripostes.

But then he remembered the hyphen in the surname.

He remembered, too, that it was not just because he was a Doctor of Divinity and an outstanding scholar that he had secured the post of Headmaster of this new and promising school. Oh, no. He had been tacitly given to understand by none other than Sir Henry Lydford himself that he would be expected to 'raise the tone of the school so that upper class parents would regard it as a modern and progressive alternative to the older but more unhealthily situated establishments, like Eton College. In short, the sons of the well-connected or the wealthy, who desired a salubrious environment for their sons, must at all costs be encouraged.

And a hyphenated name was not to be sneezed at!

Dr Chaunter cleared his throat – ever so gently – before coercing his face into the semblance of a smile.

'Yes, yes, of course. Ingleby-Maddox, a well-known County family.' The voice had the sweetness of honey. 'Hampshire Ingleby-Maddoxes is it not?'

'No,' the boy said, lazily. 'It's Wiltshire. We have a small place near Salisbury. About a thousand and five hundred acres, actually.'

In this wise was set the pattern of that Sunday afternoon tea party. Braund, Parker and Penberth were of little consequence. So far as the Reverend Doctor Cyril B. Chaunter was concerned, they scarcely existed. Only Ingleby-Maddox, Courtier and Innes – who had been able to parade a retired Colonel for a father – were of the slightest interest to the Headmaster of Lydford College. They smacked of the 'class' he was after; *they* were the stuff to give the school the reputation it needed. The others were – well, they were quite nice boys, perhaps, but in all probability they would turn out to be – in one of the Reverend Dr Chaunter's favourite expressions – nothing much more than 'passengers'. Yes, 'passengers' – those who would make very little impact as they passed through the school but who had to be tolerated, not only for the fees they brought with them but also for their value as 'ballast' when the school was open for inspection on ceremonial occasions. After all, an expanding roll-call must betoken a thriving institution.

Ashley would have been thankful to escape from the hypocrisy and humbug of this first meeting with his Headmaster were it not for the recognition that, so long as he was in the 'holy of holies', he would at least be free from the persecution of the outside world. But he had hardly set foot again in the malodorous atmosphere of the Junior Common Room when a malevolent-featured third termer named Danby, who smelt permanently of stale sweat and produced every sibilant with a shower of spittle, stalked into the room imperiously demanding, 'Now then, now then, own up – who's farted?' Needless to say this indelicate enquiry went unanswered, but Danby, fixing Ashley with a malicious gleam, went on, 'Baring wants you in the Junior Lodge. Immediately!'

Now Baring was a Praefectus – even though only a Minor one. He had a reputation, already gleefully communicated to Ashley, of being a particularly sadistic beater of new boys, and within the next quarter of an hour Ashley was to discover the aptness of that reputation. Lydford College had a *Green Book* of *Rules*, Baring said. Did Ashley know them off by heart? If not, why not? Useless to plead you had not yet had time to learn them. 'Very well, then. Bend down over that chair, boy, and I'll give you a couple to be going on with!' Thud, thud, thud – three quick steps, and then 'Thwack'. The sound was already all too familiar. Pause, for return to starting point. Then, thud, thud, thud – 'Thwack!'

'Come back tomorrow after evening preparation and I'll test you again. If you still don't know them, I'll give you six more. Now get out.'

The ignominy, the sense of injustice – 'Nobody said you had to learn the rules off by heart, and within a few days, too!' – the painful red weals on the buttocks, the forcing back of tears of anger, the hurt and frustration at not being able to hit back. Above all, the black hatred of the horrible, pock-marked Baring!

And as if that were not enough, when Ashley repaired to the Bog House to hide his tears and to inspect the damage to his buttocks, he ran straight into the one individual he least wanted to encounter – the ubiquitous Jordan. This tall, fair, crinkly-haired boy, somewhat over-developed for his fourteen years, was standing at the urine trough with his rampant penis in his hand. Seeing Ashley, he immediately grabbed the new boy by the ear, twisted it painfully, and demanded assistance in achieving a climax to his sexual self-stimulation. Ashley, peering down through the murky dimness of the Bog House, was both fascinated and repelled by this lewd demand as well as by the sight of an enormous sexual organ, flushed, fetid, waving from side to side like a hooded cobra poised and ready to strike.

Momentarily, Ashley felt tempted to comply. After all, it was a relatively painless request; for a few seconds at least, he would have this persistent tormentor at his mercy. And, having just taken a beating himself from the sadistic Baring, the level of his personal resistance was low.

But then the squalor of the situation suddenly struck him; the furtive flickering of the oil lamps; the powerful stench of the undrained liquid in the urine trough; the heavy breathing of the sexually excited schoolboy; the offensive smell of unwashed, over-stimulated flesh. It was subtly compelling – and yet it was repulsive!

Once again, Ashley wrenched himself free, and fled, leaving the angry, unejaculated Jordan to his own endeavours.

It was unfortunate for Penberth A. – although salutary for the health and well-being of Lydford College no doubt – that on the very next day the Headmaster chose to include in his usual Monday morning address to the whole assembled school a carefully worded reference to the fact that the human body should be regarded as 'a temple of God', and he gave a very pointed warning about 'the practice of self-abuse.' By itself, this homily might have gone unremarked by the largely uninterested audience but it very quickly became known that Jordan, together with several others of similar propensity, had been summoned to the H.M.'s study immediately after the conclusion of morning prayers. It was rumoured that 'someone had blabbed,' and that those now summoned to 'the Presence' were about to be expelled. Not for nothing, therefore, was Patterson V.J., a very small boy but with exceedingly sharp ears, posted to the Notice Board in the lobby outside the Headmaster's study with explicit instructions to read, and to re-read – if necessary to re-read again – every single notice thereon while, at the same time, memorising the exact number of 'Thwacks' administered and, if possible, the precise words of the 'expulsion' address.

When he eventually returned to his class room, Patterson V.J. was surrounded by a surging, eager throng of First

Formers, thirsting after information. Disappointingly, he could only report that although the miscreants had all emerged with exceptionally red faces, not one of them had been clutching a sore bottom. Worse still, the H.M. had kept his voice so low – drat him! – that his words were virtually inaudible. But Patterson *had* heard the words 'self abuse' and 'insidious insanity' – or something like that – hissed by the H.M. on several occasions. So, it was pretty obvious, in Patterson's opinion, what the chaps had got a wigging for.

And the First Form had to be satisfied with that!

The remainder of the week passed relatively quietly for Ashley. The dreaded re-examination on the *Green Book Rules* by the hateful Baring had, surprisingly, been negotiated without further violence, and the contrast between the teaching methods of the jolly but scholastically limited Miss Proudfoot and those of the learned Oxford and Cambridge graduate masters at Lydford had not proved so unbridgeable as had been feared; and he was even beginning to get accustomed to the hardness of his dormitory bed.

Then, on the following Sunday afternoon, while the married masters were at home with their families, and the bachelors were snoozing in the Masters' Common Room, and Ashley was preparing to accompany three other new boys, Courtier, Innes and Parker on the obligatory Sunday afternoon walk on Lydford Heath, he suddenly felt himself seized from behind and finally overpowered by three much bigger boys, one of whom was Jordan. Still fighting and struggling like a captured African slave, Ashley was dragged to a domitory overlooking the stable yard at the rear of the main building. There, three other junior boys, none of whom Ashley knew by name, had been similarly outnumbered and were now cowering at the mercy of their captors.

A senior boy was lolling against one of the four open windows. He casually toyed with the long, wooden handle of a clothes brush.

With exaggerated deliberation, the senior boy scrutinised

each of the frightened captives. 'Are we all here?' he drawled, with a languidness suggesting that the proceedings were almost a daily occurrence. Receiving an assent from one of his henchmen, the inquisitor suddenly stiffened. 'Right,' he barked, 'On your knees, scum.'

A vicious kick at the back of Ashley's knees buckled his legs and brought him to the floor. His neck was held in a vice-like grip, and his head forced downwards until his nose was touching the bare boards. The smell of dust and floor polish assaulted his nostrils. His head throbbed.

'Right', repeated the inquisitor. 'Presumably you all know why you're here. If not, you soon will.' He sniffed, loudly, before continuing. 'It has been reported to this Committee of Public Protection that someone has been blabbing to the Headmaster. Moreover,' he went on, with an appropriate air of judicial solemnity, 'it is confidently believed that one of you is the culprit.'

He slowly paced up and down in front of the four subjugated and perspiring victims.

'If the culprit is prepared to own up,' he continued, 'then the rest of you will be released, unscathed. On the other hand. . . .' he paused, meaningfully, 'If none of you owns up, then each one of you will receive the punishment reserved for all sneaks and cowards.' Then slowly, pointedly, 'I trust, gentlemen, that I make myself absolutely clear.'

The four forcibly prostrated figures remained silent; the seconds ticked by. No one said a word.

Even in his extremity, Ashley could not help noting the irony of the situation whereby, at the outset of this inquisition, he and his suffering colleagues had been referred to as 'scum', whereas now that they were about to be put on the rack, they had been elevated to the rank of 'gentlemen'. It made no difference to the outcome, of course. The chief inquisitor had taken up a commanding position in front of the row of unyielding renegades. Legs straddled wide, he was menacingly tapping the smooth back of the clothes brush against the palm of his hand.

'Well, gentlemen . . . I'm waiting.'

Still there came no confession; only a grunt of pain from the boy next to Ashley as his head was forced nearer to the dust.

'Did you say something, boy?'

The questioned boy obstinately shook his head. The seconds ticked by.

'Right,' said the inquisitor, at last – for the third time, 'Which of these miserable wretches shall we make an example of first, gentlemen?' and without waiting for any suggestions from his acquiescent henchmen, he went on, 'How about this reprobate, here?' He indicated Ashley. 'He looks a cantankerous little sod. Let's make an example of him.'

Once more, kicking, struggling and wrestling with every ounce of strength left in him, Ashley strove to get free as he was dragged and pushed in the direction of one of the open windows. He had no idea what they intended to do to him, but it was obvious that the window would play an important part in the punishment. While the inquisitor remained mercilessly aloof, his henchmen succeeded eventually, after a viciously bruising struggle, in forcing Ashley through the window, feet first, and leaving him hanging by his arms from the window sill. Beneath him was a fifteen foot drop to the cobblestoned stable yard below.

Presently, the inquisitor appeared at the window, clothes brush in hand.

'Now then,' he said, 'let's see what kind of stuffing you're made of. Did you, or did you not, go blabbing to the H.M. – or anyone else, for that matter – about a certain incident recently in the Bog House?'

Ashley's stubborn refusal to answer was rewarded by a sharp crack on the knuckles from the clothes brush.

'Answer me, boy!' was accompanied by another painful crack, this time on the other hand.

It seemed to Ashley that by anwering the question, either way, he was descending to the level of this monstrous demonstration of bullying. He was determined, somehow or other, to deprive them all, especially Jordan, of the satisfaction of wresting an answer from him. If he were to say 'yes',

61

he would be telling a deliberate lie, as well as playing into their hands; if he told the truth, there was no guarantee that he would be released. And even if he were released, one of the other unfortunates would be subjected to the same torture.

'Answer me, boy! Do you hear me? Answer!' Another even more painful whack from the clothes brush.

'Refuse to answer such an impertinent question,' Ashley, unwisely, managed to grunt from his precarious position.

'Impertinent! Eh? Did you hear that, gentlemen? Impertinent, by God! I'll teach you to accuse me of impertinence, you scurvy little weevil. By God, I will!'

A succession of ever more painful blows were rained down on Ashley's knuckles. He tried to avoid the impact by swinging like a pendulum, moving his hands along the sill, from one side to the other, but it was of little avail. Mostly, the blows struck home, and Ashley realised he could not hold on much longer. Already, his knuckles were bleeding; the blood was trickling down the back of his hand, staining the cuff of the fine lawn shirt which his mother had so recently laundered. He glanced down at the cobbles beneath him. It was a frightening drop. 'Hold on,' he kept murmuring to himself. 'They'll have to give up soon. They can't be such savages. . . .' But he knew he couldn't hold on. His fingers were now quite numb with pain. Each blow seemed to bite deeper and deeper into the flesh. He would have to let go; a chap could stand so much, but this was getting beyond endurance.

Perhaps he would be killed. For a few brief moments, he allowed himself to wallow in self-pity. His mother would be heartbroken, he was sure of that; Zeph Curnow would miss him too, perhaps. And what about the MacKenzie girls? Would they be sad, he wondered; Jeannie, with her lively, laughing face, and her dark brown curls; and Alethea, especially Alethea. Would she shed a tear for him? – she, with her soft, gentle smile, her silky, fair hair, and the feeling she always gave you of a confidence bestowed and a secret shared.

It was the thought of Alethea which made him determined

to survive. Pushing away from the wall with his feet, and flexing his knees as much as he could, he let go of the window sill, and tried to drop like a cat.

At precisely the moment when Ashley hit the cobbles, Mr T.R. Greenham, his House Master, drove into the yard in his spanking new gig. He was due to take evening chapel, and had come in early from his afternoon spin in order to finish correcting last Friday's Latin translations.

In a flash, he understood the significance of the scene; the open windows of the dormitory – on a freezing cold January afternoon, the figures at those windows, rapidly disappearing into the shadows; the lump that was Ashley, lying on the cobbles.

At Oxford, T.R. Greenham had only narrowly missed an Athletics 'Blue'. He could still sprint. And he rather enjoyed showing off that he could. Having quickly secured the horse, and with his driving whip still in his hand, he sprinted out of the stable yard, past the ancient library building, and then up the servant's staircase which gave access to the dormitory passage. He was just in time to see the fleeing figures of the inquisitor and most of his henchmen disappearing round the corner at the end of the corridor.

The crack of his driving whip echoed like a pistol shot. 'Stay where you are! Every one of you!' The command, staccato and imperative, carried with it a terrifying threat to the disobedient. The scuttling footsteps – all but a few – came to an abrupt halt; one or two tried to sneak away.

Mr. Greenham stalked towards the culprits. He was furious – but he was enjoying it. He loathed bullying, in every form; he thought he had caught these middle-school boys red-handed – he felt even more sure when he spotted Ashley's three fellow sufferers lurking apprehensively, like a small flock of confused shearlings, just inside the dormitory door.

'You, there,' he snapped, striding up to the group of skulking, disconcerted older boys, 'report to my study –

immediately – every one of you. Wait there, outside my door, until I return.'

He turned sharply on his heel, and strode off, back down the corridor. As soon as he had rounded the corner and descended the spiral staircase, he broke into a sprint once more.

He found the injured Ashley, bloodstained, exhausted, and gingerly rubbing an alarmingly swollen ankle.

Just over an hour later, Ashley limped down to evening chapel. He was the last to arrive, and he was supporting himself with a wooden crutch under his right arm. As he squeezed in behind Innes, into his appointed seat immediately in front of the masters' choir stalls, he felt the eyes of almost the whole school upon him. Both his hands were bandaged, one rather more heavily than the other.

'Whatever happened?' whispered an astonished Innes.

'Can't tell you now. Tell you, later,' was all Ashley was prepared to divulge.

He had barely settled into position before the first hymn was announced. With muted rustle, the choir rose; the organ breathed out the opening bars of a hauntingly beautiful melody. Then the whole school got to its feet. Encouraged by the frantic baton waving of the seemingly demented Mus. Doc., the untrained voices of a closely packed schoolboy congregation suddenly crashed forth into the opening verse of the first hymn.

'Jesus shall reign where'er the sun
Does his successive journeys run;
His Kingdom stretch from shore to shore,
Till moons shall wax and wane no more.'

'His Kingdom stretch *from shore to shore*. . . .'
In his state of stretched nerves, of heightened tension, it needed only those words to remind Ashley of his beloved homeland – to waft him back, in his imagination, to those little sandy coves along the shores of the Helford estuary

where Zeph had taught him to swim; to Porth Saxon, that small, secluded inlet where they had fished from the rocks and where Ashley knew – even though Zeph, faithfully keeping his word to 'the Mestress' had never told him – the smugglers would bring their contraband ashore; where, on a dark night just such as this, Ashley mused, glancing at the blackness beyond the stained glass windows of the ancient church, the pack ponies would be gathering from far and wide to carry the casks of best white cognac up to the Inn close by the smithy – with one to be dropped off, no doubt, at the vestry door of another village church, the one on the cliff above Parson's Beach at Mawnan Shear.

And what would he not give to be back now among his own Cornish folk; even among the smugglers with whom his mother had forbidden him to associate.

At this hour they would be preparing for their own Evensong in that lovely old church on the cliff. The persistent murmur of the sea would be in their ears; they would sit patiently while the Reverend William Peter delivered himself of his usual lengthy sermon. Some would doze; from long experience they would know that the reverend gentleman, 'ee do go on a powerful mite.' But they would not mind. The Reverend Peter had been their 'vigger' for nigh on twenty years, and they had got used to him. He was theirs.

The toneless voices of Lydford College continued to bark the words of the familiar Isaac Watts hymn;

'Blessings abound where'er He reigns:
The prisoner leaps to lose his chains,
The weary find eternal rest,
And all the sons of want are blest.'

'The prisoner leaps to lose his chains. . . .'
What a wonderful thought! He, Ashley Penberth, prisoner of Lydford College – suddenly able to leap from the invisible chains that bound him. To run . . . and to jump . . . and to be FREE! Free of the bullying Jordan; free of the sadistic, pock-marked Baring – free forever from the

silken-voiced Doctor Chaunter. But, of course, it was unthinkable; nobody ever ran away from Lydford – only cowards – and passengers!

And even if he were to run away, how could he ever face his mother – she who had made sacrifices to give him a good education, to make a man of him, to turn him into a gentleman. And Sir Andrew MacKenzie – what would he say, and what would the two girls think, especially Alethea?

'The weary find eternal rest. . . .' He could do with some of that rest, at this very moment. He was feeling tired, deflated, dejected. It seemed as though no matter how hard he tried – and he *had* tried hard during these first few days at boarding school – to maintain a cheerful outlook, he felt always surrounded by a whole concert of ill-feeling aimed at making his life a perpetual misery, and intent on bringing him down. When he tried to look happy and relaxed, they dubbed him 'too cocky', or 'a cheeky little runt' – and when, every now and then he became overwhelmed by loneliness and the utter bleakness of his situation, they would form a revolving circle around him, pulling exaggeratedly long faces and chanting, 'Grieving for the Mater, are you? Pining for Mother, eh?'

Now, as he prepared to launch forth into the last verse, 'Let every creature rise and bring . . .' and as the strains of the hymn tune ascended to the vaulted ceiling of this ancient building so redolent with an atmosphere of sanctity and peace, *that* was exactly how he felt; he longed for the comfort, the understanding and the softness of his mother. It might not be a very manly thought; he could not help that; it was how he felt at this moment.

He looked down at his bandaged hands. They would certainly serve as a reminder of this day for quite a long time to come.

He looked up again, over the top of the hymn-book held in his less heavily bandaged hand, and glanced down into the main body of the church. Jordan, he noticed, was not in his usual seat; he did not know exactly where the rest of his tormentors normally sat.

He also did not know that neither Jordan nor the inquisitor – nor any other members of the self-styled Committee of Public Protection – would be coming to chapel that evening. Mr Greenham had given them all special permission to absent themselves.

Being a kindly man at heart, Mr Greenham had recognised that, after he had finished with them, it would be far too painful for any of them to sit down.

CHAPTER SIX

The incomparable hyphen

When Mr T.R. Greenham had sprinted back to the cobbled stable yard beneath the dormitory windows he had found Ashley still rubbing a painfully swollen ankle, and at the same time examining the lacerations on both his knees. The backs of his hand were still bleeding, and he had badly grazed the palms when breaking his fall.

The Housemaster helped the boy to his feet, and then made him test his weight on the injured ankle. Ashley admitted it was extremely painful, but just bearable, he thought.

'Put your arm round my neck, then, Penberth, and we'll get you up to Mistress Chisholm. She'll soon clean you up, and then we'll see about your ankle.' Mr Greenham sounded cheerful and confident. It put fresh heart into Ashley. He felt it was quite something to be virtually carried up the staircase by the Housemaster.

Mistress Chisholm was one of those motherly women who seem destined throughout their life to look after people – not necessarily the sick, just anyone who is in need of care and attention, and perhaps a little loving. She presided over the Sick Bay at Lydford College with that mixture of clinical efficiency and warm friendliness which made every new boy look upon her treatment room as a gentle reminder of 'home', as well as a respite from the persecutions of the outside world. Even if you only had a sore thumb you would get the same soothing concern as if you had a broken ankle.

But she felt fairly certain that Ashley's ankle was not broken, she said. After gently wiggling it from side to side, she pronounced her opinion that, fortunately, it was nothing worse than badly torn ligaments, damaged when the ankle was twisted by the fall. Nevertheless, they would get a proper medical opinion when the school doctor made his routine visit in the morning.

Leaving Mistress Chisholm clucking sympathetically over Ashley's lacerated knees and hands, and binding up his wounds with her own special brand of balm and compassion, Mr Greenham felt able to return to his study. Six boys huddled outside the door. Mr Greenham ran his eyes over them. One was missing, he felt certain.

'Are you all here?' he asked, sharply.

The Inquisitor – whose name was A.E.L. Fanshawe – took it upon himself to nod. That's lie number one, thought Mr Greenham.

'Where's Jordan, then?' he snapped.

Fanshawe shrugged.

'He was one of you, was he not?' Mr Greenham shot a penetrating glance at each one of them. A row of blank faces stared back at him.

'I must have an answer,' he persisted, coldly. 'Fanshawe – I'm asking you. Was Jordan with you in that dormitory?'

Fanshawe lowered his eyes, but said nothing.

'Answer me, Fanshawe!'

The Inquisitor, now subjected to an inquisition himself, remained silent.

'I'll give you one more chance to answer my question, Fanshawe.' He enunciated with icy clarity. 'Was Jordan one of the bully party persecuting those new boys in the dormitory overlooking the stable yard?'

Fanshawe continued to regard his expensive, hand-made boots with exaggerated care. He said nothing.

'Very well, then,' Mr Greenham said, at last. 'I'll deal with you six first. Follow me.' He led the way into his study.

Had he not been so angry, Mr Greenham might even have been amused by this display of honour among rogues – he might even have admired it – but there was nothing, absolutely nothing either amusing or admirable about terrifying the life out of small boys who had only a few days before been plucked from their families. Whether or not it was his personal responsibility to punish boys in Houses other than his own, he did not care. He was determined to give these tyrants, caught virtually red-handed, a taste of the retribution they deserved.

First, he made them stand in a straight line, facing him. Then, with ever-ascending asperity in his voice, he stripped them of every vestige of personal pride in what they had done. For boys of their age and background, he said, to get hold of junior boys – outnumbering them by at least three to one – was unworthy even of a gutter urchin. It was not only dishonourable and a disgrace to their families – it was the action of a downright coward.

'That's what you are,' he spat at them, 'nothing but a bunch of cowards.'

He paced up and down in front of them, flushed with his own sense of indignation but trying to keep his anger under control.

'And now,' he concluded, not without at least a degree of relish, 'we'll see just how well you can swallow your own medicine.'

He then sent them all out of the room – to return separately, one by one. Fanshawe was instructed to come last. This was a stroke of genius – evil genius, perhaps – because it meant that Fanshawe would be listening to every sickening, whirring crack of Mr Greenham's whippy cane as it found its mark on each confederate's buttocks. Five times six is thirty – and Fanshawe had to absorb the sound of thirty well-directed strokes as he waited there, outside in the passage.

By the time it came to his turn, he had lost much of his former truculence.

'I take it, Fanshawe,' Mr Greenham began, 'that you admit to being the ringleader of this cowardly group?'

As though witnessing the firing of the faggots beneath his stake of martyrdom, Fanshawe replied, histrionically, 'I

70

admit to full responsibility, sir. The others were but minions.'

'And you realise that the whole matter will have to be reported to the Headmaster?'

Fanshawe made no reply. Instead, he gazed piously, irritatingly, as though contemplating the gateway to eternity, at the framed House photograph immediately behind and above Mr Greenham's head.

'Meanwhile,' the Housemaster went on, with pointed emphasis, '*I* am going to give *you* a suitable return – with interest – for the treatment you saw fit to mete out to the new boy, Penberth.'

He picked up the cane from his desk, waggled it three times, and then in his most commanding and authoritative voice, said: 'Fanshawe! Bend down in that corner!'

As soon as Fanshawe had sidled out of the room, clutching his painful posterior, Mr Greenham went over to his corner-cupboard, extracted a bottle and glass, and poured himself a double whisky. He needed it. Contrary to the recipient's belief, the administration of punishment can be exhausting – mentally, as well as physically – and Mr Greenham had just given a thrashing to six of Lydford's most inveterate bullies. And there was one more, at least, to be dealt with – Jordan.

But first of all, he must see the Headmaster. And that could be almost more exhausting than the thrashings.

Trevor Rupert Greenham drained the last drop from his whisky tumbler. He felt better already – fortified, and in a more relaxed frame of mind. It was wonderful what a drop of Scotch could do to a man. He went across to the coat cupboard near the window, took out his gown and his square, flat cap. He threw the cap onto his desk and slipped into his gown, adjusting it in front of the mirror. Then he unhooked his University hood from the back of the study door, and arranged it carefully to hang down his back. A final approving glance at himself in the mirror – and he was ready to tackle the H.M.

71

He picked up his flat cap, put it on his head, and went out of the room.

At the end of the passage, he espied a tall figure skulking in the shadows. It was Jordan. Like the criminal who feels compelled to return to the scene of his crime, Jordan, though realising the danger, had been drawn to the vicinity of his Housemaster's study in the hope of 'finding out what had happened to the others'. In short, Jordan was in the throes of an uncomfortable guilt reflex.

'Oh, Jordan,' said Mr Greenham, pulling up suddenly, 'I want to have a word with you.' The Housemaster swivelled on his heel, and began retracing his steps and calling over his shoulder, 'Follow me, Jordan.'

The tall, lanky Jordan, round shouldered and with a pronounced stoop, followed at a respectful distance. To say that he was filled with foreboding would be no more than the truth. He was thinly covered around the rear quarters, and he appreciated a caning even less than those will fuller provision in that area. Nevertheless, he felt a sense of relief. Secretly, he had despised himself for successfully escaping when the others had been caught by Mr Greenham. Indeed, he despised himself no less – secretly – for his propensity to display in the Bog House that particular item of anatomy with which nature had so abundantly endowed him. Escape was a normal human reaction of self-preservation; the other thing was more complicated. It sprang, partly from natural pride in the possession of such unusual equipment, and partly from a persistent desire to obtain sexual gratification seemingly unattainable on his own. He needed the company – as well as the manipulative assistance. But, secretly, he was ashamed.

It came as a great relief to him, therefore, when in front of Mr Greenham, he made a full confession.

Mr Greenham, on the other hand, was merely embarrassed. He regarded any reference to sex, or the sexual organs, as just vulgar. Good, clean, healthy living was what he understood, and the sooner he disposed of this matter of Jordan's unsavoury proclivities, and got on with the much

72

more serious aspects of Fanshawe's sadism, the better it would be for everybody.

'Well, Jordan,' he said finally, after several throat-clearings, and much nervous knee flexing. 'I'm glad you decided to make a clean breast of it. Far better to get it off your chest.' He began pacing up and down, hands clasped behind back. 'Of course, you'll have to be severely punished for your part in the window-hanging of Penberth which, I'm bound to tell you, will be reported to the Headmaster – but, er, as for the other thing. Erhumm! well, you'll just have to, er – Erhumm! – you'll just have to get that under control. I don't want to hear any more about that, d'you understand?' Jordan nodded, contritely.

'Very well,' the Housemaster went on, 'we'll get that matter wiped off the slate, here and now. So, bend over in that corner, Jordan.'

Once more the cane, still warm from its previous exertions, was flexed and set to work with its usual stinging effect.

Thus, Jordan's sins – some of them, at least – were expunged from the tally. Immediately, he went in search of Fanshawe and his similarly punished confederates to show them, by dropping his breeches and displaying the six, angry red weals striping his bottom, that he, too, had been man enough to take his medicine.

Mr Greenham, after a further restorative nip from the whisky bottle, went in the opposite direction – down to the Headmaster's study.

The Reverend Doctor C.B. Chaunter was standing by the window, magnifying glass in hand, examining a rare specimen of butterfly when, in answer to his high-pitched 'Enter,' Mr Greenham walked in to the study.

Dr Chaunter greeted him with the utmost affability. 'Oh, my dear Rupert! How delightful to see you. Do come over here and look at my *Thecla regalis*. Isn't it just superb?'

Mr Greenham knew nothing whatsoever about butter-flies.

'It belongs to the family Lycaenidae, you know,' the Headmaster continued, without waiting for a reply, 'Have you ever seen anything quite so enthralling as the delicate blue of the wing tips?'

'I have something rather important to tell you, Headmaster,' Greenham broke in.

Dr Chaunter appeared not to hear the interruption. 'And can you imagine a more sensitive shade of green – especially in the lower wings.' He held the specimen up against the light of the window, to demonstrate the full, translucent beauty of the tiny wings.

'Quite remarkable,' Greenham agreed. 'But – er – Headmaster, I'm afraid I have something to. . . .'

'Feast your eyes, my dear Rupert, on these tantalisingly exotic markings at the base of the lower wings of this incredibly beautiful little *Precis orithya wallacei*. . . .' He had picked up another specimen from the louis quinze table in the window.

'Headmaster, I have something rather unpleasant. . . .'

Dr Chaunter suddenly fixed his junior in a penetrating stare. 'My dear fellow – I'm so sorry. You were going to say something.'

'Yes, Headmaster. I have to report a very serious case of sadistic bullying.'

Dr Chaunter regarded his Housemaster through half-closed eyelids. His mouth formed itself into a tightly-sewn purse. Eventually, he put down the specimen butterfly, before gliding over to the fireplace. 'Tell me about it,' he said, softly. He motioned Rupert Greenham towards the arm-chair on the left of the fire, before sinking elegantly into the one on the right. He put his finger tips together, closed his eyes, and settled back to listen.

Without naming any of the culprits at this stage, Greenham recounted the whole story, beginning with what he had actually seen himself, then filling in the gaps from the information he had gleaned from the boys, especially Jordan.

'But I deliberately refrained from quizzing the new boy,

74

Penberth,' he admitted, 'the one who was hung out of the window. I thought he'd had enough for one day, and I therefore refrained from pressing him to inform on the others.'

The Headmaster nodded. 'I will see him,' he murmured. For several minutes he remained motionless, staring down at his outstretched legs, elegantly clad in black silk stockings, his feet in silver-buckled shoes. Then, scarcely moving his lips, and as though in some form of trance, his voice barely above a whisper, he continued. 'You say that you have dealt with these bestial creatures, Rupert – and although I think you slightly exceeded your prerogative by caning boys from other Houses, nevertheless, I applaud your prompt action. Nothing like punishment on the spot, I'm sure you agree, and thereafter no hard feelings.'

'I'm glad to know that you feel that way, Headmaster. But 'hard feelings' or not, I feel strongly that the boy who was the acknowledged ringleader must not be allowed to escape further, far more drastic punishment.' Dr Chaunter raised one eyebrow, and shot an enquiring glance at Greenham. 'What exactly do you mean, Rupert?' he asked.

'I mean, Headmaster, that in my opinion the boy must go. He has been guilty not only of causing grievous bodily harm to an entirely innocent new boy but also of hazarding the boy's life. That boy Penberth – had he hit his head on the cobbles – might easily have been killed.'

Dr Chaunter frowned deeply – and nodded. 'Who was the ringleader, Rupert?'

Now, it must here be admitted that Trevor Rupert Greenham had deliberately presented his story in a somewhat devious manner. His excuse would certainly have been that, when dealing with a devious Headmaster, one must adopt a similar method. So far, apart from disclosing the name of the new boy who had been subjected to the barbarous treatment, he had avoided mentioning any other names – he had merely admitted to the Headmaster that 'not all of the cuplrits are in my House'.

He had wanted to present to Dr Chaunter the full picture

of this heinous crime *before* declaring the name of the ring-leader, Fanshawe.

When, at last, he did so, the response was exactly as he had expected. The Headmaster stiffened. Then, very slowly he got to his feet. For a few moments he stood gazing out at the rapidly gathering twilight. As usual, when deep in thought, his eyes were half-closed. Then, with a sudden intake of breath, he turned and directed a steely-eyed stare at the Housemaster.

'Fanshawe, did you say, Greenham?' Gone was the friendly, familiar 'Rupert'. 'Fanshawe! Liggett-Fanshawe! Do you realise who the Liggett-Fanshawes are, Greenham?'

The Housemaster pretended total ignorance. ''Fraid not, Headmaster. Ought I to?'

'My dear Greenham!' The H.M.'s tone was distinctly disparaging, 'I would have thought you'd have made it your business to enquire. Fanshawe *is* a Liggett-Fanshawe. The boy's full name is Alexander Edward Liggett-Fanshawe. For some *extraordinary* reason the boy chooses to be known as A.E.L. Fanshawe. I simply cannot imagine why he should wish to divest himself of the hyphenated distinction.'

'Hyphenated or not, Headmaster,' Greenham observed, tartly, 'the boy has a very unpleasant, vicious streak in his make-up, and he has just confessed to a dangerously sadistic act. In my opinion, the boy should be expelled, immediately.'

Dr Chaunter continued to hold Greenham in an unwavering stare. His eyes had the penetrative quality of gimlets.

'Ye-es,' he replied slowly, a snake-like smoothness in his voice, 'you have already suggested that.'

Then, after a long pause, he continued, 'You do realise, Greenham, do you not . . . well, no, perhaps you do not . . . but the Liggett-Fanshawes are an extremely well-connected family. A large estate in Hampshire, I believe, and plenty of money, of course.' The Reverend Dr Cyril Chaunter sighed deeply. 'It really would be most inconvenient . . .

especially as the boy's father has virtually promised a substantial donation towards the new cricket pavilion.'

Depressingly, the conversation was proceeding precisely as Greenham had expected. If he did not actually know all the details, he had assumed, from the arrogant demeanour of the boy, that the Fanshawes were probably an exceptionally privileged family.

'I appreciate your dilemma, Headmaster, but nevertheless, I feel very strongly that, for the sake of the school's reputation, Fanshawe must be made an example of.'

'And I think you are being surprisingly obtuse, Greenham. It is the school's reputation I am thinking about.' The Headmaster buried his chin on his chest, deep in thought, and began pacing the floor like a panther. 'You are quite sure, are you,' he said, at last, 'that Liggett-Fanshawe really was the ringleader? Was there not, perhaps, some other boy who could. . . .'

This, for Greenham, was the last straw. He had never been one of Dr Chaunter's admirers and the suggestion that the blame could be shifted to the shoulders of another boy – a boy without a hyphenated surname, and of comparatively humble origins, no doubt – absolutely infuriated him. Here was this prevaricating prelate, masquerading as a devout man of God, with his powdered wig and his sweeter-than-honey tone of voice, obviously quite willing to sacrifice an innocent nobody on the altar of his precious aristocratic ideal. It was monstrous!

Barely able to disguise his feeling of contempt, Greenham said tersely, 'I'm sorry to have to say this, Headmaster, but unless Fanshawe is expelled forthwith, I shall feel bound to tender my resignation.'

Dr Chaunter halted abruptly in mid stride. Gently stroking the lobe of his right ear, he stared unflinchingly at Greenham for what seemed like a long time. Then, slowly extracting a gold watch from the fob pocket of his breeches waistband, he carefully consulted the time.

'Did you not say it was your turn to take evening chapel, Greenham?' he asked in his most honeyed tones. 'Then, I think you should be getting along there now – don't you?'

Gathering the skirts of his black frock-coat around his midriff, he stalked across to the table in the window, and resumed his intense examination of the *Precis orithya wallacei*.

CHAPTER SEVEN

Homecoming

Marianne Penberth sat on the edge of the wooden upright chair beside the Terril and Rogers range in Treworden kitchen, spreading her hands in front of the glow. Although it was nearly the end of March, there was still a distinct nip in the evening air. She felt excited, yet apprehensive. She had not set eyes on her beloved son, Ashley, since that awesome January morning when Sir Andrew MacKenzie's coachman had collected him, and taken him off for his first term at Lydford. There had been letters, of course – but that was not the same as holding the boy in her arms, kissing and hugging him, like she had always done ever since he was her baby. But perhaps, now that he'd been away at boarding school – 'to be made a man of', as Sir Andrew was so fond of saying – perhaps he would no longer like being kissed and hugged by his mother. She could not tell. They had never been separated before, and three months was quite a long time in the life of a schoolboy. She wondered whether he would be stiff and correct, giving her no more than a respectful salute – no longer her lovely, warm, friendly, curly-headed little boy – and the thought made her apprehensive.

For the hundredth time, it seemed, she glanced up again at the wooden-cased kitchen clock on the wall above the mantlepiece. The minute hand had hardly moved at all. She realised she had been doing little else for the past half-hour or so. It was stupid, she knew; it never made any difference. But she couldn't help it – and she did so wish they'd hurry up and come.

Sir Andrew had offered – kindness itself, as he always was – to pick up Ashley and his trunk, on his way back from a business trip to London. He would be putting up for the night at the *White Hart* at Launceston, as usual, and it would be no trouble to pick up the boy and his luggage the following day. Besides, he'd like to have a chat with Dr Chaunter and, possibly, the Housemaster, just to ascertain Ashley's progress, because, although he'd said nothing to Marianne, he'd heard a few rumours – and he would like to find out the truth.

It was just after half-past four when Zeph Curnow's heavy boots clattered on the cobbles outside the back door, and his excited face appeared at the window.

'They'm comin', Mistress,' he shouted, delightedly, 'I kin yur they now.' Zeph was obviously as pleased as anyone at the prospect of seeing 'young Mester Ashley' again.

Marianne threw a shawl round her shoulders, and ran out into the yard. While her farm manager kept a respectful distance, one arm resting along the top of the ivy-covered yard wall and a limp stalk of well-chewed wheat straw dangling from his mouth, the Mistress of Treworden awaited the home-coming of her son. She was wondering whether he would have grown much.

Within a few moments, Sir Andrew's carriage rumbled into the yard. But instead of the door being burst open by an eager schoolboy returning for his first Easter holiday, it was opened slowly by Sir Andrew himself, who gave a friendly greeting to Marianne and then turned to assist his passenger. Immediately, motherly instinct alerted, Marianne realised her son had been injured in some way. As she rushed forward she saw that his left leg was encased in splints from thigh to ankle. After enveloping him in her arms, hugging and kissing him – momentarily forgetting all about her earlier concern for his reaction to such a display of affection – she then held him at arms length while she looked down at his leg.

'But whatever happened?' she enquired, shooting anxious glances from her son to Sir Andrew, then back again.

Sir Andrew grimaced. 'Seems he's been in the wars a wee bit,' he observed enigmatically.

'But what? what? Tell me at once. What happened?' Marianne's voice was full of anxious, motherly concern. She had sent her beloved little boy away in good health and perfect condition, yet here he was, just three months later, with one leg in splints. What *had* they been doing to him – at this expensive school for gentlemen's sons!

'It's nothing much, really Mater,' Ashley consoled, 'Nothing to worry over, anyway.' His boyish face was flushed with the excitement of the journey and the sheer pleasure of being at home again. 'I had a bit of an accident the day before yesterday, that's all. . . .'

'That's all, you say,' his mother broke in, 'that's all, indeed! You come home with your leg in a splint – presumably it must be broken somewhere – and all you can say is that it was 'a bit of an accident'!' Her face was flushed, too; she was angry with herself for being angry – not with anyone in particular, just for being angry. She felt so thankful to have her boy home again, but it had been a shock to see him injured.

'Don't be cross, Mama,' Ashley placated. 'It was just an accident – truly. Nothing whatever to do with the school,' he added hastily, fearing lest his mother might have heard about his window-hanging ordeal. 'And it was entirely my own fault, really. We were out for our usual Sunday afternoon walk, you see – mind you, it's supposed to be voluntary but it's a bit like voluntary chapel – ' he glanced at Sir Andrew conspiratorially, 'if you don't go you'll probably get flogged. Well, as I was saying,' he continued with a laugh, 'we were out for this walk – Courtier, Braund, Innes and myself – incidentally, they're new boys, like me – and we came to this stile, you see. Well, Braund said to Courtier, who's easily the smallest of us all, that he'd wager a mug of cocoa that Courtier couldn't jump the stile straight off.'

Marianne sadly shook her head. She felt sure she knew what was coming.

'Well,' Ashley went on, obviously enjoying the telling, 'would you believe it! Little Courtier, who's a springy little chap, went and cleared it by at least a couple of inches. Then, of course, Innes had to have a go, and he managed it all right because he's quite a good high jumper, so then. . . .'

This time Marianne's head was nodding resignedly. 'I know,' she said, 'and that meant that, of course, you had to have a go.'

'But I would have been perfectly all right, Mama,' Ashley protested, 'but in my very last stride, I slipped in the mud, and instead of going over the stile I crashed right into it. Somehow I must have got my leg between the two cross bars, and then there was a horrible crack, and then . . . well, then it was a bit painful. . . .'

'Ooh, my poor boy!' Marianne enveloped her son in her arms. 'It must have been awesome!' The mere thought of the agony started the tears coursing down her cheeks. The tears were infectious; Ashley's eyes brimmed over, too, more from the realisation of his mother's distress than from the memory of his own discomfort. Mother and son clung to each other for a long moment, and then Marianne, remembering her duty as hostess to the man whose kindness seemed to know no bounds, said; 'Sir Andrew – what must you be thinking! You'll excuse us, I hope. It was all rather a shock.'

'Fully understood,' was all that Sir Andrew said.

Then Marianne dabbing away her tears with a handkerchief, went on: 'Now, tea is all ready. You will join us, I hope, Sir Andrew?'

Sir Andrew laughed. 'Have ye ever known me refuse one of your Cornish teas, Mistress Penberth?'

Marianne turned to Zephaniah Curnow who had been keeping a respectful distance during the emotional homecoming of the young master. 'And you, Zeph – you'll join us, too, won't you? After all, it's a special occasion when Master Ashley comes home, isn't it?' Knowing full well how reluctant her farm manager was to intrude whenever 'quality' was present, she added; 'You'll be very welcome, for sure, Zeph. You know that, don't you?'

'Well, thank ee, Messus. Just a cup, like. Me own tay'll be waitin' for I at 'ome, zee. But just a cup. . . .' He could never have resisted the opportunity to get first hand information about what had befallen young 'Mester Ashley'. It would be village gossip for days.

After three months of Lydford College food, the sight of his mother's tea spread out on the kitchen table was one which Ashley would savour long after the food had been eaten. The sturdy table, normally scrubbed white and bare, as a kitchen working surface should always be, was today draped with green baize over which lay an exquisitely woven lace table cloth. Only Zephaniah Curnow knew for certain where that delicate lace had come from – and he had made a solemn vow to himself not to disclose to anyone the circumstances of its clandestine, dawn arrival off the Cornish coast – but he felt tolerably sure that the Mistress had a pretty shrewd idea about its origins, as well.

But what most captured the homecoming Ashley's imagination was not the delicate tablecloth from overseas but, rather, the mouth-watering array of food set out on top of it. The massive home-cured ham on the bone, some of it already carved and curling downwards in juicy, bread-crummed slices; the succulent-looking round of tongue, as yet unsullied but crying out for the first sliver to fall to the cutting edge of the carving knife; the mound of potato salad; the crimson-magenta coloured slices of beetroot and the shredded cabbage; the wide variety of home-made pickles. And best of all, perhaps, the crackly-skinned jacket potatoes, basted with farmhouse butter and piping hot from the oven.

In the middle of the table, their contents seductively inviting, stood three elegant cut glass bowls. In the one, an enticing confection of fruit salad; in another, a wobbly, bubbly-looking chocolate blancmange; and in the third, a deliciously aromatic, brandy-based trifle – each one, of course, topped off with an enormous dollop of thick, crusty clotted cream.

83

Sir Andrew MacKenzie regarded the spread wryly. Then, cocking an eyebrow in Ashley's direction, he observed; 'A wee bit of an improvement on the normal school tea, eh?'

Ashley laughed. 'Yes, indeed, Sir Andrew. A good deal better than pease pudding gruel – with an occasional helping of hasty pudding, if you're lucky!'

Marianne smiled indulgently as she watched her son's obvious enjoyment as he plunged his knife and fork into the plateful of nourishing farmhouse food. He needed it, she thought. Looked a little bit 'peaky' – not much colour in his cheeks, she fancied. Ah, well, it was nothing that plenty of good food and fresh air wouldn't put right. And she liked the polite way he addressed Sir Andrew – deferential but not subservient – and the concern he showed that everyone else should have everything they wanted at table before hungrily attacking his own portion. Yes, he was growing into a nice lad – and growing was certainly the word. He seemed to have shot up, even in the three months since she had last seen him. More manly; quite an air of assurance, in fact. Perhaps they were doing something for him at Lydford College, after all. And so they should, she reflected, with those heavy school fees. She felt rather proud of her son – yes, she really did.

As he was leaving after tea, Sir Andrew drew her to one side, out of Ashley's earshot, and said quietly, 'Keep an eye on that leg of his. They're funny things, fractures. It'll probably be all right, but if there's any sign of trouble we'll take him up to Exeter to see Degory Logan. He's the man. Very up-to-date, so they say, and especially good on bones.' Then, noticing the look of anxiety creeping into Marianne's face, he added with a reassuring smile, 'Don't worry, my dear – or as we say *dinna fash yersel*.' His grin broadened across his red-whiskered face. 'He'll be all right. Just don't let him go putting Tiger at a five-bar gate, or anything foolish like that.'

Next morning, the first day of Ashley's Easter holiday, Zeph Curnow was up early, putting Bluebell into the shafts of the market cart. He was anticipating – quite correctly – that Master Ashley would want to have a look round the farm, and he realised that, for the time being at any rate, the mode of transport would have to be something other than Shanks's pony – or even Tiger. The light, market cart would be the answer. Even with his leg in splints, Master Ashley could get himself reasonably comfortable up on the driving seat, and with the willing little Bluebell in the shafts they would be able to get to most parts of the farm.

So, with Rover, the black and white collie, keeping a very sharp, watchful eye on everything and everybody from over the top of the footboard, and with young Master Ashley up on the driving seat beside him, Zephaniah Curnow set off to do the round of the farm. He felt elated; it was good to have the young master with him again. It had been lonely these past three months, and he was determined to make the most of Master Ashley's time at home.

'Us'll go an' see the sheep, fust, shall us,' he announced gleefully, giving Bluebell a playful flick on the rump as they rattled out of the farm yard. 'The yores and lambs be up in that ther little paddicky field, up ther by Trecombe land, you mind?'

Ashley 'minded' the field very well. Was it not up in that paddock that Zeph had taught him to ride? – had made those modest little fences of furze and broken-off tree branches, and coaxed him over his first-ever jump? And was it not in that same field that, together, they had schooled the frisky little filly, Bluebell, and broken her to the saddle as well as to harness? The memories were as fresh as they were plentiful. It was in that same paddock, too, that Ashley and the Mackenzie girls had lazed away many a summer's hour, putting their ponies over the jumps again and again – Jeannie always the recklessly daring one, Alethea less bold but determined not to be outdone by her elder sister – before sinking back into the soft warmth of the mossy, springy turf at the foot of the stone hedge. They would make up stories for each other of dragons and castles, and tall ships that sailed away in the night.

The memory made Ashley impatient to see the girls again. He wondered if they had missed him. He wondered if

Alethea would still retain that same, elusive charm which had held him in the palm of her small hand ever since that first meeting at Trevadne. He wondered. . . .

'Naow then, young Mester,' Zeph broke in, dragging Ashley's thoughts away from flouncy petticoats and bobbing curls, back to the world of farming, the man's world. . . . 'I'm aimin' to show ee as fine a crop o' spring lamb as I reckon you'd ever see.'

He pulled up outside that paddock gate. Not a ewe or a lamb was to be seen.

'Aw,' Zeph muttered, 'they'm down in t'other field, I reckon.' He jumped down from the cart, saying, 'But us'll soon have un up, though, won't us, Rover.' Immediately, Rover was at his side, leaping and barking excitedly, anticipating his orders, and as soon as Zeph told him to 'Git up round, then,' the dog was through the gate like a flash and streaking away across the field towards the gap in the hedge at the bottom. Within minutes, that miracle of understanding between shepherd and sheep dog was beginning to unfold before Ashley's eyes. It was a familiar sight. He had watched Zeph work the dog many times before, but every new occasion was a fresh delight. First, there appeared just one woolly head and prick ears – nervous, uncertain of what lay beyond the gap – then the gradually swelling chorus of high pitched bleats mingled with the throaty rumbles of the anxious, affronted mothers would herald the arrival of the whole flock, suddenly racing, jostling and leaping through the narrow opening, with the patient, controlled Rover creeping from side to side at their heels. Then, quietly and without hurry, he would bring them all up to the gate, for presentation to his master.

Yes, Ashley reflected, it was good to be back.

He remained seated in the cart, casting a youthful but relatively experienced eye over the flock of Longwools. They were in nice condition – heads well covered with wool, faces white, nostrils shiny black, ears mostly white but with an occasional black spot. And conformation was good, too – shoulders nice and level, backs broad and firm – and they had that contented looked about them which showed that Zeph was 'doing them right'.

'They're looking well,' Ashley observed, 'and a fair crop of lambs, too.'

'Oh, aah,' Zeph agreed, absently, ' 'twill do, I s'pose. So long as price stays good, like.' He leaned on the gate, eyeing the flock keenly. He was watching one particular ewe. She was limping. Presently, he climbed over the gate and began quietly threading his way through the tightly packed flock – with Rover in the background, crouching, alert and intensely watchful, ready to cut off the retreat of any ewe breaking away from the bunch. Suddenly, and with the extraordinary sixth sense which sheep seem to possess, one head came up above the rest – the head of the ewe in Zeph's sights – and the animal began struggling to get free from the flock. But Zeph was too quick for it. With a lightning thrust, his arm went down between the mass of woolly bodies, and immediately the wriggling, twisting, protesting ewe was being pulled backwards, clear of the flock, one hind leg firmly grasped above the hock by Zeph's gnarled, experienced hand.

Rover, infected by the sudden flurry of excitement, deserted his guard-post and was snapping peevishly at the captive ewe.

'Git back, there!' Zeph roared, 'Lay down, you stupid damned dog. Lay down, will you. LAY DOWN!'

Cowering, tail drooping, ashamed of his temporary lapse from grace, the collie crept back to his post, furtively glancing from flock to flock–master and then back again. Oblivious of the dog's discomfort, Zeph had expertly thrown the ewe on its back and was painlessly pinning its neck beneath the arch of his boot as he knelt at the animal's side. From a pocket of his smock he produced a razor-sharp paring knife and began carefully trimming the hoof of the right foreleg.

'I thought her were hobblin' a bit, yesterday,' he muttered, 'I reckoned 'twas time her were cotched and see'd to.'

Then there were 'The Rubies' – the dark cherry-red

North Devon cattle of which Zeph was so proud. They had to be seen and admired.

'Do ee mind they days,' Zeph reminisced, leaning over the gate, staring appreciatively at the rich red-brown animals tugging lazily at the vivid green of the spring grass, 'Do ee mind when you were no more'n a nipper, Mester Ashley, how I use'ta put ee up on the back of old Twister, an' then you'da ride un back down home after ploughin'?'

Ashley grinned. It seemed like only yesterday. 'I was a bit scared at first,' he admitted ruefully, 'but I got really fond of old Twister in the end.'

'Aw ais. Her were a good ole beast were Twister,' Zeph mused, 'specially wi' the plough. Best oxen us ever had for ploughin', I reckon.'

With the hem of his smock he wiped a persistent drip from the end of his nose.

'But I never did tell the Mestress, tho',' he went on. ' 'Bout the ridin', I mean. Her'd have just worrited herself, see. So, I never did tell her.'

Ashley grunted acknowledgement. There were quite a number of things Zeph Curnow never 'told the Mestress', he wouldn't wonder.

But it was good to be back with him again – good to be seeing once more all the old familiar landmarks, sniffing again the smells of the farm stead which to some people might seem obnoxious but which to Ashley Penberth meant, simply, 'Home'.

Oh, yes, it was good to be back – to be free from the awfulness of Lydford. It made him all the more impatient for Trevadne and the MacKenzie girls.

CHAPTER EIGHT

Naval aspirations

Miss Proudfoot, the governess, had greeted him warmly, but with formality. Alethea had shyly taken his hand. But when Jeannie burst into the room she had spontaneously flung her arms around his neck and kissed him firmly on the mouth. He had been embarrassed. After all, a chap returning from his first term at Lydford hardly expects to be kissed like that. A hug and a kiss from the Mater, certainly; a peck on the cheek by a sister, perhaps – if there's no way of avoiding it – but to be kissed by a vivacious, raven-haird beauty who smelt of lavender and rose petals, and whose figure had developed and rounded noticeably, alluringly, while he had been away at school – well, a fellow didn't expect to be kissed, full on the mouth, by a girl like that. It had sent a strange, erotic thrill coursing through his body, making his breeches feel uncomfortably tight.

He had backed away, flushed, laughing and confused; he had noticed the challenging look and the sparkle in Jeannie's eyes. He had noticed, too, that in Alethea's there was anguish and dejection. He wished he could have said something to her, there and then – something to dispel that look of sadness – but already he was being bombarded with questions about his leg and his accident. How did it happen? Out walking one Sunday afternoon with Courtier, Innes and Braund. . . . Who might they be? Three other new boys like himself. . . . And what actually happened? Jumping a stile for a wager, slipped in the mud, leg got caught somehow between the bars. . . .

'Fooling about, in fact,' Jeannie taunted.

'No, honestly. I could have cleared it easily if I hadn't slipped.'

'Was it dreadfully painful?' Alethea asked, her face crinkled with sympathy.

'Yes, it was, a bit . . . when it actually happened . . . when I crashed into the stile. But I think it was mostly the impact of hitting the blasted thing.' He glanced at Miss Proudfoot, 'Sorry, Pruddy,' he apologised with mock contrition, remembering how they used to tease her about her abhorrence of anything resembling a blasphemous expletive. 'The funny thing was,' he went on, 'I didn't feel any pain in my knee when they carried me back to the school.'

'Who carried you back?'

'The three of them. . . . Innes, Courtier and Braund. They managed awfully well, really. Somehow they succeeded in breaking off a couple of branches from a nearby ash tree – I think one of them was half broken off, anyway – and then Braund and Innes took off their jackets – they're the biggest of the three – and they threaded these branches through the sleeve . . .'

'And made a kind of stretcher!' Jeannie exclaimed, delightedly, 'How clever of them.'

'Well, it was pretty bright, I must admit,' Ashley agreed, 'And then the three of them – Courtier taking the two branch ends at my feet, the other two holding a branch end each up at my head – they managed to get me back to the school without my having to put a foot to the ground. I must say, it was awfully decent of them.'

'Who thought of the stretcher idea?' Alethea asked.

'Courtier thought of it. His father's in the Navy, and I believe they do the same sort of thing using a couple of sweeps – oars, that is. Anyway, it was Courtier's idea – and a jolly good one, too, I thought.'

'They sent for the Doctor straightaway, I hope,' Miss Proudfoot put in.

'Oh, yes. He came out that evening – reeking of brandy, of course – set it, and then put these splints on. He's a

90

cheerful old soak – ex-Naval surgeon, I believe – said I'd be as good as new before long.'

'Well,' Jeannie quipped, 'I hope he could see straight enough to fit the two ends together!'

'Was that bit rather painful?' Alethea asked.

Ashley nodded. 'Yes, it was rather. But not as painful as. . . .' He stopped short, momentarily glancing at the backs of his hands. Then he quickly went on, 'Not as painful as I thought it would be.'

Alethea noted the pause. She pondered Ashley's remark, wondering what could be more painful than the setting of a broken bone.

More than a week passed before she was able to satisfy her curiosity. It was one of those comparatively rare occasions when she was able to enjoy Ashley's company without the presence of her more effervescent – and, Alethea felt, much more attractive – elder sister. Jeannie, now a confident and highly presentable sixteen-year-old, was being called upon occasionally to accompany her father on some of his business or official functions. Today was one of them; a civic function at Truro demanded Sir Andrew's presence, and Jeannie had accompanied him as his lady. This left Alethea free to ride over to Falmouth with Ashley, to picnic on the grassy slopes below Pendennis. It was the first time, since the beginning of the holidays, they had really been alone together. The day was pure magic; fleecy lambswool clouds drifting lazily across a landscape painter's dream sky; gentle breezes fluttering the first timid leaves of Spring; hedge-banks awash with primroses.

And as they rode up over the top of Pennance Hill and looked out across the vast shimmering blueness of Falmouth Bay, there beneath them, peacefully at anchor in all its proud, tall-masted majesty, lay the Channel Squadron of the Royal Navy.

Involuntarily, Ashley tugged at Tiger's bit, 'Just look at that!' he breathed reverently. 'What a magnificent sight.'

Alethea reined her pony to a halt beside him. She was looking, not at the impressive might of His Majesty's fleet

91

but at the unmistakeable gleam of ambition in her companion's eyes.

'It's what you really want, isn't it?' she said softly with unusually mature prescience. 'It's not the farm, or the country – or even just Cornwall, is it? It's the Navy.'

'Courtier says it's a wonderfully exciting life,' Ashley mused, still gazing at the forest of masts and the intricate tracery of rigging. 'I must admit I'd like to be part of it.'

'Who's Courtier – and what does he know about it?' Alethea asked sensibly.

'He's a fellow at school. His father's in the Navy, as I think I told you. So was his grandfather. Served with our Admiral Boscawen, I believe. They called him Old Dreadnought, so Courtier says. Made a small fortune out of prize money, too,' Ashley grinned, 'so it can't be such a bad career, after all!'

They dismounted, spread Tiger's rug on the lush green turf and began munching the slices of beef, cut wafer-thin and placed between two pieces of freshly baked bread, which Alethea produced from her saddle bag.

'By Jove, but these are good,' Ashley crowed, spraying crumbs all over the rug in his enthusiasm, 'A new idea, isn't it?'

'Didn't you know,' Alethea laughed, lying back on the rug, cradling her head in the crook of her arm. 'It's called a sandwich.'

'A "sandwich"! It seems like a delicious sliver of beef between two chunks of bread to me. Why ever is it called a "sandwich"?'

Alethea waved her free hand vaguely in the direction of the fleet. 'As a future naval officer,' she quipped, 'you really ought to know.'

'Why, what's it got to do with the Navy?'

'My papa says it was invented by the First Lord of the Admiralty so that he could satisfy his hunger without having to leave the gambling table.'

'Yes, perhaps, but why. . . .'

'Why call it a sandwich?' Alethea anticipated, 'Because

the First Lord of the Admiralty happened to be the Earl of Sandwich – or so Papa says.' Her fair-skinned forehead wrinkled prettily into a frown. 'I wonder if Pruddy knows that. I must remember to ask her.'

Out of the corner of his eye, pretending not to look at her, Ashley was observing the girl at his side. She had matured appreciably during his absence at Lydford. No longer the childish ways – the slightly lisping speech, the toe-turned-in awkwardness with strangers, the babyish acceptance of 'second fiddle' to her sister and cuddly favourite of her father – all gone, or at least disappearing. In their stead, a very much emerging 'young lady', increasingly aware of the world around her and the responsibilities of privilege – her hair more than ever like a wind-blown field of ripening barley, her eyes like the sky of a cloudless June morning, and her nose, mouth and chin chiselled with the delicacy of a Michelangelo *Pieta*.

But what fascinated the young man stretched out on the mossy turf beside her was not so much her beauty and the promise of her emergent womanhood but rather that indefinable air that had surrounded her and clung to her ever since Ashley had first set eyes on her. He couldn't explain it – either to himself or anyone else. If you said 'magnetism' you would only be partially right – because magnetic power is constant, it draws you, it attracts you all the time. But there was something so elusive about Alethea; like a most desirable powder-blue butterfly, just when you thought you had it in your net it would be up and away, tantalisingly, just out of your reach. And then you would find it again, on a sprig of St Keverne heather, fluttering its pale blue wings and gently laughing at you. One more try, one more escape – but you would go on trying. Yes, you had to go on trying – even though right deep down inside you there was this feeling – this fear – that, perhaps after all, you might never make her yours.

'It's a hard life, tho' ' she was saying.

'The Navy, you mean?' Ashley replied, reluctantly coming out of his reverie.

She took another bite out of her beef sandwich and nodded. She ate prettily, he thought; so unlike Smithers who sat
opposite him at Lydford and ate with his mouth open, spitting out bits of bread and displaying the soggy mess of
unmasticated Hasty Pudding. All her movements were
pretty, he decided; she swayed attractively as she walked,
she rode easily in the saddle; ladylike, that was it. And yet,
when he threatened to pull her hair, she could pick up her
skirts and run just like a boy – faster than he could!

'Yes,' she said at last, finishing her mouthful, 'we have a
cousin who's a 'young gentleman' – or should I say 'midshipman'. . . .'

'Officer's servant is as good as anything,' Ashley suggested, 'because that's what they are.'

'Well, anyway,' Alethea went on, 'whatever's his proper
title, he's with Admiral Rodney's fleet in the West Indies,
serving under Sir Charles Douglas, I think.'

A gleam of envy crept into Ashley's eyes as he nodded,
'Yes, he's the gunnery expert; responsible for introducing
the carronade into the Navy.'

'Whatever's that?'

'The carronade?' Ashley queried, hoisting himself to a
more upright position and leaning on one elbow. 'The
carronade,' he repeated, trying to look grave and important, 'is a short naval gun with a large bore.'

'What's a bore?' Alethea asked, innocently.

'I am,' Ashley replied, unable to resist the bait, and at the
same time losing all pretence of seriousness, 'especially
when I talk about the Navy.'

'Oh, don't be silly!' Alethea chided, throwing a large
piece of sandwich at his face.

Ashley retaliated by suddenly grasping both her wrists
and pinning her back against the rug. She struggled to get
free. Playfully he let her think she was succeeding; then back
again he pinned her, several times, until at last she lay
panting and exhausted, her cheeks flushed, her eyes
shining.

She stared up into his face – the young, healthy-looking

'farmer boy' complexion, the fair, crinkly hair tousled by the wind and etched against the cerulean blue of the sky. Imperceptibly his mouth was moving closer to hers, his breath warm on her cheek, and then suddenly, impulsively, he was kissing her.

Several times before this they had kissed – playfully, when they were children sharing the same governess, playing at being bride and bridegroom, mothers and fathers, and always it had seemed right and proper that their union should be sealed with a kiss, a childish kiss, a peck on the cheek – but this was different. His lips were hard on hers – and she was experiencing a very strange, frightening sensation surging inside her.

She wriggled out of his grasp, and sat up abruptly.

'Whatever did you do that for?' she asked, looking straight into his eyes – half scoldingly, half affectionately.

'Because I wanted to,' he answered simply. 'It's something I've been wanting to do for a long time.'

'Well, you mustn't,' she said firmly.

'Why not?'

'Because. . . .'

'Because of what?'

'Just because,' she replied, with that feminine logic so baffling to the male.

'But that doesn't make sense,' he persisted.

'Things don't always have to make sense,' she countered, enigmatically.

He thought for a moment, staring out across the bay. 'Well,' he said at last, 'there are dozens of chaps at school who've got girl friends, and they often brag about the number of kisses they've had.'

'School,' she observed firmly, seeming to grasp the opportunity to change the subject, 'Lydford College – yes, tell me about it. Was it a dreadful experience for you – that first term, I mean. I believe it can be quite horrid, especially for boys who've never been away to school before.'

Sensing that it was not the moment to pursue the former much more interesting topic of conversation, Ashley lay back on the rug, and stared at the sky. A grim smile puckered his cheeks. 'Lydford College – yes, – first fortnight,' he mused. 'Rather too peppery around the nether regions, if you understand me. Got beaten – flogged, that is – several times, you see, and it began to get more than just a bit painful.'

He was feeling a curious pride, a sense of great achievement – now that it was all behind him. Nothing and nobody could ever take it away from him – that first fortnight of that first term at Lydford – and he had survived. Whatever the future might hold, it could hardly be worse than that.

As he lay there, looking up at Alethea, he was momentarily wallowing in a sensation of martyrdom. He was acutely aware, too, of the effect his words were having on her. An expression of infinite compassion had spread across her young, beautiful face, and for a split second it seemed to Ashley that her head, even against the pure blue of a cloudless sky, was circled by a soft, almost spiritual radiance.

It was a remarkable experience, yes – but it was slightly disturbing.

He blinked, sat up quickly, and then continued in a more bantering tone. 'Oh, well – you never know, it might come in useful one day, I suppose. For instance, as an officer of the Royal Navy I might find myself ordering a dozen lashes of the cat o' nine tails. At least I should understand the apprehension and the subsequent agony of the wretch being flogged.' He scratched the lobe of his right ear. 'Or some of it, anyway,' he added.

They sat silent for a while, side by side, gazing out at the impressive might of His Majesty's Navy.

'Was it almost unbearable,' Alethea said at last, breaking in on his thoughts, '– the flogging, I mean.'

'At one point, yes,' he conceded. 'At least – not exactly the flogging.'

'Tell me,' she said, turning her lovely, sympathetic eyes on him.

'Well, it's a bit difficult to explain, but . . .' he hesitated, wondering how much to divulge. Eventually he went on, 'Promise not to tell anyone. I don't want the Mater to know. She gets a little worried about such things.'

Once more those clear blue eyes washed over him, embracingly, as she assured, 'Of course I promise. You know that.'

'Well, it was when they hung me out of the dormitory window. That was a bit scary, I must confess. Chap by the name of Fanshawe . . . friendly sort of fellow . . . beat my knuckles with the back of a clothes brush . . . hoping I'd not be able to hang on.'

A sharp intake of breath confirmed Alethea's horror before Ashley continued.

'. . . Tried to make me own up to something I hadn't done. I hung on as long as I could, of course. . . .'

'And then you fell from the window!' Alethea gasped, 'and broke your leg in the fall. Is that what really happened?'

'No, no. That's the stupidest part of it. When I hit the cobbles under that window I only sprained my ankle – rather badly, admittedly – but then I had to go and do the thing properly, only a few weeks later, when jumping over a stile. Absolutely stupid, isn't it.'

'But how *awful*!' Alethea exclaimed, 'It must have been quite terrifying – the window-hanging bit I mean.' She gazed at him intently, her young, sensitive face full of compassion. 'And what absolute brutes they must be – those boys that made you hang out of the window.' She thought for a moment, frowning deeply, before enquiring, 'Does my Papa know about this – because if not, I think he ought to.'

'Oh, no!' Ashley blurted out hurriedly, 'and you must never breathe a word to him about it. He's very friendly with one of the Governors, I believe, and I should be positively crucified if anyone got to know that I'd blabbed.'

Seeking hastily to change the subject, Ashley pointed once more to the stirring sight of tall masts and fluttering sails in the Roads beneath them. 'Isn't that marvellous,' he purred, '– doesn't it make you feel tremendously proud?'

Even from a distance, the clatter of shipwrights' tools could be clearly heard, and all along the waterfront ship's officers, sailors, tallowchandlers, fishermen, boatbuilders and ropemakers – indeed everyone caught up in the throbbing life-blood of a busy port – could be seen urgently going about their business. From the slopes beneath Pendennis Castle they looked like ants on a ceaseless forage.

'And by the way,' Ashley went on, 'I've only told you all this – about the window-hanging, I mean – just to show you that I'm getting quite used to roughing it . . .' he glanced again in the direction of the Channel squadron, 'in relation to a career in the Navy, if you see what I mean.'

Alethea thought she knew only too well. Her cousin had told her that a midshipman must be able to climb to the highest point of that fearsome rigging – to spend hour after hour in the 'sky-parlour', as they called it – and even when exercising sails, a 'midi' in the tops must be wearing full dress. She knew all about a midshipman's berth – 'tween decks in the steerage, abreast the mainmast and on the larboard side – a small hole measuring about ten feet by six, and only just over five feet high, with a deal table and a brass candlestick – and very little else – for furniture.

She had heard, also, of the irrespressible high spirits which always seemed to be breaking out in the cockpit; of the battles for possession of the poop while seniors were at dinner in the wardroom; of the scrapes that the 'young gentlemen' got into during evenings ashore – and how necessary it was to have a good pair of legs with a fast turn of speed to shake off angry pursuers!

'It's an exciting life,' Alethea agreed, her eyes glinting at the thought of those hurried exits from hotel or tavern with subsequent sprints through the night back to the sanctuary of the ship, 'but it's a demanding one – and I'm just wondering how you'd get on if you had to climb to the 'tops' with an injured leg.'

'Oh, that!' Ashley scoffed, giving the wooden splint a hearty slap, 'That's nothing! In a couple of months' time that leg'll be as good as new. The old Doc said as much – and even though he's a boozy old soak, I'm sure he's right.'

As though drawn by a magnet, his gaze returned once more to the forest of masts so majestically piercing the line of the horizon, and giving his splint yet another friendly pat, he added cheerfully, 'No, no. That'll be no problem. Just give me a couple of months, and I'll be up those ratlines with the best of 'em. You'll see.'

CHAPTER NINE

A splintered tombstone

'A most delectable confection, my dear,' Colonel Innes remarked roundly, smacking his lips with appreciation. 'I hope you will convey my compliments to the cook.'

'Yes, she's done it quite well,' the colonel's lady replied, 'I gave her the recipe last week. It's one I found in Mrs. Glasse's recently published book *The Compleat Confectioner* – she calls it her *Everlasting Syllabub*. As you say, Colonel, I too find it most delectable.'

'Considerably better than old Cookie's usual suet pudding,' the colonel grunted, malevolently eyeing the almost untouched second dish in front of his wife. 'Can't say I think she deserves much praise for that.'

He drained his glass of Maderia, and then dabbed at his mouth with a white linen napkin. 'By the way Johnny,' he went on, half turning in the direction of his son, 'hounds are meeting over at Worthyvale tomorrow. What about your friend, does he like hunting?'

Johnny Innes – better known, perhaps, as Innes J.C. of Lydford College – shot an enquiring glance at his school-friend. 'How about it, Penberth? Do you get any hunting down Helford way?'

Ashley, his mouth still overfull of the justifiably maligned suet pudding, could manage no more than an affirmative nod. In due course he was able to enlighten his friend that 'Yes,' they quite often hunted with a pack of hounds at Cury.

During the Summer and Autumn terms at Lydford, Innes had become one of Ashley's friends. It was a friendship originally cemented in adversity. Together with Courtier and Braund, they had formed a quartet for mutual protection, and with Braund displaying an outstanding skill and readiness with his fists, they had eventually commanded a measure of grudging respect from their would-be tormentors. The two terms had passed relatively quietly.

Moreover, it had been Braund, Innes and Courtier who had brought Ashley back with a broken leg. That, in itself, had formed a bond between them – and in their typically gruff, schoolboy fashion they had shown a concern for Ashley's progress which had been quite touching.

Now, at the commencement of the Christmas holidays, Ashley had accepted an invitation to spend a few days with Johnny Innes and his family at their estate, Goff's Hall, near Camelford. It could only be a short stay because he wanted to be back at Treworden in good time for the usual Christmas festivities, but it was a convenient staging post on the long journey back to Falmouth, and it would give him a chance to discover a part of North Cornwall which, like many other parts of the country, was as yet unknown to him.

As the colonel had predicted, hounds met at Worthyvale Manor on the following morning. Although none of the field were known to Ashley, he was soon receiving friendly greetings from the gentry when it became apparent that he was a guest of the Innes family. It was obvious that Colonel Innes was highly respected by the squirearchy, while the farmers showed him that special brand of deference reserved for a fearless rider.

It was a crisp, sharp morning, the whole countryside powdered with a light hoar frost and shimmering beneath a bright but somewhat hazy winter sun. Far out to sea beyond Tintagel and Trebarwith Strand a long, low bank of thick cloud was slowly rolling towards the northern shore. After the stirrup cup had been served, the hunt moved off down to Slaughterbridge, but hounds then drew blank in the coppice below Tregatha. Drawing again in the woods behind Trevia, they went away on a good scent down the Lanteglos valley, skirting Colonel Innes' land, but then checked at the stream below Treforda. After casting around in the woods on the other side of the water they went away fast on a fresh scent, along the valley south of Newhall, before streaming out across the downs towards the cliffs beyond Tregragon. Already the field had thinned considerably, and when the thick bank of drizzling fog came rolling over the whole coastal region, Ashley and Johnny Innes, who had deliberately kept close together, found themselves virtually marooned in that inhospitable stretch of bleakness, somewhere between Tintagel and Port Isaac. Faintly, in the distance, hounds could still be heard giving tongue but in exactly which direction they were running was no more than an optimistic guess. Only the sound of wheeling gulls, high above the enveloping denseness of the cloud, suggested that the cliffs might not be far away.

'Nothing very pleasant about this,' Johnny remarked, as he pulled up sharply just short of a steep ravine. He peered into the blanket-like fog which had so stealthily crept up on them.

'Any idea where we are?' Ashley asked.

'Not a pile, I'm afraid. Somewhere in the region of Dinnabroad, I should say.'

'Where's Dinnabroad, for Heaven's sake? Doesn't mean a thing to me.'

'Not far from Pendoggett – which is at least something.'

'What's the something?'

'An inn – and not a bad little place, either.'

Well, as Johnny had said, that was at least something – always assuming they could find it, Ashley reflected. Anyone who has ever been caught out in the suddenness of a winter fog, either on Bodmin Moor itself, or its environs, knows just how bleak is the prospect of the hours that lie ahead. In broad, clear daylight the Moors and Downs are containable; they are within man's compass – so long as he has his own legs to carry him, if not those of a horse – but when he finds himself in the grip of a creeping, impenetrable coastal fog, a kind of mental suffocation overwhelms him. Each step he takes may be leading in the wrong direction, further and further from comfort and succour – nearer and nearer to a night beneath the shelter of a granite rock, exposed to the howling force of a freezing wind.

How desirable, therefore – how unbelievably welcome is the sight of a lantern shining into the gloom from the warmth of a friendly inn.

'If my reckoning's correct,' Johnny went on, 'it's only a couple of miles down the track, and even though it's going away from home, it'd be better than trying to catch up with hounds again. From the sound of it, they seemed to be heading for some rather deep quarries – my Pater up with them, most probably – and that could be a bit tricksy.'

'Does your Pater know about the quarries?' Ashley enquired.

'Oh, yes. You won't catch the Pater making that kind of mistake. Too canny, by a long chalk,' Johnny laughed. 'I'm not worried about him – he knows the district upside down. I'm more concerned about us. After all, Lydford wouldn't be quite the same without its two most promising pupils,' he joked, 'so I think we'd better make for the Pendoggett Inn, don't you?'

Johnny led the way slowly, away from the top of the ravine, until they came to a rough, much-pitted track.

'Unless I'm mistaken,' he observed, 'this is the main track from Delabole to Port Isaac, and if we turn right-handed we should very shortly strike Pendoggett.'

They set off at a brisker pace, now that the track was more clearly defined. It was broader, too, so they were able to ride side by side. They were both now cheerfully confident that a blazing fire and a tankard of mulled ale lay no more than a mile or so ahead of them.

But when, at last, the low outline of the inn loomed out of the fog they were surprised to find no welcoming lights blazing from the small, cottage-type windows. The place had an uncannily deserted air about it. Although the front door was closed, it was not locked. When Johnny pushed it open and, ducking his head to avoid the low door lintel, walked into the front parlour he found it empty. The embers of a log fire still smouldered in the broad, open fire-place, but there was no response when Johnny called out the landlord's name. Unwashed pewter tankards, some of them not fully drained, had been left on the shelf above the fire; a half-emptied jar of ale still stood in the dispense hatch.

'Don't know about you,' Johnny remarked, as Ashley joined him in the parlour, 'but it looks to me as though the occupants left in something of a hurry. I wonder why.'

Ashley shrugged. Being a Cornishman, he decided not to offer a solution – but he had an idea.

'Well,' Johnny concluded, after calling loudly again, and rapping his hunting crop on one of the inner doors to no effect, 'as we can't very well help ourselves to a pint of ale and raid the larder, I suppose we'd better start making for home. If we stick to the track I *think* we've just come by, and go back as far as Rockhead, then I should be able to find my way home from there, even in this filthy weather.' He peered out of the window at the gathering gloom. 'At least, I hope so.'

The place names, of course, meant little to Ashley but his friend seemed reasonably confident as, reluctantly, they left the warmth of the inn and set off once more, back along the rutted track they had just travelled.

They had been going for an hour, chatting about happenings at Lydford – Johnny commiserating with Ashley for having missed a term's cricket because of his broken leg, when Ashley, always the optimist, had cheerfully asserted his determination to play football next term, even if only in goal, in spite of the fact that it seemed to be taking an inordinately long time to get back any flexion in his knee. They had been talking thus when they became aware that the fog was thickening, and the track had become perceptibly narrower.

Vaguely, Johnny had the feeling that they were moving too far leftwards, but he had to admit out loud to Ashley that it was only the pull of his location 'bump' that told him so.

In such restricted visibility it was virtually impossible to recognise any landmark. But when they came upon another track branching off to the left, down a narrow combe and alongside a gurgling stream, Johnny suddenly stood up in his stirrups, bringing his pony to an abrupt halt.

'That looks mighty like the entrance to Trecarne,' he observed, 'even though every damned farm entrance looks pretty much the same up here in this weather. But, Goddamit! if it is, then we're miles off our route! And if there's another farm just here on the right of us, called Upton, then we're almost down to Trebarwith!'

It was then that they heard the first shout.

To begin with, they thought it was the hunt. But when a second shout was followed by cheering – wild, continuous, maniacal cheering – they realised it was no normal hunting sound. No hound ever uttered such blood-curdling screams, no hunter would greet the kill with such diabolical fervour.

'By God!' Johnny murmured, glancing at Ashley, 'I do believe it is.' He dug his heels into the pony's flanks, and set off along the track towards the sea.

Ashley followed blindly, an unwelcome curdling sensation of fear beginning to churn in the pit of his stomach. He knew not quite what he expected to see, but instinctively he felt it would be evil. The very timbre of those shouts and screams possessed the ring of the devil.

By the time they reached the cliff-top, the schooner was already beginning to break up on the rocks below. She lay on her side like a stricken sea bird, her stern and keel pointing seawards, her bow wedged firmly in the cleft of a jagged rock, a lifeless thing at the mercy of the thunderous seas around her. Her foremast had broken off and now swirled amid the floating wreckage, leaving only the stub pointing folornly skywards like a splintered tombstone, while her shrouds, like the tentacles of a dying octopus, floated aimlessly in the plunging surf. Tattered sails were strung out from writhing hull to razor sharp rock edges like the humble adornments of a poor woman's washing line.

Swarming in the sea and at the water's edge were the human vultures.

Greedily they grabbed at every bale, every cask, every wooden tea chest that floated near them. It was their harvest of the sea, and they were not to be denied. If it was solid and of any value, they grasped it; if it was a human body exhausted and struggling for the sanctuary of the shore, it would either be ignored or ruthlessly speeded to its watery grave. Nothing mattered but that the ship should be stripped of every vestige of valuable cargo. Not only the wreckers themselves but also those who had been drawn to the beach by word of mouth seemed caught up in an uncontrollable orgy of greed. Caskets of rum and brandy were broached as they floated ashore; both men and women were already so hopelessly drunk they were unable even to stagger off with their booty. For some, their life's work was ended when they toppled off the rocks and were drowned in sea water and vomit.

But for most, it was grab, relentless grab. Unmindful of their own safety, they fought not only the pounding, roaring waves but sometimes they had to fight each other when in dispute of some prized possession.

Hypnotised, mesmerised, horrified – Ashley watched from the clifftop. Right there beneath him, on a shallow ledge below, a scene which he knew he would carry with him for the rest of his life was being played out – the exhausted ship's captain, valiantly trying to protect his cargo from the marauders, was being clubbed to death by an enraged, demented wrecker.

Momentarily he remained motionless, frozen by horror to the rock on which he lay. Then, suddenly, something in his head snapped. He was up on his feet, waving his arms and shouting above the roar of the sea, calling upon the murderer to 'STOP!' He began recklessly clambering down the cliff face, but within a few steps, Johnny had grabbed him from behind.

'Come back, you fool!' he bellowed. 'Don't you understand, the bastards'll skin you alive!'

'But we can't just stand here and watch murder!' Ashley shouted back, 'That's what it is, Johnny – bloody MURDER!'

Johnny pulled him back behind the jutting rock. 'Now listen, Penberth,' he said, speaking more quietly but nonetheless urgently. 'You mean well, I know, but just two of us down there against that gang of blood-thirsty maniacs – we'd stand even less chance of survival than a couple of virgins in Hell!' He leaned back, breathlessly against the rock, drawing Ashley with him – out of sight of the wreckers below. But already one of them was shouting and pointing in their direction.

'And what's more,' Johnny went on menacingly, 'thanks to your heroics, we've been spotted. Come on, we're getting away from here – just as fast as lightning.'

The clatter of hoofs echoing from the foot of the ravine moments later confirmed that at least two horsemen had been despatched to follow and quickly silence the two youthful interlopers spotted on the cliff-top.

'Dead men tell no tales,' Johnny hissed, as he and Ashley hurriedly remounted and set off in the direction of Rockhead. 'That's their simple philosophy – which means we've got to go like the wind and outwit them. Come on! Follow me.'

At first it seemed they must be overtaken. Down on the beach visibility was still reasonably good, and the hoofbeats reverberating up through the valley suggested the wrecker's henchmen were moving at speed. But up on the higher ground the swirling, thickening fog was as much a handicap to the pursuers as to the pursued. When still a few hundred yards short of Rockhead, Johnny plunged off to the right, along a narrow footpath with encroaching gorse and heather on each side which would at least partially obscure their hoof prints. Very shortly, they emerged among the cottages of Delabole, and thereafter their tracks were lost among the many others through the village.

Once more they were able to ride side by side, and as Ashley came up abreast of Johnny he asked breathlessly,

'Oughtn't we to be alerting someone about those bastards down in the cove?'

Johnny shook his head. 'There's no one up here who'd lift a finger,' he replied gloomily, 'even supposing they're not all down there, themselves.' His sweeping gesture with his riding crop embraced the few humble cottages comprising the village. 'As you've probably guessed, despite the fog, the place isn't exactly teeming with inhabitants. Besides, it would take a whole detachment of Dragoons to nobble that bunch of villains down there, and by the time the soldiers came on the scene the wreckers would have vanished.'

'But surely there must be *something* we could do,' Ashley protested. 'It's wholesale murder going on down on that beach. Bloody murder! Surely there must be someone. . . .'

'Keep your wig on, old son! Just be thankful you aren't one of the corpses, yourself,' Johnny retorted scathingly, 'because, by God! you very nearly were!'

Ashley fumed silently. He knew full well that Johnny was right. But it seemed so hopelessly chicken-livered to sit there doing precisely nothing. The whole thing was just so absolutely BLOODY!

Sensing his friend's frustrated fury, Johnny attempted a soothing tone. 'Well, we'll tell the Pater, of course, as soon as we get home . . . and incidentally,' he continued, half turning in the saddle and cupping an ear, 'I hear no following hoof thuds, so I think we can safely assume we've shaken off the villains. Our chances of reaching home are therefore very much brighter. But, as I was saying,' he went on, resuming normal riding position, 'we'll certainly inform the Pater, and no doubt he'll report it to Bodmin. But that – well, I'm afraid that's just about all we *can* do. Personally, I shall just be bloody thankful to get home and dry.'

Ashley remained silent. He supposed Johnny was right. Perhaps there really was nothing they could do – now. But as he turned to look back over the way they had come, the vision of that struggling ship's captain reared hauntingly in his mind yet again, while the maniacal screams of the wreckers seemed forever in his ears. Under his breath, and with all the fervour of youthful zeal, he muttered; 'I know not when, and I know not how; but someday I'm going to smash that evil!

CHAPTER TEN

Degory Logan

Sir Andrew MacKenzie's coachman drew the carriage to a halt outside Mr Degory Logan's consulting rooms in Southernhay. He slithered to the ground, and opened the gleaming carriage door to allow Sir Andrew and his passengers to alight.

Almost a year had gone by since the confrontation between Ashley's knee and the unyielding stile on that unlucky Sunday afternoon walk. During the intervening months it had become uncomfortably apparent that something had gone wrong with the natural healing process. For one thing, the knee would not bend; for another, and perhaps more alarming, the injured leg was not keeping pace with the rapid growth of the good leg. Ashley was shooting upwards, but his left leg was perceptibly shorter than his right.

Mr Degory Logan was now an acknowledged expert in his field of surgery. Had he not possessed an innate love of the West Country, he would almost certainly have been a fashionable consultant in London's Wimpole Street. He had first met Sir Andrew while working for his Fellowship in Edinburgh, and they had remained on friendly terms ever since.

Since those struggling, student days he had come a long way in his profession, and as he now rose from behind his highly polished Hepplewhite desk to greet Sir Andrew, followed by Ashley and his mother, Degory Logan presented a picture of unmistakeable professional success. His coat and breeches were tailored in the latest fashion; his linen was immaculate; the proffered hand and the welcoming smile betokened nothing less than the self-assurance of a man who is well aware of his undoubted worth. He had surrounded himself with elegant trappings; the thick velvet curtains rising from carpet to decorated ceiling; the Ince and Mayhew lamp stands, the Sheraton bookcase and side tables, the collection of mezzotints adorning the walls; everything in impeccable taste. And yet beneath all the polished veneer he was still the bluff, affable extrovert – the same exuberant medical student of yesteryear.

'Come in, come in, my dear Andrew. It's altogether too long since last we met. How are ye, and equally important – perhaps even more important –' his eyes twinkled teasingly, 'how are those two lovely daughters of yours?'

'They've never been quite the same since you took them out in that racing sloop of yours,' grimaced Sir Andrew. 'I don't know what it did to them but they've been at me ever since to buy a similar boat – but a faster one, of course!'

The banter continued for a few more moments. While it obviously amused the two chief contestants – this profusion of bonhomie – it did nothing to improve Marianne's sagging morale. She had been intensely worried about Ashley's leg ever since the accident had happened, and when Sir Andrew had suggested a consultation with the best surgeon in the West Country she had been both relieved and grateful. But when the day of the appointment arrived she felt increasingly nervous. She wanted so much to do what was best for her son. She wondered what would be the right thing to wear. She wanted to make a good impression, and yet she really hadn't got any fashionable clothes. Would she be letting Sir Andrew down by her simple country talk and her even more unsophisticated country ways. It was a worry. But when all's said and done, she comforted herself, what really mattered was what the great gentleman could do to make her son's leg absolutely normal again. It was of no consequence that she felt shy, and nervous – and somehow overlooked – as these two men urbanely chaffed each other, seemingly unaware even of her presence. It mattered not at all, she told herself; indeed it lasted but a few moments only, because even now Sir Andrew was introducing her, and her son, in the easiest and friendliest of terms.

Immediately, Degory Logan was all attentiveness. When he heard how the accident had occurred he chaffed Ashley – as Jeannie had done – about 'playing the fool on a Sunday afternoon walk, eh?', and then, after recording a few general details about the boy's age and past medical history, he said cheerfully: 'Well now, if you'll just follow me into the examination room, we'll have a good look at you.'

Despite Sir Andrew's valiant attempts at light-hearted conversation, the waiting, for Marianne, seemed like an age. Her mind became a ceaseless jumble of apprehensions. What would the great man find? Had the fracture been properly set in the first place? And if not, would it now mean just a simple re-adjustment? Oh, how she hoped it would. And was he hurting her son as he probed with his expert, sensitive fingers, bending his knee perhaps further than Ashley could bear? Would she suddenly hear a scream of agony that even these thick walls could not muffle?

She tried to make sensible replies to Sir Andrew's remarks, but all the while her mind was racing ahead, fearing the worst, facing up to the inevitable. Would her beloved only child be a cripple for life? She would know, she felt sure, the moment Mr Logan came back through that door; she would be able to tell – just from the expression on his face.

But when, at last, the surgeon re-entered the room, having left Ashley in the examination room, his face was a mask. Unable to contain her anxiety, Marianne leant forward from the edge of her chair.

'Well, Doctor?' she enquired eagerly, her impatience momentarily making her forget the medical etiquette of calling him 'Mister' – in her mind he was simply the man who held the key to her son's wholeness of body, and she could think of him only as 'doctor'. But she was anxious not to appear ignorant of such niceties – if only for the sake of

Sir Andrew MacKenzie – and so she hurriedly added; 'Will he be all right, *Mr* Logan, I mean?'

Degory Logan sank into the chair behind his desk. He plucked a lemon-yellow quill pen from its holder beside the ink-well and examined its tip, minutely. He was in a quandary. The school doctor who had set the fractured femur had, unquestionably, blundered. No doubt he had done his best – his boozy, inebriated best – but the unpalatable fact remained that he had done a deplorably inexpert job.

There was really only one remedy; to break the bone again in the same place, then re-set it properly. But there were problems. In the first place, it would be devilishly painful. Since time immemorial, the medical profession had been trying to find a satisfactory way of dulling pain – asphyxia, depression of the nerves, freezing of the relevant area, opium, alcohol – they had all been tried, but none were wholly satisfactory. Secondly, during the intervening time since the accident, the normal growth in the left leg had been inhibited by the misalignment of the fractured bone at the setting. Nothing could make up for this lost time, and the boy would have one leg shorter than the other for the rest of his life.

The surgeon knew that this second factor would be the most distressing aspect for the boy's mother. And, indeed, it was a tragedy. Had more care been taken in the first place, there need never have been any noticeable interruption of normal development. But, of course, he could not actually say as much; he could not expose a fellow member of the medical profession. All he could say – and he said it with a disarming smile – was, 'A slight misalignment has developed in the leg, Mrs Penberth – nothing that can't be put right, you understand – but we'll need to have him out of action for a while.'

Immediately the spectre of hospital treatment loomed hideously in Marianne's mind. Although there was no such thing as a hospital in Cornwall, she felt sure; there had been one at Exeter for more than forty years – and there was another one at Bath, so they said – but people only went

113

into hospital when they were very ill, surely, or if they were dreadfully poor. She had a terrifying feeling, too, that people only went into hospital to die.

For several moments she could do no more than sit on the edge of her chair, nervously twisting her handkerchief and trying to pluck up courage to ask the dreaded question, 'Does it mean he'll have to go into hospital, then, doctor?'

'No, no, Mrs Penberth,' Degory Logan assured her breezily, 'there'll be no need for that.' He paused – amused by Marianne's audible sigh of relief – before continuing. 'Hospitals, Mrs Penberth, are not yet quite suitable places for . . . er . . . for young people like your son. No, no I shall not need to have him in hospital. Indeed,' he went on cheerfully, 'we shan't even need to take him from you for more than a day or so – and even then it will only be just across the fields, as it were.'

'Across the fields, Mr Logan?' Marianne queried, a puzzled frown creasing her already worried brow, 'What have the fields to do with. . . .'

'Just a manner of speaking, Mrs Penberth, nothing more. I am referring, of course, to Trevadne, Sir Andrew MacKenzie's residence which is, I believe, not far from your farm at Treworden.' Degory Logan's smile could not have been more reassuring. 'In other words, not more than a few fields away.'

Marianne nodded – though still perplexed.

'You are very fortunate in having such a good friend and neighbour as Sir Andrew MacKenzie,' the surgeon continued, 'and he has made what I think you'll agree is an excellent suggestion, Mrs Penberth. His idea is that I should come down to Trevadne for a few days' shooting, and perhaps a day or two's hunting, – he seems to think I'm in need of a little relaxation in your lovely Cornish countryside – and while I'm staying at Trevadne I can perform the necessary re-alignment of young Ashley's broken leg.'

'Oh, yes, doctor . . . I mean, Mr Logan . . . . that would be exceedingly kind, I'm sure,' Marianne began, 'but why would it. . . .'

'Don't mention it,' Degory Logan cut in, 'I assure you, Mrs Penberth, it's a pleasure for me to be able to assist any friend of Sir Andrew's – and with those two charming daughters of his eager to look after your son, to say nothing of Miss Proudfoot and the rest of the Trevadne staff, the lad could scarcely be in better hands.'

Degory Logan leant back in his chair, clasped his hands behind his head, and beamed at the anxious mother.

' 'Tis a very kind suggestion I'm sure,' Marianne began, 'but would it not be possible for the operation to be performed at home, at Treworden, doctor? I mean, is it truly needful for the boy to be away at Trevadne? I feel sure I could look after him well enough at home.'

All Degory Logan said – and he said it with one of his most winning smiles – was, 'I'm quite sure you could, Mrs Penberth. But it would be better for me to have him at Trevadne.'

What he did not say was that he had discussed the matter with Sir Andrew; he had told him that, in order to correct the bungling ineptitude of the school doctor – but he did not put it in quite those words – he would be forced to break the leg again so that he could re-set it properly. The process would undoubtedly be painful – but there was no alternative. And although there had been many experiments, no one had yet discovered the secret of total anaesthesia.

Inevitably in such cases, the patient reacted with extreme vocal distress; not for long, it must be understood, but nevertheless, stridently.

It would be insensitive to allow the mother to be within earshot.

Sir Andrew had fully understood; they had formed a plan. Degory Logan would perform the operation at Trevadne while Sir Andrew ensured that Marianne stayed at home.

'There's just one other thing I ought to mention, Mrs Penberth,' the surgeon continued, almost as an afterthought, 'and that is that during the past year – since the accident, that is – there's been a slight retardation of

115

growth in the injured leg; it's inevitable with children, especially when they are growing rapidly, and I'm afraid there's nothing we can do about that. It's just not possible to make up for lost time, as it were.'

A sharp intake of breath revealed Marianne's concern. 'But what exactly does that mean, Mr Logan?' she asked anxiously. 'Will he always be. . . .' She could not bring herself to say 'a cripple' – she could not bear to think that her boy, her precious Ashley who, but a few years ago, it seemed, was a perfectly formed baby in her arms, could not now, in the hands of this skilful man, once more be made perfect.

Degory Logan, sympathising with her distress, continued quietly, 'It means, Mrs Penberth, that Ashley's left leg will always be just a little bit shorter than his right. Not much, I'm glad to say – thanks to the fact that you've come to see me now – even though,' he added in an undertone 'I would have preferred it a little sooner.'

'But never mind,' he went on, encouragingly, 'we shall be able to make a considerable improvement in the knee flexion, and the slight disparity in length of leg can easily be adjusted by having the heel of his left boot or shoe built up a little bit.'

Once more he bestowed upon his patient's mother his most reassuring smile. 'So you see, Mrs Penberth, you really have nothing to worry about. Your Ashley is a fine-looking boy – and, unless I'm very much mistaken, he's going to grow into an exceptionally handsome young man.' He glanced enquiringly at Sir Andrew who by now had joined them. 'How about it, then, Andrew, don't you agree?'

Sir Andrew was in no doubt. 'Och, yes. Of course he's a fine fella. And my two wee girlies will just love having the laddie to look after.' He emitted a short, staccato laugh – rather like an exploding firework. 'Ha! But those two will be all over him – wi' their flethrin' an' their fisslin'. Why, in no time at all they'll have quite spoilt the laddie wi' pettlin', I shouldn't wonder.'

He was remembering at that moment the party at Trevadne last Christmas. The two girls and Miss Proudfoot had organised it. It had been a great success; party games, masks and paper hats, charades and *tableaux vivants* – and at the every end of the evening, a game – invented by the two sisters with help from Ashley – which they had called 'Hubba'.

'Hubba!' Sir Andrew had expostulated, 'What the de'il might that be?'

The girls were eager to explain. 'It's the call made by the – what did you say he's called, Ashley?'

'The "Huer",' Ashley had explained. 'He's the watchman posted up on the cliff to spot the approaching schools of pilchards. . . .'

'And when he sees the fish all swarmed-up close together,' Jeannie had enthused, '– so that the fishermen can go out with their nets and catch them – then he cries "Hubba"!'

'Oh, aye,' Sir Andrew had said, doubtfully, 'and wha' exactly is the game ye have in mind, then – and why is it called this "Hubba"?'

'Well, Papa,' Alethea then explained, her eyes sparkling mischievously, 'first of all, one of us goes away and hides – in the smallest and most inaccessible place possible. . . .

'And then,' Jeannie had elaborated, 'after the servants have dowsed the lights – or most of them, anyway – the rest of us try to find the one who's hiding.'

'Oh, aye,' Sir Andrew had observed with suspicion, 'and wha' then?'

'Well, then, we all swarm up together closely – like the pilchards!'

'And the last one to join the swarm,' Alethea had concluded triumphantly, 'shouts "Hubba"!'

It was only later, long after the cry of 'Hubba' had been sounded – and when he had surprised his elder daughter, Jeannie, in the darkest corner of a passage, her arms around Ashley in a passionate embrace – that Sir Andrew realised,

117

with something of a shock, just how much his firstborn had grown up; and also just how youthfully handsome young Penberth had become.

It was then that he decided it was high time, now that peace between England and France had once more been restored, that Jeannie should pay an extended visit to the MacKenzie cousins at their house in Paris, or at their chateau in the country near Morlaix.

It would give those two ardent young lovers a chance to cool down.

No sooner had Marianne agreed to the operation being done at Trevadne than she changed her mind. She had been persuaded – swept along – by Sir Andrew's kindness and the aura of omnipotence which in her mind surrounded Degory Logan. But Ashley was her boy – it was her very own and only son they were talking about, and although she felt sure they meant it for the best, nevertheless if anything painful like an operation was necessary, then it was going to be done in her house and under her care.

So she put her foot down.

Degory Logan exchanged a meaningful glance with Sir Andrew which said 'Leave it to me; I'm used to this kind of thing.'

Turning to Marianne once more, he said blandly, 'That's quite in order, Mrs Penberth. I fully understand your feelings, and I know that you desire only what is the very best for your son. Indeed, I was thinking of just that when I suggested carrying out the orthopaedy in Sir Andrew's residence. You see, Mrs Penberth, I know the room which would be made available to me at Trevadne; it is one which I am quite sure the Trevadne staff would be able to make ready, to my complete satisfaction, for the operation.'

He glanced again, pointedly, at Sir Andrew before continuing in a mock self-deprecatory tone, 'My medical friends tend to laugh at me in this respect, Mrs Penberth – indeed, I believe they call me pernickety Logan – but I

118

insist on total cleanliness and hygiene. The room must be cleared of all furniture, carpets and curtains; the floor and the walls must be scrubbed; the operating table must be spotless.'

Sir Andrew stifled an emergent grin. Despite Degory's reputation for hygienic conditions – he was way ahead of his time, but he had been trained in Scotland where they were beginning to understand such matters – Sir Andrew suspected that the degree of cleanliness specified would hardly be necessary for an orthopaedic operation of this type.

But he had recognised the ploy. By requiring such high standards, the surgeon was hoping to deflect Marianne from her request that the operation be performed at her own home, Treworden.

And he succeeded – as he usually did.

The prospect of scrubbing the ancient walls of Treworden farmhouse, already flaking with age; of removing furniture and carpets, scrubbing the floor – well, she supposed they might be able to do it with the help of Zephanaiah and his wife, Marianne was thinking, – but it was all rather daunting. And what about light? The Treworden windows were small; even on a bright sunny day they never let in a great deal of light.

And what about nursing Ashley afterwards; would she know what to do – supposing anything went wrong? If the surgeon was going to stay on for a while at Trevadne, he would be on hand in case of emergency – like Ashley slipping on wet kitchen flagstones, or falling down.

Besides, it would be quite a feather in his cap for Ashley to be looked after by the MacKenzie girls, by the MacKenzie staff. And Zeph would drive her over every day in the market cart. So, perhaps after all, it would be better that way; better for Ashley – and that was what really mattered.

So, after a little more heart-searching, she gave in. Yes, Sir Andrew, she would be grateful to accept the kind offer – because it was best for Ashley.

A fortnight later she was packing Ashley's night clothes

into a small portmanteau – it was older and shabbier than she would have wished the MacKenzie servants to see, but she couldn't help that.

In order that the boy should miss as little of the new term as possible, Degory Logan had agreed, at Sir Andrew's special request, to come down to Cornwall in January – despite the appalling travelling conditions. Now that he had arrived, he wished to perform the operation as soon as the room could be got ready.

All the next day, while the surgeon relaxed after his tiring journey, the Trevadne housemaids went to work on the room known among the family as 'the prophet's chamber', not because it was particularly small – and it certainly had more furniture than just a bed, a table, a stool and a candlestick – but because it overlooked the wall, as did the room prepared by the Shunammite woman for the prophet, Elisha. All morning those servants washed over walls and ceiling; all morning they were down on hands and knees, scrubbing floorboards.

Down in the kitchen one of the footmen was scouring a plain deal table until it was white. When it was dry it was carried up to 'the prophet's chamber'.

All was now ready.

Next morning, early, Degory Logan mixed a preparation of opium in spirit of wine. He handed it to Ashley.

At the first signs of drowsiness, Ashley was led from the principal guest bedroom along to 'the prophet's chamber' by both Jeannie and Alethea, each girl holding one of his hands. Never before had he felt so much like a lamb being led to the slaughter.

Even since his arrival the previous day, brought over by Zeph Curnow in the market cart, along with his carefully packed portmanteau, the two sisters had fussed over him, and cossetted him more like a pair of heavenly angels than the two vibrant, laughing, teasing girls he had been brought up with.

And now, as they entered the operating room, they each informed the renowned surgeon that they intended to remain with their patient throughout his ordeal. Degory Logan demurred. Miss Proudfoot, who professed some nursing experience, was at his side. She would constitute sufficient unprofessional assistance, he felt. However, if the girls could be relied upon to act sensibly and not be affected by the patient's momentary expressions of pain, then they might possibly perform a useful function by keeping the patient calm.

To Jeannie, the words 'the patient's momentary expressions of pain' meant but one thing – agonised screams. She realised just why, at this very moment, her father was propelling Ashley's mother on a tour of the greenhouses – well out of earshot of the house. And in the realisation of what Ashley was about to endure, she suddenly felt overcome with faintness.

'I. . . . I'm sorry, Mr Logan,' she faltered, 'but I. . . . I can't . . .' and then, brushing one hand across her forehead, she stumbled from the room.

Degory Logan quietly nodded approval. Glancing at Alethea and then at Miss Proudfoot, he grunted, 'And if either of you two feel the same, I shall quite understand.'

Miss Proudfoot shifted nervously from one foot to the other. 'If you'll excuse me for just a moment, sir, I'll see that Miss Jeannie is all right – and then I'll return.'

As she hurried from the room, Degory Logan began running his strong but sensitive fingers over Ashley's injured leg. 'And now, my lad,' he assured, in his most positive tone, 'we're going to put this old leg of yours right, once and for all, eh?'

Drowsily, Ashley signified that he had heard, and that he approved. He was very conscious of the warming comfort of Alethea's hand gripping his. She was standing at the head of the table, smiling encouragement. She knew that Degory Logan was putting something under Ashley's knee, raising it from the table. She dare not look.

'You'll feel a sharp pain, my boy,' Degory was saying, 'but I just want you to be brave – and then it'll all be over.'

The words penetrated Ashley's brain only thinly – but

121

just enough to resurrect the memory of Lydford College, the fall from the window, the acute pain as he hit the cobbled yard. Strangely, the memory was a comfort; nothing could be worse than that first fortnight at Lydford. He had lived through it, and he had survived.

He looked up at Alethea. Her lovely blue eyes, so full of sympathy and compassion, were fixed on his, willing him to be brave. He would be brave; he would show her he could be brave.

Out of the corner of her eyes Alethea saw that Pruddy had quietly returned; that she now stood on the opposite side of the table, one had laid gently on Ashley's shoulder.

Out of the corner of her eyes, too, she was aware that Degory Logan had reached for what she thought was a heavy instrument. Again, she dared not to look.

Suddenly, there was a sickening crack! – and with a heart-rending scream, Ashley shot upwards.

'Hold him!' the surgeon rasped, 'Hold him steady while I. . . .' His powerful fingers quickly went to work on a young leg which had already suffered too much.

For Ashley, gripping Alethea's hand, his face contorted with pain, the agony became unbearable. He could stand no more – 'Aagh!' – and then an angel of mercy came and carried him off into a dead faint.

CHAPTER ELEVEN

Signed on

The waiting was the same; only the waiting room was different.

Three years had slipped by since Ashley had been left in Degory Logan's examination room in Exeter while, in the room next door, his fate was being decided.

Most surgeons would probably have thought it best to leave well alone; after all, the boy was not in pain, and there was still at least some flexion in the knee.

But Degory Logan was no ordinary man. Like Edward Jenner and several other friends, he had been privileged to sit at the feet of the great John Hunter at his house in Jermyn Street while he lectured on the theory and practice of surgery. Though Hunter was naturally a cautious man, and the hesitancy of his delivery had made his lectures hard to follow, Degory Logan had nevertheless been tremendously impressed. He had been seized with a desire to progress in his chosen field, to develop new techniques, to open up fresh avenues of research.

He understood all too well that a boy of Ashley's age had a lot more growing to do, and unless something was done to correct the misplacement of those bones, the disparity in length between left and right leg would become more and more embarrassingly acute.

Moreover, he had taken a great liking to the lad. The thought of this sturdy, fair-haired boy – with his short, slightly upturned nose and his vivid blue eyes – his friend Sir Andrew's protégé – becoming a severely handicapped cripple, even a laughing-stock, was not only a painful prospect, it was a challenge to his medical skill.

He had been determined to do something for the boy – determined to succeed.

The fact that the operation was ultimately a success was at least partly due to Tub Richards. He had been sent for the day after Ashley, his leg rendered immobile by strong wooden splints, had been returned to the luxury of the main guest bedroom and the attentive ministrations of both Jeannie and Alethea.

Thomas Richards – nicknamed Tub in recognition of his barrel-shaped size – kept the smithy alongside *The Red Lion Inn* at Mawnan. He had known Ashley, as he was accustomed to say, 'ever sin' ee were a nipper', and many a time had shod Ashley's pony, Tiger.

Wearing his best Sunday clothes, he had presented himself at Trevadne at ten o-clock in the morning, as commanded by Sir Andrew MacKenzie, and was duly taken upstairs by one of the footmen to the bedroom in which Ashley was recovering. After touching his now diminishing forelock, first to Sir Andrew and then to Mr Degory Logan, he turned to the prostrate figure in the four-poster bed.

'Why, Mester Ashley, zur, I nivver thought to find ee yere, zur – an' in such a pickle, like,' he remarked, a warm but sympathetic smile creasing his florid cheeks. 'What be doin' thur, then? Taken a tip out huntin', or somethin'?'

Ashley smiled back, wanly. 'This kind gentleman here – Mr Degory Logan – has been putting my leg to rights; the one I broke at school, remember?'

'Aw, ah,' was the all-embracing response, 'I see'd ee were sick, like.'

'Well, now then, Richards,' Sir Andrew broke in, 'Mr Logan, the surgeon, wants you to make an iron splint for young Penberth, here.'

'An iron splint, zur,' Tub Richards repeated, bewildered.

'That's right. D'you think you can make up a thing like that?

'Aw, ais, zur,' responded Tub doubtfully. 'I'll do

anythin' to oblige, zur. A hyan splint, did ee say, zur?'

'That's it,' Degory Logan confirmed, taking a piece of paper from his pocket, 'Like this.'

Overnight, the surgeon had made a meticulous drawing of what he wanted, clearly indicating the exact measurements. The blacksmith – now looking anything but black in his freshly laundered smock – studied the drawing carefully.

The seconds ticked by. 'Well,' asked Sir Andrew at last, 'Can you make that up, d'you think?'

Tub Richards continued to pore over the sketch intensely, tracing each line with his soot-ingrained forefinger. Eventually, he lifted his head and looked at the surgeon. 'And ee'll want un jointed, like, 'bout half-way down?'

'That's it,' Degory confirmed, 'so that it will swing easily at the knee. And it'll be held in position by those leather straps,' he went on. 'Will you be able to make up those, as well?'

The blacksmith nodded. 'Aw, ah. Jabe Medlycott, the saddler'll make un up for I, I 'spec.'

'And don't forget that boss – or stud – at the bottom of each iron,' the surgeon enjoined, 'They are to be fitted in to the heel of the boot – slotted in, if you understand me, and held in position by that leather strap around the ankle. Is that clear?'

Once more Tub Richards touched his receding forelock to the gentleman, 'I quite understand ee, zur. An' I'll be pleased to make un up for Mester Amos's boy,' he said, before backing deferentially out of the room.

That was all three years ago, Ashley reflected; three years during which, in fulfilment of his promise to Degory Logan, he had been obliged to wear an iron splint. It was heavy, it was cumbersome – and it made him horribly conspicuous – but at least it had prevented any damage to the bones which the surgeon had so skilfully re-knitted together.

For the first two weeks after the operation, Ashley had remained at Trevadne, Sir Andrew having made a spare room available to Marianne especially so that she might be near her son.

But during those weeks, while fretting at being made to stay in bed all day, it was not so much the constant concern of his mother that Ashley found so affecting – sadly, a boy on the threshold of manhood all too frequently takes a mother's love for granted – far more so was it the tender expressions of devotion with which the MacKenzie sisters surrounded him.

Nothing, it seemed, was too much trouble; indeed, they would vie with each other for the pleasure of bringing him as wide a variety of delicacies as they could conjure – from kitchen, from greenhouse and from fruit store.

They smoothed his pillow – even though it was scarcely rumpled; they stroked his brow – whether or not it was overheated; they whiled away the time for him by playing at cards or dice or dominoes. They sang to him – even at that early age Alethea had a most movingly beautiful singing voice – and every now and then, upon the flimsiest of excuses, Jeannie would plant her soft lips upon his in what she successfully persuaded herself – if nobody else – was nothing more than just a sister-like kiss.

But it was disturbing. Although genuinely fond of Jeannie – how could he not be; she was such fun to be with, so lively, so amusing, so irrepressibly vivacious – nevertheless Ashley was acutely aware that by responding to her girlish advances, no matter how playful they might appear, he was being hurtful to Alethea.

And of all people, apart from his mother, he least wanted to hurt Alethea; she who had befriended him that first day of lessons with Miss Proudfoot; she with whom he had shared the most important secrets of childhood; she who had nursed him so recently with a tenderness deeper than that of anyone else, and of whom Degory Logan had observed, as he watched her ministering to his needs, that she seemed to have a natural vocation for the task.

Subsequently it had not helped matters when, on the eve of being taken to Paris to stay with those cousins and to be invested with a Parisian 'finish', Jeannie had cleverly contrived to be alone with Ashley in the conservatory beyond the dining room at Trevadne.

In that emotional half hour Jeannie had been uncharacteristically tearful.

'Say that you'll miss me, Ashley,' she had pleaded. 'Say that you will – because I'm going away for a long, long time. And who knows,' she added, in the tones of a born tragedienne, 'who knows whether I shall ever see you again?'

And when Ashley had replied, with youthful blustering embarrassment that 'Of course she would be missed. What did she expect? It wouldn't be at all the same without her', she had clung to him, saying 'Oh, Ashley! But why do you hold back from me like this. You must know that I love you – and you really love me, don't you? You know that you do.'

It was difficult; tantalising, in fact, for a rapidly maturing fifteen-year-old schoolboy to be thus confronted by such a fully developed, precociously seductive seventeen-year-old beauty. It was no coincidence, of course, that Jeannie had chosen, for that last evening before her departure, her most daringly low-cut gown. She would be away for almost a year, and she was determined to leave Ashley with a lingering impression of her attractions.

It should be no surprise, therefore, that in a last farewell embrace, her arms entwined around his neck, her half-exposed breasts pressed tightly against his satin waist-coat, Ashley should feel a great surge of hitherto unexperienced desire to possess her utterly, to crush her to him, to devour her. . . .

It was also no coincidence that at that very moment Sir Andrew – his impending presence announced by a muffled cough – should enter the conservatory on the pretext of admiring his orchids. Cigar well lit, kilt swinging rhythmically above knees bristling with gingery hairs, he sauntered between cyprepediums and odontoglossoms pausing every now and then to inspect a rare bloom. Out of the corner of his eye he noted with satisfaction that his excitingly beautiful daughter and her young swain had hurriedly disengaged themselves from each other and now stood discreetly, merely holding hands and pretending to admire the plants.

Though embarrassed and frustrated at the time, Ashley had to admit on reflection that the interruption had been timely. It had prevented him becoming too involved with Jeannie. Unquestionably she aroused him strongly in a purely physical sense – far more so than Alethea had ever done – but his love for Alethea was set on a different plane, pitched at a higher note. If Jeannie was physical, then Alethea was metaphysical – or so it seemed to Ashley; rather like one of Dr Chaunter's abstruse sermons preached from the text 'Before Abraham was, I AM'. It was all rather confusing.

But there was nothing of the milk-sop about Alethea. Oh, no. If her outward appearance might seem like the cool beauty of an arum lily, Ashley knew it to be no more than a cloak for a warm spirit and a generous heart. And as if to confound the lily-like impression still further, Alethea could hawk and ride with the best, and was never happier than when involved in some outrageous practical joke.

That he loved her, Ashley had no doubt; he always had – so long as he could remember – and he always would. But sometimes he wondered whether she was really beyond his reach – and whether he loved her because she was unobtainable.

By contrast, Jeannie stirred in him more basic thoughts. She was a child of nature – refined, yet of the earth, earthy. The attraction was impelling. But it was harder to understand – this feeling he had for Jeannie – and deep down in the recesses of his mind it fanned an ember of guilt. He should not be desiring her in this way when he knew perfectly well that he really loved Alethea.

It was just over two weeks later that there arrived at Treworden a letter from Paris. It was from Sir Andrew. Marianne read it aloud to her son. Characteristically, it was short and to the point. It said, 'Arrived safely yesterday afternoon. Good crossing, comfortable cabin. This morning I took Jeannie to the *Rue des Petits Champs* where she was affectionately welcomed by the cousins. The parting for the poor wee girlie was tearful, but I am sure my decision was the right one. I am going now to spend a few days with my brother, Ranald, at Fontanelle, but I hope to be back at Trevadne by the end of next week.'

Poor 'wee' Jeannie, Ashley mused. Although England had been at peace with France for a considerable time it was known that Prime Minister Pitt scorned the idea that, just because she had been regarded as the traditional enemy in the past, France must always remain so in the future. Indeed it was rumoured, so Sir Andrew said, that a commerical treaty between the two countries was being planned, as a result of which travel without passports would be possible. But despite all these good intentions France had never been noted for friendly feelings towards the English.

Poor 'wee' Jeannie! Had she been despatched to this unfriendly country only to give her 'finish' – fluency in the French language and close acquaintance with courtly manners and deportment – or was it because of him, Ashley? Had Sir Andrew, with his practised helmsman's eye, seen which way the wind was blowing? Had he decided that a mere tenant farmer's son was no suitable match for his eldest daughter, and so packed her off to France where fields were fresher, pastures greener? Somehow, it didn't sound quite like Sir Andrew, Ashley thought; it was out of character for a man of such liberal views.

More likely, he concluded, Sir Andrew was well aware of how headstrong his beloved first-born could be. If she wanted something – or somebody – she would allow nothing to stand in her way. But the English Channel was a sizeable ditch to jump! Besides, a year in France would do her good, broaden her education, add a new lustre to those shiny, dark curls on her head.

Was that what Sir Andrew was thinking, Ashley wondered? Or could it be that he found it hurtful to see the crestfallen look on Alethea's face when Jeannie was displaying her most captivating ways in front of Ashley. For, although he would never have admitted it, not even to himself, Alethea was undoubtedly her father's favourite. She was his baby; the last tangible link with the woman whose smile had been as the evening sunshine and whose laughter could dispel a mountain of gloom – the wife he had loved so passionately but for so short a time. Alethea was her last gift to him; she was extra-specially precious.

Whatever might or might not be Sir Andrew's thoughts and motives, the facts of the moment, so far as Ashley Penberth was concerned, were plain enough.

Jeannie was now in Paris while Ashley sat nervously on the edge of his chair in the sparsely furnished waiting room.

Again it was Sir Andrew who had arranged it. Always willing to use his influence on Marianne's behalf, he had contacted one of his many friends in high places and pulled the necessary strings.

To become an officer in the Royal Navy you either had to enter under the patronage of the Captain of one of His Majesty's Ships, or of some other officer; or you could obtain a warrant of entry from the Admiralty after passing through the Naval Academy at Portsmouth.

Provided you had the right kind of friends, preferably in Parliament, it was not difficult, but while Sir Andrew was blessed with several influential contacts both in the House of Lord's and in the armed services, he thought it advisable for Ashley to be properly trained at the Academy.

Ever since receiving the letter from the Admiralty requiring his attendance for interview by the Selection Board at Portsmouth Dockyard, Ashley had been building on dreams. Following in the footsteps of Boscawen, Cornwall's most famous sailor; serving under men like Hawke, chasing the French fleet down to Quiberon Bay and then, despite a raging Biscay storm, thrillingly defying all the maxims of seamanship by going in after them, into a harbour abounding with reefs and shoals, a gale blowing astern and a lee shore ahead. Ashley knew the story. Enough to make any Cornish boy's blood tingle.

And just think of the prestige. An officer in one of His Majesty's Ships. The Royal Navy! And the uniform, too. Gone were the days, so Courtier said, when an officer could dress as he pleased – striped flannel jacket, red breeches and check shirt would have been good enough in the past – but not now. Why, there were even Captains nowadays who'd dismiss any midshipman caught on shore without his uniform.

And what about the MacKenzie girls – would they not be proud of him in his uniform? Would not even Sir Andrew himself regard an officer of the Royal Navy as a worthy suitor for one of his daughters?

But why did he say 'daughters' – not 'daughter', he frowned. Of course there was only one daughter, as far as he was concerned, the one he truly loved – Alethea. Why then was he thinking of them both?

His thoughts were abruptly terminated by a fearsome summons from the door. 'If you please, sir. Follow me.'

The awful moment had arrived – the one he had been dreading for at least the last half hour. The muscles of his stomach contracted, became as though cauterised; as he followed the smartly dressed seaman down the long narrow passage the prospect of vomiting seemed not only a strong possibility but a positive relief. However, by the time the highly varnished door to the interview room was being pushed open, Ashley had succeeded in bringing his jangling nerves under some kind of control. It was unfortunate, though, that the distance between the doorway and the applicant's chair in front of the interviewing Board was considerable. Ashley did his level best as he walked that distance to conceal his limp. Degory Logan had performed his task with skill. He had corrected the bungling efforts of the school doctor, and he had achieved a much improved degree of flexion in the knee. But nothing could make up for the lost growth of bone during those intervening months, and the left leg was now at least two inches shorter than the right. Moreover, in order to strengthen the leg and prevent any further damage, Mr Logan had prescribed a jointed splint to be worn at all times. With this, and the specially made-up heel of his boot, it was impossible for Ashley not to walk with a slight limp.

Now, as he crossed that awesome divide of carpeted floorboards, he felt painfully aware that the Board Chairman, watching him closely, had spotted it.

'Your name is – er – Penberth, I believe,' he began gruffly, but not unkindly. 'Ashley Penberth, is that right?' the shaggy grey eyebrows almost curtained the steely-blue eyes.

'Yes, sir,' Ashley replied smartly, trying to forget the pounding of his pulse.

'And you come from Cornwall, eh what? Near Falmouth, is that correct?'

Again Ashley gave what he hoped was a brisk, seamanlike response. The Chairman nodded, scrutinizing the face in front of him. He liked the look of the lad; good officer material, he would think. Came from the right part of the country, too. There was just one reservation. . . .

However, the usual hoops of an interview must be gone through first, the usual questions. . . . Had the boy had a good journey? How had he travelled? Put the lad at his ease. Then hand the questioning over to other members of the Board. What school was he at? Hobbies? Special interests? Why did he want to join the Navy? All very familiar stuff – generally rather boring. But the more the Chairman saw of this applicant, the better he liked him. A potential Officer's Servant, or 'midshipman' of the right calibre – intelligent, courageous and full of tenacity, the type that would hang on – like Hawke – and never let the enemy get away. In fact, just what the Navy was looking for. Sadly, though, there was that limp, that built-up boot heel.

'You do realise, Penberth,' he said, taking over the interview once more, 'that an Officer's Servant must be a very agile young gentleman.'

Here it comes, Ashley thought. But he answered briskly, firmly, 'Yes, sir. I do understand that.'

The Chairman peered over the top of his gold-rimmed spectacles. 'They have to be able to swarm up shrouds and man the yards. . . .'

'Yes, sir.'

'More often than not at lightning speed. . . .'

'I fully understand, sir.'

The steely-blue eyes almost disappeared beneath the eyebrows. The look was penetrating – but the voice was kindly. 'Correct me if I am wrong, but when you entered the room just now I thought I detected a slight limp. Just a temporary inconvenience, is it? An injury at – er – football, perhaps?'

That was virtually the end of the interview – and the end of Ashley's dreams. The truth had to be admitted. The Chairman expressed polite sympathy, thanked Ashley for his attendance, and declared that the Board's findings would be communicated to him in due course.

As he left the room Ashley felt it no longer necessary even to try to disguise his disability.

A fortnight later the letter arrived, saying that The Lords Commissioners of the Admiralty had now considered the application of Mr A. Penberth. They thanked him for the offer of his services but regretted. . . .

It was only small comfort when Sir Andrew MacKenzie, trying to mitigate Ashley's acute disappointment, recounted how a young acquaintance of his serving in one of His Majesty's ships at the tender age of thirteen had fallen from aloft and been killed instantaneously.

It merely evoked a silent prayer of thanksgiving from Marianne that the Navy had rejected her son.

But that was all nearly two years past. In the meanwhile, having left Lydford with few regrets at the age of sixteen, Ashley had been content to stay at home and help farm Treworden. Zeph was delighted, of course; although he was always glad of Ashley's assistance, what he treasured most was the companionship. As of old, they did most of the work together – the hard work first; the hedging and ditching,

133

the ploughing and sowing, the harvesting, the milking and the shepherding; and because the two of them together made the work that much lighter they found time to slip down to Porth Navas where *Heatherbelle*, the gaffer they had built together, rode beckoningly at her moorings. Sometimes they would sail eastwards across Falmouth Bay, to the fishing grounds beyond St. Anthony Head; occasionally, when the weather was right and they had plenty of time – and without saying a word to Marianne – they would round Black Head and the Lizard, and be away down to the Carter stronghold within the shelter of Cudden Point.

They did most things together, yes; but when Ashley donned his high-collared velvet coat, his many-wreathed cravat, which Sir Andrew had taught him how to tie, his best breeches, silk hose and silver buckled shoes in preparation for a visit to the MacKenzies at Trevadne, it was Zeph who gave the new mare Tansy her number one grooming. He had a special slap on the rump for her when he'd finished; and he had a special wink for Ashley when he came to give him a leg up.

And the Mackenzie girls were more lovely than ever. Jeannie had returned from Paris, more polished, more *soigné* perhaps, but still the same vibrant, demanding, evocatively sensual Jeannie, while Alethea had developed into a soft, willowy, ingenue with hair more than ever the colour of ripening corn.

But things could not go on as they were, Ashley realised, delightful though they had become. Farm prices were falling, last year's corn harvest had been poor, and the potato crop had been heavily infested with blight. Despite plenty of sound farming advice from Sir Andrew – and Zeph thought he had been dropping in at Treworden rather more frequently than was strictly necessary from an agricultural point of view – the inescapable fact was emerging that the income from the farm was not enough to support both Zeph and Ashley, either now or in the foreseeable future. One of them would have to find other employment – and Ashley was determined that it should not have to be Zeph. No longer young, Zeph had served his mother faithfully ever since Amos Penberth had been drowned. No man had been more faithful to his late Master's memory and, if Ashley could possibly help it, Zeph Curnow would not be the one looking for a new situation.

So, without prompting or assistance from anyone, Ashley decided to seek employment in an alternative branch of the King's service. The Navy had rejected him; the Army would almost certainly do the same – and in any case, he loathed the thought of the Army almost as much as the prospect of working indoors. The high-rise stool of the office clerk was not for him. Better by far the life of an agricultural labourer with a half-loaf of bread and a hunk of cheese of your dinner, and a hessian sack as a rain-coat. Better to face the rigours of frost and snow, wind and rain, than be caught like a rat in a cage, scratching away forever at a ledger for trivialities. No, no – for him the ceiling must be the open sky, his walls nothing higher than a Cornish hedge, and the ink for his quill nothing blacker than the thundering Cornish seas.

It did not have the status of the Navy, and it certainly would not make him rich. Jeannie might not like it, and Alethea – well, he hoped Alethea would understand. In any case, it might not matter because already there was talk of sending her away to be 'finished' in Paris, like Jeannie.

He would be unpopular in the district, of course. He fully realised that. But the prospect hardly bothered him at all. There had been plenty of unpopularity at school – the wounded animal hounded by the healthy ones. He'd seen it scores of times on the farm and in the wild and, apart from one or two notable exceptions, human nature seemed very little different.

And his former friends at Lydford – Courtier now a midshipman in the Navy, Johnny Innes following his father into the Army – would be embarrassed. 'Poor old Penberth. Deuced hard cheese, really. Distinctly 'infra dig' don't you know.' Oh, yes, he could almost hear them saying it.

But it would have two overriding advantages; he would

be able to live at home and look after his mother, and it would mean that Zeph could stay on the farm.

And if, in addition, it provided him with a chance to hit back at the likes of these fiendish devils who had lured an innocent Dutch skipper onto the rocks at Trebarwith, clubbing him to death as he tried to defend his cargo – if he could bring such men to justice, then that would be enough.

Yet another waiting room door opened. An emaciated figure, more like a ghost than a man, teetered on the threshold, beckoning to Ashley.

'The Assistant Controller will see you now,' the man croaked. 'Follow me'. Ashley was becoming accustomed to the procedure. He followed the wraith-like attendant along a short well-lit passage towards a varnished door bearing, in yellowed lettering, the legend. 'Ass't Controller'. It struck him, as he proceeded along the corridor and entered the room, that in the extensive use of varnish His Majesty's Revenue establishments were not far behind those of the Royal Navy. Doors and panelling shone like polished apples. At least the two services had that much in common.

The Assistant Controller was sitting behind a desk of modest proportions and of non-descript period. It was purely functional. At his back a bow-shaped window overlooked the harbour; on his right-hand side, at a smaller table, sat a clerk with paper, ink and a quill pen in front of him. Neither man looked up as Ashley entered.

Eventually, after what seemed an inordinately long silence – supposedly to emphasise the vast gulf in status between the interviewer and the candidate – the Assistant Controller glanced in Ashley's direction.

'Your name?' The voice had the quality of a frog.

'Penberth, sir.'

'Where do you live?' The face, on the other hand, had the leathery texture of a toad.

'Near Falmouth, sir,'

'Be precise, man.' There were large warts on forehead, nose and left cheek.

'Treworden Farm, Mawnan, Near Falmouth,' Ashley almost snapped. He was finding it hard to say 'sir'.

The toad-face looked up. 'You live on a farm then. Why aren't you farming?'

A difficult question. To anyone else – the Navy Board, perhaps – Ashley might have been willing to admit to 'hard times' but he somehow found it difficult to do so to a toad.

'I wish to be on His Majesty's Service,' he replied. It sounded dreadfully priggish, but it was the best he could do. At least it was half true.

'Why not the Navy, then?' toad-face snarled. Ashley knew he was trapped. Best thing to own up.

'I tried, sir, but they rejected me.'

'Why?'

Ashley explained. No point in trying to hide anything.

Toad-face picked his nose, thoughfully. 'What's wrong with your leg?' he said eventually.

'It's a bit shorter than the other.' How many times he wondered wearily would he have to say that during his lifetime.

'Hmph,' the toad croaked. 'Well, I suppose you can ride a horse?'

Ashley explained that he had been able to ride almost before he could walk.

'You can provide your own horse, eh?'

'Yes, sir.'

'And pistols? You'll have to be armed, you know.'

The pair of flinklocks suspended on the wall above the fireplace in the drawing room at Treworden would suffice, for a start.

'Yes, indeed. I can be armed.'

'You'll have to be prepared to use 'em, you understand.' Toad-face glared out of the window. 'Make no mistake, they're first class bastards you'll be dealing with. They'll get you if you don't get them first.'

'I fully understand, sir.' The job was beginning to look quite promising. Nothing to match up with a naval engagement, perhaps, but a couple of loaded pistols would certainly add spice to the appointment.

The toad sat staring at Ashley for a full sixty seconds, looking him up and down, and rhythmically inflating his cheeks like a puff-adder. Then he opened a drawer at the side of his desk and withdrew a parchment-like piece of paper. He flicked it across towards Ashley with an invitation to read it before completing and signing it in the appropriate places.

In handsomely illuminated copper-plate writing the document declared that:-

'I, ... of . . . . in the County of Cornwall do solemnly swear that I will be faithful and just to His Majesty King George in the execution of the Trust in me reposed as a Riding Officer on the account of ye Customs. So Help me God.

Signed . . . .

Sworn before me on This. . . . . Day of the month . . . . . . in ye Year of our Lord Seventeen Hundred and Eighty . . . . . .

. . . . Compt.'

Ashley took the proffered quill pen from the Assistant Controller and, after a moment's hesitation, completed the blank spaces in the top line. He paused once more before signing away his freedom – but then he remembered it would kept Zeph in his job, and so he signed it. He handed it back to the 'Asst. Compt' who slowly and meticulously entered the day, the month and the year of the 'swearing' before appending his flamboyant signature. A look of utter distaste crept over his leathery features as he reluctantly added the 'Asst' in front of the 'Compt'. It seemed to be saying, 'After all these years, still only assistant to that bloody old fool of a Controller!'

'You will report to the officer-in-charge at Falmouth, Captain J.H. Breward. . . .' He paused, to see whether the name meant anything to this newest of Riding Officers. However, observing that it caused not so much as a flicker of recognition, he leaned across the desk until his face came unpleasantly close to Ashley's, saying 'You will report to Captain Breward on Monday morning next, first thing. Do

138

you understand?' his breath, as it wafted across the desk, smelt profoundly horrible. 'He will inform you as to your duties and your District.'

He leaned back in his chair, regarding Ashley from beneath hooded eyelids. His toad-like face creased itself into a slow, venomous smile.

'Captain Breward. Yes,' he went on reflectively, the smile having grown into a mirthless grin, 'an excellent officer. Most conscientious. I'm sure you're going to get along *extremely* well with him.'

He seemed to be licking his lips with relish at the mere thought of that encounter.

CHAPTER TWELVE

Brandywine Hero

Once again, Ashley was waiting. It seemed that if you wanted to serve His Majesty, King George the Third, you had to get used to waiting.

But this time it was somewhat different. There were no varnished walls or polished floor, no tangible reminders of past naval glories, no portraits of celebrated sea-dogs glowering from on high. It was not a proper waiting room at all; it was the outer office of the uninspiring, pillared Customs House in Falmouth.

Over by the window, which looked out across the mouth of the Penryn river and the lower waters of the Carrick Roads, the clerk to the Collector of Customs busied himself at a battered wooden desk. He was a cheerful, round-faced little man of some fifty summers, with a barrel-shaped figure and a wooden leg. The top of his bald head shone like an ivory-knobbed dandy cane, and his cheeks resembled a pair of well buffed apples. His name was Matthew Reynolds. A Londoner by birth and upbringing – if the squalid scramble for existence in eighteenth century London's dockland could be so described – he had been *shanghaied* into the Navy while carousing in a Wapping tavern. Almost before he realised what was happening he had found himself serving in one of the frigates of Admiral Boscawen's squadron. It was while chasing the French, off Cape Lagos, that a stray shot had carried away most of the lower part of his left leg, leaving him – after some very rough and ready naval surgery – with nothing below the left knee except a strapped-on wooden stump.

But it had not left him bitter or downhearted in any way. In fact, he had considered himself extremely lucky merely to be alive. Not even the loss of half a leg could diminish his natural cheerfulness or his unquenchable optimism. When the squadron had returned to Falmouth, he had been paid off at his own request. The Navy, he knew, would have little further use for him, and besides, during one of his earlier visits to the port, he had espied a comely wench behind the bar of *The Five Pilchards*, and he had a fancy to drop anchor in her back parlour. She, too, was as round as a pumpkin, and although she had taken a good deal of persuading in the first place, he had eventually bowled her over in the tap room.

They had lived happily ever after in a two room cottage, one up and one down, at the back of Arwenack.

Of course, it had been necessary for him to get a job – a shore job, mind, because his wooden leg made sea-going a cumbersome business – and although Fanny, his little pumpkin wife, was quite willing to carry on behind the bar at *The Five Pilchards* for the time being, it wouldn't have been right – or indeed, possible – for them both to live indefinitely on her slender earnings.

So, when the vacancy for a clerk to the Collector of Customs had come up, Mattie had put in for it. It would suit him nicely, he thought; as near to the sea and ships as he could hope to get without being too closely involved. And his service in the Royal Navy ought to be an advantage, too, he reckoned.

The fact that Fanny was well known to the Customs staff was also an advantage – even if it did mean that she had to dangle the plum of her virtue rather precariously in front of the Collector's eyes in order to land the job for her husband. But she had managed it – without letting the plum actually drop – and Mattie Reynolds was soon installed behind that rough-hewn wooden desk in the Collector's outer office.

But that was in the days of the 'old' Collector.

'Things is a lot different now,' Mattie offered, conversationally, while Ashley awaited the arrival of his new chief. 'That was in the old days, you understand – in the days of

Mr Faraday, the old Collector. Very nice man, really. Easy goin' type of gentleman, if you know what I mean.'

'Oh, yes,' Ashley was encouraged. This was just the kind of conversation he wanted. He had taken an immediate liking to Mattie, and he felt sure that, given suitable encouragement, this friendly, cheerful little man could provide some very useful background information.

'Yes,' Mattie obligingly continued, a bit too easy-goin', some might have said. A bit too friendly with the fisherfolk – them as goes fishin' across the channel to *Rusco*, as they calls it,' Mattie treated Ashley to the broadest of winks, 'and Mr Faraday, he was mighty fond of a drop o' brandy see. But them as are up at the top, like – the higher-ups in London, if you know what I mean – they wanted a bit more action, like, and less o' the 'all boys together', as you might say. I reckon the Government had been pushin' them, see. Too much contraband comin' in to the country, an' not enough revenue, see. So, that's why they sent down Cap'n Breward, I reckon. Sort of straighten things out a bit, see.'

Ashley was beginning to see the picture quite clearly: an easy-going, friendly Collector, fond of the booze himself was all too ready to turn a blind eye when a *run* was being made, while up in London some bright fellow of a politician calculated that if the appropriate duty had been paid on all the goods smuggled into Falmouth alone during the course of a single year, the money received would have been more than twice the amount of land tax for the whole of the kingdom. Small wonder if it was being said in influential circles 'We've got a whole army of officials down there in Cornwall for the sole purpose of catching these renegade smugglers; then why, in Heaven's name, aren't they catching them? What the blithering blazes do they think they're doing! Sitting on their arses doing nothing – or worse still, being bribed to keep out of the way!'

The fact that the 'army' was totally inadequate to the size of the task made no difference. Action was demanded; the smugglers must be caught and hauled before the magistrates. Parliament must be satisfied that positive action was being taken to put a stop to this debilitating drain on the country's revenue.

So, in deference to such pressure from on high a 'new man' had been put in at Falmouth. The easy-going Faraday had been put out to grass; Captain James Henry Breward had been put in his place.

'What's he like?' Ashley enquired.

'Wot, Cap'n Breward?' Mattie replied, delighted to be asked, and busily transferring some papers from one side of his desk – and then back again. 'Well, o' course, you know who 'e is, don't you.'

Ashley shook his head encouragingly.

'Oh, well,' Mattie went on, rocking his head from side to side, 'he's the one wot would ha' won the war if only they'd done wot 'e told 'em.'

'Which war was that?'

'Why, the one against them American colonies of ours. You know – what to they call it? – the American War of Independence, isn't it?'

'The one we've just lost,' Ashley suggested.

'Yes, that's the one. Well, 'e was with Lord Cornwallis at the battle of Brandywine, see. The Battle o' Brandywine Creek, I think they called it. I've no doubt you'll be 'earing all about it from his nibs, hisself, afore long.'

'He likes to talk about it, then, does he?'

Mattie chuckled throatily. 'Well, he's certainly told me a good many times, I'm tellin' yer.' He straightened his back, puffed out his chest, and contorted his mouth into what he felt was its most disdainful, military snarl. He was about to give Ashley an imitation of his future boss.

' "There we was, Reynolds," he says to me, "on the march from Princeton to Trenton, in pursuit of Washington's five thousand. The road was a quagmire, Reynolds, a positive qua'mire" ' Mattie deliberately slurred the word, ' "troops sinking to their knees in the mud, guns gettin' hopelessly bogged down – and all the time we were bein' shot at by Washington's long-rifle fire, you understand Reynolds." "Yes, sir" I says, and then he goes on, ''And how far do you think it is from Princeton to Trenton, Reynolds?'' he ask. ''I'm sure I don't know, sir'' I says. ''Ten miles, Reynolds'' he bellows. ''Only ten bloody miles, Reynolds – an' it took us the whole day to get there! Just think o' that!'' '

Mattie glanced across at Ashley to make sure this histrionic masterpiece was being appreciated. Interpreting Ashley's amused smile as being one of deep interest, he continued, ' ''Well, then,'' the Cap'n says, ''even though the troops were tired, having tramped through that mud all day, Sir William Erskine, the Quartermaster General and I . . .'' ' Mattie paused and glanced at Ashley once more, 'You'll note that, Mr Penberth, ''The Quartermaster General and *I* . . . ''yes, *we* urged General Lord Cornwallis to attack the Americans, even though it was nearly five o'clock in the evening an' the troops was tired. We reckoned that we had Washington on the run, *we* did, but Lord Cornwallis didn't like night fighting especially on soggy ground in unknown country, so he called off the hunt and said we'd bag the fox in the morning.'' '

'And did they?' Ashley asked, now genuinely interested.

'Neow!' Mattie derided, 'They let old 'Never-tell-a-lie' give 'em the slip, they did. And 'e wasn't 'arf crafty, was old Washington. He kep' his camp fires burnin' all night, so the Cap'n says – kept about four 'undred men behind to tend the fires and keep up reg'lar patrols, an' so on – and then 'e muffles the wheels of 'is hartillery in blankets so as they won't be heard, and then he slips away. . . .'

But before Mattie Reynolds had time to finish the sentence, Captain Breward burst into the room.

'Mornin' Cap'n,' said Mattie pleasantly enough, 'This is Mr Penberth, the new Rid. . . .'

'Yes, yes, I know,' broke in the Captain, testily. 'I'll see him shortly.' He began thumbing through the papers on Mattie's desk, all hustle and self-importance.

'I was just tellin' Mr Penberth about your. . . .' Mattie began, seeking to put the Captain in a flattered frame of mind, but once again Breward cut him short.

'I know, I know. I heard you. Telling him how Cornwallis lost a golden opportunity to catch Washington, and finish the Revolution, once and for all. And all because he ignored mine and Sir William Erskine's advice!'

He kicked open the door of his own office, crashed through the doorway, and then kicked the door shut again.

Mattie Reynolds drew a deep and profoundly disapproving breath.

'See what I mean,' he said, turning to Ashley. 'You can just visualize it, can't you. Lord Cornwallis taking the advice of one of 'is hinfantry captains.'

He snorted disparagingly – and if there had been a spittoon, he would have spat.

'Is he always like that?' Ashley asked.

Mattie nodded. 'If that man had his way, he'd have God up there salutin' 'im every mornin', and askin' for 'is orders.'

Ashley laughed. 'And polishing his boots as well, I wouldn't wonder.'

Mattie suppressed a smile. 'I reckon you've got 'im summed up all right. Just as well to be forewarned.'

At that moment, the comparative peace of the office was shattered by a raucous shout so penetrating that the dividing wall seemed in danger of being demolished.

'R E Y N O L D S !' the voice bellowed, 'Bring that new man in now.'

'Aye, aye, sir,' was Mattie's instinctive response. He stumped across the room, beckoning Ashley to follow. Then opening the door of the inner office, and with rather obvious deliberation, he announced; 'Mister Penberth, sir.' He bestowed an encouraging wink on Ashley as he went past, before quietly closing the door.

Without looking up from the report he was apparently studying, Captain Breward, with a gesture more appropriate to a dismissal rather than to a welcome, motioned Ashley to a vacant chair. Once more, while the Captain read on, Ashley waited. To make everyone wait was, Ashley concluded, an essential part of every official's armour. It

145

made the official feel big and important; it was intended to make the other person feel nervous and small. But Ashley had become so accustomed to it that it had no effect on him whatever. It merely gave him the opportunity, in this case, to study the man in front of him.

Captain James Henry Breward was the son of a lowly-paid London solicitor's clerk. He was the eldest of the family of seven boys and two girls, and there had never been enough food or clothes to go round; everything had been in short supply. Fiendishly ambitious from the earliest age, he had been determined to get on in life – and it mattered little to him who he trod on in the process, or how hard. Because he was the eldest, he always had to be first at everything – besides, if you got there first, you were sure to get the best of the pickings. Nothing must get in his way; even a closed door had to be kicked open.

He had joined the army in the ranks at sixteen, and had eventually been commissioned in the field. And because service in America was unpopular, promotion was rapid. He had played a significant part in the opening skirmish of the American revolution when some seven hundred grenadiers and light infantry, regarded as the elite of the British Army, had been ordered to destroy gunpowder and stores at the village of Concord. They had been met on the edge of Lexington Green by a small but defiant band of straggling colonial militia, gathered at sunrise, more to make a moral protest than to engage in hostilities, and less than one tenth of the British in numbers; and a scuffle had broken out when the British moved in to disarm the Americans. Some of the British became over-excited; a few scattered shots were fired; then a volley was loosed off by a British platoon. The American War of Independence, which was to last for the next eight years, had begun.

'So you think you're going to be the new Riding Officer, eh?' The tone of voice was taunting; the lips had curled into a disparaging snarl. J.H. Breward had put down the papers he had been reading. He was welcoming the new recruit.

Without waiting for Ashley to reply, he went on: 'I told

146

them up there you'd be no bloody good to me.' He paused, watching for the expected response from a cowering victim. Then, with the inveterate instincts of the bully, he pressed home the advantage.

'No bloody good at all, I told them.' The snarl gave way to a smile of ill-disguised contempt. 'Not the slightest bit o' bloody good because, as far as I can see –' he flicked disdainfully at the papers he had been reading, 'you've had no experience of Preventative work, whatever.' He shook his head, disbelievingly, and shrugged his shoulders. The smile had become almost sympathetic; nothing like making the junior feel an incompetent fool.

'Not a bit o' bloody good,' he repeated. 'I told them so, up at Headquarters – but, of course, they never listen to common sense up there.'

'They had plenty of opportunity to find out,' Ashley remarked coolly.

'Find out what?' snapped Breward, sensing insubordination.

'That I'd had no experience of Preventive work, and whether I'd be any bl . . . – any good at the job.'

Captain Breward made a derisory noise, like a pig finding the trough empty. Come to think of it, Ashley mused, he was rather like a pig – but not quite so fat. His face had the same *lardy* sort of pallor of the Long White Lop-eards back at Treworden. His nose was different, of course; not like the turned up snout of a hog, but large and rather bulbous, like a lump of lard stuck on his cheeks at the last moment, and supporting a pair of owlish-looking spectacles. Thick, greying hair was scraped back off his forehead, and beneath a neatly trimmed silver moustache was the full-lipped brutal-looking mouth of the bully.

'*They* couldn't solve a bloody riddle even though the clues were as thick as confetti,' Breward snorted. 'Why, I don't suppose any of them has the slightest idea of what hard Preventive work is really like. All they want is results. Plenty of prosecutions – and convictions, mark you. Any bloody fool can get a prosecution – if he keeps his eyes and

147

ears open – but to get a conviction by a Cornish jury is a very different kettle of fish. Why, there's literally hundreds of smugglin' bastards down here who ought to have been strung up to a gibbet years ago – but can you ever get a Cornish jury to agree? Not bloody likely! They're all far too afraid for their own skins.'

Ashley observed the Captain with mounting distaste. Every Cornish instinct within him flared defiance. He was all too well aware that there were many unsavoury characters involved in 'the trade', not only in the smuggling of brandy and gin, tobacco and lace, but also in the transmission of information to a foreign enemy – spying, to say no less. And they were in defiance of the law – it was the duty of the King's men to bring them to justice. But to take pleasure in seeing one dangling from a gibbet – well, that was another matter.

As though reading his thoughts, Captain Breward remarked, 'You're Cornish, yourself, I suppose.' And when Ashley replied with a thinly veiled contemptuous nod, Breward spread his hands in simulated dismay, and said, 'There you are! I told them so, up at Headquarters. A Cornish-man among the Cornish! No bloody good at all!' He slumped in his chair, feigning total despair. Then, after a carefully calculated silence, and from beneath a hand held wearily to his brow as he studied the new entrant's papers, he remarked in a voice barely above a whisper, 'And I'll wager a hundred to one that you've never even heard a shot fired in anger . . . let alone actually fired one, yourself.'

He sat there, hunched, slumped – the very picture of dejection. Then, pulling himself up into a more commanding position, he fixed Ashley with a penetrating stare. 'Well,' he said at last, with a shrug that was intended to suggest that he was washing his hands of the whole affair, 'I suppose we'll have to have you. God knows, we're short of troops in these parts, so I suppose we'll have to make what we can of you.'

He got up and walked over to the map pinned to the wall. Picking up a cane from a nearby chair, and straddling his legs with his back to Ashley, he gave what he considered a convincing demonstration of the great field commander laying down battle strategy.

'You'll ride the river and coastline from Gweek round to Cadgwith – and inland from a line Helston – Garras – Traboe Cross, and then on down to Cadgwith. That'll take in the hamlets of Mawgan, Manaccan and St. Keverne. You'll find a fistful of rogues down there, I can assure you – both on the coast and inland. I want you to catch 'em all, and then, by God, we'll string 'em up. Yes, string 'em up, d'you understand.'

He turned and pointed his cane menacingly at Ashley. 'And you'll need to be watching those buggers down at Trengarth. As slippery a bunch of devils as ever landed a keg, I can tell you. And I want *you* to catch 'em at it – redhanded! Understand.'

He sank down into his chair once more, leaned back against the wall, and tapped the cane across the palm of his left hand.

'You'll have Pedloe on one side of you; he works from Falmouth up to Truro, and down to Gweek. On your other side you'll have Tom Dyer working from Cadgwith, down to the Lizard Point, and then up to Mullion. Old Nat Woodstock rides the coast from Mullion up to Porthleven – but he's no bloody good either, so that makes two of you.' Under his breath he added, 'If ever a man had a "gentleman's agreement" with a bunch of smugglers, it's Nathaniel Woodstock.'

Then, as if reading from a book, Captain Breward continued, 'Your duties are simple enough; to patrol your district, both by day and also by night. Obviously, you'll vary your patrols – sometimes by day, sometimes by night. You must never let the bastards get to know your routine. You will visit every town and village in your district, and search out any likely places where contraband might be hidden.

You must maintain contact with your colleagues, both on land and also in the Revenue cruisers – I will be instructing you on that in due course – and, it is of the utmost importance that you keep a journal of daily journeys, times of arrival and departure. The clerk, Reynolds, will show you how the journal is to be kept – and I will be inspecting it, from time to time. Is that all quite clear?'

'Yes, sir, thank you. Quite clear.'

Captain Breward got to his feet. He straightened his shoulders, puffed out his chest. He stared at Ashley through his owlish spectacles perched slightly awry on his lard-like nose.

'Very well, Penberth – you may stand down now.'

Asley recognised the dismissal, and got up to go. As he was walking towards the door, the Captain's voice suddenly barked; 'Wait a minute.'

Ashley turned to face him.

'What's the matter with your leg?' Breward snapped. 'You're limping.'

The same wearisome question; the same perfunctory reply.

'I broke it while I was at school. One leg's a bit shorter than the other.'

A golden opportunity for histrionics – too good to be missed – and Breward seized it. Placing one hand to his forehead in a gesture of utter despair, he sank to his chair once more. 'Oh, my God!' he moaned, 'not that as well, surely! Not only do they send me someone who's still wet behind the ears, but they send me a cripple into the bargain!'

He paused, just long enough to allow his words to have their full effect – and then, in a voice riddled with self-pity, he added, 'I told those silly buggers that you'd be no bloody good to me . . . I told them!'

With these encouraging words still ringing in his head, Ashley set forth on his first day as one of His Majesty's Riding Officers in the county of Cornwall. It was, however, no mere coincidence that his chosen route should take him near Trevadne – because he had promised Alethea that he would call in and tell her how the interview had gone, as soon as possible.

But Alethea was strolling in the orchard with her father

when Ashley arrived at the house. It was Jeannie therefore who received him, reclining on a chaise-longue in the withdrawing room and reading the poems of a rising young Scottish poet, Robert Burns. She was wearing one of the gowns recently brought back from Paris. Distinctly *avant garde*, it was Grecian in style, very full, very flowing, and made from a thin diaphanous material. So thin and so gossamer, in fact, that as it fell in rippling swathes from bodice to ankle-length hem the voluptuous outline of Jeannie's young, exciting body was clearly discernible. It was disturbing. Ashley found it very difficult to drag his eyes away from those shapely thighs – even when, eventually, Alethea came in from the garden.

CHAPTER THIRTEEN

On His Majesty's Service

On the high ground just south of Roskorwell, Ashley leaned back in the saddle, gave a checking jerk on the reins, and brought Puncher to a halt. He had been riding all day.

Behind him stretched the broad expanse of Falmouth Bay, shimmering and glinting beneath a cloudless June sky. Ahead, nestling between protecting bluffs on each side, lay the tiny fishing village of Porthallow.

As much to ease his muscles as to obtain a better view, Ashley stood erect in the stirrups and gazed down at the cluster of cottages huddled together at the head of the cove. In the hot afternoon sunshine nothing stirred. The usual number of small fishing vessels lay, like exhausted fish, tilted to one side on their beaching timbers and with bows drawn shorewards as though gasping for refreshment and revival from the windlass.

Strung out from the back door of one of the cottages, and clearly visible from all angles of the cove, was a clothes line of washing. Conspicuous among the greys and whites of smocks and undergarments was a bright red shirt. It flapped languidly in the gentle breeze of a peerless afternoon.

Ashley smiled. 'D'you see that, Puncher,' he said, companionably addressing the horse as he frequently did on these lonely rides. 'I think I know what that means.'

Puncher responded by dragging at a fresh tuft of grass and then jerking his head upwards at the sound of Ashley's voice. Momentarily he appeared to be looking in the right direction but very soon he was waggling his head, jingling his bridle impatiently, before returning to the patch of fresh pasture of his feet.

Ashley sank back into the saddle, resting one elbow on the pommel, absorbing the simple beauty of the typically Cornish scene below. Presently a grey-haired woman emerged from the back door of the cottage and began gathering the bone-dry garments from the washing line into a tattered rush basket.

'Now this might be interesting,' Ashley breathed softly, 'Look, Puncher. Watch this.'

Again Puncher's head came up. This time he caught sight of the moving figure; his ears pricked forward as he watched the woman move slowly along the line. She gathered in all the garments, except the bright red shirt. It remained, fluttering gently, like a solitary beacon against the green background of the hill beyond.

As she was about to re-enter the cottage, the woman glanced up in Ashley's direction. Something caught her attention; the brass buttons on Ashley's jacket glinting through the screening blackthorn bush, perhaps, or the jingle of Puncher's bit and bridle as he munched a succulent mouthful. Whatever it was, it made her hesitate. Then, with rolling, bow-legged purposefulness she made her way to the end of the cottage garden to get a better look. Having satisfied her curiosity she turned on her heel and went back towards the cottage.

On the way she took down the bright red shirt.

'There you are, Puncher,' Ashley chuckled. 'What did I tell you? We've been spotted all right – and the signal's been removed.'

But Puncher seemed uninterested; he had returned to the luscious pathside forage. His head shot up again, however, when a few moments later a young boy came out of the cottage, jumped on the back of a pony grazing the adjoining field, and galloped away up the hill towards St. Keverne.

Ashley smiled. 'There he goes,' he said to the munching, uninterested Puncher. 'Just as I thought. Before long, everyone in the neighbourhood will be warned that the

Riding Officer's on the prowl. That is,' he added with a rueful grin, 'if they aren't aware of it already.'

He gave a tug on the reins, pulling the reluctant cob away from his impromptu feed and setting him off down the steep, treacherous path leading to Porthallow.

It was a pity, of course, that they had been spotted. But it couldn't be helped. In the countryside – particularly the Cornish seaboard – nothing unusual went unobserved. Even when he paused at the stream to allow Puncher to drink, Ashley knew that behind almost every cottage window in Porthallow a pair of eyes would be watching.

An old man standing in his cottage doorway, his wizened, salt-encrusted face screwed tightly around the stub of a broken pipe, gave Ashley a friendly nod. No point in upsetting the 'King's Men', the old man's grin seemed to be saying – especially if you've got a keg or two of 'cousin jacky' hidden under the stairs.

'Good Luck to him,' Ashley mused. If it helped the old chap to keep out the winter's cold, or to make a shilling or two for a few small luxuries, so be it. As far as he, Ashley, was concerned it was the big fish he was after – the ones with an extensive smuggling organisation, and those who were getting rich at the expense of the country's revenue. Above all the criminals who had a vested interest in luring well-laden ships to their doom.

Ashley checked, as he rode past the old man's cottage. 'Good day, to you.' he called out.

'Good day to ee,' the old man responded.

'Not a bad un for the time o' year,' Ashley observed.

'Naw, naw. Us've seed wuss.'

Ashley sat, relaxed in the saddle. Puncher played with his bit. It was the usual pause before the usual question.

'Any smuggling going on in these parts?' Ashley asked, with no more than a semblance of smile.

The old man's grin split his wrinkled face from ear to hair-tufted ear.

'Naw, naw,' he chuckled, 'there be none o' that round these yer parts.'

Ashley grinned back. 'No, I thought not. Nothing but fishing, eh?'

'Tha's reet, Mester,' the old man nodded, trying hard not to give his customary wink. 'Nothin' but a bit o' fishin'.'

Ashley laughed out loud; the old man continued to grin. Each was finding the interlude highly amusing; each knew that the other knew who was doing the lying.

With a wave of his riding crop Ashley bade the old man 'Good-day', and set Puncher at the mountainous cliffside path leading up out of Porthallow towards Porthoustock. As they climbed the rough, flinty track which skirted the sheer drop to the rocks below, Ashley felt doubly grateful for the power and surefootedness of the cob between his knees. Puncher's head was going up and down with the rhythm of a steam piston; the tremendous strength of his hindquarters came quivering up through the saddle as man and horse steadily mounted the treacherous hillside. Not for the first time was Ashley appreciating the quality of Puncher's company. In a world where everyone's hand was against the 'King's men', the unquestioning loyalty of the horse provided no shallow comfort.

At the top of the stiff climb, where the ground levels off into a small plateau above Porthkerris beach, Ashley slid from the saddle. Leaving Puncher to sample a patch of well-shaded pasture, he threaded his way through the newly uncurled bracken until he reached the cliff edge. The hot smell of summer gorse wafted into his nostrils. Away to the North, the whole immaculate sweep of the coastal scene lay before him like an artist's canvas – the majestic grandeur of Rosemullion Head, the snakelike persistance of Nare Point, each guarding in its own immovable way the entrance to the Helford River. In the near distance, shrouded by the gossamer veil of a coastal haze, cattle and sheep grazed peacefully beneath Penare; seagulls wheeled lazily from cliff-face to gently rippling water, and then back again.

Ashley lay down in the bracken and, cradling the back of

his head in his hands, he stared up into the vastness of the azure sky. This Preventive business, he reflected; it really couldn't be such a bad occupation if it took a fellow to places like this. Who else, other than His Majesty's Government, would actually pay a man to ride the countryside he loved. True, the word 'pay' was almost a joke, and the prospect of putting Cornish smugglers behind bars didn't exactly overflow with attraction but, so far, he had managed to give a fairly convincing appearance of doing the job without actually bringing anyone before the Courts. Unfortunately this happy state of affairs could not be allowed to last much longer. He was well aware of that. Captain Breward had been making ugly noises about the lack of any prosecutions coming from the St. Keverne district. Everyone knew that the whole of the coast right round from Helford village down to Coverack and beyond was a hotbed of smugglers, and in Captain Breward's opinion it was about time the buggers were dangling from a gibbet. 'String 'em up, Penberth. String 'em up, I say,' was the Captain's repeated command – but in his heart of hearts Penberth A. had serious doubts about his ability to carry out the Captain's order.

Nevertheless, he recognised that if he wished to keep the job – and times were becoming increasingly hard in the countryside – he would have to make a very serious effort to put at least one bunch of smugglers in the dock. He shuddered – quickly putting the unwelcome thought behind him. Today, on this gloriously sunny June afternoon, he would concentrate on the good things of life: the early morning ride along the creek-side track between Gweek and Mawgan beneath the delicate pale green ceiling of the freshly sprung beech leaves; the idyllic beauty of the winding paths around the headwaters of the Trelowarren inlet; the hedgerows between Manaccan and Helford village – a riot of purple-magenta foxgloves and campion, the creamy tracery of 'Queen Anne's lace', and the brilliant wax yellow of buttercups. Even in the dead of winter that wooded ride from Gweek to Mawgan was silently, mysteriously beautiful. Occasionally a squirrel would go leaping and swinging high up in the feathery branches of a beech tree, every movement expressing more eloquently than mere words the uncomplicated joy of just being alive. Every now and again the silence of those mysterious woods would be broken by the insistent 'Rat-a-tat-tat' of a woodpecker; and when at last the earth stretched, yawned and finally awoke into Spring, then the soft covering of fallen beech leaves would give way to a seemingly endless carpet of bluebells.

Yes, if you loved the countryside, as Ashley did, the job had its compensations. Socially, of course, it carried very little prestige; indeed, to be one of 'the King's Men', or more colloquially, 'a searcher', was to be labelled in the eyes of many nothing less than a social pariah.

Surprisingly, Ashley reflected, neither Jeannie nor Alethea were among the many – at least so it seemed. To Jeannie it was no more than a temporary aberration – something to be glossed over with the merriest of laughs. It mattered little to her how Ashley chose to earn his living – just so long as he remained the curly-headed little boy who had grown into the handsomely desirable young man.

His mother cared only for two things; that her son should still be living at home with her, even though so much of his duty required him to work during the night hours; secondly, that he was working on the side of the law not against it. Although she had failed to keep him away from 'the trade' entirely, at least he was working to prevent it.

Sir Andrew, on the other hand, maintained an enigmatic aloofness.

But it was Alethea's reaction that interested Ashley the most. She cared not one whit for the social aspect. Her only concern seemed to be for his safety. She knew that, only a few years ago, Preventive officer Odgers at Porthleven had been shot dead by smugglers while trying to do his duty. She knew, too, that Odgers wasn't the only one of 'the King's Men' to have been summarily despatched by the 'gentlemen of the trade'. There were many other unrecorded incidents – like the one where the two Riding Officers, Hallam and Corcoran, working together between Portscatho and Portloe had suprised a gang of smugglers making a 'run' of goods into Veryan. Hopelessly outnumbered, the two Officers had nevertheless put up a brave fight against the bludgeons and knives of their assailants but were eventually overpowered, then bound with ropes and left lying, half dead, among the rocks and bracken on the cliffside. Had it not been for the resourcefulness of the younger, fitter Corcoran who managed to free himself by sawing the binding rope against the jagged edge of a nearby rock, both men would have perished from exposure.

It was tales like these that frightened Alethea. Ashley smiled at the recollection of her concern. She had grown into such a lovely girl, especially during the last few years. Not the stunning, vibrant, vivacious beauty that was Jeannie. Not the kind of girl always ready with a witty riposte, always able to turn a solemn occasion into one of hilarity. No – but there was a captivating softness about her, a kind of will-o-the-wisp charm; one moment you felt sure you had her in the palm of your hand, but then she was gone.

'But she *is* pretty,' Marianne had said to her son, one evening after returning from dinner at Trevadne, 'perhaps not so startlingly beautiful as her sister, but she'm very attractive, to my way of thinking.'

Ashley, deep in thought, had nodded agreement.

'I s'pose 'tis something to do with that very slight Scottish accent of hers,' his mother continued. 'So soft, it is, I can hardly hear what she'm sayin'. Don't quite know why but the sound of that voice puts me in mind of a Highland mist, or something.' She had chuckled, with that rich, gurgling Devonian laugh of hers. 'Which is quite ridiklus, really, because I've never seen such a thing in me life – never having been up-country further than Taun'on.'

Ashley had smiled appreciation, warmly. He had loved that laugh of hers ever since he could remember. They were sitting at the kitchen table, hugging a mug of hot cocoa, mulling over the evening at Trevadne. Not often would Marianne accept an invitation to take dinner with Sir Andrew MacKenzie and his two daughters. They were undoubtedly 'the quality', and she always felt slightly uncomfortable, just a little bit out of place. She much preferred Sir Andrew's company in her own home. She could look after him there, fuss over him – and besides, she knew just where everything was. But every now and then she would agree to visit Trevadne on a social footing because she felt it would further her son's chances with one or other of the MacKenzie girls. She wouldn't really mind which. They were both nice girls; either would make a truly excellent catch for her boy; but from the far away look that came into his eyes whenever her name was mentioned, she knew that it was Alethea who haunted Ashley's dreams.

'Yes,' he had agreed, musingly, 'she certainly is very beautiful. But there's a sadness there, too. I don't know quite what it is or how to describe . . .' his voice had trailed off into the realms of silent contemplation.

And his mother – as loving, caring mothers will – had sought to resolve the mystery by saying, simply, 'Well then, Ashley, you must just find a way to make her happy.'

Now, as he lay back comfortably on a bed of bracken on the cliff above Porthoustock, staring up at the sky, he was remembering his mother's straightforward solution. He let out a snort of affectionate disavowal. 'Just like Mother! She thinks it's all so simple.'

Yet, there was nothing either simple or straightforward about Alethea. Even though they had grown up together, there were times when Ashely found her quite baffling. That she was capable of a deep, all-embracing love he felt sure; equally surely he knew that he had not yet found the way to unleash it. If he could but find the key. . . .

He rolled over on to his side, plucked a fresh stem of grass, then got to his feet. He had work to do, he reminded himself. He wasn't paid – pittance though it might be – to

159

lie about in idyllic surroundings, just thinking about the women in his life.

He remounted Puncher and set off along the cliffside track, down into Porthoustock, then inland towards St. Keverne.

Over the years, St. Keverne had acquired an unsavoury reputation for lawlessness and unruly behaviour. It was well-known to be swarming with smugglers. Even the inn right next to the church, *The Three Tuns*, had taken its name from the three barrels of contraband liquor purloined by a 15th century vicar from a wreck down on the Manacles – or so they said. And it was common knowledge that a boatload of St. Keverne smugglers had nearly succeeded in bashing out the brains of Penzance Customs Officers who had tried to intercept them. Admittedly, that was some years ago; but it seemed like only the other day that a gang of P'roustock men had landed the colossal haul of two hundred and eighteen ankers of brandy in one night. It was well known; the problem was to catch them at it – red-handed.

And that was precisely what Ashley had been instructed to do.

The task was formidable; he had no illusions about that. Almost everyone in a coastal village seemed to be 'in it'. Despite the 1766 Act which provided a reward of £50 for information leading to the arrest and conviction of any person engaged in smuggling, it was more than anyone's life was worth to give the game away in a small community like St. Keverne. To turn King's Evidence was the shortest route to a knife in the back on a dark night.

As a result of this confraternity among villagers, the life of a King's man was a lonely one, to say the least.

So far, though, Ashley had not been subjected to violence. On the contrary, most people he had encountered while riding the district were quite friendly. Too friendly, in fact. It made you wonder just what they were up to behind your back.

The afternoon was already well advanced by the time

Ashley rode into St. Keverne. He had been dawdling; he had to admit it; up there on the cliff above P'roustock, day-dreaming about Alethea, and it was now too late to ride on down to Cadgwith, his original intention.

He began looking round for somewhere to put up for the night.

Over there, across the square, facing the church was *The White Hart*, a handsome-looking public house which had recently acquired, so Ashley had heard, a modest but nonetheless unusual local renown. The owner's son, Charles Incledon, was the possessor of a quite remarkable singing voice. In Cornwall there were many fine voices, of course, but Charles Incledon's was exceptional. While singing in the St. Keverne church choir he had so impressed a visiting Canon that before long he was being installed as a member of the Exeter cathedral choir. And it was there that an Assize judge had been so moved by the boy's rendering of '*Let my complaint come before Thee*' it had brought tears to his eyes – and a gift of five guineas to the singer.

But Charles, restless by nature, had soon grown tired of his studies and had run away to sea. Enlisting as a midshipman in the Navy, he had served under Captain Cleland in *HMS Formidable* and then later in *HMS Raisonable* under Captain Lord Harvey. Encouraged by his officers, he left the Navy to seek his fortune on the stage, and after appearing at Southampton as Alphonso in *Castle of Andalusia*, and than as Edwin in *Robin Hood* at Bath, he was now making a name for himself at Vauxhall Gardens. The St. Keverne chorister had become the best ballad singer in the country.

All this Ashley knew from hearsay – an oft-told tale of the local boy making good – and although *The White Hart* undoubtedly had its attractions, it was the inn beside the church that caught his attention – *The Three Tuns* with its steeply sloping thatched roof and its inn sign depicting that renegade old parson with his barrels of contraband liquor. It had a homely, inviting look.

And there was something about its cobbled forecourt and

stableyard, its outhouses and their close proximity to the church overlooking the sea that suggested it as the most likely rendezvous for the transaction of a particular type of business.

Ashley decided to follow his instinct.

He clattered over the cobbles, saw to Puncher's stabling – and then entered *The Three Tuns Inn*.

CHAPTER FOURTEEN

The Three Tuns Inn

Anticipating that his arrival in the village would by now have been well advertised, Ashley was surprised to find, as he stalked into the small, intimate bar of *The Three Tuns Inn*, that his presence was apparently unexpected. He felt sure the boy seen cantering off up the hill out of Porthallow had gone on ahead to warn the residents of St. Keverne that the Riding Officer was on the prowl. It would have been nothing unusual.

But judging by the look of genuine surprise on the pretty, oval-shaped face of the barmaid as he entered, the message had not yet been relayed to *The Three Tuns*. From beneath long dark eyelashes she regarded him coolly. In one hand she held a pewter tankard from which she sipped occasionally; in the other she held an old woollen stocking with which she lightly buffed the already highly polished bar top.

Ashley stood in the middle of the room surveying his surroundings. Nothing remarkable; blackened ceiling, dun coloured walls, half-panelled with varnished timber and relieved only by a faded picture of sheep being driven through a gate. In the far corner, a high-backed wooden settle facing the empty fireplace, and a few roughly made chairs pushed up against the walls. Nothing to suggest the presence of contraband goods. Nothing unusual in that, either. You had to look for the stuff – and in the most unlikely places; tobacco in the hollowed out section of a ship's mast or a wooden door lintel, silks wound round a woman's waist beneath her skirt where it was thought no Riding Officer would dare to probe, tea in that little broken down wooden casket beneath a pile of straw, and brandy – well, brandy almost anywhere, best French cognac in kegs buried deep in that mound of grain up in the barn loft, or under the woodlump by the back door, or down in that cave at the foot of the cliff. There was no limit to the ingenuity of the free traders. And the Riding Officer, often outnumbered by as much as a hundred to one, had to be a match for them.

Ashley regarded the barmaid – and the barmaid coldly returned his stare. She was observing every detail of his attire; the black tricorn hat, the cream silk cravat, the sky-blue riding coat, the light beige coloured well-cut breeches, and the black leather riding boots. He made an impressive figure. An aggresive figure even; for at his waist were holstered a pair of flintlock pistols, and from his broad leather belt dangled a naval-type cutlass.

For several seconds while the noisy tick of the clock above the bar emphasised the silence, barmaid and Riding Officer sized each other up. A comely wench, Ashley thought, with her black hair peeping out prettily from beneath that fluffy white mob cap with the red ribbon threaded through it. But a bit cheeky, he wouldn't wonder – considering the challenging way she was looking at him with those large, lustrous eyes. She was making it abundantly clear that she didn't care very much for what she saw. Doubtless she would need putting in her place before very much longer.

'Kindly inform the landlord I wish to see him,' he demanded, coldly.

The merest expression of amusement twitched the corners of his mouth as he watched the girl bristle. It was nothing new. In the comparatively short time he'd been working for His Majesty, King George III, trying to preserve for him the revenue to pay for, among other things, a Royal Navy to protect the inhabitants of his kingdom, Ashley had learnt to absorb like a sponge the dislike – and in some cases the downright hatred – of those who thought only of themselves. He understood their feelings. Everyone expected His Majesty's protection; only the very few gave a moment's thought to just how it was to be paid for.

'Am I right in thinkin' you require to see Mister William Trenethy, the landlord of this establishment?' the barmaid enquired tartly, summoning as much dignity as she knew how.

'You are – and I do,' was the curt reply.

'Then I must ask you to find a civil tongue in your head!' Very deliberately she hitched the skirt of her magenta-coloured dress above her silver buckled shoes, and with her head held at its most disdainful angle, she swept imperiously out of the bar.

Ashley smiled. Obviously he had offended the lady. He wondered who she was and where she came from. It was the nature of his business to visit public houses, from Gweek right round to Cadgwith, searching for contraband, but he had never before encountered a barmaid quite like this one. She had a certain something – a *je ne sais quoi* – a dignified bearing, perhaps. It was hard to put a finger on it. And she was prettier than most, too – very much prettier. Strange to find such an attractive wench serving behind the bar of a country inn on the Lizard.

The Riding Officer's smile broadened as he listened to what he was not intended to hear. *Sotto voce*, the girl was hissing: 'There's a very rude man in the bar says he wants to see you, Will. All dressed up in some kind of uniform, he is – with pistols and a sword. Don't like the look of him, not one little bit, I don't.'

'Sssshh! Rosie,' came the reply. 'For the lawd's sake, ssshhh!'

As a member of the Parish Church choir, Rose Roskruge had often been complimented by the vicar on the power and clarity of her singing voice. It reached to the further-most corners of the building, he would say, and it had the resonance of a well-cast bell. But there were times when the landlord of *The Three Tuns Inn*, Will Trenethy, whose nerves were not of the strongest, rather wished his barmaid would speak less loudly. Now, gesticulating for her to keep her voice down, he hissed back:

165

'I know, I know. I see'd him come. Tis the Ridin' Officer. He'm yere to search the place, I 'spec.'

'Well, that's as maybe,' Rose retorted, forsaking all attempts at speaking softly, 'but it's certainly no excuse for rudeness.'

'Sssh, sshhh!' Will anguished, shifting nervously from one foot to the other, 'You mustn't speak so loud, Rosie. You must be civil to the man. I want ee to be nicey – I want ee to study un.'

The snort that greeted this injunction broadened the Riding Officer's grin still further. Evidently the lass was not only pretty, she was spirited as well.

'Study un! Ha!' Ashley heard her explode, 'I'll as lief study the man as fly to the moon. What *he* needs is a lesson in good manners, not a bit o' studyin'. The sooner he learns to show a little common courtesy to a maid, the better it'll be for he.'

It was meant to be heard – and Ashley heard it, every word. He quickly turned his back to the bar, and looked out of the window. It would not do for the landlord to discover him, face wreathed in a broad grin, rocking with silent laughter. No, no. This was serious business – His Majesty's business – and it must be treated accordingly.

By the time an obsequious Will Trenethy came sidling round the doorway at the back of the bar, Ashley's face was once more a mask.

'You wanted to see I, zur, I do believe,' landlord Will began, nervously fingering the corners of his mouth. 'T'were the maid, yere, that do tell I – me maid, Rosie, if you understand, like.'

'Yes, yes. I quite understand,' Ashley barked, 'I told her to tell you.'

The barmaid had followed as far as the doorway. She leaned against the upright, eyeing the Riding Officer sourly.

Glancing at Rose, Will Trenethy observed, 'Her forgot to say the name, zur.'

'She could hardly have done so,' Ashley replied coldly,

'because she never enquired.' He smiled mirthlessly at Rose who curled her lips into a withering sneer. It was intended to be demolishing, Ashley thought, but in fact he found it rather attractive. He turned his attention to the landlord once more.

'The name is Penberth,' he informed, speaking rapidly, 'Ashley Penberth, His Majesty's Riding Officer for this district.'

'Aw, ais,' Will Trenethy snivelled. 'You'm the Ridin' Officer, then.'

'That's what I said.'

'Aw, ais – then you'm new to these yere parts, I 'spec.'

Ashley nodded, rocking back and forth on his heels, appraising the mouth-fingering landlord.

Will Trenethy continued, 'Us useta have a different genelman come round. By the name o' Craddock I think 'twas. Very nice genelman, he were. Very easy to get along wi', like.'

'Yes,' Ashley thought, 'and gave you no trouble, I've no doubt.' It would have been nothing unusual. All around the coast there were Customs officers whose gaze could be diverted by the gleam of a gold sovereign or a few tubs of cousin jacky. The Board of Customs was all too well aware of it. Parliament had been prodding. Of every three barrels of cognac or Geneva coming into the country, at least two had yielded not a penny piece of duty. Something had to be done about it. And that's why men like Captain Breward were being recruited – 'To catch the buggers, and string 'em up!' – and also young men like himself, Ashley supposed.

'But he haven't been around for quite some time,' Will was saying, his eyes shifting uneasily between barmaid and Riding Officer, 'I've not see'd un for quite a while.'

'He's retired,' Ashley informed tonelessly.

'Oh, ah. He'm re-tired, then.' Will nodded sagely, trying not to make his disappointment too apparent. 'An' you do be the one takin' his place, like?'

'That's right.'

The landlord shot a meaningful glance at Rose – who missed the significance because she was examining her nails – and then continued unctuously, 'Well, zur, be there something I could be gettin' for ee – like a pint o' best porter, p'raps?'

'No thank you, not just now. But I shall be wanting to have a look at your cellar.'

'Zertainly, zur. Just as you say,' Will replied, staring fixedly at the Riding Officer and dabbing weakly at his lips with the fingertips of his right hand. He looked just like a rabbit caught by a stoat, Ashley thought. For a moment he felt quite sorry for the fellow.

But he said, briskly enough, 'Very well, then. Shall we make a start.' He stood in the centre of the room, gently tapping the side of one boot with his riding whip. Will continued to stare, making no move. Ashley tapped, rhythmically – waiting; Will stared. The boot-tapping grew perceptibly more impatient; still the landlord stood, lip-fingering, irresolute, mesmerised.

Rose it was who, looking up from her manicure, eventually broke the impasse.

'The gentleman says he wants to see the cellar,' she reminded, with exaggerated interest. And then, throwing a contemptuous look at the Riding Officer, she added, 'Shall you be showin' un – or no?'

The sound of Rose's voice seemed to bring Will out of his coma. He began shifting nervously again from one foot to the other; he picked up Rose's woollen duster, pretending to remove a drip of ale from the already highly polished bar top. Ashley recognised the signs; anything to delay the inevitable.

'Ooh, ah!' Will managed at last, 'The cellar, ais. The genelman wishes to see the cellar, Rosie. Do ee take un down, then, an' show un.'

Rose looked up, astonished. 'Me? The cellar? You know I never go down to that dreadful place, Will.'

'T'would be nice if you were to show the officer,' Will smarmed.

Rose responded with a short, throaty laugh. 'Not likely,' she snorted. 'What, me go down that musty old place! An' with me new dress on! You must be dreamin'.'

The landlord cringed. 'T'would be nice, though, Rosie.'

'Nothin' nice about it at all, Will. Damp, dirty old place, and you know it. . . .' Then she suddenly realised the significance of Will's entreaty. A wicked gleam came into her eye. Oh, yes – a chance to teach this arrogant Riding Officer a lesson, perhaps. 'Nothing but a cob-webby old dungeon of a place full o' 'Duty Paid' liquor barrels, eh,' she added maliciously.

But she caught Will's eye – and winked prodigiously. The deception was on. She would enjoy making a fool of this overbearing official.

'Well, if I must, I must, I 'spose,' she agreed, lifting the hem on her dress well clear of the floor. 'Come along then, we may as well get it over and done with. The sooner we can return to our normal peaceful ways, the better pleased I shall be.' She flashed a petulant glance at Ashley as she opened the bar hatch to let him come through. 'If you will kindly step this way, sir,' she invited, her ringing voice mockingly deferential.

Ashley, who had been thoroughly enjoying the pantomime, followed the barmaid down the cellar stairs. She had a good figure, he thought – a pretty hair line, a slender neck. He wondered where the landlord had found her; she could hardly be his daughter. Altogether too fine-boned, too refined.

The cellar was damp, musty and full of cobwebs, as Rose had accurately described it. But there were signs of some very recent activity – not much, Ashley smiled wryly, because there hadn't been a great deal of time. The galloping young messenger from Porthoustock could scarcely have given more than ten minutes warning. But in that time, Will Trenethy of *The Three Tuns Inn*, St. Keverne, had been busy. All the most readily accessible tubs, ankers and barrels were clearly labelled 'Duty Paid' – much too clearly, Ashley thought, and there were far more than could possibly be required by a small country inn. But there was no law governing quantity – at least, not that he was aware of.

'Yes, yes, I can see those quite clearly,' he snapped, as Will confidently indicated the most prominent ankers at the front of the rack, 'I'm more interested in some of those at the back, there.'

Foolishly, Will tried to draw his attention to a harmless barrel of home-brewed ale. 'Like this one, yere, p'raps?'

The sharp smack of whip against riding boot echoed round the cellar. Clearly, the Riding Officer had a short temper. But his voice was exaggeratedly considerate as he replied, 'No - o, not that one, thank you, Mr. Trenethy. I'm not really interested in your ale.' He was moving slowly to the far end of the cellar – like a cat stalking its prey, Rose thought. It was stealthy. She hated him.

In the brief moment his back was turned, she felt something pressed into her hand. She looked at Will. No words were spoken – but she knew what to do.

'I'd like to have a look at this one,' the Riding Officer was saying, 'Just get it down for me, will you, Mr. Trenethy.'

His tone was conciliation itself. It was no coincidence that he happened to be pointing at the most inaccessible anker in the cellar.

He stood, gently whip-tapping the side of his boot, while Will struggled. Rose watched, incredulous.

'The brute!' she thought, inwardly fuming, 'he's not going to lift a finger!'

She waited – until she could bear it no longer. Then with a look at the Riding Officer that would have plunged a dagger right through his sky-blue jacket, she went forward.

'Here, Will,' she began, 'that be far too heavy for ee to manhandle on your own. And as there doesn't appear to be anyone else to help ee,' she added, her voice ringing with sarcasm, 'allow *me* to give you a hand.'

Ashley stood, motionless – apart from the gentle, rhythmical boot tapping. A faint smile curled his lips. He knew exactly what the barmaid was thinking – 'The mannerless bastard – stands there and lets a woman do the dirty work. Huh, no gentleman, he!'

He sympathised. It was something he had to endure. There was no end to the tricks these people would invent in order to cheat the Revenue, and if you once started to do the manhandling yourself, you'd very soon become the laughing stock of the tricksters. 'Ooh, ah, us had un away on a wild goose chase, all right! Hee, hee, hee. . . .' Ashley could just hear the laughter echoing round every inn in the district.

And then what would Captain Breward say!

With every instinct urging him to assist the frail, struggling landlord and his pretty little barmaid in her dark magenta silk dress, he nevertheless remained apparently unmoved. It was while the keg was being, with difficulty, lowered to the ground that the Riding Officer observed the barmaid slap something on its side. He also noticed the nasty pluck on the bodice of the dress, caught by the sharp edge of a rusty cooper's nail.

'Ohh! Just look at that!' she wailed, 'and my new dress, too. First time on to-day! Ohh. . . .' She examined the damage, her eyes filling with tears.

In the next minute her anger got the better of her. Turning to the Riding Officer, her eyes blazing, she flared at him. 'Well, *now* are you satisfied!'

It was hard. She looked so pretty in her rage. Ashley scrutinised the label so very recently slapped on to the side of the keg. It was seared and yellowed, expertly forged – and it bore the legend 'DUTY PAID'. He enveloped her in a long penetrating sideways stare. Yes, she was a comely lass. He felt greatly tempted to pretend satisfaction, to conclude the search. But a fleeting smirk of triumph flashing across her face caused him to change his mind.

He straightened up and surveyed the cellar once more. 'No,' he said enigmatically, 'not quite satisfied yet.'

His gaze eventually fastened on a mound of something over in the far corner, of indeterminate shape and covered by a tattered lugsail. It was very dusty and cobwebbed.

'I think we'll have a look at that,' he announced, stalking towards it, 'Just remove that cover, will you.'

'Aw, that be just a heap o' empty barrels, thur,' Will volunteered, 'There be nothin' to see under thur.'

Ashley permitted a sardonic smile to linger around his lips. How many times had he heard that remark before!

'Nevertheless, be so good as to remove that cover,' he snapped. 'I wish to see what is beneath it.'

Will Trenethy – spindle-shanked, scrawny-armed and frail of structure – began struggling with the coarse, heavy lugsail. 'I don't say but there might'n be one or two that edn empty, like,' he muttered, 'but 'twould'n be many.'

Rose was watching the smile on the handsome Riding Officer's face. It had openly broadened into a cynical grin. No doubt he was quietly congratulating himself on having located a lucrative pile of contraband, and eagerly anticipating the financial reward for its seizure. She looked from one man to the other – from the imperious, lip-curling arrogance of the unhelpful officer on the one hand, to the slight, wasting figure of the landlord on the other. She was remembering the story of her rescue from the sea – and suddenly the gall boiled over within her.

Grinding her teeth, and throwing aside all concern for her clothes, she scrambled over the litter of broken crates and upturned barrels to where Will wrestled with the lugsail. 'Leave it to me, Will', she enjoined, 'I'm a bit younger 'n you. You've suffered enough, already. I'll do it.'

She had started hauling at the heavy-salt-encrusted sail-cloth, breaking fingernails as she did so, when she felt a firm restraining hand on her arm. Even a Riding Officer is human – sometimes – and the sight of that angry figure in the pristine-fresh magenta silk dress, scrabbling with that dirty lugsail, had melted his necessarily stern, official's heart.

'Allow me, ma'am,' the voice said, not unkindly. But she would have none of it. Angrily, perversely, she tried to brush his hand aside. It gripped her arm the more strongly.

'No, ma'am. You, too, have suffered enough. I should

hate to think of that pretty dress being further damaged.'

Gently but firmly he propelled her away from the sail-covered mound. As he did so, he relieved her of the 'DUTY PAID' labels that Will had so recently thrust into her hand.

With a smile that was both warm and humorous, he said, 'And you'll not be needing those now ma'am'.

CHAPTER FIFTEEN

Lanteague

Carriages began arriving soon after eight o'clock. From every window in Lanteague's imposing façade, lights blazed. They twinkled invitingly through the fir trees surrounding the mansion; they welcomed the gentry to the Ball.

Colonel Sir Francis and Lady Arabella Bouchier stood in the main hall, beneath one of the glittering chandeliers, receiving their guests. They were the host and hostess, as they had been for many years past, at the annual Hunt Ball.

The chandelier beneath which they stood, along with four others of equal splendour, one at each corner of the hall, had been lowered for cleaning and re-candling that very morning. Each piece of delicately cut crystal – the pear-drops, the lobes, the dagger-blades – had been removed, washed in soapy water, dried, polished and lovingly re-assembled by an army of servants specially recruited for the task. Four times a year – at Christmas, at Lady Day, at Michaelmas, and just before the Hunt Ball at Candlemas – the same group of women, drawn from the surrounding estate cottages, would descend upon the Manor for this special task. They had come to regard those chandeliers as if they were their own property.

Now, those mountain peaks of cascading crystal, hauled once more to their lofty eminence, whispered and jingled like excited fairies, and sent a shower of rainbow-coloured reflections to the ballroom below.

Colonel Bouchier, Master of Foxhounds and resplendent in hunting pink, and Lady Bouchier, wearing the cream

174

muslin confection so recently created by her new seamstress, stood in the centre of the room, graciously receiving their guests.

A tall major-domo in dark blue velvet cut-away jacket, white breeches and black, silver-buckled shoes was making the announcements.

'His Worship, Mayor Hocking and Mistress Hocking – Colonel, Sir Arthur Julian and his Lady – His Honour, Judge Bown and Miss Amelia Bown –'

There was a pause; the guests were arriving slowly. The roads leading to Lanteague were rough and pot-holed even in summer; in winter, carriage wheels sank deep into the mud. But they came. Such a prestigious affair as the Lanteague Ball was not to be missed – at least not by anyone who regarded himself as anyone.

Soon the major-domo was clearing his throat once more; 'The Honourable Justin St. Ormonde and his Lady – Mister Clement Vivian and Mistress Vivian – Sir Andrew MacKenzie and Miss Jean MacKenzie. . . .'

The major-domo was bending low, inclining his ear, making certain he announced the next arrivals correctly. He straightened. 'Miss Alethea MacKenzie and Mister Ashley Penberth.'

Alethea had made sure Ashley was properly announced. It was unusual, to say the least, for a Riding Officer of His Majesty's Customs Service to be among the guests at such an exclusive occasion. But Ashley was her squire. How he earned his living was of no consequence to her, whatsoever. He had been her friend and admirer ever since those early days with Pruddy, their governess at Trevadne, and that was enough for her. She was not the kind of girl to forsake a friend.

And tonight, Ashley would swear, she was looking more beautiful than ever – and yet somehow even more elusive. Every now and then there came a look into her eyes which made Ashley feel, with a creeping numbness, that her thoughts were elsewhere. They were not on him. Mostly, she would be gay, light-hearted and amusing and her

175

mind – her heart even, Ashley dared hope – was centred on himself. But then that faraway look would return. When it did, it made him wonder whether among the many visitors to Trevadne there had come some blade – some gayer, more exciting, more eligible, yes, much more eligible squire – to captivate her heart and engage her thoughts. She could have any one of so many. Why then should she choose a tenant farmer's son who, in spite of his upper class education, had been able to find employment no more prestigious than that of a Riding Officer in His Majesty's Customs? Instinctively, he knew the answer. It was because they had grown up together; because she understood his background and his circumstances; because by nature she was infinitely sympathetic. True to the highest principles of her class, she scorned such trivial distinctions as those between one occupation and another. It mattered to her not one whit what a man did, nor who he was; her concern was only that he should be true to himself.

All this Ashley knew – and loved. No man could have a truer, more loyal – or more lovely – friend. Yet, every now and then came that faraway look.

But tonight she was his, and his alone. Of that he felt sure. In her pale blue, short Polonese gown with uncovered petticoat and bunched-up overskirt with three delicate puffs behind, she was drawing admiring glances from all round the now rapidly filling ballroom. Her fine-textured, corn-coloured hair was swept backwards and upwards into a plaited coil on the crown of her head, but the whole rather severe effect was softened by tendrils of small curls rippling down the side of each cheek. The low, square-cut bodice of her dress, with its elaborately puffed sleeves and silk rouleaux trimming, emphasised quite dazzlingly the smoothness of her slender neck and shoulders.

High up in the minstrels' gallery the orchestra was making those peculiar squeaks and groans which foretell a sudden bursting forth into melody. Family greeted family; the babble of voices rose to a crescendo; an unmistakable air of expectancy filled the ballroom. The major-domo's voice, powerful enough to reach the four corners of a barrack square, could still be heard above the clamour – but only just.

'Major and Mrs Hansford-Phelips, Miss Louisa Hansford-Phelips, Miss Georgina Hansford-Phelips.'

Not only had those magnificent chandeliers been subjected to routine cleaning, the whole hall had been swept and garnished. On each side of a large open fireplace, in which now blazed a crackling log fire, the gardeners had mounted an impressive array of hot-house plants, brought in that very morning from the greenhouses and the conservatory.

'The Reverend William Peter and Mrs Peter; Doctor and Mrs Cantley; Miss Grace Cantley; Mr Degory Logan . . .'

Ashley swivelled round on his heel. Degory Logan!

'The man who operated on my knee,' he smiled. 'All the way down from Exeter, too!'

'Oh, he'll be staying with Doctor Cantley, I expect,' Alethea suggested, 'They've been friends for years. Papa will be glad to see him.'

Already Degory Logan and Sir Andrew MacKenzie were greeting each other cordially, and Jeannie was flashing her lovely dark eyes at the bachelor surgeon. 'I wonder how many dances she'll steal from poor Grace Cantley,' Ashley wondered. He felt sorry for the rather plain, doctor's daughter. He knew only too well how attractive – how seductive – Jeannie could be. Even the debonair, man-of-the-world Degory Logan would find her blandishments hard to resist.

'You must speak with Mr Logan,' Alethea was saying, 'He'll be interested to see how well you've recovered.'

Taking Ashley firmly by the arm, she led him towards the group in which her father and Degory Logan were indulging in their usual light-hearted banter.

'Mr Logan, sir,' Alethea interrupted, 'behold! Your star patient.'

The eminent surgeon swung round. 'My dear Alethea,' he beamed, sweeping her an exaggerated bow, taking her hand and pressing it to his lips. 'How perfectly delightful to see you again after so long.' He stood back, holding both her hands, surveying appreciatively the vision before him. 'Lovelier than ever! But of course! I should have expected it. And what did you say, my dear – something about a patient of mine?' Reluctantly he dragged his gaze from the girl who so obviously enchanted him, saying 'Ah, yes, the face is familiar. . . .'

But at that moment, Ashley's attention was suddenly distracted by the major-domo's voice announcing, 'Captain Farquharson . . . Lieutenant Liggett-Fanshawe. . . . Cornet Rushford. Prebendary and Mrs. . . .'

Ashley heard no more. Trying hard to attend to what Degory Logan was saying, and to make polite, intelligent replies, he could not prevent his thoughts leaping backwards – back to that first term at Lydford – to the boy who had hung him out of the dormitory window and beaten his knuckles with a clothes brush. Liggett-Fanshawe! Could it possibly be the same?

Unquestionably, it was. Older, of course, moustachioed and a little heavier round the jowls, he still contrived to look elegantly distinguished in his Dragoon officer's uniform – dark blue jacket, red collar, cuffs and turnbacks with silver frogs and edgings, white kerseymere breeches, black boots and steel spurs. At his side – or more precisely, a half pace to the rear but straining at the leash like an eager puppy – was a much younger Dragoon, fresh-faced, sandy-haired, not much more than a school-boy. Cornet Rushford presumably. How typical, Ashley mused – Liggett-Fanshawe with a junior henchman at his side.

Whether by accident or design, the two Dragoons seemed to be moving towards the MacKenzie group. Deliberately Ashley turned away, facing Degory Logan, concentrating on what the surgeon was saying. At this moment, with Alethea on his arm, and feeling slightly self-conscious among the squirearchy of the county, the very last thing he wanted was a confrontation with Liggett-Fanshawe. He felt, rather than saw, the two Dragoons pause as they came

178

near. They had halted right behind his back. There could be no mistaking the sudden look of recognition in Degory Logan's eyes. Then came the voice, the same casual, drawling voice; the intervening years melted like rain-washed snow; Ashley was back at Lydford.

'Egad! but I do declare,' drawled the voice, 'Mr Logan himself. Well, what a delightful coincidence!' A slight click of the heels, a deferential bow, and the introductions had begun. Liggett-Fanshawe, it seemed, had subjected himself to Degory Logan's care following an accident in the hunting field. The surgeon, a naturally friendly, out-going man, and never one to eschew the fleshpots, had become very much *persona grata* with the Liggett-Fanshawes. He had enjoyed several shooting week-ends with them on their Dorset estate.

'Oh, ah, Degory,' the voice drawled on with exquisite politeness, 'may I introduce my junior, Cornet Rushford – er, recently joined the Troop, and stationed with us at Helston, don't y'know.'

Briskly, enthusiastically, Cornet Rushford stepped forward. It was all part of the excitement of army life – rubbing shoulders with the gentry at fashionable occasions. If you couldn't have action – and that was what he most craved for – then showing off his dashing, silver – epauletted uniform at county balls was at least a promising alternative. And that fair-haired girl, there, on that civilian's arm – well, she was positively stunning. Enough to turn the head of any young cornet of Dragoons. And, by Jove! so was her sister – that one with the dark curls tumbling own off the top of her head – the one standing there beside that impressive-looking Scotsman in a kilt. Yes, indeed! Life was full of promise. He felt the blood flooding his cheeks as he bowed low, first to Jeannie MacKenzie, then to Alethea.

Meanwhile, Degory Logan was moving slowly round the group, effecting the introductions, Lieutenant Liggett-Fanshawe and Cornet Rushford in his wake. He halted in front of Ashley.

179

'And this,' he was saying in his warm, friendly voice, 'is a young friend of mine, Ashley Penberth.'

Nearly ten years had elapsed since Dr Cyril Bernard Chaunter, his arm metaphorically twisted by Housemaster T. Rupert Greenham and others, had been forced to expel from Lydford College one of his most aristocratic – and, therefore, most desirable – pupils. Ashley Penberth had been indirectly the cause of that dismissal. True, the Headmaster had tried to soften the expulsion by allowing the culprit to finish the term – it had been put about that Liggett-Fanshawe would be leaving in order to attend a more exalted establishment – but just about everyone at the school knew perfectly well that the boy had been asked to leave. Now, after a lapse of ten years, how would he react on being confronted with the instrument of his disgrace?

As there was now no way the confrontation could be avoided, Ashley awaited the response with a kind of grim resolution. However Liggett-Fanshawe might react, he, Ashley Penberth, would stand his ground.

'Egad!' the Dragoon Lieutenant replied languidly, after the briefest hesitation, 'I do declare we've met before, eh, Penberth?'

Urbane as ever, Ashley thought. Faced with a ticklish situation, Liggett-Fanshawe would rely on good manners and his impeccable pedigree to brazen it out. He was already casting admiring glances at Alethea.

'I do believe we have met before,' Ashley agreed, an enigmatic smile playing about his lips. 'Would it have been at Lydford, perhaps?'

The Dragoon Lieutenant side-stepped the enquiry by appearing not to hear. Instead, with a disarming smile, he said, 'Well, deuced good to see you again, Penberth,' and with a very direct look in Alethea's direction, he added, 'I shall look forward to seeing something of you while I'm stationed in these parts, eh what?'

With a very low bow to the MacKenzie group – and with Cornet Rushford in deferential attendance – he melted away into the ever-growing throng of guests.

By now the orchestra had completed to its satisfaction the preliminary squeaks and squawks, and the conductor, pince-nez slighly askew, had turned to face his audience. Tapping the top of the gallery balustrade with his baton, he announced the first dance to be a Cotillion.

Alethea, Ashley, Jeannie and Sir Andrew MacKenzie joined two other couples in a square and, with the opening bars of the music, they commenced the first change.

'Who is your friend?' Alethea enquired as she and Ashley came together.

'Liggett-Fanshawe,' he replied, amused at the description of 'friend'. 'We were at Lydford together – for a short while.'

They separated, swaying away from each other in the second change. Ashley now partnered Jeannie. She was smiling, that wicked smile of hers that said so many things – that reminded him of the day when, together, they had tried to catch a falling leaf, the same falling leaf, twisting and spiralling down from the tall trees at Polwheveral. He could remember even the dress she was wearing – the pale blue stripey dress with little embroidered sprigs of red, yellow and brown. And he was remembering too, how they had stumbled into that shallow, mossy ditch, how he had felt the honeyed warmth of her breath on his face, the closeness of her lissom body – and how he had so very nearly lost his head!

The memory caused him a twinge of guilt. Why should that be, he wondered. Because of Alethea? Yes, of course. And yet there had never been anything resembling a betrothal between them. A tacit understanding, perhaps – but nothing more – even though he loved her – and he felt sure he did love her – always had, in fact, ever since that first shy meeting in the study at Trevadne. But it bothered him sometimes that he should feel, occasionally, so strongly attracted by others – like Jeannie, for instance, and like. . . .

Again he was partnering Alethea.

'I seem to remember the name,' Alethea said. 'Wasn't he

181

the sadistic bully who made you hang out of the dormitory window and then hit your knuckles with a hair brush?'

So she had remembered it, Ashley thought, almost every detail. Just like her, he mused. Jeannie, if she had remembered it at all, would have dismissed it as a fleeting episode of schoolboy stupidity, to be banished from the mind as quickly as possible in favour of the much more exciting present moment. Today and tomorrow were for Jeannie; yesteryear only to be recalled if it evoked happy memories. With Alethea it was quite different. Impressions bit deeper, lasted longer. Perhaps it had something to do with her conviction that her own birth had been responsible for her mother's early death. She had never been told as much, Ashley knew – at least, not in so many words – but that she thought it, deep down in her heart, he felt sure. Introspective – that was the word he was searching for – but not depressingly so. That was part of her charm. She could be as gay and lighthearted as anyone – as Jeannie, for instance – but every now and then she would retreat into herself – into a world where no one else could follow.

But tonight she was in party mood – swaying gracefully in time with the music, gliding in and out of the square, smiling, curtseying – and looking, as she nearly always did, like a very desirable but fragile example of Meissen china. Yet that delicate image, Ashley knew, was deceptive. When she wanted to she could pick up her skirts and run like the wind, and she was a quite fearless rider.

'Strange,' she was saying, 'because he doesn't look like a bully, now.' She glanced in the direction of Liggett-Fanshawe who was dancing in the square next to theirs.

'Does the leopard ever change his spots?' Ashley observed darkly. Then his face creased into a wry smile as he added. 'Oh, no. I'm probably maligning the fellow. He'll have grown out of all that, I expect.'

The Cotillion came to an end. The dancers dispersed, mingled, conversed. Old acquaintances were renewed, freshened, polished – and in some cases rather thankfully stowed away for another year. New friendships were forged – and for the young, even the not-so-young, the first tender shoots of romance came peeping nervously, excitingly through the protoplasm of social decorum.

Almost immediately further baton-tapping from the minstrels gallery heralded the announcement: 'My Lords, Ladies and Gentlemen – the next dance will be a Minuet.'

Easily the most popular ballroom dance for well over a hundred years, the announcement of the first Minuet was greeted with an audible murmur of approval. Gracefully, elegantly, the dancers began forming up into open couples. After ceremonial bows saluting spectators as well as partners, each couple began moving with dainty little steps across the ballroom floor.

'What brings him to these outlandish parts?' Alethea enquired, gliding prettily to the right.

'Liggett-Fanshawe, you mean?' Ashley queried, drawing his partner backward, and then forward to the left. 'Dragoon duty, I suppose. I heard they were sending down a Troop.'

Forward again, then backward, in quarter turns they moved.

'For what purpose, do you think?' she asked.

Above the gentle stream of lilting music, he uttered the one word, 'Smugglers.'

She frowned – the smallest frown. Then she smiled up into his face saying, 'He might be able to help you, then.'

'Yes, I suppose he might.' It was his turn to frown.

Sensing his resistance to the idea of seeking assistance from someone who had once been a sworn enemy, she raised one eyebrow quizzically, enquiring 'And would you feel able to accept help from him?'

'Of course,' he agreed, the frown deepening. 'If it should be necessary.' He rather wished she would think less about Liggett-Fanshawe.

Approaching and retreating, searching and evading, they glided together, they swayed apart.

She saw that her question had disturbed him. She took his hand. She changed the subject.

'I think Papa is getting rather fond of your mama,' she observed, with a conspiratorial wink. 'Have you noticed?'

He studied her from beneath his dark, bristly eyebrows. An enigmatic smile hovered round his mouth. Wickedly, he said, 'No, I hadn't noticed.'

'But you must have,' she chided, 'it's written all over their faces.'

Constantly on the move, mincing, gliding – one moment side by side, then facing each other – yet scarcely progressing a single step.

'Why did she not come to the ball tonight?' she asked.

He laughed and shook his head. 'She says she doesn't dance. Besides, she'd feel out of place amidst all this finery.'

'Oh, what nonsense,' Alethea scoffed. 'You know that's not true.'

'*I* do – I know it's not so. But then she's my mama; I'm likely to be a bit biased.'

Together – apart; seeking, then losing; face to face for a brief moment, then gliding past each other in the time-honoured play of courtship; so they danced. Always elegant, never hurried.

'It would be nice for Papa,' Alethea mused dreamily, 'he's so lonely. Neither Jeannie nor I can ever give him the companionship he needs.' Then the far-away look came into her soft eyes as she added, 'But, of course, it must be founded on love.'

They merged together, hand in hand, facing each other – like gentle wavelets jousting in a summer sea – and as, briefly, he held her eyes in his, he murmured deeply, feelingly, 'Yes, it must be love.'

It was as they swayed away from each other once more that he caught sight of Rose Roskruge.

She was standing with a little huddle of household servants in a narrow doorway leading from the ballroom. Clearly the servants had been given permission to watch the dancing, so long as they did not obtrude. But why on earth was Rose standing there with them, Ashley wondered. While the servants were clearly distinguished by their white aprons and caps – some of the kitchenmaids still wore their blue and white striped calico day dresses – Rose was conspicuous in an absolutely black dress. That it suited her particularly well, with its close-fitting bodice and flowing skirt, Ashley noted only by the way; he was momentarily more interested in why she was there at all. She could hardly have been recruited as temporary barmaid for the evening; if so, why was she lurking there with the household menials.

Indeed, it was his involuntary 'Godstrewth! Fancy that!' that caused Alethea to shoot an enquiring glance at him as they came together once more.

'Oh, nothing, really,' he explained, half-apologetically, 'I've just seen someone I never expected to see here, that's all.'

'One of the guests, you mean?'

'Well, no – not exactly. I mean no, definitely not. She's over there, among the servants. And yet I didn't think she was employed here.'

'You know her?' Alethea enquired rather doubtfully.

'Oh, yes. She's the barmaid at *The Three Tuns Inn* at St. Keverne.'

Alethea's ingenuous blue eyes regarded him levelly. 'You've encountered her in the course of your official duty, I suppose?'

He nodded. He was about to explain that, in his opinion, she was no ordinary barmaid; that as a child she had been saved from a shipwreck on the Manacles but that her mother had perished; and that she had been brought up by a childless couple, Sampson and Amia Roskruge, in the village of St. Keverne. But then he checked himself.

He was remembering how he had learnt all this. He had been riding the coast from Cadgwith when he had surprised her bathing in a small, sandy cove between Porthoustock and Porthallow. He had been angry with her a few days beforehand because, following their first meeting at *The Three Tuns Inn*, she had tried to attract his attention his coastal ride by waving her floppy-brimmed hat almost right in front of Puncher's eyes. The horse had shied away sharply, unseating his master. Riding Officer, Ashley Penberth, had not been amused.

But when he saw the girl again, drying herself beside a rock down in that sandy cove, he had relented. Also, he had found himself inordinately disturbed by the beauty of her young body so clearly outlined by her clinging wet bathing gown.

It was the memory, once again vividly in his mind, of those ripe young breasts, those subtly rounded hips, those shapely thighs, that now stayed further explanation.

'I'm rather surprised to see her here, that's all,' he concluded, trying to banish that vision from his thoughts. 'But it's really a matter of absolutely no consequence whatsoever.'

He smiled as reassuringly as he could, his attention once more fully restored to the partner whose hand he held.

Forward, backward – turning slightly – approach and retreat. Gliding – swaying – together and apart. Together and apart. Dainty movements, mincing steps. Forward, backward. Together and apart.

So the dance progressed – full of elegance and charm. Only once or twice did Ashley allow his glance to stray towards that narrow doorway – to that demure figure in the plain black dress. And when he did, it ruffled his conscience – just a little bit. It bothered him. Alethea was undoubtedly the girl he loved; he knew that, felt sure of it. Why then did he also feel that catch in his breath, that slight quickening of heartbeat whenever he looked at the barmaid of *The Three Tuns Inn*? It was a nuisance; he must learn to control it. Alethea was the girl for him.

When the first Minuet drew majestically to its close it was followed, after a suitable interval, by a Gavotte, and as the circles formed up, Ashley was somewhat dismayed to find that Degory Logan had invited Liggett-Fanshawe to join the suite. The Dragoon was partnered with Jeannie MacKenzie, and as the couple separated from the circle to perform their short solo, it was abundantly clear that Lieutenant Liggett-Fanshawe was bent on ingratiating himself with the Mac-Kenzie family.

The Gavotte was followed by another Cotillion, and after that came the second Minuet. Then it was time for supper.

By now, Liggett-Fanshawe had so successfully insinuated himself with Jeannie that both he and Cornet Rushford were invited to join the MacKenzies, the Cantleys and Degory Logan at the buffet. It was while they were all sipping Colonel Bouchier's deliciously cool champagne that Ashley espied another army officer bearing down on the two Dragoons. Even at this comparatively early hour, this gentleman had already imbibed rather more champagne than was good for him. The glass in his hand was barely half full and yet somehow he contrived to spill the contents down his scarlet tunic, single epauletted on right shoulder – silver-braiding around buttonholes. He was not an attractive sight.

Instinctively, it seemed, – and with a pregnant glance between them – the two sisters, Jeannie and Alethea moved away, putting the menfolk between themselves and the semi-inebriate officer.

Answering Ashley's unspoken enquiry, both girls simultaneously whispered, 'Colonel Bouchier's nephew.' It was Jeannie who elaborated, her mouth close to his ear, her warm, honeyed breath on his cheek. '46th Foot, just been gazetted Captain. Obviously celebrating. Definitely *not* to be encouraged!'

Then she moved away, took hold of both his hands and, with the familiarity born of long acquaintance, she smiled coquettishly, saying, 'Shall we dance, Mr Penberth?'

As they regained the ballroom, hand in hand, the minstrel conductor was just announcing what everyone, it seemed, had been waiting for – a Country dance, ''Thread-the-Needle.''

This was the signal for the 'pink' coated hunting fraternity to shed their inhibitions. They streamed on to the ballroom floor, wildly cavorting around each other, whooping and prancing, and blaring their hunting horns as they pretended to gallop across open country.

If some of the more sedate burgesses, in their brocaded

silk frock coats – in blues and greens, in buffs and in burgundies, with their high collars and heavy, turned-back cuffs – if they, in their cultured elegance looked askance at the antics of their bucolic brethren, the brilliantly uniformed military officers lacked nothing of the hunters' exuberance. The Colonel's champagne was taking effect; fully-grown men were acting like children. Undoubtedly, the party was beginning to warm up.

It was while whole-heartedly entering into the spirit of a gallopade with Jeannie that Ashley caught sight of Colonel Bouchier's nephew, the newly promoted Captain Loxley-Gregg, weaving his way unsteadily in the direction of that doorway from which Rose was watching the fun. Spilling champagne as he went, his face was flushed, and there was a very determined gleam in his eye.

The dancers had scarcely completed a full circle of the room before the freely perspiring Captain was seen to be dragging a reluctant figure in a plain black dress on to the ballroom floor.

'*Ah, mon Dieu!*' Jeannie exclaimed with alarm, '*C'est impardonnable!* Do you see what is happening? He is forcing the poor girl to dance with him. Lady Bouchier will be furious!'

It was true. The inanely grinning Captain was pulling Rose on to the dance floor.

'I do not know the girl's name,' Jeannie was saying, 'but she is the young seamstress recently engaged by Lady Bouchier. She has given much satisfaction, I understand. But now, I'm afraid, she is the unwilling servant in the young master's hands. And Lady Bouchier will not be the only one to be furious.'

But when some minutes later Ashley returned to the ballroom with Alethea once more as his partner, Rose appeared to be enjoying herself. The orchestra conductor, Ulrich Fieldman, spurred on by the infectious gaiety of the country dance, decided to spring a surprise on the dancers. He announced that he would now play music, learned during student days in Vienna, for a dance called the Waltz. Pulling from a pocket in his embroidered silk waistcoat a piece of crumpled paper, he said, 'And this, my Lords, Ladies and Gentlemen, is what the great poet Goethe says about the Waltz in his novel *Die Leben des Jungen Werthers* recently published.' He unfolded the paper and read: ' "Never have I moved so lightly. I was no longer a human being. To hold the most adorable creature in one's arms and fly around like the wind, so that everything around us fades away. . . ." '

He folded the piece of paper and replaced it in his waistcoat pocket. 'And that, Ladies and Gentlemen, is what Johann Wolfgang von Goethe says of the waltz. Now, I play for you the music.'

Raising his baton once more, he launched his minstrels into the exciting new tempo. Few of the revellers knew the correct steps, but the more observant very quickly realised that the waltz was but a progression from the well-known Gavotte. Soon, they were all whirling and twirling – 'flying around like the wind' – in an ecstasy of new-found abandon. None more so than a flushed, excited Rose Roskruge.

Heedless of tomorrow's consequences, oblivious of the disapproving stares from the 'quality' as she circled with her besotted partner, she was dancing with a flamboyant gaiety to rival the best. She seemed particularly determined to be noticed by one of the guests – and to make sure of it, she danced right under his very nose.

In the early hours of the following morning, among the cyprepediums and odontoglossoms in the moonlit warmth of the conservatory at Trevadne, Ashley once more held the 'most adorable creature' in his arms. There was no music. There were no dancers. They were alone.

Almost imperceptibly they began to dance again. In the brickwork pathways between plant benches, and with the heady perform of exotic flowers all round them, they began waltzing once more; slowly at first, and careful of Alethea's bunched overskirt, but then, as the imaginary music built up to its pulsating crescendo, they twirled and swayed, round and round, until as Goethe described, 'everything around us fades away. . . .'

Sadly, though, it was the music in their ears that faded away – it returned once more to the monotonous drip, drip, drip of the down-pipe above the water butt, and the shingled staging over the ground-trough. Slowly the magic began to disappear.

And as if to hold forever the bewitching memory of that moment, Alethea moved closer to Ashley, her face up-tilted to his. She felt his arms tighten around her, drawing her ever closer. The lingering tang of champagne was in his breath as his lips brushed hers; his fingers explored the contours of her tight-fitting bodice. Alarmed by the strange sensation welling up within her as she felt the hardness of his body pressed against hers, she tried to pull away. But he would not let her go. As his lips became ever more demanding, so the panic within her mounted. And yet she did not wish him to stop; she wanted him to go on and on and on – and that was the dreadful realisation. She knew she should not be enjoying it. All her careful upbringing had taught her that no girl of birth and breeding should ever enjoy such delightful abandon. And yet she did, she did, she did. . . .!

But it just *had* to stop. It was wicked – even though it had the taste of Heaven.

She wrenched herself free of his embrace, and went indoors.

Later, riding back to Treworden beneath a frosty, star-flecked sky, Ashley's mind was troubled. He knew that he loved Alethea – the adorable creature so recently in his arms – and yet his thoughts would keep returning to Lanteague, wondering just what was happening to the seamstress in the plain black dress.

CHAPTER SIXTEEN

A most unwelcome guest

A cloud of blue tobacco smoke ascended lazily to the yellowed ceiling of *The Three Tuns Inn*. Sullied clay pipes projected like beaks from the wizened faces of the evening regulars perched along the high-backed settle. Will Trenethy was behind the bar.

He seemed even more on edge than usual. Frequent nervous fingering of his mouth in between polishing pewter tankards had left a dark ring around his lips, giving him a slightly ludicrous expression. He pecked at the ale in his tankard; he repeatedly shifted from one foot to the other; for no apparent reason he kept glancing over his shoulder.

Unlike the landlord, the regulars were relaxed, convivial. Old men, all of them, they were in their usual places to discuss, to disseminate – and often to exaggerate – village news and local gossip.

'Her's nivver bin the same since the church were struck,' observed Aaron Polter, prune-faced, and sitting at the far end of the settle, 'Nivver!'

'In the great storm of '71 you mean,' Will suggested, seeking to control his nerves by joining the conversation.

'Aw, no, 'tweren't '71, Will. 'Twere early part o' '70, I do mind – end o' Jen'y or early Febbery,' prune-face corrected, 'an' right in the middle o' Sunday mornin' Service, 'twas. Vigger were in the middle o' the Lit'ny Service when there were the loudest clap o' thunder you ever did hear. Like the crack o' doom, 'twere. Just like the endin' o' the world.'

'Aw, ais,' Jacob Maliken wheezed, 'I mind un well,

'twere a terrible storm. Tore the church spire right down to the ground.'

'Aw, 'twere more'n just a storm, Jacob,' Aaron protested, ' 'twere lightnin'. Struck by lightnin', twas.'

'Aw, ais,' chorused the other three on the settle, ' 'twas lightnin', all right.'

' 'Twere just like a thunderbolt from the Lord,' Tom Milren observed sagely, 'as though vigger'd bin sayin' what 'e oughtn't to.'

' 'Twas a Judgement, all right,' Jackson Pentecost added lugubriously, his clay pipe whistling each time he drew breath, 'a terrible Judgement from on high.'

The mention of 'judgement' sent landlord Will Trenethy into a renewed outburst of nervous anxiety. One hand flew to his mouth, fingering, dabbing his lips. As he poured himself a fresh pint, his hand visibly shook.

'But no one was killed,' he suggested, trying to sound cheerful, ' 'twas only a warnin', like.'

'As, ais, but vigger were badly shooken,' Aaron propounded, 'And as for his sister, why her was struck down terrible. Taken for dead, her was. Her's nivver bin the same since. Nivver.'

'Aw, ah,' agreed Jacob Maliken, 'I mind un well. Lyin' there in vigger's arms, wi' her shoes an' stockin's burnt right through by the fire an' brimstone, they was – right away up as far as 'er garters.'

The mere mention of the Reverend Anthony Williams' sister and her garters immediately evoked a gust of bawdy laughter. The little old men, perched like sparrows on a branch, rocked back and forth with salacious enjoyment.

'But you'm wrong on one point,' interposed Will Trenethy, always a stickler for accuracy, 'the Reverend Williams, he be Rector Williams, an' that be a pile higher than a vigger, as you know well 'nough.'

Jacob Maliken screwed his face into a replica of a dried fig. 'Whether he'm a vigger or a rictor makes not a beanpole o' difference,' he protested, 'I'm tellin' you, just as sure as I'm yere, vigger's sister were showin' her garters!'

'Aw, an' 'er was, too,' Jackson Pentecost affirmed strongly, 'I mind un well. They was pink an' silky, wi' a brave bit o' red ribbon on 'em – quite saucy, like, I mind.'

This was too much for the regulars. As nearly as their venerable age allowed, they erupted into paroxysms of spluttering mirth. When, at last, the tempest of thigh-slapping and asthmatic coughing subsided, Tom Milren, after making full use of the nearby spittoon, managed to enquire:

'Speakin' o' saucy pink garters, Will. . . .' further thigh-slapping and gales of laughter – 'Speakin' o' they, where be our Rosie tonight, then?'

'Aw, ais, Will,' chorused the others, 'where do Rosie be, then?'

'Her'll be along shortly, I 'spec,' Will affirmed, none too pleased at the lewd innuendo. 'She'm a bit late this evenin', that's all. I 'spec she've bin out fishin' wi' her daddy. But her'll be along.'

He unhookd a pewter tankard from above the bar and began polishing it vigorously. It relieved his feelings; absorbed some of his pent-up anxiety.

'And none of this yer 'silky pink garters' while Rosie's about, mind,' he added, warningly.

'Aw, no, Will,' Jacob Maliken grinned mischievously, 'her's too much of a leddy for any o' that sort o' talk.'

'Aw, ais,' agreed Tom Milren, giving Jackson Pentecost a provocative nudge, 'her'm too much of a leddy – speshly sin' her's bin workin' up at the big house, eh?'

'Up at the Colonel's place, aw ais,' Jacob chortled, 'up at Lanteague, eh? Very frenly wi' the Colonel's nevvy, unless I be much mistook. How is it they call un – Cap'n Loxley-Legs, or somethin', edn it?'

More nudging and sniggering as, with the mildness of an angel, Jackson Pentecost observed, 'They'm both very fond o' dancin', I do believe – and speshly the bit that do come atterwards!'

'Aw, ah!' his three cronies nodded knowingly, 'the bit that come atterwards, eh. Aw, ais.'

' 'Tez the best bit of all!' affirmed Jacob Maliken through an enveloping smoke cloud, 'Aizily the best!'

'Oh, ah,' encouraged his friends, agog for the next utterance.

But Jacob was taking his time. His lips quivered at the prospect of his own wit; the blackened stem of his clay pipe rattled against what was left of his teeth. He enjoyed keeping his friends waiting.

Unable to endure the suspense any longer, Jackson Pentecost enquired, 'An' why be that, then Jake?'

Jacob drew on his pipe. 'Why be that the best bit do ee say? Well, I'll tell ee. 'Tez the bit when the pinky silk garters gets pulled off, that's why.'

Sallies of this nature were almost too much for the little old men. Doubled up with laughter, they coughed and spluttered so violently that even their hold on the perch became precarious. When at last the crescendo of asthmatic wheezing subsided, they sat for several moments savouring Jacob's wit and remembering, as best they could, the far off days when they, themselves, had removed a frilly garter from a maiden's shapely thigh.

Eventually, and in more sober fashion, Aaron Polter remarked slyly, 'I do believe our Rosie'll nivver be the same agin. Nivver!'

'Aw, ah?' queried his confederates, sensing further titillating disclosures, 'Why be that, then?'

'Ah – h – h, you may well enquire,' Aaron continued darkly, ' 'twas the night o' that ther Ball up at Lanteague where Rosie'd gone to work for her Ladyship. Do ee mind what I'm referrin' to?'

'Aw, ais,' Tom Milren volunteered on behalf of his fellow listeners, 'Us do mind un well.'

'Well,' Aaron continued, leaning confidentially towards the other three, ' 'twas like this yer. . . .'

At this point Will Trenethy decided that he must intervene. He had known Rosie all her life. He had even helped in her rescue from the shipwreck down there on the Manacles when Sampson and Amia Roskruge had taken her into their home as a tiny baby and brought her up as their own. Rose Mary Roskruge they had christened her – vicar had made it all legal, like – and on the fly-leaf of her christening Prayer Book he had written, 'They shall lift up their voice, they shall sing for the majesty of the Lord, they shall cry aloud from the sea.' 'Isaiah, 24 v 14.' It was appropriate, Will thought, because Rose had a lovely singing voice, and, of course, she had come out of the sea.

So he said firmly – as firmly, that is, as his uncertain nerves would allow, – 'That be 'nough o' that, then. You'd best leave Rosie out of it.'

After all, she was still his barmaid, his employee, and although she had left him temporarily for what she considered to be the more exalted position of seamstress to Lady Bouchier, she had undoubtedly suffered a terrible experience at the hands of the Colonel's newly promoted nephew, Captain Loxley-Gregg. Nobody knew exactly what had occurred – apart from those most intimately concerned, of course, – but when in the early morning after the Ball it was discovered that the seamstress had fled, and when, later, a succession of whip-cracks and blood-curdling screams were heard issuing from the Colonel's study, the servants at Lanteague had little doubt but that someone was being horsewhipped. It was typical of the Colonel to inflict summary punishment on someone caught misbehaving himself under his roof, but who could be the unfortunate miscreant, and what had been his crime?

They remembered the Colonel's nephew dragging the unwilling seamstress on to the dance floor, forcing his attentions upon her. Lively imaginations needed no more than a few seconds to fill in the missing details.

True or false, by the time the news reached the village, Rose had unquestionably been subjected to the fate worse than death. In short, she was a fallen woman.

So said the village gossips. But Will Trenethy was fond of Rose; she was a good girl, and he would not allow calumny to be spoken of her in his hearing. Whether or not she had indeed lost her maidenhead to the demands of a lecherous

Captain of the 46th Foot he did not know; it would be too indelicate, even in the sometimes bawdy atmosphere of the tavern, to enquire. Moreover, had he done so, Rose would have responded with a painful back-answer, he felt sure. And her parents, Sampson and Amia Roskruge – as well as their close friends, the Tripconeys of Trevallack – had remained persistently tight-lipped about the whole affair. It was said that Wilmot Tripconey had accompanied Sampson to Lanteague to demand retribution from the Colonel – and that eventually they had received satisfaction. Whether or not there had been any connection between their visit and the sounds of stinging whip-cracks heard coming from the Colonel's study they would not say, but the servants, despite having been sworn to secrecy, had let it be known that when Captain Loxley-Gregg left that same morning, in a hurry and without saying his 'goodbyes', he appeared to be walking with considerable discomfort.

For all that, Will Trenethy thought to himself sometimes, it was rather a pity that if Rose *had* to be deprived of her virtue, she hadn't been able to surrender it to someone of whom she was really fond, or – and this he furtively stored away in his devious mind – in the furtherance of some worthy cause.

But that was no reason why her name should be denigrated by this rascally bunch of little old lechers.

So, squaring his bent, sloping shoulders as best he could, he repeated, 'Yes, indeed, I would require you gen'lmen to leave Rose's name out of it. There be no occasion to go repeatin' malicious gossip. Rose be a good girl, an' I wont be hearin' nothin' agin her. Unnerstand.'

He continued polishing the tankard vigorously, his face pinched and disapproving, and he had only just returned the shining tankard to its hook when the latch of the back door sounded, and Rose hurried in.

Her cheeks were flushed, her eyes shining. Will thought she'd never looked prettier. All the old sparkle, missing ever since her return from Lanteague, was back again. She drew her employer into the back kitchen, out of earshot of the regulars, and said, rather breathlessly;

'The Ridin' Officer's in the village, Will. Did you know?'

Like a rabbit mesmerised by a stoat, Will Trenethy stared back at her. One hand flew to his mouth and began dabbing at his lower lip. The pewter grime transferred itself from fingers to lip, giving his face an even more macabre expression.

'Where's he to, then? Which way's he comin'? Where'd you see un, Rosie?' The questions babbled out.

'He overtook me, comin' up from Rosenithon.' She was unable to disguise the excitement in her voice.

'Did he speak?'

'No, no. He just rode on. Didn't recognise me, I 'spec,' she said, disappointed. Then she suddenly brightened. 'But he'm bound to come here, isn't he?'

Will gripped her shoulders. 'That'm just what us don't want, Rosie,' he hissed. 'Us just can't have un comin' here tonight. Oh, Lordy me! Not to-night! *Not to-night*!!'

He paced back and forth, wringing his hands one minute, dabbing at his mouth the next. Then he gripped Rose by the shoulders once more. 'Listen, Rosie. You'm a good girl – a very good girl – allus have bin – but us'll be needin' your help tonight, Rosie, like us've never needed it before, see.'

'Why, Will? What's on tonight then?'

'Hab'n your daddy told ee?'

Rose shook her head, only half concentrating on what Will was saying. Her thoughts were on that backview of a rider in a sky-blue jacket and a black tricorn hat as he had just trotted past her. She was savouring the prospect that very soon she might be seeing Ashley Penberth once more.

'No,' she said absently, 'Dad never talks to me about that sort of thing – if that's what you mean.'

'Oh, but Rosie,' Will went on, his voice shot through with nervous anxiety, ' 'tis the biggest run us've ever attempted. Tis more'n two hundred ankers we'm expectin'. P'raps I shouldn't be tellin' ee all this, but everything's all made ready – 'bout fifty pack ponies waitin' down at

P'roustock, an' more'n a hundred carriers'll be gatherin' there, too – an' then there be old Dolly Jago up there on the quoits, waitin' to pass on my signal, an'. . . .'

'But what's all this got to do with me, Will?' Rose cut in, genuinely puzzled. 'You know I never get involved in that sort of thing.'

'That's quite correct, Rosie, an' nor should ee. Your daddy always made me promise not to get ee caught up in anythin' like that, but us do need ee tonight, Rosie. Us'll need ee terrible if that thur Ridin' Officer do come pokin' 'is nose in just where he in't wanted.'

Rose shot him a suspicious glance. 'And just how do I come into the matter?'

' 'Tis like this, Rosie,' the landlord replied, straining to appear winsome. 'If he do come here – an' I've no doubt he will – I want ee to study un. Be real nice to un.'

'Yes,' Rose agreed guardedly, 'and then what?'

'Well, if he want to put up yere for the night, like, 'twouldn't do for we to turn un away, see, 'cos he'd be bound to suspect somethin' – smell a rat, like. So, I just wants ee to make up to un a bit. Take good care of un. Keep un up in his bedroom, like, so's he don't come pryin' into things as don't consarn un.' Will Trenethy flexed his eye-brows suggestively, as he added, 'So's he don't *want* to come pryin' . . . if you sees what I mean.'

'Oh no,' Rose retorted sharply. 'There'll be none of that! Just because of what happened up at Lanteague, you seem to think I'll be easy come by. . . .'

'Aw, naw, naw, Rosie,' Will protested, ' 'tis nothin' like that. . . .'

'Oh, yes it is,' Rose flared, 'I know 'xactly what you'm thinking – yes, you an' all the others like you. You think I'm a fallen woman, don't you, and next time ready for anybody. No point in caring. Well, I'll bid you be so good as to mind your own business, thank you, an' I'll be mindin' mine.'

With a defiant shake of her head, she lifted the hem of her dark blue silk skirt above her silver buckled shoes and swept out of the kitchen, into the bar. She was greeted by the little old regulars warmly and with some ribaldry. But she was in no mood for ribaldry. Incensed by Will's presumption, she knew only too well he had merely expressed what all the rest of the village were thinking.

To give vent to her rising anger and resentment she picked up the old stocking from under the bar and began polishing the bar top vigorously. Then she turned to the mirror at the back of the bar, adjusted her pretty little mob cap. While she was patting an unruly curl into place she heard the stableyard door being pushed open. Immediately, like a swath of hay falling to the sickle, the babble of conversation died away. Rose turned – to see a familiar figure in a sky-blue jacket and black tricorn hat striding towards the bar. The regulars sat silent, regarding the 'King's Man' with suspicion, with hostility. Aaron Polter spat, pointedly, into the spittoon beside the settle. The inference was not lost on the Riding Officer. He smiled wryly. He was quite used to it. People love to take a shy at authority, always had, always would. Sometimes it's an over-ripe tomato or a putrid egg; sometimes a gob of phlegm – not often in your face, fortunately, but as near to your feet as possible. It was a healthy sign, Ashley reflected; a demonstration of rugged independence, a perquisite of freedom. He took no offence.

'Good evening, Mistress Rose,' he greeted affably, 'a pleasant surprise to see you again.'

So, he had remembered, Rose thought forlornly; remembered that she had left *The Three Tuns* to go to Lanteague, and was now back again. He would have heard the gossip. In his eyes, like all the rest of the village, she was now a fallen angel.

'A pleasant surprise to see you, too, zur,' she rejoined, flashing him a sad little smile. 'Is there anything I can get you?'

'Indeed. Be so good as to pour me a pint of landlord Trenethy's best porter, if you please, Rose.' He eased the black tricorn from his head and laid it on the bar. With a quite irrational surge of affection she noticed the red mark it

199

had left across his forehead. It reminded her of the day he had surprised her in the little cove beyond Porthoustock. He had dismounted and joined her on the grassy plateau above the rocks. She had felt embarrassed, sitting there in her wet bathing gown, so voluminous when in the water yet so figure-clinging when out of it. He had lain there on the soft, springy turf, his head against a rock, his half-closed eyes seeming to devour the contours of her body. He had removed his hat then, and there had been that red ring around his forehead. They had talked. She had told him of her unusual upbringing, of her unknown ancestry; he had told her how his father, also, had been wrecked on the Manacles. And in those brief moments of self-revelation and discovery, she knew she had fallen in love.

'Thank you, Rose,' he was saying, as she handed him his well-filled tankard. 'Is the good landlord at home? If so, ask him to prepare a room for me, will you. I intend staying overnight.'

Rose smiled inwardly. She knew just how welcome this request would be to her employer – but she fully intended to see that he acquiesced.

'Yes, sir,' she replied in her best front parlour accent, 'I will inform Mr Trenethy you will be staying the night.'

CHAPTER SEVENTEEN

Blazed Off

Will Trenethy, hovering anxiously near the doorway, heard every word. From the tone of Rose's voice he could tell she was more than just pleased to see the Riding Officer. He felt hugely relieved.

Normally, a girl who become friendly with a 'King's Man' would be regarded as a traitor to the village. But Will Trenethy prided himself he was smarter than that. Never one to waste a favourable puff of wind, he reckoned he knew how to turn his barmaid's particular affection to everyone else's advantage.

But firstly he must make sure she had a plentiful supply of 'Will's Special Brew' with which to ply her handsome friend.

He went down into the cellar.

In the bar Ashley was beginning to enjoy himself. After riding all day in the hot, mid-summer sunshine, the long draught of best porter now diffusing through his body was bringing an increasingly pleasant feeling of relaxation. And the close proximity of a smiling Rosie was certainly no detraction from his pleasure. Leaning against the bar, her bare, well-rounded forearms folded beneath her bosom, she displayed to fullest advantage the provocative charms of her decolletage. Oh, yes; he was glad he had decided to put up for the night at *The Three Tuns Inn*.

'Come now, Mistress Rose,' he said cheerfully, 'these gentlemen here could do with a re-fill, I'm sure.' He swept the row of little old men with an all-embracing gesture. 'They're looking rather parched – just like the countryside in this hot, dry weather. Fill 'em up, then Rose – at my expense. And don't forget to pour one for yourself.'

As though blown off their perch by a sudden tornado, the four regulars were at the bar with their hastily emptied tankards, murmuring 'Well, thank ee, zur. Thank ee very much.'

Rose, too, flashed an appreciative smile at the munificent Riding Officer, and began pouring from the 'Black Jack' on the bar. While she was re-filling the row of tankards Will Trenethy emerged from the cellar, a look of pious innocence on his face, a jug of foaming liquid in his hand.

'Aha, Landlord Will Trenethy!' Ashley greeted, by now full of the spirit of largesse. 'One for him, too, please Rosie. I'm sure he'll relish a drop of liquid down a dried-up throat.' He noticed how Will's hand was shaking as he placed the jug on the bar at Rose's elbow.

'Aw, thank ee, Zur,' Will responded, 'And I'd like ee to try a drop o' my special, yere. I just brought un up for ee to sample. 'Tis one I brew for special occasions, like – an' I'd be proud to know your opinion.'

Ashley smiled inwardly. It was a fairly common ploy – to flatter the 'King's Man', to make him a little drunk, even. But he was quite used to it. He had a good strong head – and the offerings were sometimes rather exceptional.

He drained his tankard, and Rose re-filled it with Will's 'Special'. Then she disappeared into the kitchen to prepare his supper.

'Your good health, landlord,' Ashley toasted. 'And yours, too, zur,' his beneficiaries chorused.

Ashley drank deeply, swilling the liquid around his mouth before swallowing. His audience stood silent, tankards poised, awaiting the verdict.

'Umm,' he said eventually. 'Very good, landlord.' He licked his lips in appreciation. 'And fairly potent, too, I should say.'

'Aw, 'tis that, all right,' volunteered Jacob Maliken, leading his companions back to their usual perch on the settle. ' 'Tis Will's best, edn it, Will?'

202

'Aw, ais,' agreed Aaron Polter, ' 'Tis strong stuff. 'Tis no good for boys. Only fit for men to drink, is Will's special.' He winked heavily in Tom Milren's direction.

'Too true, too true,' Tom responded, sensing the bait. 'You'm best not be drinkin' too much o' Will's 'Special', Master, or you'll be like a ship wi'out a rudder.'

'Aw, ais,' joined in Jackson Pentecost, ' 'Tis strong enough. 'Tis only fit for men, not boys.'

Ashley nodded, grinning. 'Only men, eh?' He up-ended his tankard, before bringing it down with a resounding smack. 'Same again, then, landlord,' he demanded, wickedly – defiantly. 'And a re-fill for these gentlemen and yourself when you're ready.'

With alacrity Will complied with the command, brushing aside Ashley's proffered payment. The House could stand a few pints of cheap ale so long as the Riding Officer had plenty of the 'Special'.

Once more, healths were drunk all round, clay pipes re-lit, tongues loosened.

'Well, gentlemen,' Ashley was saying, viewing his companions with an increasing sense of bonhomie, 'what's the local gossip? What's afoot?'

The question was not to Will's liking. It was the word 'afoot' that had an ominous ring. Somehow it smacked of danger, so he sought to divert the conversation into more promising channels.

'We was just rememberin' ' he smirked, 'what happened when the church spire was blown down in the great thunderstorm of February '70, an' how the vicar's sister lost her modesty. . . .'

'Lost her what?' Ashley asked, intrigued. Will's 'Special' was beginning to have a delightfully mellowing effect. The conversation sounded promising – just right for the mood.

'An' her did, too,' Jacob Maliken supported, warming to the chance of telling the story again, 'her had a hole in her stockin' and her was showin' her garters, too.'

Once more the mention of the unfortunate lady's stockings and garters produced a cataclysm of asthmatic laughter. The little old men were savouring anew the vision of that titillating memory. The embellishments grew, unchecked, as each one added to the telling of the story until, by the end, scarcely an item of feminine underwear remained unexamined, uncommented upon.

The conversation had reached the height – or the depth – of bawdy speculation when Rose returned to say that the Riding Officer's supper was ready.

'I've laid it up in the guest bedroom where it'll be nice an' quiet for you, not down here among all these scallywags.' She surveyed the row of flushed faces along the settle reprovingly – but there was an affectionate twinkle in her eyes. Then she turned to the Riding Officer, saying, 'Now, if you'll follow me, zur, I'll show ee to your room.' Only an observant onlooker would have noticed the potent look that flashed from landlord to barmaid as, with a deliberate rustle of skirts, she swept past him and began mounting the stairs. The Riding Officer, for his part, was far too busy bidding a good evening to his new-found friends to notice anything like that.

But as he followed Rose up the narrow wooden staircase his eyes were drawn appreciatively to the trim pair of ankles ahead of him. The more easily to mount the steep stairs, Rose had hitched her skirt well clear of her silver-buckled shoes. It was as much as any man was normally permitted to see – but although he was having difficulty in focussing properly, it was enought to remind Ashley Penberth of another occasion, a different place.

He was remembering yet again the day when, returning from an official ride down to Cadgwith, he had come upon her bathing in that small cove near Porthoustock. She had shivered as she sat beside him in her clammy, wet bathing gown, and when he had suggested she might like to change into something drier and warmer she had gratefully disappeared behind a cluster of large rocks. The turf on the little plateau above was sea-washed soft, and he had settled back against a smooth boulder, half closing his eyes.

But the rocks behind which Rose was drying herself did

not provide an impenetrable screen. There were a few fissures – one or two cracks. Of course, no man worthy to be called a gentleman would ever have dreamed of becoming, in the circumstances, anything so base as a Peeping Tom, but Ashley. . . .

Well, by seeking a more comfortable position for his head, he had found himself able to view as never before the soft, voluptuous curves of a young nubile body – a perfect model for a Titian or a Botticelli – 'A Naiad at her toilet', perhaps, or more simply, 'The Bather'.

It had been a disturbingly unforgettable picture.

Now, as he mounted the stairs behind those trim ankles and that uplifted skirt, the sensuous memory came flooding back. The ripe young breasts, dark-nippled and up-tilted, bravely thrusting heavenwards as the wet, clinging gown was peeled over the bather's head; the smooth, rounded hips; the shapely thighs, seductively revealed as the long, ankle-length bathing drawers were lowered. It had aroused within his loins the powerful sensation of raw sexual desire.

And he had felt guilty. Not because he was observing, uninvited, something he was never meant to see, but guilty nevertheless. Guilty because of Alethea. He loved Alethea; he felt sure of that. And yet, at that disturbing moment he had felt an almost overpowering desire to possess, wholly and ecstatically, that young body being unclothed behind those rocks. Quickly, firmly, he had put away the thought – 'Get thee behind me, Satan!' – tried to banish it from his mind, but it had remained – subdued, subjugated, but never entirely stifled.

The stairs he was now climbing seemed inordinately steep. Even the looped lanyard, substituting for a handrail to the stairs, seemed to be swaying. Or was his head swimming a bit? Surely a few tankards of ale would never have this effect – never had before. Must be just because he was tired; riding all day, nothing much to eat since breakfast. Must be that. Be all right with a good supper inside him; something to soak up the liquid. Be quite all right after that.

Rose had laid supper on a small table by the window.

Even in the gathering twilight the view was quite breathtaking. In the right-hand foreground the battlemented tower supporting the recently re-built church spire stood sharply etched against the fading brilliance of the sunset. In the background, the immaculate, curving sweep of Falmouth Bay completed the window picture. Already the lights of Pendennis Castle and the houses nestling around the harbour twinkled across the darkening water.

A plate of cold ham, pickles, beetroot and a mountain of potato salad stood beckoningly on the table. Beside it Rose had placed yet another brimming tankard of ale.

She was standing attentively beside the table as Ashley, with some difficulty, crossed the room. 'I trust everything's to your liking, sir?' she asked, smilingly. 'If there be anything else you require . . . well, we can always do our best . . . even if we haven't got it,' she added with a merry laugh.

Ashley grasped her hand – as much to steady himself as to express appreciation.

'That's just shplendid, Rosie,' he praised, his voice already beginning to slur, 'exactly, what I like . . . cold ham, p-potato salad and p-pickles. . . . You have done well, Rosie . . . really couldn't have done better.'

But he was not thinking of the food on the table. Though the haze was thickening, he could still see clearly enough to know that the girl standing quietly beside him was infinitely desirable. At that moment she represented for him everything a red-blooded male could wish for. He lusted after her in his heart, exceedingly.

'I think you'll find you've got all you need, sir,' she was saying, 'but if there's anything else, just let me know. . . .' Then, seeing the expression in his eyes, she withdrew her hand from his, and with a half-smile added, 'I'll be up again shortly with a nice creamy trifle I've been mixing for you.' With a swish of her skirts she left the room and went downstairs.

Having divested himself of his riding jacket, Ashley plunged his hands into the earthenware wash basin. The cool water, splashed over face and neck, momentarily restored his senses. He could think clearly again – at least, more clearly than for some time. He sat down at the table, extracted from their leather case the bone-handled knife and fork he always carried with him when 'riding', and plunged them into the succulent ham. Rosie had certainly catered for his hunger in one physical sense. Would that she might. . . . He pulled himself up short and stared out of the window. Though darkness was rapidly closing in, cooling the stifling heat of the day, he could still just make out the strange shape of the Quoit beyond Rosenithon, silhouetted against the blue-black vastness of the sea. Rosenithon; that was the little hamlet where Rose lived, he mused. Rose's home – Thorn Cottage, she had told him – the small, picturesque mud and hair building overlooking Godrevy beach to which Sampson and Amia Roskruge had carried that bundle, rescued from the sea nearly twenty years ago, and which they had christened 'Rose' – for no other reason than because Sampson had said she looked 'just like a fresh-sprung rose'. Who was she, he wondered? Would she ever know?

As though drawn by the tentacles of conscience he found his gaze swinging round to the north. There, less than ten miles away as the crow might fly, across the Helford River, stood the mansion of Trevadne – and Alethea. A pang of guilt shot through his befuddled mind. What was he doing here in this small country inn, with more liquor drunk than was good for him, and already entertaining the most sensual thoughts towards the barmaid, while away to the north and not ten miles distant was the dreamy Alethea – the girl he had always loved?

But the sobering effect of the cold water on his face and neck was already wearing off. He found it hard to think. Moral considerations were an effort; he was thankful when Rose returned with her special concoction of a creamy trifle. As intended, it was delicious; it was also Ashley felt sure, liberally infused with cognac.

While he was devouring it with relish, Rose turned down

the bed. Afterwards she stayed, chatting – just as she had done on that grassy plateau above the cove at Porthoustock. She was fingering the gold-enamelled locket she had shown him as they chatted that day. It was a *Toutin* he thought, made in Paris, 17th century, and it had a pair of miniatures inside – French aristocrats, he had suggested, and she had wondered whether they might be her ancestors.

Her soothing voice as she now cleared away the remnants of the meal became further and further away. It was a delightful sensation. Nothing mattered. And because the room seemed to be spinning round and round when he got up from the table he was glad of Rose's helping hand as he steered unsteadily for the bed. Nor did he make any protest when she slowly, coaxingly began to divest him of his clothes. The years in-between were slipping away; he was back in his bedroom at Treworden being put to bed as a child. It was happiness itself; relaxed, carefree and warm – and someone was looking after him. And even if the raftered ceiling above his head kept moving like a flotsam-strewn ocean swell, it mattered not; he was safely stretched out on the flock mattress of a large double bed.

It mattered not either that at that moment he thought he heard, in the distance of his consciousness, the sound of trotting ponies. Where were they going? Down to Godrevy beach? To meet an incoming schooner laden with contraband? He half-struggled to raise himself on one elbow. But then he fell back again. The effort was too much. Besides, he had heard another, much more welcome sound – the rustle of a silk-taffeta dress being pulled over its wearer's head. He propped himself up on the pillow – just as he had done against that rock above the cove at Porthoustock. Frustratingly, his vision was becoming blurred again; he tried hard to steady the room, to see more clearly the revelations beneath the dress, the shapely figure coming towards him in nothing more than gartered stockings and a thin chemise.

Then he felt the warmth of her body against his as she slid beneath the coverlet on the bed.

* * *

The life of a Riding Officer provided few compensations; driving rain and sleet lashing the Cornish coast in the depth of winter was definitely not one of them; nor was the feeling of loneliness, the knowledge that just about every man's hand was agin you – that if you were unfortunate enough to surprise a landing party bringing contraband ashore you would almost certainly be outnumbered by at least fifty to one. Nevertheless, you had to do your duty.

If, however, a red-blooded young officer were to find himself, by some rare good fortune, alongside a most attractive young maid beneath a coverlet in an isolated Cornish village – and if at the same time he were to hear the thunder of trotting ponies going about their unlawful business – might he not be forgiven if, just that once, he deliberately turned a deaf ear – *and let the cursed ponies thunder by*!

* * *

Downstairs, Will Trenethy was tidying up the now deserted bar. The regulars had all left – gone to their appointed stations, confident that Will Trenethy could handle a tricky situation. In turn, Will had every confidence in Rosie. She never did anything by halves. She would protect her father from discovery, no matter what the cost – and Will had a shrewd suspicion that in this particular instance the payment might not be too unwelcome. In a little while, he would carry out his part in the well-tried plan; but first of all he must allow Rosie time to accomplish hers.

He dried the last tankard and hung it on the hook above the bar. Then he went to the foot of the stairs and stood irresolutely fingering his mouth, and listening. No sound came from upstairs. All was silent – rather too silent, he thought. But then, you never could tell with young folk these days.

With a final shake of his head he went through to the kitchen, picked up the candle – the special one with the outsize wick, the one kept specially for the purpose because it threw out the brightest light – and placed it in the shiny brass candlestick.

He took down a taper from the mantelpiece, kindled it from the dying embers in the kitchen range, and lit the candle.

Then he slowly mounted the stairs.

He paused outside the guest bedroom, one ear to the keyhole. A sensuous smile of satisfaction crept over his face as he heard the bed creak. He fingered his lower lip appreciatively. Rosie, he guessed, was competently fulfilling her part of the hurriedly arranged plan. She understood, as well as anyone – even though she might not approve – how essential to success was her part in the emergency plan; she knew that while the laces, the silks, the 'baccy', the tea and the brandy were being brought ashore and carried inland, the 'King's Man' must be very much otherwise engaged.

And that, Will Trenethy congratulated himself, was precisely what was taking place in the guest bedroom at this very moment.

He tip-toed along to the adjoining room. There, from the small window in the far corner, the Giant Quoits, the massive prehistoric tomb-stones beyond Rosenithon, could still be seen. Silvered and eerie in the brilliant moonlight, they stood as a centuries-old landmark between *The Three Tuns Inn* and the sea. Will opened the window to obtain a clearer view. Even as he did so, a shadowy figure could be observed moving stealthily at the foot of the stones. Will nodded with satisfaction; Dolly Jago had obviously taken up her usual post in the well-tried plan.

Having placed the large candle in the window, Will let it burn freely for several seconds, allowing the flame to reach its full height. Then, in time-honoured fashion, he moved it from side to side across the open window.

A few minutes later a bright lantern could be seen swinging from the topmost stone of the Quoits. Dolly Jago had picked up the signal and was faithfully transmitting to the waiting schooner the vital message that the coast was clear.

Will Trenethy's essential task having been successfully completed, his curiosity about another matter got the better of him. He wondered just exactly what was going on in the bedroom next door.

Leaving the candle burning brightly in the open window to reassure the watching Dolly Jago that all was well, Will Trenethy sidled across the room. He pressed one ear to the partition wall. Disappointingly, he could hear nothing – nothing except the scurryings and scratchings of rats and mice up in the roof thatch. The bedroom keyhole, he decided, would make a better vantage point. From there he had already derived suggestive pleasures at hearing the bed creak. What further sounds of erotic ecstacy might he not enjoy if he were to return there now? To his deprived imagination the prospect was positively titillating.

He crept back along the short passage and knelt down once more, his ear close to the keyhole of the guest's bedroom door. For the time being, he had done his part; the vital message had gone forth that the 'King's Man' was now safely 'taken care of', and that, as a result, the coast was clear. The 'run' could now begin.

In the meantime, why should he not wallow for a few brief moments in the luxury of sensualism, devouring such delight as he could from the creaks and reverberations filtering through the guest room keyhole.

But he had been careless. The gentle on-shore breeze that tempered the stifling heat of the night was just strong enough, every now and then, to flutter the window curtains of the Inn.

Was it, then, just a chance puff of that gentle breeze that blew curtain towards flame, flame towards curtain? – or might it not have been the zephyr of a watching guardian angel, jealous for the virtue of her son?

Whether of heavenly origin or not, the result was unquestionably terrestrial. Within seconds the parched, faded curtain was ablaze. Moments later the flames, billowing through the open window, were licking the tinder-dry thatch of the overhanging roof.

Simultaneously, as the smell of burning reached Will Trenethy's nostrils, someone in the village square below shouted 'Fire!' Obeying an immediate instinct, Will rushed back to the room he had just left. Already some of the

meagre furnishings were alight; he had time only to grab a
few precious possessions he kept in his bedroom. Then,
hammering on the door first, shouting 'Fire, FIRE!' he
burst into the guest's bedroom. Leaving the occupants hurriedly scrambling into their clothes, he dashed downstairs to
unbolt the front door. Already excited villagers were
forming into a human chain and the first buckets of water
were being passed from hand to hand. Steadily the chain
grew, the buckets of water increased, but so did the fire.

Ashley's immediate thought as he stumbled, half
drunkenly, down the narrow staircase after Rose, his head
pounding as though hit by a stone-crusher's hammer, was
for Puncher. At all costs he must save his faithful companion. Emerging on to the cobbled courtyard in front of the
inn he could see that already the flames were relentlessly
devouring the thatch roof. Sparks flew in every direction; it
could only be a matter of time before one of them set alight
the bone-dry thatch above the stables.

Puncher and the other two horses must be got out immediately. Even now smoke was swirling in through the open
top half of the stable door, and the terrified animals were
crashing about inside, flailing at walls and partitions,
pounding the cobbled floor. The sound of the pathetic
whinnying acted like a cold douche on Ashley's befuddled
brain. Useless just to open the door and let the horses out;
they would go wild with fear, madly charging hither and
thither within the confines of the stable yard, probably
injuring themselves, possibly even breaking a leg. They
must first be caught, in the stable – then quietly led out
through the gate at the far end of the yard.

Ashley was into the stable like a flash, calming Puncher
by the familiar sound of his voice, eventually grasping his
halter. But the other two horses still had to be dealt with.
They were plunging dangerously as the crackling, spitting,
hissing sounds of the blazing roof timbers became more and
more frightening. Great tufts of flaming thatch were slithering down into the stable yard, and although quickly
beaten out with spades, forks, or anything else the helpers

could lay hands on, the heat in the yard was becoming unbearable.

Someone had followed him into the stable, Ashley realised, but in the rapidly thickening, eddying smoke he was unable at first to make out who it was. Then, with a surge of admiration, he realised it was Rose – fearlessly grappling with a pair of panic-stricken horses. Daunting task though it was, together they succeeded in getting the animals under control so that they could be led out through the gate at the lower end of the yard and into the field below the church.

By now, the roof of *The Three Tuns Inn* was properly ablaze. Great tongues of flame were licking the blackness of the night, sparks shot skywards, higher and higher, almost to the height of the church tower itself, then cascading to the ground in a myriad of white-hot fragments. The whole village was illuminated; and the whole village, it seemed, was out there, helping. Miraculously, ladders were appearing from nowhere, to be set up against the adjoining shop building; intrepid firefighters scrambled as high as the heat would allow, while bucket after bucket of water was passed up to them. Everyone was fighting to save *The Three Tuns Inn* – and as soon as he had seen to the horses' safety, Ashley, with Rose at his side, was in there with them, fighting as hard as anyone.

But, remorselessly, the fire was spreading.

Three miles out in Falmouth Bay the master of an incoming schooner let slip an unprintable oath. Then he closed his telescope with a snap.

'What the de'il do they think they're doing?' he exploded, angrily. 'First, they gie us the 'Coast is clear' signal, as plain as could be – and now, only a few minutes later, the stupid bletherers are blazin' us off! What the Hell are they up to!'

He moved to the ship's rail, putting his telescope to his eye once more. The blaze on shore was unmistakable; and it was growing more brilliant by the minute.

Turning to the man at the wheel, the skipper added resignedly, 'Och, weil. We'd best hae naething to do wi' em. Put the helm doon, Jamie, and set course for Bessy's. Those Carter laddies 'll handle the cargo for us. They've never failed us yet.'

The helmsman did as he was bid, setting the ship on a Sou-Sou-Westerly course. Though 'blazed off', they were being neither hunted nor even followed, so he was able to steer well clear of the Manacles.

CHAPTER EIGHTEEN

Mr. de Wynn's

Jeremiah Shoemaker eased his rotundity between the tables in de Wynn's Coffee House and sat down in his usual window seat. He was puffing and blowing more than he should; he was putting on weight, and he knew it. His wife was always on about it; telling him he ought to take more exercise. Instead of going across by boat from Flushing to Falmouth every morning to have coffee with his fellow Packet Ship commanders, he ought to be taking the dog for a walk, she said; round Trefusis Point as far as Mylor Church, then up the hill to Tregew before dropping down into Flushing once more. It was a lovely walk, she told him, and it would do him a world of good. He was getting too fat, she scolded – and there were no two ways about it.

But Jeremiah Shoemaker, despite increasing girth, was a happy man. Born in British North America, where his family had found sanctuary from religious persecution in Europe, he subsequently joined the Royal Navy only to find himself fighting against his native land during the war of American Independence. When eventually the war ended, Jeremiah saw that promotion would inevitably be slow in the Navy, and he had therefore set about obtaining, with the help of his wife's influential family, the command of one of H.M. Postmaster General's Packet Ships based at Falmouth.

Life was good for a packet commander in the 1780's – after the war ended in '83, that is. Although basic pay from the Post Office was no more than moderate, as was to be expected, a packet commander could gross a very considerable yearly income by way of passenger receipts, private trading and various more dubious practices that went under the name of 'adventures'.

Captain Jeremiah Shoemaker made full use of all such opportunities – and, as a result, he was doing very nicely.

Sitting now in his usual window seat at Mr de Wynn's Coffee House, he gazed out across the harbour at his elegant waterside residence in Flushing. It had been while on a visit to Falmouth as a junior officer in the Royal Navy that he had first seen and fallen in love not only with a Flushing girl but also with the village itself. He had made a vow that one day he would live there.

Mr de Wynn sidled up to the table. 'Good morning, Captain Shoemaker,' he ingratiated, 'and how fares the Captain this morning?' It was the familiar greeting – bowing, hand-wringing, obsequious; the greeting reserved for Mr de Wynn's most important customers. Mr de Wynn was no fool. During the past fifty years Falmouth had been growing apace – at the last count there were well over five hundred dwellings, housing some two and a half thousand inhabitants – and Mr de Wynn had been quick to recognise the commercial possibilities of the town. Accordingly, with the foresight of a true entrepreneur, he had built himself a hotel overlooking the harbour, with wharves, stables and a coach house at the rear.

He had also been quick to appreciate that the prosperity of the town depended very largely on the development and expansion of the Packet Service, and that among his wealthiest customers would be the packet ship commanders. He lost no time, therefore, in putting all the services of his hotel at their disposal, especially the bow-fronted room opening on to the street leading to the Church of St. Charles the Martyr. This room, with its multi-paned bow window at the front as well as its smaller window overlooking the harbour at the back, was known locally as de Wynn's Coffee House, and the owner was particularly gratified to find that it had become the acknowledged meeting place for Packet Ship Captains awaiting their orders.

It did not bother him, therefore, when the only response received from Captain Shoemaker on this beautifully sunny morning was little more than a grunt and a friendly nod. Packet Captains who lived in desirable houses across the water in Flushing were not only wealthy, they were also very important. Without the constant comings and goings of the Packet ships to all parts of the globe – to Vigo, Lisbon and Cadiz, to Halifax, New York and Bermuda, to Charleston, Savanna and Vera Cruz – the town of Falmouth would be still be no more than the fisherman's haven formerly known as Pennycomequick, or the 'Smithick' which, at the suggestion of Sir Walter Raleigh, the Killigrew family had so successfully developed and which now was one of the largest towns in the land.

'And will you be taking your coffee at once, Captain?' the attentive Mr de Wynn enquired, 'or would you prefer to. . . .?'

'No, no,' Captain Shoemaker dismissed, with a wave of a fat, much be-ringed hand, 'I'll wait. Cap'n Pickersgill and Cap'n McKinley are even now along at the Agent's office collecting their orders. I have no doubt they will be joining me very shortly.'

'Very good, Captain,' de Wynn bowed. 'You shall have my personal attention as soon as the other gentlemen arrive.'

Although he employed two maids, Ruby Trevithick and Lowdy Pascoe, to serve in the coffee room as well as in the hotel, Mr de Wynn always preferred to serve important customers himself – and these, of course, included his Packet captains.

He hovered attentively by Captain Shoemaker's table. 'And your good lady wife, Captain?' he enquired solicitously, endeavouring to prolong the conversation with one of his most influential customers, 'she continues to enjoy good health, I trust.'

Off-handedly the Captain replied, 'Mrs Shoemaker is in excellent health, I'm happy to say. She takes good care of herself.' He added, with just the semblance of a derisive snort, 'She *walks*, you know.'

Mr de Wynn sniggered sympathetically. 'It's becoming quite *de rigueur* among the ladies of fashion over in Flushing, I understand.' He never lost an opportunity to flatter his important patrons – and it was definitely the *ton* to live on the opposite side of the harbour.

'I don't know about *de rigger*,' Captain Shoemaker snorted loudly, 'but at least it gives my dog Bundle a bit of exercise.'

Mr de Wynn nodded, knowingly. He was well aware that Captain Shoemaker had a great admiration for Admiral Rodney under whom he had served in the West Indies at the beginning of the decade, and it was well known among Rodney's fellow officers that the great Admiral had inspired an exceptional degree of devotion in his dog, Loup. Accordingly, as Rodney had his Loup, so Captain Shoemaker had his Bundle of Mischief, subsequently shortened to Bundle. It was fashionable for a lady of substance to be seen out walking a dog, and Mrs Shoemaker, along with the other packet commander wives, liked to be very much in the fashion. Besides, the exercise helped to keep her hour-glass figure in its enviably attractive shape.

'Aha, there you are, Pickersgill!' Shoemaker roared, as a tall beanpole of a man entered the Coffee House from the Church Street doorway and snaked his way towards the table by the window. 'Where is it to be, then – Lisbon or the Med.?'

Captain Stanley Pickersgill subsided into the chair opposite Shoemaker, stretching his long, thin legs in front of him. His brown frock with high-stand collar and small round cuffs, his double-breasted square-cut waistcoat, his nankeen breeches buckled below the knee with large oval buckles – definitely *haut ton* for the year – his waistcoat-matching snuff-coloured stockings and his high-tongued, bluntly pointed shoes left no doubt but that the commander of the packet ship *Moonraker* was something of a dandy.

'Neither!' Captain Pickersgill replied, pulling a long face, 'It's Jamaica.'

'Oh, my Heavenly Saints!' exploded Shoemaker, rocking

his tubby little body from side to side with thinly concealed amusement, 'Not again, surely! And just when we're running into the best of the English summer.'

'Four months away from home,' Pickersgill grimaced, 'and more important than the weather, just when I'm beginning to bring Kerenza to heel.' He shot a darkly meaningful glance at his fellow packet commander.

Shoemaker chuckled, sympathetically. 'Making her realise on which side her bread's buttered, eh? – and liberally buttered, too, if I know anything about you, Captain Pickersgill.'

'More to the point,' Pickersgill grunted, 'making her understand *who's* buttering it!'

Shoemaker nodded vehemently, but then with a sly grin, added, 'You must admit, though, Captain, your wife really is a very pretty woman – a very pretty woman indeed. You mustn't be surprised if the drones swarm around the honeypot when you're away at sea.'

Both Ruby Trevithick and Lowdy Pascoe, listening behind the long velvet curtains screening the kitchen quarters, edged a little closer. It was one of the perquisites of being a serving maid to be able to pick up little snippets of gossip. Unfortunately for them, however, this illuminating side-shaft on Captain Pickersgill's wife was interrupted by the arrival of a third Falmouth Packet Ship commander.

'Oho, there, you rascals!' he greeted, swaggering truculently towards the vacant chair by the window, 'I thought I'd find ee here.' Out of breath and perspiring freely, he threw his *chapeau bras* cocked hat to the ever-attendant Mr de Wynn, and thankfully took the weight off his feet.

Anson McKinley was even more grossly proportioned than his friend Jeremiah Shoemaker. In his younger days he had been nicknamed Hanzum McKinley, but not any longer. The lucrative West Indies run for his ship, the *Lady Isabella*, with its single fare to Jamaica of sixty three pounds, its back-handers from passengers in return for privileges aboard, its profits from private trading and bald-faced smuggling, had made Captain Anson McKinley one of the richest men in the district.

But the years of easy living, mostly ashore, had all too revoltingly taken their toll. As he now jellied into Mr de Wynn's largest arm chair – it was always known as 'Cap'n McKinley's chair', and anyone else so foolish as to occupy it elicited not only a very disapproving stare from Mr de Wynn himself but also a pointed delay in service from his maids – as he spilled over the arms of the chair, Anson McKinley presented a masterly portrait of self-indulgence.

His Macaroni cravat hung loosely beneath the rolls of his numerous chins; his single-breasted, short-skirted waistcoat, no longer adequate to the task of covering his distended belly, was held precariously by a single, over-strained button, while his white buckskin breeches, drum-tight around bulging thighs, were held at the knee by dangling blue ribbon ties.

From a pocket above the small falls of his breeches, the flap of which only just preserved his modesty with the aid of yet three more over-strained buttons, dangled a broader sky-blue ribbon attached to an ostentatious fob.

Within seconds of Captain McKinley's arrival, Mr de Wynn was in ingratiating attendance. He always made a point of serving Captain McKinley personally, partly because he felt that important customers like Packet Captains should be accorded the highest service, but mainly because if Ruby or Lowdy stood attentively beside him, Captain McKinley would invariably try to run his hand under their skirts, stroking their thighs and pinching their bottoms. The girls didn't care for it – at least, not from Captain McKinley. With the lean and hungry-looking Captain Pickersgill it might have been a different matter – but he always kept his hands to himself.

'Good morning, Captain McKinley,' Mr de Wynn purred, 'and how is the Captain this morning?' The enquiry was acknowledged with a mere wave of a pudgy hand. 'And Mrs McKinley is well, I trow?' the proprietor of the coffee house persevered in his most polished tones.

McKinley nodded. Mrs McKinley's health was not a subject he cared to dwell upon; in fact, he did not expend much thought on Mrs McKinley at all. He had other more absorbing interests elsewhere.

'Bring the coffee,' he ordered, through thick, bulbous lips, 'and make it *tooty sweety*, Wynn.'

Mr de Wynn melted into the shadows of his culinary precincts, emerging a few moments later with a fresh supply of steaming coffee.

'Honduras coffee this morning, gentlemen,' he informed proudly, pouring the dark aromatic liquid from a highly polished copper pot. 'Sugar and cream on the table, as usual.' Discreetly he then moved back into the shadows – but not, of course, out of earshot. After all, his Packet Captains were by far the best disseminators of news and scandal, both local as well as worldwide.

'Cap'n Pickersgill's got his orders,' Shoemaker remarked, addressing McKinley.

'Oh, so ye have, have ee,' McKinley croaked. 'Been down to Bell's Court this mornin', eh? And what did they tell ee, then?'

Pickersgill uttered with disgust the one word 'Jamaica.'

'Well, Blister my tripes!' exploded McKinley. 'The devils are giving you no rest from the Indies run, then, are they?' He called for the cigar tray, selected one of the largest, waited for de Wynn to supply a light before continuing; 'What about crew? You'll be havin' difficulty there, I wouldn't wonder. The buggers don't care for these long trips, do 'em.'

'Nor do they like being restricted in their adventures,' observed Shoemaker.

Pickersgill nodded firmly. 'No, indeed they don't. But after Robinson's experience, we have to be so damnably careful.'

Mr de Wynn, out of sight but well within earshot, smiled knowingly to himself. He remembered the case very clearly; and it wasn't all that long ago, either. Captain Robinson of the *Expedition* had been dismissed the service for allowing iron ballast to be replaced by a corresponding weight of fruit taken on board at Lisbon. He pleaded that his crew had done it without his permission but his defence was not accepted, and as a result he lost his job.

Captain McKinley waved his cigar airily. 'Give 'em an extra shilling for the trip, Cap'n Pickersgill, and turn a blind eye to the goods they bring aboard – within reason, of course. After all, Robinson's four tons of ballast was goin' it a bit! You can't go lettin' the buggers upset the trim o' the ship.'

'The trouble with paying one crew a bit more,' put in Captain Shoemaker, 'is that it then upsets the others.'

'Oh, well,' McKinley dismissed, with another wave of the cigar, 'you just can't satisfy the bastards, no matter what you pay 'em. And in any case, Cap'n Pickersgill, you'll not be aboard, will ee? Surely, you'll be handin' over once gain to your Mate – you'll be lettin' him take her across, won't ee?'

Pickersgill shook his head. 'It's not quite as simple as you make it sound, Cap'n McKinley. I've already had shore leave covering the last two sailings, and the Post Office authorities are getting distinctly prickly about any further extensions.'

'Are they, Begad!' McKinley snorted. 'Just let 'em try that sort o' nonsense with me! I'll soon show 'em the door.' He puffed furiously at his cigar, making it glow like the anger he was obviously feeling.

'And I'll tell you this much,' he went on confidentially, leaning forward as far as his tight breeches would allow, 'the Packet Agent would find his purse weighing considerably lighter if he was so foolish as to try that game with me!'

His two confederates chuckled politely, Captain Shoemaker observing diplomatically, 'We don't all possess the same weight of financial punch as you do, Cap'n.' Then, in more serious vein, he continued, 'But Cap'n Pickersgill's quite right. The Postmaster General is known to be concerned about the increasing number of absentee Packet commanders . . .'

'What damned bloody cheek!' expostulated McKinley.

'. . . and the rumour is,' Shoemaker persisted, 'that it'll not be long before it becomes a case of 'Sail – or be sacked!''

McKinley's purple jowls wobbled with indignation. 'Sail, or be sacked, indeed! What infernal insolence! Who the bloody 'ell do they think they are! And where the even bloodier 'ell do they think they'd be if it weren't for us Packet captains, eh? Answer me that one!' He sank back into his chair, exhausted by his own vehemence.

'That may be so,' Pickersgill rejoined soberly, 'but the fact remains . . . ''them as pays the piper calls the tune.'' '

'Well, you're not going, surely,' McKinley remonstrated, 'Not just to satisfy those shits at the Post Office!'

Again, Pickersgill shook his head. 'Got no excuse to remain ashore,' he said.

'Well, but . . . well, dammit,' McKinley blustered, 'can't you plead something . . . can't you say your wife's pregnant, or something?'

Pickersgill shrugged, stealing a furtive glance in Shoemaker's direction, 'Unfortunately she isn't,' he said rather sadly.

'Well then, man,' McKinley spluttered, 'for God's sake, pull yer bloody cock out and get busy!'

This outburst of lewdness was greeted by all three with guffaws of the coarsest type of laughter during which Pickersgill was heard to mutter, ruefully, that he ony wished to Hell he could . . . however, further speculation about such interesting possibilities, including an offer of gratuitous assistance *in loco maritus*, as it were, from Captain McKinley, in order to provide Captain Pickersgill with an excuse for staying ashore, was interrupted by the emergence from the kitchen shadows of Mr de Wynn, enquiring whether a replenishment of the coffee pot was needed.

Mr de Wynn, while welcoming the prestige conferred upon his establishment by men of such wealth and renown – as well as their money, of course, – had no liking for bawdiness, and whenever he thought the conversation or behaviour of his customers was beginning to get out of hand he would politely intervene in this way.

And it had the desired effect because, after disdainfully waving the enquiry aside, Captain McKinley continued in more sober tones. 'Well,' he enquired of his companions, 'What's new?'

Still chuckling quietly at the thought of Captain McKinley assisting Captain Pickersgill in the achievement of his wife's pregnancy, Captain Shoemaker crossed one expensively breeched leg over the other and settled himself more comfortably for a bit of gossip.

'You heard about the lark down at St. Keverne the other night, I suppose?' he asked.

Captain Pickersgill grinned approval of the change of subject.

'St. Keverne?' Captain McKinley queried, raising a quizzical eyebrow, 'No. What sort of lark was that, then?'

'One of the taverns there,' Shoemaker enlightened, *The Three Tuns* I think they call it – it went up in smoke a couple of nights ago.'

'Pooh!' McKinley scoffed, 'there's nothing unusual about that, Cap'n Shoemaker. These old inns with thatched roofs are like tinder boxes – positively like tinder boxes, I say. They're frequently catching fire.'

Captain Shoemaker's eyes twinkled. He winked at Captain Pickersgill. 'Ah, yes. But this one was different.'

Sensing a whiff of scandal, Captain McKinley leaned forward expectantly. 'Something different, ha? Tell us about it.'

Shoemaker and Pickersgill also leant forward, joining McKinley in a confidential huddle. A silly grin played round each man's lips as Shoemaker began, 'Well, it happened like this.'

Mr de Wynn moved a step closer. He busied himself, quietly re-arranging the clean cups and saucers on the dumb-waiter in the corner. Whenever his important customers adopted anything resembling a conspiratorial attitude, he always made it his business to be well within earshot. He usually managed to pick up a few tit-bits of scandal. Sometimes they could prove quite useful.

'. . . one of the largest and most lucrative adventures ever attempted,' he heard Captain Shoemaker recounting, '. . . liquor, 'baccy, silks . . . that sort of thing. . . .'

Mr de Wynn sidled out among the empty tables, gently flipping with a duster, gradually moving closer.

'. . . everything all arranged,' the Captain went on, barely above a whisper, '. . . ponies ordered, landing and carrying parties converging on P'roustock . . . sale to be conducted in the cellar of *The Three Tuns* that very night . . . when, Blister my Tripes! but who should turn up but this new Riding Officer from Mawnan or somewhere.'

'Ha!' exploded McKinley, slapping a fleshy thigh in appreciation. 'That put the cat among the sea birds, eh!!'

'And what happened then?' Pickersgill asked, a sardonic smile creasing his dark, handsome face. 'Had they by any chance got a barmaid?'

Shoemaker nodded vigorously. Pickersgill's smile broadened into a wicked grin. 'The old trick, I suppose?'

'Exactly!' Shoemaker agreed. 'A few pints o' harmless-looking porter – but with a few drops of India Berry added – and then the trollop does the rest. Takes him upstairs, lifts her skirts . . . and that's him taken care of for an hour or so.'

Eyes popping, mouth slavering, Captain McKinley leaned even further forward, asking, 'And is that what happened?'

Captain Shoemaker nodded. 'But with a slight difference,' he continued. 'This young Riding Officer fella – apparently he's not the usual cut for the job – well-eddicated kind of a young 'un, got friends in high places, or so they say. . . .'

Captain Pickersgill grunted. 'Hmph! A fellow like that wouldn't be interested in a common tavern whore, surely?'

'Ah, no. That's the difference,' Shoemaker explained, 'There are plenty of those available, as we know – like that rough 'n ready wench along at The King's Arms here, in town. . . .'

Captain McKinley shifted uncomfortably at the reminder of this slattern.

'. . . but this young Riding Officer's had plenty of experience of that sort, so they say, and never done anything but refuse the bait – apparently they trailed a sleazy piece in front of him down at Manaccan or somewhere, but he fooled them and seized twenty ankers of cognac before it could be dispersed. But this barmaid at St. Keverne, well, she must be a pile different. Pretty as a picture, they do say . . . and with a figure to make your mouth water.'

Captain McKinley gleamed. '*Which* tavern did you say this was, Cap'n Shoemaker?'

'*The Three Tuns* at St. Keverne, Cap'n, I understand.'

'And this bird? Did she. . . .?' Captain McKinley gestured the lifting of a young maid's skirts, licking fat lips as he did so.

Captain Shoemaker, to Captain McKinley's lascivious delight, winked agreement. 'The story goes,' he went on, 'that the Riding Officer, pretending to be as drunk as a Lord, allows himself to be beguiled up to the guest bedroom of the inn. . . .'

'Yes, yes,' McKinley urged, agog, 'and then what?'

'Well, as soon as the landlord was satisfied that his barmaid was about to do her duty, he signalled from the adjoining bedroom that the ''coast is clear'' in the usual fashion. . . .'

Even Captain Pickersgill was now getting interested, 'And then what happened?' he smirked.

'Well then, apparently, wishing to make sure all was going according to plan in the guest bedroom, this landlord fella indulged his fancy for a little bit of key-holing, if you follow me. . . .'

'Yes, yes, we follow you, Cap'n,' McKinley nodded, edging forward in his chair, 'and what did he see?'

Captain Shoemaker was enjoying his role as raconteur. He was in no hurry to conclude his tale. 'Well, of course,' he teased, 'a key-hole is a very small aperture. . . .'

'Yes, yes, we quite understand that, Cap'n, Shoemaker,'

McKinley pressed, 'but what did he . . . did he actually see the maid lifting her. . . .?' Again he mimed the titillating revelation.

'Not so fast, Cap'n McKinley, not so fast,' Shoemaker counselled, 'Only the landlord himself knows exactly what he saw, and no doubt he'll be keeping that little tit-bit to himself, but whatever it was, it must have excited him a rare pile because the next thing he knew, the roof of the inn was ablaze!'

'Oh, my Lordy!' interjected McKinley.

'Left a candle unattended somewhere,' Pickersgill suggested.

'Precisely,' Shoemaker confirmed, 'that's exactly what had happened, so I'm told. He'd been signalling to the look-out on the coast, and then left the candle burning naked while he peeped through the key-hole.'

Captain McKinley gave one thigh a resounding slap as he rocked his grossly overfed body back and forth. 'Egad, man! but that's a rich story. I like that greatly. And that old Peeping Tom landlord got the kind of eyeful he never expected. Hee, hee, hee.'

'But the richest part of it all,' went on Captain Shoemaker, savouring the denouement of his tale, 'was that the incoming vessel, loaded to the gunwales with contraband, saw the flames shooting skywards from the blazing roof of the inn and naturally thought she was being 'Blazed Off!', – and then, Blister my Tripes! if she didn't get picked up and chased by a Revenue cutter down in Mount's Bay.'

'Ooh, my Lordy!' McKinley anguished, 'was she captured?'

'No, no, I haven't heard so,' Shoemaker assured, 'she managed to give 'em the slip, and was last seen heading back to France.'

Captain Pickersgill's face creased into a wry grin. 'And all because this Riding Officer fellow was in bed with a strumpet!'

'Oh, yes,' McKinley enquired with genuine interest, 'what happened to the little bird?'

'Oh, she was all right,' Shoemaker confirmed, '– or so I understand – even though the Inn was burnt to a cinder. And, incidentally,' he went on, turning to Pickersgill, 'the girl was apparently no strumpet. Rather a superior type of young lady, so they say – not the usual type of barmaid, at all.'

'Then why was she mixed up in that sort of thing,' Pickersgill asked, ' – luring the Revenue man up to the bedroom, and all that?'

'Evidently, because her father was heavily implicated in the run – there's some story about the father, I believe – saved her from drowning as a child, or something. Whatever the reason,' Shoemaker continued, 'she evidently feels under some special obligation to him, and therefore felt obliged to keep the Riding Officer very fully occupied.'

A lecherous gleam crept into Captain McKinley's eyes. 'Lucky Riding Officer!' he commented enviously.

'Ye-es,' Shoemaker speculated reflectively, 'and quite a handsome fellow, I understand.'

Captain McKinley stroked his fleshy jowls, also reflectively. 'And knows what's good for him, by the sound of it.'

Captain Pickersgill had been reflecting as well – but from a rather different angle. 'Hmm,' he mused, 'and a useful man to have on the job, I would say, wouldn't you, gentlemen?'

It took a moment for the innuendo to be appreciated by the other two. And then, 'From our point of view, you mean,' McKinley chuckled. 'Oh, definitely, – from our point of view, a very useful man.'

'Indeed,' Shoemaker concluded, 'a man deserving of every encouragement – eh, gentlemen?'

This all-embracing conclusion from Shoemaker was greeted by a rumble of deep-throated chuckles from the other two, but their conspiratorial mirth was interrupted by the tinkling of the bell above the entrance door, announcing the arrival of another customer.

His Majesty's Collector of Customs for Falmouth, James Henry Breward, had been instructed by his wife to purchase ¼ lb of Mr de Wynn's best ground coffee.

He had been thus instructed by Mrs Breward not merely because she appreciated good coffee but even more so because she liked to be able to boast to her friends that she always purchased from de Wynn's. It gave her, she felt, a certain standing. De Wynn's was undoubtedly the best coffee house in the county, frequented as she knew by all those wealthy Packet Captains, and Mrs Breward was on the look out for a little bit of prestige. She wanted her husband, recently appointed to his important office of Collector of Customs, to be seen to be on friendly terms with all the best people in the town.

At present, she and her husband were renting a modest abode in Falmouth, but she was well aware that the 'quality' lived in those attractive Queen Anne houses on the other side of the harbour, at Flushing.

Mrs Breward coveted one of those houses. Not because, facing due south, as they did, and looking straight out over the water, they caught all the best of the day's sunshine, but because – much more importantly – it would put her right up alongside all those fashionable sea captain's wives.

Accordingly, James Henry Breward had been instructed to 'keep well in' with the Packet commanders, and to leave no pebble unturned in a search for a suitable property to rent in Flushing.

It was precisely because she knew the Packet Captains foregathered so regularly at de Wynn's Coffee House that Mrs Breward had sent her husband there to make his purchase. Not a large quantity, mark you, because James Henry Breward was inclined to be stingy with the housekeeping money, but just enough to show her friends that she bought only from the best.

Having made his modest purchase at the coffee counter, Captain Breward now eased his way towards the three sea captains seated in the window. '*Good morning*, gentlemen,' he greeted, pretending complete surprise at finding them there, 'I trust I find you all in the best of health. My word,' he went on, through the stony silence, 'the smell of that coffee is exceptionally good this morning. Mind if I join you in a dish?'

He knew his wife would never forgive him if he ignored even the smallest opportunity of extending his acquaintance with these powerful men.

Captains Shoemaker and Pickersgill had already had some dealings with the new Collector of Customs, but Captain McKinley had always made it his business to steer a course well clear of any officials. He distrusted them profoundly. Besides, they were usually of rather poor 'quality' – servants, in fact, and definitely not up to the society in which he chose to class himself. He conveniently forgot, of course, that he, himself, was a servant of the Postmaster General – albeit a very wealthy one.

He saw nothing to change his opinion as he surveyed the man, perfunctorily introduced by Captain Shoemaker, now drawing up a chair to their table. Lard-like face, piggy eyes behind metal-rimmed spectacles, a now out-of-fashion 'Major' wig with two corkscrews curls tied at the nape of the neck and forming a double queue behind; heavy features, thick brutal-looking lips now curled into an ingratiating smile. Captain McKinley took it all in, and with uncharacteristic percipience, came to an instant conclusion – the man was probably a bully; he was certainly a toady.

Nevertheless, Captain McKinley, despite his bluster, his easy living and his lecherous mind, was no fool. His own skin was what mattered most. If there had to be Customs men, then it was prudent to be on good terms with them; butter them up a bit; draw them, not *quite* into one's own society, but to the fringe of it; make them then feel it to be an unpardonable breach of the social code not to look the other way at the appropriate time; tempt them with the prospect of social advancement, but never actually try to bribe them. If you played your cards right, you could always achieve the same ends without wasting good money.

Captain McKinley's florid cheeks curled into a smile as he turned to Breward, saying; 'My friend, Captain Shoemaker has just been telling me about the singular success of your man down at . . . er . . . whereabouts did you say it was, Cap'n Shoemaker?'

The enquiry was accompanied by a nudge and prodigious winks which Captain Shoemaker, his tubby little body wriggling appreciatively at the prospect of a bit of fun at Breward's expense, was quick to return.

'Oh, ah – down at St. Keverne, Captain,' he replied with exaggerated gravity, 'just inland from the Manacles, don't you know.'

'Why, yes, of course,' McKinley purred, 'St. Keverne – with its tall church spire – one of the best known landmarks along the coast. Ye-es, a quite remarkably skilful coup your man achieved down there – almost a case of *legerdemain*, you might say.' Captain McKinley prided himself on being able to produce the telling phrase, the *bon mot*, appropriate to the occasion. He was not, he was fond of telling himself, quite like other men; appreciably above them in intellectuality, if he had to be honest. Now, with slightly raised eyebrows and a look of mild surprise on his flabby face, he went on, 'And he did it all on his own, too, I understand.'

Significant, smiling glances were flashing between Captains Shoemaker and Pickersgill as they watched Breward shifting uncomfortably in his chair. He was grinning vacantly, and nodding, anxious to conceal his ignorance. He hadn't the faintest idea what they were talking about.

'But then of course,' McKinley was saying, bestowing on Breward one of his most flattering smiles, 'I'm sure you must know a great deal more about it than we do, Mister . . . er . . . er . . . I'm afraid I didn't quite catch your name. . . .'

'Breward,' the Collector of Customs enlightened, 'Captain J.H. Breward.'

'Oho!' McKinley chaffed, simulating fraternal bonhomie, 'Another old sea dog, eh?'

'No, no, Captain,' Pickersgill intervened hurriedly – all Pickersgill's reactions were inclined to be jerky – 'Mister . . . er . . . Captain . . . er . . . Breward is not one of us, no . . . er . . . he's an army man. Is that not so, Mr Breward?'

Breward nodded. 'That's correct. The old 46th.'

'Well, well now, but how very interesting,' McKinley cooed, oozing further deception, 'an army man, eh? And now you've decided to sheathe the sword and collect His Majesty's revenue instead, is that it?'

Again Breward nodded. 'Very little future in the army after Yorktown,' he said gloomily.

'Oh, yes,' McKinley mused, 'Yorktown – of painful memory, eh? When we lost our American colonies. . . .'

Breward shook his head sadly. 'And we could have *won* the bloody war four years earlier, at Brandywine, if only . . .'

'Brandywine!' Shoemaker exclaimed, 'Well, Blister my Tripes! but I had an uncle at Brandywine. '77, wasn't it?'

The opportunity was too good to miss, and Breward seized it. Clearly, these influential Packet Captains knew something he didn't; about St. Keverne – presumably about Riding Officer Penberth, one of his own officers, and he knew nothing about it. To continue that conversation would merely disclose his ignorance of some action – considered highly meritorious by these important men – relating to an officer under his authority. Confession of ignorance would be damaging to his image in the eyes of the very men he was most anxious to impress. But here was a chance to change the subject, to talk about a profession of which these bloated, overpaid, yet enviable sea captains knew nothing. He would show them, by God! – these men in powdered wigs, well-cut clothes and expensive footwear. What did they know of the hard slog of campaigning in a foreign land; of the quagmire of the road between Princeton and Trenton, for instance, with the troops sinking to their knees as they tried to haul their guns through the mud; what did they know of the blood, and the sweat, and the sheer exhaustion of war! He'd tell them, by God! – he'd bloody well tell them!

And yet – there was that house across the water in Flushing.

Only they could help him to achieve his wife's ambition. He must be careful.

'Brandywine' he repeated, looking at Captain Shoemaker, 'Yes, September '77. Which regiment?'

Shoemaker laughed. 'Oh, nothing you'd recognise, I think. You see, he was on the other side.'

'Against us, you mean.'

'Exactly. My grandfather emigrated to British North America – ooh, about a hundred years ago, I suppose,' Shoemaker explained, 'and although my father eventually came to England, his brothers remained in America.'

Now it was Breward's chance to show interest. He grasped it. 'How very strange, Captain,' he purred, 'and so when war broke out. . . .'

'Precisely,' Shoemaker affirmed. 'They found themselves fighting the British, my uncle being a high-ranking officer in Washington's army. But, by all accounts, you fellas gave them one hell of a drubbing at Brandywine Creek!'

Breward despairingly shook his head. 'But we let them off the hook, I'm afraid – oh yes, we let 'em off the hook, all right!'

Sensing a grand opportunity to butter up the Collector of Customs, as he intended, Captain McKinley regarded Breward with a mock-indulgent smile. 'It must have been a most interesting battle, Mister . . . er . . . Captain . . . er,' he fumbled. 'Perhaps you would be good enough to favour us with your description of how it went?'

Breward leaned forward, eager to impress the town's most influential citizens. 'Well, yes . . . if you really are interested?'

'But of course we're interested,' McKinley encouraged, 'of course we are. Aren't we, gentlemen?' From beneath a quizzically cocked eyebrow he shot a meaningful glance at his friends.

'Well, then,' Breward began, pointedly moving his coffee cup away to his left, 'it all started here, a place called Kennet Square, not far from Chad's Ford. At four o-clock in the morning, Generals Howe and Cornwallis led a force of seven thousand men out of the square and along the banks of Brandywine Creek. After marching for about twelve miles, we crossed the creek at Jeffry's Ford . . . just about here.' He placed the sugar bowl at 'Jeffry's Ford'.

Mr de Wynn left the coffee room and went down to the kitchen. He had heard these battle descriptions before; they usually took rather a long time.

He felt sure that a fresh pot of coffee would be required very soon.

CHAPTER NINETEEN

The Glory that was Osbourne's Hill

'Mornin', Mr Penberth,' Mattie greeted, beamingly, from behind the much-scored wooden desk in the Collector's outer office. 'Not a bad one for the time o' year, I s'pose. Might be better, might be worse. But there's good weather on the way, sir,' he added brightly. 'I can feel it in me knees.'

That was Mattie all over, Ashley reflected. Always cheerful, ever the optimist, he had proved to be the one glowing star in the sombre firmament of King George's Customs at Falmouth. Despite the temptations of an international port, rapidly growing in prosperity; despite the frequent attempts to grease the palm of his hand with bribes; and notwithstanding the pretentious asipirations of his chief, Mattie Reynolds had never lost his simple, rough-hewn sense of proportion. Perhaps even more endearing, he had retained – with the merry encouragement of his pumpkin-shaped wife and the good-natured taunts of customers at *The Five Pilchards* tavern – his irrepressible, London-bred sense of humour. In short, he was the one person Ashley looked forward to seeing each Friday morning when he rode into the office, to write up his past week's log and to receive any official instructions for the week ahead.

'The chief's bin askin' for you,' Mattie grimaced. 'Wants ter see you as soon as you comes in, he says. You know what he's like – everythin' got to be done – not to-day, mind, nor termorrer – but the day before that, if you get my meanin'.'

Ashley responded with a rueful nod. Evidently, Captain

Breward knew the worst. News travelled fast across the Cornish countryside, and in the few days since the roof of *The Three Tuns Inn* had blazed aloft into the night sky at St. Keverne, word would have got around. The whole story, luridly embellished of course, would have delighted the gossip-hungry ears of the Captain. Ashley could almost hear his censure; 'Dereliction of duty, eh? Bloody well caught with ya breeches down, ha! In *flagrante delicto* in fact. By God! but I'll have ya bloody balls off for this!'

It was exactly the kind of incident Captain Breward had been hoping for; confirmation of his forcefully expressed opinion that 'You'll be no bloody good to me. I told them up at H.Q. that you'd be no bloody good.'

Expulsion from the Service with ignomy – that's what it would mean; just like Fanshawe at Lydford College all those years ago. Strange, Ashley mused, how the wheels of life so often seem to come full circle.

He stood for a while, his back to Mattie Reynolds, silently staring out of the window – brooding.

Had it been worth it? There was no use pretending he hadn't known what they were about – down there at *The Three Tuns* that evening. Or at least, he'd suspected it. 'Get the fellow drunk' they would have said, 'and 'tice him up to bed wi' a wench.' They'd tried it on him before; not at *The Three Tuns*, of course, but on each former occasion the bait had been far from enticing and he had felt no reluctance in giving them short shrift.

But the barmaid at St. Keverne was different. He had found her more attractive than he cared to admit. Even now the scented memory of her was still disturbingly fresh – the softness and warmth of her body as she slipped beside him under the bed-cover. Worse still, perhaps, was the recurring hope that, even though she would certainly have persuaded herself she acted purely out of loyalty and a sense of duty, she had not found the experience wholly distasteful.

He drew a deep breath at the recollection, squared his shoulders and stared out across the harbour. Had it been worth it; in the face of all the rumours which must now be circulating, and with the immediate prospect of being given the sack, had it really been worth it?

How was he going to explain away his dismissal – to his mother, to Sir Andrew who had been such a stand-by throughout his life, but above all, to Alethea? For the very first time, the mere thought of Alethea made him wince – yes, wince; not with shame, perhaps, because he could not bring himself to regard this new feeling he had for Rose Roskruge as being shameful, but it was disloyal. Ever since he could remember, he had loved Alethea; and even though there had been times when her sister, Jeannie, had tempted him sorely, he had always clung to his love for Alethea. How could he now, with honesty, ever face her again – she who was so beautiful in spirit as well as in body, and who was so manifestly pure. Would she be able to forgive him – for just one lapse from grace – would she? And a yet more searing doubt – would he mind so terribly if she could not?

Angry with himself, and for his confusion, he kicked the skirting board at his feet. To fall from grace was so easy; to *accept* forgiveness, so damnably hard.

'Excuse me, sir,' he heard Mattie's voice behind him, 'but I was just wonderin' if . . . .'

Ashley swung round on his heel, glad to be distracted from his thoughts. 'Wondering what, Mattie?'

'Well, sir, I'm not sure as I knows how to put this, sir, but . . .' Mattie faltered, fearing to offend.

'To put what?' Ashley's expression clouded with foreboding.

'Well, sir,' eventually Mattie went on, 'I did hear there was a bit o' somethin' down at St. Kerverne the other night – you know how things gets talked about, sir, 'specially in somewhere like *The Five Pilchards* – a bit o' somethin' rather unusual, if you know what I mean.'

Ashley nodded gloomily. 'So you've heard it, too, have you.'

'Well, sir,' Mattie went on cheerfully, and with gathering assurance, 'bein' an old sailor, meself, sir, and havin' travelled the world all over an' seen a good many goin's-on, as you might say –' he paused for a moment, then continued tentatively, 'I do hope you're not thinkin' I'm bein' pertinent, sir . . . ?'

Ashley shook his head. 'No, no, certainly not. Please carry on.'

'Well, sir, I was just wonderin' if p'raps you was worritin' over what Captain Breward's goin' to say.'

Ashley nodded. 'Yes, as a matter of fact, I am.'

The anxious look on Mattie's face cleared. 'In that case, sir, I think I may have a little bit o' good news for you.'

Ashley, who had been staring gloomily at his black leather top boots, looked up hopefully. 'Oh, yes,' he encouraged, 'tell me.'

Mattie left the desk behind which he had been sitting and stumped across the floor to be closer to Ashley.

Lowering his voice, he went on confidentially, 'Well, it's like this, sir. You knows little Lowdy Pascoe – her wot works for Mr de Wynn at his hotel and coffee house, just along the street from 'ere, sir.'

Ashley might not know Lowdy Pascoe but he certainly knew de Wynn's Coffee House.

'Well, sir,' Mattie went on, *sotto voce*, 'as well as workin' for Mr de Wynn durin' the daytime, her an' Ruby her friend, well, they helps out the Missus an' me of an evenin' down at *The Pilchards*, see – on alternate evenin's like, although they both helps out when we're busy, see.'

Once again Ashley nodded. He couldn't quite see how the nocturnal activities of these two girls could resolve his dilemma, but never mind; Mattie's impish expression clearly suggested further revelations were to come.

Glancing over his shoulder to make sure the Collector's door was tight shut, Mattie proceeded, 'Well, it's like this 'ere, sir. Last evenin', while Lowdy was helpin' with the wash-up, she was tellin' the Missus an' me about how durin' that very mornin' three o' Mr de Wynn's best customers, Cap'n McKinley, Cap'n Shoemaker and Cap'n Pickersgill, was takin' their usual dish o' coffee, like they do almost every mornin', see, and Lowdy – well, sir, she over-heard them gentlemen tellin' about the blaze down at St. Keverne.'

Watching the effect this account was producing, Mattie thought he detected a deepening of the unhappy frown which was already clouding Ashley's face, and instinctively he hesitated to go on. During the comparatively short time they had been associated in H.M. Customs, Mattie had formed a great liking for the new member of Captain Breward's staff – indeed, he had been remarking to his wife only recently just how much he had taken to 'that young Mr Penberth', and as he had no liking whatsoever for Captain Breward, nor for any other members of the Customs staff, for that matter, he was particularly anxious not to hurt or embarrass the one colleague he really did like.

So, in an apologetic tone, he said, 'I do hope you doesn't think I'm speakin' out of turn, sir?'

Receiving immediate reassurance from Ashley, Mattie continued, 'Well, sir, as I was sayin', Lowdy hears these Packet Captains tellin' about this 'ere fire, an' how the King's man was . . . er . . . on the premises, as you might say, when who should come into the Coffee House but . . .' he jerked his head in the direction of the Collector's door, 'his nibs, hisself.'

Ashley smiled grimly. 'Here it comes!' he thought. But out loud, he said, 'Yes, Mattie, what then?'

Mattie was unable to prevent a mischievous grin illuminating his well-scrubbed, enthusiastic little face. 'Well, sir, both Lowdy an' Ruby made sure they was well within hearshot because they thought . . . well, sir, . . . they guessed it might have somethin' to do with you, sir, and knowin' as they do that you an' me works for the same gentleman, as you might say, they took pertikler note o' what was said.'

'Oh, yes,' said Ashley, growing interested, 'and what *did* they say?'

'Well, sir,' Mattie went on, really getting into his stride, 'Lowdy thought – an' Ruby did agree with her, she said –

239

that them Packet gentlemen had decided to have a bit o' fun with our Captain Breward, see, pertikly seein' as how none o' them's too partial towards anyone connected with the Customs, like.'

'Not unusual,' Ashley commented wryly.

'Well, sir,' Mattie hurried on, 'Lowdy says she didn't think them Packet commanders was too pleased when his nibs . . .' again a jerk of the head towards the Collector's office, '. . . she didn't think they was impressed all that wonderful when 'e come an' joined 'em for coffee, like . . . she thinks he's tryin' to get it in good with their comp'ny, if you understands me. Any'ow, Lowdy says that before his nibs has had time to take a sip of 'is coffee, them Packet Captains is sayin' how they considered the Ridin' Officer for the St. Keverne district had done a right good job in blazin' off a big ship comin' in to land contraband goods, sir.'

Ashley's eyebrows shot up in surprise. 'A right good job, eh?'

'Yes, sir,' Mattie confirmed. He could hardly contain his delight. His gnome-like features screwed themselves into a replica of a wrinkled pippin. 'And what's more, sir,' he went on, now grinning unashamedly, 'both Lowdy an' Ruby was of the opinion that them Packet gentlemen were havin' a right game wi' the Collector . . . so much so, sir, that they had 'im not knowin' whether 'e was comin' or goin'.'

This entertaining discourse was rudely interrrupted by the familiar shout of 'REYNOLDS!' – the Collector's normal method of summoning his clerk.

Before responding, Mattie whispered hurriedly, 'I'm only mentionin' this, sir, 'cause I thinks you may find things is a little bit better than you's fearin'.'

Then he stumped across the room and opened the Collector's door.

Ashley heard the familiarly petulant voice demanding , 'Is that bloody Riding Officer. . . .' Then, realising that the door was open, the voice dropped in mid-sentence to, 'Has Mr Penberth arrived yet, Reynolds?'

Mattie's wink as Ashley passed him, going into Breward's office, was barely concealed. It clearly said 'Good luck, sir.'

Captain James Henry Breward was sitting at his desk very deliberately writing. Without looking up he motioned Ashley to a chair. He continued writing. It was all part of making the junior officer feel unimportant. By now Ashley was quite used to it. He crossed his legs and just sat there, waiting . . . waiting.

When eventually Breward looked up from his writing, a crafty, almost admiring smile creased his singularly unattractive face.

'By God! Penberth,' he began, the smile broadening into a fiendish grin, 'you didn't half put the cat among the canaries down at St. Keverne recently.'

The grin turned into a penetrating stare – half-believing, half-questioning.

'Indeed?' Ashley parried, non-commitally.

'My tripes, but you did!' Breward continued, 'My friends tell me that one of the biggest shipments of contraband – brandy, silks, tobacco, the whole bloody lot, in fact – was planned to be run from Godrevy or P'roustock that night, but then you turned up in their midst.' The piercing stare became more intense, trying to elicit the truth without disclosing ignorance. Receiving a blank response from an unusually poker-faced Ashley, Breward continued, 'And when the buggers realised a Riding Officer was on the prowl, they were so anxious to blaze-off the incoming vessel that the stupid shits set fire to the roof of *The Three Tuns Inn*!'

Again the penetrative, questioning stare. 'That *is* what happened, isn't it?'

'Oh, yes,' Ashley affirmed, glad to be able to state the truth without giving anything away, 'I'm afraid the Inn *was* badly damaged by fire.'

'And you had nothing to do with that, I hope?' Breward asked guardedly, seeking facts but nervous of being in any way implicated officially.

241

Ashley shook his head. 'The fire was entirely accidental,' he replied laconically.

Breward's relief was transparent. The mirthless smile returned. So long as he, personally, could evade responsibility for the actions of his juniors he was well content – unless of course they redounded to his credit. Then, most surely, he would bask in the sunny praises of his superiors.

'You heard, of course, what happened to the schooner,' he asked, still probing, '. . . I'm referring to the ship those idiots blazed off?'

'She rounded the Lizard, I believe,' Ashley said, '. . . probably making for the Carter stronghold, down at Bessy's Cove.'

'Why go all that way round?' Breward queried, still testing his subordinate, 'Why not Coverack or Cadgwith?'

'Too close at hand,' Ashley responded, 'and besides, only the Carters could handle a large cargo at short notice.'

Breward drummed the desk top with the fingers of his right hand, thinking. Useful piece of local knowledge, that, he thought to himself. Perhaps this educated bastard, Penberth, might be of some small value, after all. And hadn't those Packet Captains mentioned something about 'friends in high places'. . . .

His mouth curled itself into something resembling a pleasant smile, as he said, 'As a matter of fact, Penberth, you're quite right. They did round the Lizard, and they may well have been heading down towards Cudden Point and the Carter's coves – but they ran right into the arms, or the grappling irons as you might say, of a Revenue Cruiser on a routine sweep of Mounts Bay.'

'They got her, then, did they?' Ashley asked, with genuine enthusiasm.

Breward hunched his shoulders, slumped in his chair, slowly shook his head. 'No, they bloody well didn't. They gave chase, of course – but the schooner was too quick for 'em. Led 'em one hell of a dance – all over the place – but eventually they lost 'em. Last seen heading back towards the French coast. And the silly buggers didn't even get her name.'

'They'd not have bothered too much about that,' Ashley commented, 'Names of ships don't mean a great deal in this game.'

'Why not!' Breward snapped.

'Because the next time she comes over, she'll almost certainly be wearing a different name,' Ashley asserted. 'They usually keep a set of false names stowed away in the lockers, and they'll hang out whichever one they think will confuse us most.'

Breward picked his nose, depositing the extraction on the floor beside his chair. 'Hmmm . . .' he mused. 'You seem to know a lot about it.' The tone was unmistakably accusing.

Ashley smiled inwardly. 'One learns those sort of things, you know, sir . . . just by listening.'

Breward hoisted one white-stockinged leg on to the edge of the desk; then followed it with the other, crossing his ankles and slouching down into his chair. He pulled a toothpick from his waistcoat pocket and began picking his teeth. 'Hmmm . . .' he murmured again, ruminatively, 'crafty set of buggers, aren't they.'

He sat for a while, idly raking around with the toothpick, staring into space. Then, like a jack-in-the-box, he shot out of his chair and stalked across the room to the window overlooking the harbour and the distant view of Flushing. Long and hard he gazed at those Georgian waterside houses. Perhaps this fellow, Penberth, wasn't quite such a bloody fool, after all. Friends in high places, did they say – those Packet Captains. Something about courting a baronet's daughter. Might be politic to humour the fellow. Hmmm. Friends in high places, eh?

Still staring out of the window, Breward said aloud, 'But those half-baked ninnies in the Revenue cruiser had to go and let 'em get away – let 'em slip right through their bloody fingers!'

He turned on his heel and returned to his desk, glancing

sideways at Ashley with a new interest. Friends in high places, eh? . . . and, after all, the man had just called him 'sir'.

He slumped down into his chair once more, emitting a long-drawn-out sigh. 'Let 'em get away, huh. Just like we did at Brandywine. Did I ever tell you?'

It was 'the chief' being expansive – and although Ashley had heard the story from Mattie, he decided that, in the present circumstances, it might be prudent to pretend otherwise. He shook his head.

'Autumn of '77, it was,' Breward went on, '. . . in fact I was telling some friends of mine only the other day.' He put his feet up on the desk once more, and with finger tips tapping rhythmically, he settled down to indulge in reminiscence. 'We'd had to make a twelve mile slog up to Jeffry's Ford before we could cross the bloody Brandywine Creek, and then we had to march all the way up to the top of Osbourne's Hill where we formed up in line of battle. We had the guards on the right, I remember, the grenadiers in the centre next to the light infantry, and on the left we had the foreigners, the Anspach and Hessian Jagers, all grouped behind a belt of trees and hidden from the enemy. My God!' Breward exclaimed, warming to his tale, 'but it was a bloody marvellous sight! Especially when we emerged from those woods in the early part of the afternoon – Cornwallis and Howe like ramrods astride their horses, their red coats, gold lace edgings and gold epaulettes making a brilliant contrast to the dark tree trunks behind them. But what must really have put the fear of God into the rabble of an army down below us was the sight of the British bayonets gleaming in the sunshine!'

And so the story had continued: the band striking up *The British Grenadiers* as the precision-formed columns marched remorselessly down the slope of Osbourne's Hill – no irregularity, no wavering, no hurry. On and on they went, with all the arrogance of highly disciplined troops. All around them the slaughter was appalling – but still the British moved forward, and had it not been for the onset of darkness the whole of Washington's ragged army might well have been destroyed.

'But once again the bastards got away,' Breward snorted indignantly. 'Cornwallis never did like night fighting – always preferred to have a good night's sleep and then 'bag the fox in the morning'. Ha! But by that time it was nearly always too late; the buggers had slipped away in the night!'

Again Breward disconsolately picked his nose, flicking the extracted substance across the room. 'And after that, winter set in, and Cornwallis decided to go home on leave. And then. . . .' he shrugged expressively, 'almost exactly four years later, he allowed himself to be cornered at Yorktown, and we'd lost the whole bloody war!'

Something told the silent Ashley that the Battle of Brandywine Creek had been Captain Breward's finest hour. It seemed such an ironic twist of fate that he should now be reduced to chasing renegade Cornishmen smuggling that very commodity after which the creek and the battle had been named.

It was perhaps even more unfortunate that among those Packet Captains whose society he so assiduously cultivated, he was rapidly acquiring the sobriquet, 'The Brandywine bore'.

CHAPTER TWENTY

The hooting of an owl

Jeannie Mackenzie was reclining on a chaise-longue by an open window in the drawing room at Trevadne. A cool, summer-evening breeze wafted in from the garden, gently rippling the long, elegant floor-to-ceiling curtains. A book of Burn's poetical works was open on her lap. She had just been reading the opening sentence of the Preface to the First, or Kilmarnock, Edition, dated July, 1786, 'The following trifles are not the production of the Poet, who, with all the advantages of learned art, and, perhaps, amid the elegancies and idleness of upper life, looks down for a rural theme to Theocritus or Virgil. . . .'

She then turned the pages until her eyes lighted on one of her favourites – 'Address to the Unco Guid or the Rigidly Righteous' – and, with a wry smile playing about her lips, she read:-

> O ye wha are sae guid yoursel',
> Sae pious and sae holy,
> Ye've nought to do but mark and tell
> Your neibours' fauts and folly.

Like everyone else, it seemed, she had heard the rumours about strange happenings at St. Keverne, and because she felt sure Ashley was feeling ashamed to show his face at Trevadne, she had sent a special message inviting him to dine with them that evening.

Alethea might well be upset by the gossip – poor, darling innocent little sister with the corn coloured hair and the trusting blue eyes – of course she would be hurt by the rumour that her beloved Ashley had been seduced by a bar-maid at St. Keverne. Of course she would. But she, Jeannie, would show him there was no intention on her part to 'mark and tell' his 'fauts and folly'. No, no, indeed; she, with her Parisian education and worldly experience was not shocked, as her little sister was, by such transitory *affaires d'amour*. After all, a man must learn, sometime; far better that he should cut his baby teeth in the nursery than in the salon. 'Besides,' she mused, coquettishly preening her hair in front of an imaginary mirror, 'it makes a man that much more attractive if he possesses a certain amount of experience.'

So, she had seized the opportunity afforded by her father's extended absence on business – to arrange a small dinner party, consisting of herself, Alethea and Ashley – and a rather dashing young Light Dragoon officer, temporarily stationed at Helston, who had recently been paying a great deal of attention to her sister. She thought it might have a salutary effect on relationships all round if Ashley were to meet this handsome Lieutenant who, at that very moment, was taking a turn in the rose garden with the demure and increasingly lovely Alethea at his side.

As she idly riffled through the pages of the Burns poetry Jeannie's mind returned to the words of the Preface – '. . . with all the advantages of learned art . . . amid the elegancies and idleness of upper life . . .' Her life, exactly. But she had no need of Theocritus or Virgil to provide her 'rural theme' because, with his simple country enthusiasms, Ashley would provide it for her. Not for the first time her fingers flicked the pages until she found what, she had to admit, was at least one of her favourites:

> 'When first I saw fair Jeanie's face,
> I couldna tell what ail'd me. . . .
> She's aye sae bonny, blithe and gay,. . . .'

– and at that moment the footman formally announced, 'Mister Ashley Penberth, Miss MacKenzie.' And Ashley limped into the room.

He looked unusually shy and ill at ease, Jeannie thought. It amused her. 'Guiltily wondering if the rumour's reached us yet,' she speculated, a faint smile parting her lips, but she immediately sought to dispel his embarrassment by planting a warm, intimately welcoming kiss on his mouth.

In fact, she was in the middle of this display of extrovert affection when Alethea and her escort stepped in through the open French window.

Ashley took the scene in at a glance; the attractive blush suffusing Alethea's cheeks as she greeted him with downcast eyes; the brilliantly uniformed Dragoon officer with the languid, insolent expression standing so closely beside her, his dark blue jacket with its crimson, silver lace-trimmed collar, cuffs and turnbacks, his immaculately cut white kerseymere breeches, his shiny black boots and steel spurs emphasising, as nothing else could, the ordinariness of Ashley's civilian attire.

But already Jeannie was effecting the introductions. 'Ashley, dear,' she was saying, casually slipping her arm through his, 'I rather think you know Lieutenant Liggett-Fanshawe?'

Ashley nodded. 'Yes, we have met before.'

'Oh, really?' the Lieutenant drawled. The voice was deliberately casual, the half-smile totally without mirth. The eyes flickered ceiling-wards as he disclaimed, 'Frightfully sorry. 'Fraid I don't recall.'

'At the Lanteague Ball, perhaps?' Jeannie suggested airily.

Ashley gave a short laugh. 'Yes, that's quite correct – but it so happens that we were also at school together.' He faced the Lieutenant squarely, grasping the limply extended hand and gripping it rather more fiercely than he would normally have done. 'At Lydford – remember?'

'Egad! But so we were,' Fanshawe grimaced, gingerly withdrawing the lace-cuffed hand from the painful grip, 'What a fantastic memory you have, Penberth!'

Then, with an elegant wave, dismissing an unpleasant recollection, he added, 'Long, long time ago, though – eh, what?'

248

Ashley had been watching Alethea's reaction. Had she deliberately chosen to forget that peerless Spring day, on the slopes below Pendennis Castle, when they had shared a picnic 'sandwich' lunch together; when they had discussed his hopes for a naval career; and how the tears had welled up in her lovely, compassionate blue eyes as he told her about the window-hanging incident at Lydford, and the fellow 'by the name of Fanshawe' who'd been the instigator.

Did she remember all that – including the very first, fumbling but grown-up kiss that had preceded it? Did she remember? Or did she prefer, now that the same Fanshawe – Liggett-Fanshawe – had grown into such a personable and eligible young officer who was so clearly attracted to her – did she now prefer to forget?

Ashley felt a little pain stabbing at his heart as he looked at the two of them standing there together – she so lovely, so composed, the earlier deep blush now faded but still colouring the pale cream of her complexion, while the Lieutenant stood so possessively close to her, languidly self assured in his glittering, silver-tasselled uniform.

Why should she not prefer to forget; why should she not prefer Liggett-Fanshawe – even though the polished exterior might still cloak the instincts of a sadistic bully? After all, an officer of Light Dragoons would represent a very much more suitable match for a MacKenzie of Trevadne than someone as unpopular and unfashionable as a Riding Officer in His Majestry's Customs Service – and one who, according to rumour, was easy prey for any voluptuous barmaid!

Put bluntly, it was a difference of class – and Ashley was well aware of it.

Breaking an awkward silence, Jeannie observed casually, 'Lieutenant Liggett-Fanshawe is stationed at Helston. I do believe he thinks we must all be barbarians, living in such an isolated part of the country – really I do.' And then she added gaily, 'Which, of course, we are – aren't we, Ashley?'

She draped herself gracefully along one end of a *canapé*

covered in Aubusson tapestry and motioned the others also to be seated.

'But of course we are,' Ashley retorted, sinking into one of the Louis Quinze *fauteuils*, 'completely uncivilised!' And then turning to the Lieutenant, he asked, 'And for how long will you be here, do you think, Fanshawe?'

'Not too long,' the Lieutenant drawled. But then, glancing sideways at Alethea with whom, somewhat presumptuously, he was sharing the two-seater *causeuse*, he added, 'But just long enough, I hope. . . .' He carefully examined the back of his hands and his well-manicured finger nails before continuing, 'It seems that your Mr Borlase – of Penzance, is it – it seems he's been pleading with General Onslow to send some soldiery down into these parts.'

'Oh, yes,' Ashley remarked, his interest aroused, 'for any particular purpose?'

Fanshawe's eyes flickered ceilingwards once more – an affectation Ashley remembered from schooldays. 'It seems that the coasts around here are swarming with smugglers,' the Lieutenant explained, 'and the Government's getting a bit upset about all the revenue being lost. Frightfully tedious, of course – but the Government must have its money to pay for its toys. Like the army, for instance – especially as things are looking a little fragile across the water.'

'In France, you mean?' Alethea asked, without looking at him directly.

'Exactly, my dear lady,' Fanshawe agreed, bestowing an indulgent smile on her. 'But mark you, these smuggler fellas with their contacts in Brittany and the Channel Islands could prove very useful if we get drawn into war with France once more – which, I feel bound to say, does now seem rather likely.'

'The Prime Minister's doing his best to keep out of it,' Ashley observed. 'He's constantly trying to preserve friendship between our two countries.'

'And Edmund Burke hates the Revolution,' Jeannie added.

'But not Mr Fox,' Alethea stoutly maintained. 'He

thinks the fall of the Bastille was quite the best thing that's happened in the whole history of mankind!'

'*Mister* Fox!' Jeannie scoffed, ' – the drunken old fool! He does nothing but carouse with the Prince of Wales and encourage his extravagance!'

'He's *not* a drunken old fool!' Alethea flared, her cheeks reddening perceptibly, 'He loves liberty and the freedom of the human spirit.'

'And I suppose it was that same human spirit that prompted the mob of harridans to threaten the lives of their King and Queen at Versailles,' Jeannie retorted, 'before dragging them back, humiliatingly, to Paris and virtual imprisonment. Was *that* an example of this freedom of the human spirit!'

'They wanted to have their King and Queen in their midst,' Alethea parried.

'Ha!' Jeannie ridiculed, 'such touching concern! And I suppose it was the same concern,' she went on scathingly, 'shown by those women who forced their way into the Queen's bedroom – having first murdered the guards, be it noted – and then stabbed their filthy pikes into the bed just in case their Queen – whom they chose to call 'the Austrian whore' – might be hiding beneath the coverlet. Most *touching* concern, I *must* say.'

'It had *nothing* to do with *concern* and you know it,' flamed Alethea. 'It was raw, unalleviated hunger!'

'Hunger! Pah!!' Jeannie retaliated unfeelingly, 'What does Mirabeau know of hunger. . . .'

'He's dead, anyway,' Alethea corrected – irritatingly, coming from a younger sister.

'Yes, yes, I know he's dead,' Jeannie continued, beginning to flare. 'All right, then, what *did* Mirabeau know of hunger? – what does that huge butcher-like man, Danton, know of hunger? – and what does that horrible little lawyer from Arras, the one they call the 'Incorruptible', abstemious though he may be – what does *he* know of hunger?'

'*They* weren't at Versailles,' Alethea countered.

251

'That's not the point,' Jeannie retorted, her voice becoming more and more strident. 'They're the leaders . . . the rabble-rousers . . . the ones inflaming the mob to do these terrible things! And if you'd take the trouble to read Burke's *Reflections* you'd realise how serious this Revolution is becoming. 'The age of chivalry is gone' he says, 'and the glory of Europe is extinguished forever'.

'Oh, *very* dramatic,' countered her sister, 'but chivalry and glory are no substitutes for food!. . . . And although I may not have read Burke, I have at least read Rousseau, and he preaches a faith in the essential goodness of human nature when uncorrupted by tyranny.'

'There you are!' crowed Jeannie, spreading her hands expressively, '– tyranny! And what do you call the action of those fishwives at Versailles if it wasn't tyranny? And when Lafayette persuaded the Queen of France to step out on to the balcony with her young family, and the mob hurled insults at her and shouted 'No children, no children!' was *that* a display of the essential goodness of human nature, might I ask?!'

Ashley chuckled inwardly. The two sisters hadn't changed, really – hardly at all. He could remember so well those childhood days when they frequently squabbled – usually over trifles – each one looking prettier and prettier the more angry they became, and dear old Pruddy continually trying to pour oil on the turbulent schoolroom waters.

But the temperature was rising, he thought; he recognised the familiar signals; he decided it was time for him to 'do a Pruddy' himself, so he said:

'But seriously, the Duke of Brunswick's advance on the Meuse must surely have convinced those French revolutionaries that they can't win. After all – eighty thousand men, seasoned Austrian and Prussian troops – that's a very formidable army. My guess is, it'll all be over in a few months, and the king of France'll be back on his throne again.'

'Precisely!' the royalist Jeannie agreed. 'The Duke of

Brunswick has specifically stated that he fully intends to restore all King Louis's former powers.'

'Proud words!' murmured Liggett-Fanshawe sceptically, 'I hope he's able to fulfil his intentions. But the French are proud, too, don't forget. And they're obviously very much annoyed by Pitt's stubborn refusal to get involved in the war – so far. Do you know,' the Lieutenant continued, clearly enjoying the role of knowledgeable informant, 'that for years now there have been French agents in this country actively sowing the seeds of revolution. There's a fella by the name o' Chauvelin, a French envoy, who's recently been denounced for fosterin' seditious ideas among members of the Constitutional Clubs – a perfect pest of a man, I tell you. Someone ought to string the fella to a lamp post and give him a good thrashin'.'

'Shades of Lydford,' Ashley thought with a grim smile. He glanced across at Alethea – wondering if she was thinking the same. Fleetingly she returned his gaze – then quickly lowered her eyes.

Throughout dinner the conversation seldom strayed far from the turbulent state of the French nation and the indignities to which its monarchy had been subjected. Every aspect of the developing situation was discussed.

With the *hors d'oeuvre* they recapitulated the *Jeu de Paume* – Mirabeau and the Tennis Court Oath.

The soup was enlivened by the rabble-rousing antics of Camille Desmoulins in the gardens of the Palais Royale, and by the time the *entrée* was served, the Bastille had been stormed!

Ironically, perhaps – if not prophetically – it was while they plunged knife and fork into *Canard à l'orange* – a recipe 'borrowed' by Jeannie from her French cousins – that Lieutenant Liggett-Fanshawe began recounting the almost unbelievable mishaps and frustrations surrounding the escape of the royal family from Paris, and their subsequent attempt to flee the country.

'Caught like sitting ducks at Varennes,' he snorted, elegantly toying with a *haricot vert*. 'And the story going the rounds of the regiment,' he went on maliciously, 'is that it was a detachment of dragoons – French dragoons, of course – that made the initial blunder.'

He glanced at Alethea, to make sure he had her full attention. Then he went on again, 'Apparently, Colonel the Duc de Choiseul was sent with his squadron to meet the royal party at Pont de Sommeville and escort it to a place called Stenay where Bouille and his regiments would be waiting to take them across the border, and to safety.'

'And then what happened?' Jeannie interjected, already getting rather bored with the military details.

'Well, then,' the Lieutenant continued, taking his time and enjoying the sound of his well-modulated voice, 'in an attempt to allay suspicions at Pont de Sommeville, old Choiseul had been putting it about that his dragoons were there merely to protect Bouille's pay wagons. But, of all the stupid things! – the pay wagons had already passed through the town, and the townspeople were well aware of it! Not surprisingly they became a trifle suspicious. In fact, they became so agitated that poor old Choiseul and his squadron had to pull out.'

Dabbing his mouth with the edge of his starched white napkin he paused once again, savouring the impact of his words.

'Well, then,' he continued, 'as everyone knows, the King was recognised at Ste Menehould – despite being disguised as a very portly *Baroness de Korff*. . . .'

'Which, in itself, would have required an ocean of ingenuity!' quipped Jeannie.

'Disguising the King, you mean? Indeed it would!' the Lieutenant agreed, 'and whoever was responsible can't have done it very well. . . .'

'It was Count Fersen, surely?' Alethea interjected.

'Oh, yes. . . .' Jeannie breathed, caressingly, 'Count Fersen . . . *such* a romantic figure!'

'The Queen's lover,' Alethea said bluntly.

'And why not?' Jeannie queried, tartly. 'Married to such a clumsy dolt of a man – albeit a good-natured one – a woman of Queen 'toinette's gay, pleasure-loving personality needs – well, she needs, shall we say, a little diversion,' – she flashed the merest smile, fleetingly, coquettishly, in Ashley's direction – 'an occasional variation on a familiar theme.'

'Far too much "pleasure loving", in my opinion,' Alethea remarked with uncharacteristic asperity. 'Playing at milk-maids during the day-time, and dancing all night!'

'And what would you have her do?' Jeannie taunted, 'Spend the whole day at her lovely little *Petit Trianon*, reading *Du Contrat social*, and thinking pious thoughts about the Rights of Man!'

'At least she might have taken the trouble to find out more about her adopted country and the conditions in which the *canaille*, as I'm sure she calls them, are forced to live,' Alethea retorted.

'But of *course* you can't expect her to know about such mundanities,' Jeannie dismissed, provocatively. 'All her life she's lived in a gilded cage – all those Hapsburgs are the same. . . .'

'And a dreadfully stuffy cage, by all accounts,' Ashley murmured.

'That may well be,' Jeannie conceded, 'but it's the only thing she's ever known, and you can't expect her to act as midwife to all the nation's troubles.'

'Troubles!!' Alethea flashed at her sister, 'You call hunger – stark, gnawing hunger – just "troubles", do you! And I suppose it was entirely understandable that she should suggest to the starving millions that if they had no bread then why didn't they eat cake!'

A natural sense of justice prompted Ashley to demur. 'There's really no evidence that she actually said that, surely?'

Alethea rounded on him, her eyes seething with hostility. It had nothing to do with what he had just said, Ashley recognised; it was what he had done. Her pent-up anger had found its watershed.

'Of *course* she said it! It's absolutely *typical* of her!' she

255

flared. 'She neither knows nor cares what goes on around her so long as she has her play-acting and a never-ending succession of State Balls.'

'They do say she cares overmuch for dancing,' Liggett-Fanshawe interpolated, seeking to ingratiate himself with his new-found love. But then he had to spoil it by adding, with obvious admiration, 'And I understand she displays a very dainty toe in a Gavotte.'

Alethea seized on the reference. 'Well, she'll have very little opportunity to do that *now* – now that they're virtual prisoners in the Tuileries.'

It was the defiant note of satisfaction that puzzled Ashley. Where was the characteristic tolerance, the underlying rivulet of sympathy? Why had she so suddenly turned against the French monarchy – why so enamoured of Rousseau's Ideal State? He had never known her in this vein before. It was as though she had been stung into a burning mood of revolt. Like those revolutionaries in Paris – not sure exactly what it was they wanted but boiling with discontent; storming the hated symbol of monarchical power, the Bastille, and demanding the Governor's head on a pike-staff; metaphorically, Alethea was demanding some-one's head, also.

And Ashley thought he knew whose head it was. His own.

In her eyes he had not just disappointed her, he had failed her. Unlike her more worldly sister who might readily for-give a single indiscretion – because she was able to recog-nise a similar failing in herself – Alethea's threshold of forgiveness, through immaturity as much as natural inclination, precluded any surrender to the sins of the flesh. The Rubicon must not be crossed!

'You were saying, Lieutenant,' Jeannie broke in, reverting to her role as a good hostess, '. . . before we were treated to this lively dissertation . . . you were telling us about that ill-fated flight to Varennes. Pray, continue. . . .'

Once more Liggett-Fanshawe lightly dabbed his mouth with his napkin. He was pleased to be offered the conversa-tional saddle again.

'I was remarking how ineffective must have been the King's disguise as the *Baroness de Korff* because he was recognised at Ste Menehould by the postmaster, named Drouet, who hastily summoned a meeting at the town hall.'

Lieutenant Liggett-Fanshawe of the Light Dragoons paused while the sweet course – pancakes soused in flaming cognac, another 'borrowed' recipe – was served. Then, receiving appropriate encouragement from his hostess, he continued:

'Yes, it was all rather sad, really, because up to that point the escape – organised, as you say,' he smiled approvingly at Alethea, 'by the Swedish gentleman, Count Fersen, Marie Antoinette's most fervent admirer – purely platonic, of course, you understand –' he winked wickedly at Jeannie, '– yes, up to that point the plan had worked reasonably well. I expect you know the story?'

Jeannie did – but seeking to be the perfect hostess she denied anything more than a purely superficial knowledge and invited him to continue.

'I have the story from a fellow dragoon who was out there at the time and who has a close contact with the royal family. As you know, it all happened just over a year ago – on the 20th June to be exact. I remember that date because when my friend told me the story, I thought it so remarkable that I wrote it all down in a notebook – a log book, really, in which I record anything that strikes me as interesting.' He toyed dilettantishly with his pancake; he enjoyed the taste of cognac but eschewed the thicker, more starchy parts of the pancake. 'Apparently, everything went according to plan to begin with,' he went on, having assured himself that he had everyone's full attention, 'Shortly before nine-o-clock in the evening, an ordinary hackney coach drew up in a courtyard near the Tuileries and took its place among other hackneys waiting for hire. But the driver was no ordinary coachman. It was Fersen.

'Inside the palace, the Queen was waking her two children and getting them dressed in the disguises made by their governess, Madame de Tourzel. Then, carrying the little

Dauphin in her arms and followed by her daughter, Madame Royale, and the governess, she led the way down a secret staircase and out into the courtyard where she hoped Fersen was waiting. Panic! For a few awful moments she couldn't see him anywhere.' The Lieutenant histrionically demonstrated the panic. Then asked, 'Am I boring you?'

'No, no,' chorussed Jeannie and her sister – Alethea rather less enthusiastically – 'Please go on.'

'Well, at last Marie Antoinette spotted her paramour . . . yes? . . . no, just her devoted friend. . . . Count Fersen, and together they swiftly and silently bundled the two children and the governess into the coach. Fersen jumped up on to the box, touched up the horses, and this very unusual coachman with his even stranger fare clattered out of the courtyard and into the gathering darkness.'

Lieutenant Liggett-Fanshawe sipped his wine before continuing. 'Back in the Palace once more, Marie Antoinette prepared to go to bed as though nothing unusual was afoot. Deliberate subterfuge, don't y'know. She apparently gave precise orders for the next day, retired to her bedchamber and dismissed her ladies for the night. Likewise the King, having concluded an interview with Lafayette, went off to bed also. You can just picture the scene – candles being extinguished, servants retiring to their quarters, the whole household settling down for the night. So far so good; no one suspected anything.'

The Lieutenant took another sip of wine; he held his audience in the palm of his hand, he felt; he could take his time.

'Presently,' he went on at last, 'the King and Queen were out of bed again, hurriedly donning their disguises, and with Madame Elizabeth, the King's sister, they made their way – separately, so as not to arouse suspicion – to the agreed meeting place with Fersen in the Rue de l'Echelle. Madame Elizabeth arrived first, then the King, but although they waited and waited there was no sign of the Queen. Panic once more! But, at last, she appeared, on the verge of tears, having completely lost her way.'

'Typical,' murmured Alethea. 'Didn't even know her own city!'

'Be quiet, sister,' Jeannie admonished. 'Don't spoil a good story.'

'Truth proving stranger than fiction,' Ashley commented.

'Do go on, Lieutenant,' Jeannie urged.

'Well, at last Fersen had got them all together – the King, the Queen, their two children, the King's sister, and the governess – all in the hackney coach, and it must have been with a big sigh of relief, I suspect, that he set off out of Paris on the long journey to the frontier – and to freedom for the royals.

'But now we come to Fersen's only mistake. Sad, really, because it was a mistake born of love.'

He dabbed with the napkin again – seeking to add suspense to the drama.

'Because of the long journey ahead,' he went on, 'and ever concerned for the comfort of the woman he loved and the exalted position to which she had been born, Fersen had arranged for a big new Berline to be made specially for the journey. It was to be driven out of Paris by his servants earlier in the evening to an agreed meeting point on the road to Meaux. But there was no sign of it when Fersen and his royal fugitives reached the spot. Valuable time was lost searching for the wretched thing, up and down the road, until at last it was found, lanterns extinguished sensibly, but further on down the road. By now Fersen was getting anxious. The first light of dawn was already appearing on the horizon; they were getting badly behind time. But the King could not, and the Queen would not, be hurried; not, that is, if it could be avoided. It was beneath royal dignity – and, in any case, they were now safely out of Paris. Nevertheless, Fersen understood the urgency, and after persuading his royal charges into the shining new coach as quickly as he could, he set off for Bondy where he had arranged for a relay of six horses to be awaiting them. So far, apart from the exasperating delays, nothing had miscarried.'

Liggett-Fanshawe, handsomely uniformed Dragoon officer and *raconteur extraordinaire* sighed dramatically; slowly shook his head. 'But just when these royal fugitives, fleeing for their lives, should have been thundering across France in the fastest vehicle available, taking with them only the barest necessities of life, . . . what were they doing? They were lumbering slowly along in this huge and most conspicuous new Berline piled high with useless royal luggage.'

The raconteur drained his glass. 'The rest of this sad story you probably know. When they finally reached Pont de Sommeville, there was no sign of Choiseul – as I said earlier, Colonel the Duke had been obliged to pull out because the inhabitants were becoming too inquisitive; the royal party had missed him by as little as twenty minutes.

Further on, at Ste Menehould, the King was recognised by the postmaster, who galloped off through the night to raise the alarm, and by the time that lumbering great Berline reached Varennes there was a road-block barring the way!'

'And that was the end of it?' Ashley enquired.

'Absolutely, Penberth. As I've alreay said, caught like sitting ducks.'

'Did they not even try and make a dash for it?'

Again the Lieutenant shook his head, sadly. ' 'Fraid not. I understand though that a Captain Deslons, having left his troop of a hundred men on the far side of the barricade, offered to cut a way out for the fugitives if the King would but give the order.'

'And did he?' Even Alethea was eager to know.

'No, no,' the Lieutenant smirked. 'Poor old Louis! Once again he couldn't make up his mind.'

'And so they dragged him and his family back to Paris,' Jeannie added succinctly, 'and shut them up in the Tuileries. Disgraceful!'

'Oh, I don't know,' Alethea differed, 'I think they *deserved* to be taught a lesson.'

Again, Ashley was surprised by the vehemence with which she spoke. It was so unlike Alethea.

'Rather more than just a lesson!' Jeannie retaliated. 'To restrain a monarch in that way amounts to imprisonment. I don't think the future looks at all promising for them.'

'Oh, nonsense!' Alethea derided, 'You just don't know what you're talking about. Brissot, Vergniaud and all the rest of the Girondins will never let anything happen to the Royal Family – nothing serious, anyway. You know that perfectly well, and cousin Marie says they are becoming more and more powerful. They have very strong humanitarian instincts, and Marie feels certain they will prevail.'

Ashley sensed a renewal of sisterly combat. He decided to head it off by changing the subject. Twirling his wine glass thoughtfully, and looking straight at Liggett-Fanshawe, he commented, dryly, 'I thought you said the blunder was made by that French colonel of dragoons. . . . Colonel, the Duc de Choiseul, wasn't it . . . but surely the main blunder was the choice of that heavy vehicle and the resulting slow progress, and the Colonel could hardly be blamed for that.'

Clearly, the Lieutenant disliked his story being called in question. 'The blunder, my dear Penberth,' he replied, dismissing the interruption with a wave of the hand, 'lay in not ascertaining that the pay wagons had already gone through the town.' Then turning to Jeannie, he observed, 'But I rather agree with your assessment of the French monarchy's prospects. Unpromising, to say the very least. Indeed, I'd not care to be in their dancing slippers, myself.'

'Nonsese!' Alethea exclaimed, 'I think you're all *far* too pessimistic! Jacobins, Girondists, Danton, Robespierre, they're all politicals, and they're all in Paris. Marie says in her letters that in the countryside, especially around Morlaix, near where their chateau is, the people don't concern themselves overmuch with such things. It's Brittany, you see,' she added by way of explanation to the Lieutenant, 'and the Bretons have never really accepted that they're part of France; they resent having to take orders from Paris. So, life goes on as it always has, Marie says, and there's absolutely no talk of war with England, or any nonsense like that. In any event,' she concluded defiantly, 'I shall be able to see for myself when I go over to stay with them, shortly.'

Ashley frowned deeply. 'You're not thinking of going to France now, surely?'

'But of course! Why ever not?' There was cold defiance in her voice. For the first time that evening, she looked straight into his eyes, unwaveringly.

Ashley shook his head. 'Is that wise – at this time, I mean?'

'Yes,' she said flatly. 'I need a change. I need to get right away for a while – to collect my thoughts, and to smooth myself out.'

Again that unflinching, defiant look as she challenged, 'After all, what is there to keep me here? Really nothing – at least, not at the moment.'

Disregarding the thinly disguised censure of himself, Ashley persisted, 'But at this particular time! . . . with all the uncertainty over there!' In his deeply-felt anxiety he even sought confirmation from Liggett-Fanshawe.

With a suitably lugubrious expression, the Lieutenant nodded agreement. 'Positively feel bound to support you, Penberth. Dashed unwise, I do aver.'

But Alethea made light of their fears. There were still many English and Scottish families living in France who had faith in the country's future. The MacKenzies of St. Pol de Leon were among them. Forced to escape from Scotland after the battle of Glenshiel, they had fled to France, eventually finding sanctuary in the picturesque Chateau Fontanelle overlooking the Morlaix estuary and bounded by some of the most productive land in Brittany. They would not be leaving their country homestead, she said – no matter what Messieurs Danton and Robespierre might decree.

'And so,' she concluded, with a laugh as fragile as a piece of bone china, 'if they are not afraid, then why sould I be? Besides, my cousins have been begging me to go and stay with them for a long time, and I don't intend to disappoint them.'

*　　*　　*

262

Half an hour after midnight, Ashley rode out of Trevadne forecourt and headed for home.

But instead of turning right, up to High Cross and the shortest way back to Treworden, he turned left, down towards Porth Navas. He, too, was feeling in the need of time to think – to get the bits and pieces of his soul together, to understand the promptings of his heart.

So, he had decided to ride back the long way round – along by the creek, up through the wooded valley to Bosaneth, and then home across the fields. It would give Puncher the chance to stretch his legs, too.

As he dropped down through the tall trees above Pol-wheveral, he came to the brook where he and Jeannie, both of them at the exciting age of growing physical awareness, had chased and caught a falling leaf; and then, triumphantly clutching their prize, had rolled together in the soft mossy bed of the brookside.

He pulled up for a moment and sat loosely in the saddle, remembering the occasion and listening to the soothing burble of the water trickling over the rocks.

From high up in the trees above him came the melancholy hoot of an owl. It was nothing unusual. On his frequent rides through the night on normal official business, the hooting of an owl had become a welcome sound – a reminder that during his lonely vigil he was not the only living thing still awake.

But tonight, as he sat astride the faithful Puncher in the eerie stillness of Polwheveral woods, that owl seemed to Ashley to be hooting a warning.

CHAPTER TWENTY ONE

A Shot in the Dark

Emerging from his reverie, Ashley set Puncher slowly picking his way down through the trees to Porth Navas. The faithful cob needed no guiding; he could find his way home from almost any point on either side of the Helford river – a comforting thought, Ashley often reflected, for a master liable to be seriously wounded in the course of his official duty.

Moreover it allowed Ashley to immerse himself in his innermost thoughts, as he was now doing, without bothering too much about where he was going.

High above his head the tall trees, their branches grown so thickly together that they almost obscured the three-quarter moon, rustled and whispered mysteriously. All round him the pungency of pine bark, mingled with the first heady scents of wild buddleia, pervaded the cool night air. It was a night of timeless beauty – a moment to search and restore one's soul.

Alethea. He must think about her. She had looked so lovely tonight in her elaborately embroidered, full skirted gown, the dark blue of the silk high-lighting most effectively the colour of her hair. But her manner had been so strange; there had been a totally uncharacteristic stridency in her voice; there had been no tolerance, no forgiveness in her eyes.

That it was all on account of him he had little doubt. The local gossips had been busy-needled in their embroidery of a juicy tale, and Alethea had believed what she heard. Brought up as she had been on the vision of a knight in shining armour, she would find it hard, if not impossible to forgive a fall from grace. Some women were like that. Perhaps not Jeannie – but then Jeannie had been 'baptised' in the sensuous waters of Parisian society. Jeannie would understand – Jeannie would forgive. And Jeannie was so undeniably attractive.

And yet, deep down in the innermost recesses of his natural inclination, Ashley craved the purity of Alethea. Even though the longing for her made him feel both unworthy and, somehow, unclean – he could not deny it. He needed the purifying balm of her approbation, the cleansing dew of her love. Above all, he felt the need to deserve it.

At least he wanted to love and be loved by the Alethea he thought he knew – not the strident, taut-strung apostle of revolutionary vehemence she had sought to portray this evening. That was not the true Alethea; that was not the little girl who had taken his hand and made him sit by her side on that very first occasion of their meeting in the 'schoolroom' at Trevadne; that was not the youthful 'nurse' who had tended him so lovingly after that painful operation on his leg.

This evening they had seen a different Alethea; an Alethea determined to alienate herself from her sister, to uphold the ideology of an Ideal State, and to decry the profligacy of the Bourbon court. It was an Alethea bruised by recent experience but still seeking perfection. And Ashley knew it was all largely his fault.

Or was it? Might it not have something to do with her new found friendship with Liggett-Fanshawe. That she was pretending to be enamoured of him – trying hard to give the appearance of a romance – was, to Ashley, abundantly clear, even though at first the sight of them together had been hurtful. It was her way of giving him a slap in the face – and he couldn't blame her.

But Liggett-Fanshawe! Of all people! To have driven her into the arms of another man – a better man, a socially more acceptable suitor, – though painful would at least have been tolerable. But Liggett-Fanshawe!

And yet, why not? Was he, Ashley, not being over-dramatic about the whole thing? After all, Liggett-Fanshawe had a top class pedigree; indeed, for a daughter of Sir Andrew MacKenzie, he might seem an ideal match. Besides, just because he had displayed all the characteristics of an odious bully in his youth, there was really no reason to assume that he would remain the same all his life. In all probability he had completely grown out of it by now.

All the same, there was something about the man. . . .

These thoughts were interrupted by Puncher suddenly checking in his stride. His head came up, and even in the darkness his leaf-shaped ears, pricked in alertness, were clearly outlined against the moonlit background. His head was turned towards the creek. Ashley listened, but could hear nothing. From long experience, however, he had learnt that Puncher's ears were sharper than his own – and Puncher had never been wrong.

Down there by the creek – possibly on the water of the creek itself – something unusual was afoot. And Puncher had heard it.

Ashley sat for a moment, straining his ears. Nothing. Absolute silence – apart from the gentle stirring of the trees and the occasional scurryings of some small nocturnal animal.

But then he heard it. The rythmical creak of a rowlock, the swish of an oar blade in water.

On a moonlit night – or on any other night – it was a sound to make a Riding Officer's stomach turn over. Inescapably, it was the moment of decision. He could take action, here and now, or he could put spurs to his horse and gallop away as fast as he could in the opposite direction.

'Whereabouts were you, Penberth, at 1.15 a.m. on the morning of so and so' Captain Breward would ask, 'when sixty three ankers of brandy were brought ashore at Porth Navas?'

The answer could be simple as well as truthful, 'Oh, I was a good five miles away, checking the security of our Customs Store up at Gweek.'

Oh, yes, you could do just that; you could say just that. After all, who could blame you. Smugglers were invariably armed; almost certainly you would be heavily outnumbered. What chance would you stand? Many were the instances of Riding Officers being set upon and brutally beaten while trying to seize a cargo of contrband – indeed, only quite recently one of them was overpowered by a gang of ruffians, roped to a rock on the cliffside and left to die of exposure.

So, if you were sensible, you looked the other way – and you would live to sleep comfortably in your bed.

The alternative was less attractive. You could gather up what courage you possessed – and go in and do your duty.

With a 'Tchk, tchk' click of the tongue, Ashley urged Puncher forward, moving slowly down towards the creek. He decided to take the western side of the Trewince arm, to keep Puncher's hoof thuds muffled by the softer turf on that side of the creek, and to make for the cover of Calamansack Wood. From that vantage point he would be able to see what was astir without himself being observed.

By now, the sound of rhythmically dipping oars was becoming increasingly clear; as each pull brought the boat nearer, so the biliary juices in Ashley's stomach tasted more and more unpleasantly sour. A dryness was developing in his throat, too, as he faced up to what had all the makings of an inevitable confrontation.

But as the prow of the vessel appeared round Pedn Billy headland, excitement took over from fear. The adrenalin started to flow.

Expecting to see a small boat pulled by one man, Ashley was suprised to see that it was a two-man gig. This was something new. Hitherto, contraband had almost invariably been brought over from Roscoff in fast-sailing luggers – with a fair wind, it took little more than ten hours – but there had always been the frustrating possibility, especially on a night such as this, of being virtually becalmed in the middle of the English Channel. This could mean the most irritating delay, and the upsetting of pre-arranged plans, and it had recently been rumoured that in order to circumvent this problem – particularly during the summer months – several of the younger and stronger members of 'the trade' had been using gigs to row the goods over.

The rowers were hugging the western shore, taking full advantage of the shadows cast by the tall Calamansack trees, but as the boat passed through a narrow shaft of moonlight, the clearly visible, tell-tale mounds in both bow and stern, although covered by canvas, strongly suggested that contraband was on board.

And beneath those canvas coverings, as well as kegs of brandy and Geneva, there would almost certainly be fire-arms, primed, loaded and ready for use in defence of a valuable cargo.

At first, from the way the boat was coming in, Ashley guessed the intention was either to come all the way up the Trewince arm – Trewince being the probable distribution point for the goods in due course – or to make the landing in the small inlet directly opposite Perran Cove but on the Calamansack side of the creek – for ultimate storage in and around the buildings of Higher Calamansack farm.

In either case, Ashley would be on the same side of the creek as the landing contrabanders and would therefore have no excuse for avoiding a confrontation.

Despite being, strictly speaking, 'off duty', for his evening engagement at Trevadne – although, according to Captain Breward, a Riding Officer was *never* 'off duty' if he happened to come across contraband goods – Ashley never rode anywhere at night unarmed. As was his wont, he had with him tonight the brass-barrelled, Walter's blunderbuss pistol with a spring-operated bayonet which he invariably carried with him in a specially made saddle holster. It was a useful weapon, because although the widening of the barrel towards the muzzle had little effect in spreading the shot, the gun made a deafening noise when fired. In addition, in cavalry-type holsters fixed to the front of the saddle, Ashley always carried a pair of matching flintlock pistols which, when on search duties, he would remove from the saddle and holster at his belt.

And tonight, as on all other evening social occasions, he carried in the pocket of his jacket a little brass-barrelled Twigg pocket pistol with a short triangular bayonet under the barrel.

Each weapon had its special use; the blunderbuss for its frightening effect, the saddle or belt flintlocks for their more deadly aim, and the little pocket pistol with its snap-up bayonet for use in a tight corner.

While he waited to see just where the gig would come ashore, Ashley primed, loaded and rammed each weapon. Because of the time taken to reload, it was important to have each gun ready for immediate use.

Watching the boat glide along the creekside, and steeling himself for the rapidly approaching moment of action, Ashley was surprised to see the vessel swing across towards the opposite bank. Clearly, the smugglers were intending to run the cargo from Perran Cove – probably to be stored in the ancient Chapel of Budockvean. This was an interesting development, Ashley thought – quite apart from the fact that it removed, at least temporarily, the imminence of a bloody engagement. He had not previously thought of that Chapel as being a convenient storehouse for contraband. But when you came to think about it, tucked away as it was so near the water yet sheltering beneath the mantle of ecclesiastical respectability, it could be seen as an ideal location. Well worth a surprise search!

But that had to be for another day. The immediate question was how best to deal with these two contrabanders who were about to land their cargo on the opposite side of the creek in the soft mud of Perran Cove.

The thought flashed across Ashley's mind that it was a heaven-sent opportunity to do nothing; to steal away into the night – no one would know – and creep back to the safety and comfort of a feather bed. He would have every excuse; after all, officially it was not his district – his district was on the far side of the Helford River – and furthermore, he was really off duty. So, yes indeed, there was every reasonable excuse for doing nothing – nothing more than to observe, and then slink away.

There was just one problem. He was paid – pittance though it might be – to uphold the law, to seize smuggled merchandise, and to apprehend the smuggler. True, it was only a little matter of conscience – and there were many who found no difficulty in squaring that! – but for some, just occasionally, it pricked!

And with that dinner conversation still fresh in his memory – the contemptuous sneers of Liggett-Fanshawe, the thinly veiled disapproval and disdain in Alethea's eyes, and . . . and . . . and, yes, the provocative challenge to excel which radiated from Jeannie – with these recollections in his mind, Ashley was in no mood for flight. Besides, the excitement of the chase was already coursing through his veins.

He gently urged Puncher forward a few paces while trying to formulate a plan of action. He pulled up directly opposite Perran Cove.

Already the two men, tired though they must have been after rowing across from Roscoff, were commencing to unload their cargo. If the plan forming in his mind were to succeed, Ashley must act at once. Still seated astride Puncher, he unholstered the blunderbuss, pulled back the flintlock arm to the full-cock position, and then bent forward in the saddle. Puncher, like the good Riding Officer's mount that he was, had been trained by his master not to over-react at the sound of gunfire. But he liked to have warning. And so, with a few whispered words of calm and a friendly pat on the neck, Ashley showed him the gun. Then he pointed the weapon in the air – and fired.

The noise was shattering! – the effects immediate and electrifying! The heads of the two smugglers came up over the gunwale of the gig like rabbits startled in long grass. Like rabbits, too, they appeared to be mesmerised by the sheer unexpected suddenness of the shock. They peered into the darkness – uncertain what to do; whether to remain with their rich pickings, or bolt for safety in the burrow.

Even the well-schooled Puncher shot into the air; began prancing sideways. Calming him, Ashley headed back along the creekside, firing in the direction of the gig but deliberately aiming high, first one of the saddle-holster pistols and then the other, thus sowing in the minds of the smugglers, he hoped, the belief that 'the Revenue men' were out in some force.

It worked. After the third shot, one of the men hoarsely shouted the single word 'Sarchers! – and both of them set off up the path to the Chapel, running for their lives.

That gave Ashley the breathing space he needed. They would be back, he felt certain – re-inforced and ready to fight for their hard won illicit cargo – but it would take time. And when they *did* return, it would be in considerable strength; he would be hopelessly outnumbered, and so he had to work quickly.

Replacing the blunderbuss and the two pistols in their holsters, he then slipped from the saddle. After removing the little Twigg pocket pistol from his jacket pocket, he stuffed it into the top of his breeches. Then he rummaged around in his other pockets until he found what he wanted. Using the saddle flap as a writing surface he scribbled a note on a rough piece of paper and wedged it into the stirrup-leather, under the flap, where he knew Zeph would look for it.

He then took off his jacket, folded it neatly, loosened the saddle girth, and wedged the jacket securely under the saddle. Removing his boots and stockings next, he stuffed the stockings into the boots, and with a piece of cord which he invariably carried in his saddle-bag, he fastened the boots firmly to the saddle itself.

Giving Puncher a resounding slap on the rump, and with a friendly but authoritative 'Home, home, lad,' he sent the faithful cob reluctantly trotting back towards Porth Navas – only to see the horse come to a halt a few yards away, turn, and watch what his master was doing.

But Ashley did not worry. He knew that eventually

Puncher would make his way back to Treworden where Zeph, seeing the boots and jacket, would look for the message.

Treading gingerly over the muddy stones and sharp-edged oyster shells of the creekside, Ashley moved to the water's edge and waded in. As soon as he was knee deep he removed the Twigg flinklock from his breeches top, put it between his teeth, and then, as quietly as possible, melted into the cool waters of the creek.

Swimming like a dog with a stick in its mouth, he was soon across to the other side, placing the flintlock, safe and dry, in the stern of the gig, and then grasping the starboard gunwale.

A couple of powerful heaves – and the boat floated off the soft sand, stern first, and into deeper water.

Swinging the bow round to face the mouth of the creek, Ashley began propelling the boat forward, keeping to the starboard side – the side furthest from Perran Cove – so that he would have the protection of the hull between himself and the retaliation he felt sure would soon come from the enraged smugglers.

It was a wise precaution. He had already reached Pedn Billy, the rocky promontory guarding the entrance to the creek, when he heard running footsteps coming down from the Chapel.

Then, floating across the water, came the voices; 'Well, shit me breeks! But where'm the bloody boat gone?'

'Aw, 'tis they bloody revenue buggers!'

'I know *tha*', you stoopid shitter! But where'm the bo. . . . Aw, there 'tis. There, look. Driftin' towards the river.'

'Yere I say! Her'm not driftin'. Tidn possible. 'Tis agin the tide. Tide's still comin' in.'

'You'm right, Jabe. 'Tis agin the tide.'

'Well, how's her movin' like that, then? Tell me that. There aint no one in the boat . . . at least not so far's I can see.'

' 'Tis they revenue buggers, I reckon.'

272

'Aw, shut up, Zack!'

'But how's her movin' then?'

'Her's bein' pushed, I reckon.'

'Listen! There's someone pushin' her. Swimmin', like. I can hear un.'

' 'Tis they revenue buggers, like I said.'

'Aw, shut up! you stupe!! Yere, Jabe, give the bastards a blast. We'll flush 'em out wi' a bit o' gunshot.'

Jabe required no second invitation. Immediately, a flash of fire, a puff of smoke, a crack reverberating through the trees – and a splinter fizzed from the top of the gunwale.

Ashley kept his head down, and pressed on.

The schooldays accident to his leg had deprived him of the chance to excel at any of the running sports but he had made up for it, at least in part, by becoming an exceptionally strong swimmer. Working on the farm with Zeph, for as far back as he could remember, he had developed tremendously powerful chest and arm muscles, and the fact that one leg happened to be considerably shorter than the other made no difference in the water. He might not be much of a sprinter over land, but in water there were very few who could catch him.

Despite the contra-flow of the tide, he was making good progress, swimming hard with both legs and his right arm while dragging the gig along with his left, and by the time the smuggling party had realised they were about to lose their 'adventure', Ashley was almost out into the main stream of the Helford River. Once there, he knew that the tide would be in his favour, washing him upstream and taking him out of range of the guns.

A further burst of firing greeted him as he swept past the projecting Pedn Billy, but he kept his head well down and the shots thudded harmlessly into the portside timbers of the gig. But then he heard what he had been expecting much sooner, a voice saying:

'Fetch a boat, Jabe. We'll cotch the bloody shitters in the river.'

'Aw, arse,' came the reply, 'but what about the rest of 'em. Where'm they to?'

'They'm hidin', I spec.'

'Aw, shit! Zack. Nebber mind the rest of 'em. Get after that bloody gig!'

But by the time the villains had obeyed their leader's injunction, Ashley was well out into the mainstream of the Helford River. It was now safe for him to climb aboard. As anyone who has tried it will know, to clamber over the side of a craft with a fair depth of freeboard, is not the easiest of tasks, but by using the immense power in his arms to full effect, Ashley was quickly over the side and grasping the oars.

There was little time to lose. While his pursuers would almost certainly have two men pulling an unloaded boat, Ashley must propel, single-handed, a two-man gig weighed down with contraband.

It was not long before he saw that his guess was correct; round the corner of the Calamansack Woods appeared a small craft, pulled by two oarsmen. A third figure could be seen, sitting in the stern. The silhouette of a long-barrelled hunting rifle could just be distinguised slung over his shoulder.

A single shot from that accurate weapon could be enough! – enough to secure for the contrabanders the safety of their cargo; enough to reduce by one the already thinly spread complement of His Majesty's Riding Officers.

But only if the marksman could get within range.

At the moment, Ashley knew he was safe. The distance between the two boats was too great, but unless he could maintain that distance, at least as far as Mawgan Creek, he would become, as Liggett-Fanshawe had described the French King at Varennes, like a sitting duck to be shot at.

And the odds were three against one; two men's strength to pull the hunter's craft, the third ready to take deadly aim.

But they had to catch their quarry first; and the man with the rifle would need to get a very steady sighting down that long barrel. Not an easy shot from a moving boat.

Some comfort there, perhaps – even though it did seem that the hunter's were closing the gap.

By the same strengths of chest, arms and back muscles which made him an unusually powerful swimmer, Ashley was also an exceptionally strong rower. Taught by Zeph Curnow from the very earliest age, there were few only who could now match Ashley as an oarsman. Fate had deprived him of one strength but she had replaced it with another, in abundance.

Added to his natural power and skill with a boat, coupled with a basic determination to survive, there was something else that drove him on. Not the highest of motives, he would have been the first to admit, but a powerful incentive, nevertheless.

At their very first meeting, Breward had told him, in bald-faced fashion, that as a Riding Officer he would be, in his considered opinion, 'no bloody good' at the job.

Now Ashley Penberth was a Cornishman, through and through, and for a Cornishman to be told by an up-country upstart that he was 'no bloody good' was an insult hard to bear. By nature an easy-going person, Ashley had been stung, like it or not, by this derogatory appraisal of his ability. Normally slow to anger, there had been fermenting in his soul a deep-seated loathing for this man, Breward. It would not be putting it too strongly, regrettable though it might be, to say that he seethed with an unavenged hatred of the man.

That the true story of the 'affair' at *The Three Tuns*, St. Keverne, had reflected no glory upon himself, Ashley readily admitted – the fact that the Packet Captains had apparently persuaded Breward otherwise was nothing but a monumental joke, an example of how those influential burgesses enjoyed displaying their contempt for official-dom – and ever since then Ashley had been actively seeking a chance to prove Breward wrong.

The feeling of hatred for Breward, reprehensible though it may seem to those who regard such an emotion as being purely destructive, was at least part of the driving force which now kept Ashley pulling so powerfully on the oars. If he could but remain beyond the range of that hunting rifle, and stay alive – undoubtedly the most urgent incentive – he could make an official seizure of contraband, and by so doing, throw Breward's condemnation in his face!

Whoever dares suggest that revenge is not sweet!

Ashley ground his teeth, determined to succeed. The gig, though relatively light in weight, was proving a hard pull; easy, perhaps for two men rhythmically propelling the craft without hurry. But loaded up with kegs of liquor it was a hand-blistering task for a single pair of oars.

And was he holding his own against his pursuers? In the semi-darkness it was difficult to judge. Already well past Groyne Point, and now leaving Tremayne quay away on the port side, he would soon be approaching the entrance to Mawgan Creek. Another moment of decision loomed. If the gap was gradually being closed by his pursuers, his best chance of survival would be to abandon the gig at the Bishop's Quay and seek sanctuary within the walls of Saint Martin's Nunnery. But that would mean surrendering his hard won prize.

Like most criminals, the smugglers had made one mistake. Almost certainly they would have caught their prey had they left the third man – the one with the rifle – on shore. His weight in the stern of the boat was making the crucial difference between success and failure. They had brought him along to do the shooting – just one shot – if not to kill, then at least to wing the fleeing bird. But so far they had not been able to get near enough to allow him a really close shot. They would have done better to leave him and his weight behind – and taken on the wildfowling themselves.

Although it was some reassurance to hear them cursing and swearing to this effect – the oarsmen blaming the marksman for his weight, the marksman blaming the oarsmen for not rowing hard enough – it was no comfort to Ashley to see that the first streaks of dawn were already piercing the eastern sky. It was getting lighter by the moment. And although it was still dark enough to make taking aim a difficult task, nevertheless Ashley hugged the shadows of Bonallack Wood for as long as he could. Eventually he must emerge into the unshadowed stretch of water preceding Constantine Quay and the final run up to Gweek, and it was there that he would present the clearest target for his assailants.

It would be their last chance of success. They had already come further upstream than expected; they would surely never risk coming within gunshot range of the Custom House store on the quayside.

As both boats emerged into the clearer light – the fugitive so near to his refuge, the hunters so close to their kill – Ashley was alarmed, despite having expected it, to see the marksman raise his rifle and draw a bead on his target.

Fleetingly, Ashley contemplated slithering to the bottom of the boat, out of the marksman's sights; taking cover behind the mound of kegs in the stern.

No sooner had the thought occurred than it was banished. It would mean surrender. The marksman, temporarily losing sight of his victim, would merely lower his rifle – and wait. The oarsmen would then overtake the gig at their leisure. There they would find His Majesty's Riding Officer cowering behind their own contraband. A most ignoble end.

No, no. His only chance still lay in flight. Keep going. Keep out of range. Hands blistered and bleeding, arms, back and leg muscles crying out with the pain of his exertions, nevertheless he must keep on rowing – harder, harder, harder! – no matter what the physical cost.

Through the mist of sweat pouring into his eyes, he watched the marksman take steady aim. . . .

CHAPTER TWENTY TWO

Touché

Zeph Curnow swung one leg over the side of the bed, and yawned. It was getting light. The birds were in full chorus. Time to get up.

He swung the other leg out, and stretched. It was an unwise movement. Almost immediately he was seized with an excruciatingly painful spasm of cramp in his left leg. It lasted for what seemed an eternity. Then, mercifully, as it always does, the agony began very slowly to subside.

Exhausted by the sheer effort of withstanding the pain, he lay back on the feather mattress, panting.

'Gettin' old, I 'spose,' he muttered disgustedly. 'That be what tez – gettin' old!'

His wife lying beside him, her face more than ever like a polished russet apple but now shining beneath untidy wisps of greying hair, put out a hand from under the warmth of the coarse woollen blanket, and patted her husband. It soothed him. Not that anything known to man or beast can alleviate the breath-seizing agony of a really bad cramp, but it's a comfort to know that someone is at hand. At least, it was to Zeph Curnow. Among the many 'blessings of this life' for which he gave 'most humble and hearty thanks' to his Maker as he knelt each Sunday evening in Mawnan Church, the first in order of precedence in his mind was undoubtedly his wife – except, that is, on those occasions long ago when they'd been having an argument.

Too often in those days, she felt, he would absent himself from the connubial feathered bliss for several nights on end, and although she had been under the strictest instructions to inform any nosey enquirer that he had merely 'gone a-fishin' ', she knew perfectly well that he and his revered 'Mester', the late Mr Amos Penberth, had really 'gone a-smugglin' ', instead.

They'd had arguments about it. She'd said that no good would come of it. And on such occasions she had inevitably come rather lower down the order of precedence in Zeph Curnow's prayers.

But, of course, she had been proved right; sadly right. And as a result, ever since then – almost without exception – she had regained her pre-eminent situation at the forefront of her husband's thanksgivings. From that sad day forth Zephaniah Curnow had given up smuggling.

That is not to say, however, that there were not times when he missed it – missed that special excitement on a moonlit night of stealing silently into a secluded cove, running the precious 'moonshine' ashore, loading it on to the backs of the waiting ponies to be taken upalong the narrow track to *The Red Lion Inn* at Mawnan. And doing it all under the very noses of the Preventatives!

Now, as he lay back on the bed, regaining his breath and recovering from the exhaustion of cramp, his thoughts went back to that last ill-fated return trip from Roscoff all those years ago: the excitement of the chase when they were picked up by that revenue cruiser and the 'Mester' decided to make a run for it, through the Manacles. And how the gamble had so nearly paid off! They had come through the narrow, dangerous channel between the Manacle rocks and Manacle Point, apparently quite safely, and the dreaded Carn Dhu rocks were already slipping astern when the 'Mester' decided to go about and make for the open sea. And then it had all gone wrong. The arms of the rudder had sheared, and almost simultaneously the whole rudder blade had broken away.

Involuntarily, Zeph closed his eyes, trying to blot out the memory; the fighting for his life in those pounding waves, the miracle of his survival, the awesome task of telling his employer's wife that she had become a widow. And then the birth of her baby son: the boy, now grown to full manhood, who in order that Zeph might remain undisturbed on the land at Treworden, had taken employment with those very same Preventatives whom his father had so delighted in bamboozling.

As he lay there now, massaging the still painful muscles in his thigh, an unusual, unexpected sound filtered through the early morning chorus of the birds. Hoof beats! Coming nearer.

Gingerly he raised himself again to a sitting position on the edge of the bed.

'Sounds mighty like our Puncher,' he said, turning to his still snoozing wife.

'An' what of it?' she observed sleepily. 'Mester do often-times come home at strange hours.'

Zeph's face screwed itself up like a crushed lobster pot. 'Somethin's different, too,' he murmured. 'Tedn soundin' like it should.'

Gripping his so recently contorted thigh, he hobbled across the bare-boarded floor to the tiny window over-looking the yard, and peered out.

'Well, blister m'tripes!' he exclaimed. ' 'Tis Puncher sure 'nough. But nobbidy ridin' un! An' Mester's boots a-danglin' from the saddle!'

Zeph's wife sat up with a jerk. 'Nobody ridin' un!' she repeated, coming wide awake. 'Where be Mester to, then?'

Zeph was already pulling his farm smock over his night-shirt; struggling into his boots. 'I dunno,' he said, with urgency, 'Us must find out!'

He clattered down the steep, narrow staircase, leaving his wife pulling on her day clothes. Out in the yard, Puncher was whinnying plaintively; pounding the cobbles. Zeph caught hold of the loose reins and began stroking the velvet of the cob's nose, soothing him. But Puncher would have none of it. He kept swinging his head round towards the saddle, jingling his bit, scuffing the cobbles with the hoof of his left hand leg.

Seeing the jacket under the saddle, it took only seconds

for Zeph to interpret the message, and while an upstairs window of the farmhouse was being flung open for Marianne to call out, 'What is it, Zeph? What's the matter with Puncher?' Zeph had found the piece of paper under the saddle flap.

Now, Zeph was no scholar – never had a day's schooling in his life. But he understood pictures, and could recognise certain place names. Ashley knew this: also, that when it came to using his wits, Zeph was as sharp as a needle.

On the scrap of rough paper Ashley had hurriedly sketched a long barrelled flintlock rifle with an unusual-looking trigger guard. Below that he had written just two words:- 'Gweek C.H. – HURRY!'

'Aw, ais. 'Tis the Fergie he'm wantin',' Zeph murmured to himself, ' 'tis the Fergie, all right.'

By now he had been joined in the yard by both his wife and his employer – his wife fully dressed, the Mistress still in her night robes with a shawl thrown round her shoulders.

'What is it, Zeph? What does it say?' Marianne asked, taking the scrap of paper and peering at it in the pale dawn light. 'And what's this gun for? Why the gun? He's been up at Trevadne – a dinner party – surely they're not going off on a shooting expedition, or something! Not at this time of the morning, surely! Duck shooting at Gweek, could it be?'

Zeph scratched his head. 'I'm sure I don't know, Mestress, – 'cept I do know he'm wantin' the Fergie.'

'The Ferguson rifle, you mean,' Marianne interpreted, 'the one on the wall in the kitchen?'

'That be the one, Mestress,' Zeph nodded, 'and ee wants un quickish, if I understand un aright. But what be they figures alongside the Gweek bit, do ee think, mmm?'

Marianne looked again. 'C.H. . . .' she murmured, looking at Zeph's wife for inspiration, then 'C. . . . Oh, no! Customs House! That's what it stands for.' Her hand flew to her mouth. 'Oh, dear! That means trouble. And 'HURRY'! Oh, my!' Then, quickly recovering, she went on, 'Down to Gweek, then, Zeph – as fast as you can go.'

'Will ee fetch the Fergie, Mestress, or shall. . . .' Zeph queried. But before the words were out of his mouth, his wife was hurrying towards the farmhouse kitchen, 'I'll fetch un,' she said, obviously glad to be doing something positive.

Drawing her shawl more closely around her shoulders, Marianne watched Zeph remove the blunderbuss from the saddle holster. With mounting alarm she heard him murmur, 'Aw, ais. Her's bin fired, all right. 'Tis business Mester Ashley's been about, then.' Hobbling back into his cottage, he muttered, 'Get me powder, a minute, an' reload. Her might come in handy, again.'

Emerging with his powder flask at the same time as his wife brought out the rifle from the farmhouse kitchen, Zeph began priming the blunderbuss.

'Why should he need the rifle as well as that noisy thing?' Marianne asked anxiously, 'Surely he can't be caught up in a battle!'

Zeph shook his head. 'I'm sure I don't know, mmm. But there's one thing I can tell ee, that there Fergie, she'm a mighty akkerit weapon. Her's quick for the re-loadin', see – an' if anythin' come in Mester Ashley's sights when he've got that gun in his hands, well. . . .'

The sentence remained unfinished, but the implication was clear.

With a remarkably agile spring, Zeph leaped up on to Puncher's back, and gathering the reins into his powerful, rough-skinned hands, he looked down, first at his patient, long-suffering little wife, and then at Marianne. Seeing the look of intense anxiety on her face, he said in that old, reassuring way of his, 'Don't ee worrit yersel, Mestress. I'll bring un back all right – like I allus used to.'

He dug his heels into Puncher's flanks, and clattered out of the yard.

The smile on the rubicund face behind the desk in the Collector's outer office stretched from ear to ear. Had it not been for the limitations of facial anatomy, it would probably have stretched even further. Mattie Reynolds was hugely amused.

And it was all because of little Lowdy Pascoe.

'Mister de Wynn's lady wife's been ill, see,' Lowdy was saying, 'and so Mr de Wynn called in at th' apothecary's this morning an' asked Mr Wilson to make un up a potion, like. But just when Mr de Wynn was goin' out to collect the medicine, who should come in for their mornin' coffee an' gossip but the three Packet Cap'ns that Mr de Wynn likes to serve, hisself. An' then, of course, they gets talkin', see, an' Mr de Wynn, he don't like to miss any o' the goin's on, like, 'cause he thinks he might miss a bit o' scandal.'

'Yes, that's right, Lowdy,' Mattie put in, just to let the girl get her breath, 'that'll be Cap'n McKinley, Cap'n Shoemaker and Cap'n Smithson, I 'spect.'

Lowdy shook her head. 'Not Cap'n Smithson,' she corrected, 'Cap'n Pickersgill.' Then went on eagerly, 'Well, Mr de Wynn, he waited an' waited, an' all the time them Captains was talkin' and talkin', an' Mr de Wynn, he couldn' seem able to drag hisself away. So, in the end, seein' that me an' Ruby wasn't busy, he tells me to go along to th' apothecary an' fetch the potion for un.'

Mattie grinned encouragingly, sensing that more was to come. 'So that's how you managed to slip out for a while.'

Lowdy swallowed and nodded at the same time. 'Tha's right. But I just had to come along an' tell ee, 'cause you know what, the Packet gentlemen have been talkin' about your Mr Penberth.' The mere pronouncing of Ashley's name caused a blush of colour on Lowdy's impish face.

'Oh, yes,' Mattie grinned, 'and what've they bin sayin', Lowdy?'

' 'Tis ever so excitin', Mr Reynolds,' Lowdy enthused, 'an' I ain't too sure o' the rights o' it, mind, but it do seem that our Mister. . . . I mean *your* Mister Penberth, he've taken a prize, or somethin' . . . upturned some smugglers, it seems . . . over on the Helford like. An' there was some shootin', so they say . . . an' ever so many tubs o' brandy, I think 'twas, locked up at Gweek.'

Mattie's eyebrows almost went off the top of his forehead. 'Our Mr Penberth, you say?'

Lowdy giggled again, and blushed. 'Ruby an' me, we think he'm ever so hanzum. Don't ee agree, Mr Reynolds?'

'Why, yes,' Mattie nodded proudly, 'very fine genelman, Mr Penberth. But what about this seizure, then, Lowdy? Tell me about that.'

'Well, the best bit is,' Lowdy continued, hugging the apothecary's potion to her chest, 'while them Cap'ns was tellin' about it – they seem to get the news of everythin' afore the rest of us – well while them was tellin' how Mister Penberth had foxed they villains – an' Ruby an' me thinks we knows who they be – while they was tellin', like, who should come in an' join 'em but your Cap'n Breward!'

'And what did *he* say?' Mattie enquired.

'Oh, he were *de*lighted,' Lowdy glowed, 'Said he'd always knowed what a good officer Mr Penberth'd make. Had a fair pile to do with appointin' him, or somethin', so he said. Mind you, Mr Reynolds,' Lowdy cautioned, 'them Packet Captains wasn't all that pleased! Ruby an' me could tell that, an' no mistakin' – even tho' they was pretendin' to be on the side of the law, like. O' course, they always do – 'specially when that Captain Breward's anywhere abouts.'

Mattie laughed. 'Oh, yes, indeed! They like to be thought respectable citizens – very much so – when it suits 'em.'

Lowdy gazed, unseeingly, out of the Customs House window. A dreamy look clouded her eyes, as she said, 'Ooh, but your Mr Penberth, Mr Reynolds! Oo-ooh! But he'm so hanzum, so strong! Why, Ruby an' me,' she giggled coyly, 'we wouldn't mind if he. . . .'

Mattie leaned across the desk and tried to give her a smack on the bottom. He missed – but grinning broadly, he said, 'Never you mind about that, then, my girl. You'd best be cuttin' along – or you'll have Mr de Wynn after you.'

And then as the pert little figure minced out of the room,

he added, 'But thanks for lookin' in, Lowdy.'

He was still grinning when, a few moments later, Captain Breward burst through the outer office like a gale of wind, demanding, 'Tell Penberth I want to see him as soon as he comes in.' He then kicked open the door of his own office, slamming it loudly behind him.'

But Mattie Reynolds was not dismayed. The Captain *always* came in like a strong sou'westerly, and he *always* kicked open his office door. It did not necessarily mean that Ashley – or anyone else, for that matter – was in for a wigging.

And when, for the first time ever, he heard the Captain whistling a cheerful tune, Mattie felt doubly reassured.

'Mornin', Mr Penberth,' he was saying brightly when shortly afterwards, Ashley came in. 'Not a bad day for the time o' year, I suppose – might be better, might be worse,' was the familiar greeting, but then he added, 'Oh, and – er – the Captain's wantin' to see you as soon as you comes in, sir.'

Ashley nodded rather wearily. 'Same as usual, I suppose.'

Mattie's broadest grin returned. 'Well, no sir. Not quite the same as usual, this mornin', sir. I think you may be findin' the Captain in quite a good mood today. Somethin' to do with a handsome seizure last night, would it be, sir?' he twinkled.

Ashley regarded the Collector's clerk – the only man in H.M. Customs he really liked – with a look of good-humoured surprise. 'So the news has reached you already, has it?'

But before Mattie could reply, the Collector's voice bawling 'R E Y N O L D S!' shattered the calm. Mattie stumped over to the Collector's door and opened it. 'Did you call, sir?'

'Of course I bloody well called! What's the matter with you, man?' Breward snorted. 'Are you deaf as well as crippled!?'

'No, sir,' replied Mattie, with unquenchable cheerfulness, 'I came as quick as I could, sir.'

'Well, has that bloody . . .' Breward checked himself, ill-humouredly, 'Has Penberth come in yet?'

'Yes, sir. He's just this minute stepped in.'

'Well, I thought I told you to send him in to me as soon as he arrived!' Breward said petulantly.

'He's only just this very minute come in, sir,' Mattie replied stubbornly.

'I know, I know! You've already *said* that!' Breward barked, and before Mattie had time to turn on the wooden stump of his left leg, the Collector was sneering, 'Well, come on, man! Don't stand there, gaping! Send the bloody Riding Officer in!'

Mattie began to wonder whether perhaps he'd misinterpreted that cheerful whistling, and he flashed a warning look of surprise at Ashley as he went past him into the Collector's office.

Of even greater surprise to Ashley was the sudden change in Breward's tone as soon as the door was closed.

'Quite a handy little skirmish you had last night, I hear,' he began, motioning Ashley to the only arm-chair in the room – the one normally offered solely to those he regarded as important, 'and once again, all on your own, too!'

The lard-face dripped with unaccustomed benevolence; the spectre was quite unnerving. 'Tell me about it, Penberth,' Breward purred. 'Tell me about it.'

Recovering from the sudden and unwonted display of bonhomie, Ashley described the events of the night. 'It was really quite simple, as a matter of·fact. I heard the tell-tale sounds of activity down in Porth Navas Creek, and curiosity got the better of me . . .'

'You were responding to the call of duty, of course. Very praiseworthy,' Breward put in.

Ashley let that go without comment, preferring not to disclose that he was returning from a dinner party at Trevadne, but went on, 'These two rascals had obviously rowed across either from Roscoff or one of the Channel Islands, in a gig well laden with contraband. . . .'

'And you quite properly seized the cargo, eh?' Breward

leaned back in his chair; clasped his hands behind his head; regarded his junior narrowly.

'That was the problem,' Ashley continued. 'It was a two to one situation for a start, with the probability of re-inforcement on their side once the shooting began. So, I decided to stay on my side of the creek but to try to give the impression that there were at least three of us they'd have to contend with.'

Breward nodded sagely, clearly wishing to indicate the understanding and approval of a born strategist. 'Good thinking, Penberth. Yes, good thinking. And what next?'

'Well, first of all I let fly with the blunderbuss I always carry,' Ashley explained, 'and as you know it's a shattering sound at any time, but it seems even louder in the middle of the night and when totally unexpected.'

Breward's eyes narrowed even further. Ashley felt them boring into him. 'Go on,' Breward said. 'What then?'

'Well, as I say, to give the impression we were out in some force, I fired off my two saddle holster pistols from different places along the creek. That really did send them racing up the combe – for reinforcements, I felt sure. So, I only had a limited time to get hold of the gig.'

By now, Breward was unashamedly interested. 'And how did you do that? The boat was on the other side of the creek, wasn't it?'

'Nothing for it – I just had to swim across and grab hold of it.'

'You're a strong swimmer, I presume?' Breward quizzed.

'Fortunately, yes,' Ashley nodded. 'Not much good over land – but satisfactory in or on the water.'

Breward's face became a pious blank, deliberately registering nothing at this brief reference to Ashley's physical shortcoming. He merely uttered a clipped, 'And what then?'

'Luckily I managed to drag the boat out into the main-stream of the Helford, where the tide was in flood,' Ashley explained, 'and as soon as I felt beyond their range, I clambered aboard and rowed for my life!'

'They were shooting at you?' Breward asked.

Ashley nodded. 'Oh, yes, they took a few pot shots while I was still within range.'

'That's important,' Breward snapped. 'As you know, shooting at a revenue officer is a *hanging* offence. Remember that. If we can catch the bastards, we can string 'em up!'

A rueful smile crept over Ashley's face. 'Yes, they certainly had a go at me! But as I made sure I had the hull of the gig between me and their guns, the shooting was mostly ineffective – although the larboard side of the boat took a few splinters!'

Thereafter, in response to a bombardment of questions, Ashley described the subsequent race up the Helford River, and the successful landing of the contraband goods at the Gweek storehouse.

'You managed to shake them off, then?' Breward asked.

Ashley grinned wryly. 'We frightened 'em off, really.'

'We?' Breward queried. 'Who else was with you?'

'Zeph Curnow,' Ashley informed. 'He's our farm manager at Treworden. Yes, it was really Zeph Curnow and the Ferguson rifle that did it. . . .'

'The Ferguson rifle!' Breward barked. 'How in Hell did that come into it?'

'That was the lucky stroke,' Ashley went on. 'I got a message up to Zeph to meet me at Gweek, and to bring the Ferguson – it's a breech-loading rifle given to me a few years ago by Sir Andrew MacKenzie, a neighbour and very good friend of ours, up at Trevadne – and by the time I finally made the port of Gweek, Zeph had raced down on Puncher, and was awaiting me behind the parapet of the bridge. And, my word, but how glad I was to see him!'

Breward, whose mouth had dropped open at the mention of 'farm manager' and friendship with Sir Andrew MacKenzie, suddenly sat bolt-upright and asked:

'But what about the Ferguson rifle?'

'As you may know,' Ashley began, 'the Ferguson rifle is capable of firing. . . .'

'I know, I know!' Breward interrupted, testily, 'it has a firing capacity of four shots a minute, demonstrated years ago to those blockheads at Army H.Q. by Captain Ferguson, himself – and in the most atrocious conditions of wind and rain, mark you – yet those stupid warlords only agreed to the formation of a 100-man unit, commanded by Ferguson, to be sent out to our American colony in '77.'

The former Captain of Foot paused to dab his mouth with a folded handkerchief. Then, fixing Ashley with a menacing stare, he went on;

'I tell you, I saw them!' he thundered, 'I was *there*! The very first time they went into action was at Brandywine. And I was there. Down that hill they marched, firing as they went – four bloody shots a minute! Never before seen anything like it! By God, but it made the rest of us seem like 16th century arquebusiers!'

Wagging an admonitory finger at his junior officer, Captain Breward continued, 'I tell you, Penberth, if every regiment of Foot lined up at the top of Osbourne's Hill had been armed with Ferguson rifles, we'd have finished off the war that very same day! There we were, the flower of the British army, with Washington's rag-tag troops – the rabble in arms, they called 'em – down there at the bottom of the hill. . . .'

Ashley settled back, prepared for another long exposition of the battle of Brandywine Creek. 'The Brandywine bore in full swing yet again!' the Packet Captains would have said.

But, in fact, Breward stopped short of another full account of the famous battle. Instead, and to his credit, he seemed to realise that this, though trivial by comparison, was someone else's moment of triumph.

He looked straight at Ashley, and said, 'You did well, Penberth – to effect a seizure of that cargo, I mean. Yes, you acquitted yourself commendably.' He tried hard to screw his lard-face into the semblance of a smile.

Ashley nodded his appreciation – remained seated, wondering whether the interview was over, or whether there would be some sting in the tail. Breward picked up a piece of paper from his desk and began reading it. Eventually, he looked up, saying 'That will be all, Penberth. You may stand down now.'

Mattie Reynolds was studiously engaged at his desk, pretending to be hard at work, too busy to have been listening, when Ashley emerged from the Collector's office. But his great liking for 'young Mr Penberth' got the better of him, and when he looked up at Ashley the very warmest of smiles was illuminating his round, enthusiastic little face.

'Beg pardon, Mr Penberth,' he began, respectfully, 'an' I hopes you don't think it wrong of me – but I couldn't help hearin' a bit o' what the Captain's bin sayin'. . . .'

Ashley opened his eyes wide – gave Mattie an admonishing wag of the finger – then smiled understanding encouragement.

'Well, sir,' Mattie went on, 'I couldn't help rememberin' what the Captain says to you when you came for your first interview. . . .'

'About me being no bloody good as a Riding Officer, you mean?'

'That's it, sir. That's just what he did say. I remember it as if it was only yesterday. 'No bloody good!' that's what 'e says, 'No bloody good at all', 'e says, if you'll pardon my language, sir. An' when I gets home that night, I says to the missus, 'That Mister Breward!', I says. . . .' Mattie checked himself. 'Well, never mind about that now, sir,' he went on. 'But I can't 'elp sayin' but 'ow glad I am to think you've certainly made 'im in there,' he jerked his head disparagingly in the direction of the Collector's office, 'bloomin' well eat 'is words for 'is dinner.'

Ashley laughed out loud. 'Yes, you're right, there, I reckon, Mattie,' he agreed, giving him a friendly dig in the ribs. 'Let's see, now – what's the word they use – 'Touché', isn't it? Yes, I think that would be appropriate.'

Mattie grinned broadly, furiously nodding his head. He wasn't too sure what the word meant, but it didn't really matter because as 'young Mr Penberth' went out into the morning sunshine, Mattie heard him whistling a cheerful tune.

Yes, he had a great liking for Mr Penberth. He was glad he'd made the Collector eat his words.

But '*Touché*' – now that was a funny word, wasn't it? Ah well, you never knew what you could pick up with a bit o' schoolin', did you?

CHAPTER TWENTY THREE

A Dark Encounter

When Ashley set out for Helston several weeks later the sky was heavily overcast, and there was a hint of mizzle in the air. It had turned much colder.

Captain Breward had laid it down very firmly that fellow Riding Officers must keep in touch with each other; from time to time they must be seen riding the district together – especially if any 'rough stuff' was in the offing.

Accordingly every Tuesday evening Ashley would ride to *The Angel* at Helston to meet Nathaniel Woodstock for a tankard of ale and an exchange of news.

Now Nat Woodstock could hardly be described as everyone's idea of a zealous Customs Officer. Indeed, had not Breward himself described Woodstock as 'no bloody good, either', which, together with Ashley Penberth, made two of a kind, and had he not gone on to suggest that Woodstock was 'hand-in-glove' with the Mullion smugglers?

While it was perfectly true that Nat would never be guilty of over-exertion on behalf of His Majesty's Revenue, he nevertheless had his good points. For one thing, he was dependable – even if the only thing you could depend on was that he would be late for an appointment. But he would undoubtedly arrive in the end. Just when your patience had frayed to the point of combustion, he would come rumbling in, rhythmically swaying from side to side, his battered tricorn set rakishly over one eye, and looking, for all the world, like some great galleon in full sail, but with its Royals and Topgallants somehow caught up in the shrouds.

In short, Nat Woodstock was an amiable giant – a bit over-fond of a drop o' best cognac and a game of back-gammon in the *Kiddleywink*, perhaps, but a likeable character for all that.

On arrival at *The Angel*, therefore, Ashley was in no great hurry. He knew Nat would not be waiting. Having seen to Puncher's nosebag, he was groping his way across the cobbled yard towards the side entrance to the inn when a hooded figure glided from the shadow of the ancient hotel wall. He felt a touch on his sleeve. Instinctively he drew back, feeling for his pistol – at the same time peering through the murky gloom, trying to see who it was. But the face, deeply shadowed within the hooded cloak, was unidentifiable.

Then came the voice, low-pitched, melodious and faintly provocative, whispering, 'Hullo!' The one word was enough. Immediately, Ashley recognised the voice of Rose Roskruge.

'Good God! Rosie!' he exclaimed in astonishment, 'What the devil are you. . . .'

'Ssssh!' Rosie hissed. 'Keep your voice down – and no names or places, please!'

'Why, what's this all about?'

'Listen!' she went on, drawing him into the deep shadow of the wall, 'I had to see you. It's urgent.'

Wild thoughts began racing through Ashley's mind. What did she have to see him about – why so secret, why so urgent? Nearly three months had gone by since the night of the fire. He had not seen her in the meantime, deliberately steering well clear of St. Keverne – if for no other reason than to save them both from embarrassment.

But now, suddenly, his spirits plummeted. The worst had occurred. She was about to inform him that she was preg-nant. That single night at *The Three Tuns Inn* – when know-ingly he had allowed himself to be beguiled, not only from the paths of righteousness but also from the lonely road of duty – had been enough. What else could it be?

And the irony was that he could remember so little

293

about it. If he had begotten the child now developing in Rose's womb, he had only a hazy recollection of the moment when the seed had been planted. All he could now vaguely recall was a semi-besotted vision of Rose pulling her dress over her head, and standing before him in nothing but her black stockings, purple garters and scant chemise – and then there came the warmth of her body against his.

It would be almost, if not quite, true to say that like the biblical character, Lot, hiding in that mountain cave above Zoar and made helplessly drunk by a virginal daughter intent on preserving her father's seed, 'he perceived not when she lay down, nor when she arose'. But unlike Lot, he had been aroused from his blissful slumbers by an agitated Rose, clutching her dress against her bosom, and shouting 'Fire!' The room had been rapidly filling with smoke; the noise and heat of the crackling, blazing thatch roof had been terrifying.

It had seemed like the vengeance of God!

Strangely, though, in that twinkling of an eye when past, present and future all seem distilled into one fleeting moment of the mind's awareness, he felt no shame at the recollection of that night.

If what he now suspected Rose had come to tell him were true, everything in his life henceforward would be different. Friendship with the MacKenzie family, including of course his long-cherished romance with Alethea, would cool to the point of freezing; his mother would be bitterly disappointed; in all probability he, himself, would be condemned to spend the rest of his working life in a job he had come to detest, merely to support the mother of his child.

Yet, surprisingly, after the initial momentary shock of contemplation, he found that none of this seemed to him to matter. Instead of feeling annoyed, frustrated – cheated, even – as so many others had in similar circumstances, he experienced only a deep sense of wonder that within the complex structure of Rose's physically desirable body there should now be growing a part of himself.

The only cause for sadness – at least so far as he was

concerned – lay in the fact that when in due course the child did arrive – Rose's child, his child – he would have so little remembrance of the moment of its begetting.

He turned to Rose; took her arm, and feeling an involuntary shiver pass through her, he said gently,

'It's really rather cold out here, Rosie. Let us go into the hotel where it's warm.'

To his great surprise she took a quick step away, disengaging her arm. 'Oh, no!' she burst out. 'I daren't be seen in there with you!'

'Why not?'

'You don't understand,' she whispered urgently. 'It's the Sithney gang.'

'The Sithney gang!' Ashley echoed incredulously. 'Are you telling me it's not. . . .'

'Oh, yes it is,' Rose interrupted, misunderstanding the unfinished question, 'it's the Sithney gang, for certain – and they'd be slittin' my throat from ear to ear if they saw me tellin' you.'

'But . . . telling me what?'

'Here – come over here a minute.' She pulled him into the darkest shadow. 'Now listen,' she continued, keeping her voice down but speaking rapidly. 'There's a large ship – a brig, I believe she is – on her way up from Portugal, or Spain, or somewhere, and she'm loaded with a fair cargo of wines and oranges and valuable jewellery, 'tis believed. The word is that she'm in trouble of some kind, and she'm aimin' to put in to Falmouth for repairs, see. She'm a lame dog, like, and she'm tryin' to limp back to a kennel, if you understand.'

Ashley grunted acknowledgement. He understood well enough. Vivid projections were already racing across the screen of his mind, as Rose continued.

' 'Tis the Sithney gang'll be there for certain, and you know what they'm like, I 'spec. 'Tis they you should be after – not honest traders like we.'

Ashley chuckled inwardly – a moment of light relief in a challenging situation – as much for the realisation that he was not about to become a reluctant father as for Rose's comic idea of 'honest trading'. Honest indeed! Thousands of barrels of contraband liquour brought ashore each year without so much as a penny piece of duty being paid. And yet, they were honest enough in their own eyes – merely performing a necessary and compassionate service to the community. The fact that King George was deprived of the revenue wherewith to pay for a Royal Navy to protect our shores, or an army to repel invaders – such as those Spaniards who landed at Mousehole in 1595 and burnt the church at Paul – oh well, that was really none of their business. That was a matter for politicians – 'not for the likes of we', and Ashley was amused how the urgency of her message had caused Rose to slip back into the local vernacular.

But, mention of the Sithney gang; *that* was different. They were wreckers.

Ever since that day up on the North coast, when he and his school friend, Johnny Innes, had stood helplessly by while a ship's captain and crew were bludgeoned to death, Ashley's hatred of wreckers had grown with a festering intensity. He longed for a chance to do something about it; to hit it, and to hit it hard!

Now, as he spoke, his voice reflected the cold, implacable determination stirring within him.

'What about the Sithney gang, then, Rosie?'

'Why, that be just what I come into Helston for to tell ee,' she hissed back, impatiently. 'I knew you'd be here to meet your friend. So, as soon's I got wind of it, I jumps on my little Belle an' I comes ridin' in as fast's I could.' She paused for a second to catch her breath. At the same time she drew Ashley closer before continuing. 'Listen. Unless I be very much mistaken, they'll be down there with the lamp and mule – on the track along the cliff-top 'tween Chyvarloe and Chyanvounder – know where I mean?'

Ashley murmured agreement.

'Well, then,' Rose went on, lowering her voice still further, 'they'll be aimin' to draw that ship on to the rocks down under Halzephron Cliff – Hell's Cliff, that is – you know where?'

A sudden thrill of excitement mixed with fear went juddering down Ashley's spine. He recognised the moment; real action this time. The longed for chance to strike at those cowards and villains who, for the sake of an anker of spirits or a bale of silk, would batter an exhausted sailor to death. No time to lose; no time to wait for Nathaniel Woodstock – even though his assistance would be valuable.

'Thanks, Rosie,' he growled. 'Thanks for telling me. Must go at once. Not a moment to lose.'

Rose gripped his arm, detaining him. 'Don't ee go lettin' on 'twas I that told ee, mind,' she pleaded, 'or it'll be *my* dead body you'll see floatin' in the sea at P'roustock.'

Ashley drew her towards him, his face very close to hers. 'If any of those bastards so much as lays a finger on you, Rosie,' he hissed, 'I swear, before God, I'll have his guts laid out on the fish quay before morning!'

In the darkness and with the warmth of his breath still fresh on her cheek, Rose smiled. She had always regarded her Riding Officer, Ashley Penberth, as one of the 'gentlemanly sort'. She had never before heard him swear quite like that. She rather like it.

But before she could utter another word, he was gone – disappearing into the stable. Moments later he was clattering past her, out of the cobbled yard and turning left down Coinagehall Street.

There hadn't even been time to wish him 'Good Luck'. She felt cheated.

Then she had an idea.

At the bottom of the hill, just before the lane branches off to Porthleven, Ashley recognised the rotund outline of Nathaniel Woodstock slowly ambling towards their rendezvous. The sheer size of the man seemed to dwarf the willing cob between his knees. As usual, his hat was well down over one eye, and he was singing. Clearly he had been visiting one of his well-stocked cronies.

'How do, my friend,' he greeted, in his warm, drowsy

voice. 'And how fares Mester Ashley Penberth this night, eh?'

'Listen, Nat,' Ashley replied, pulling an already excited Puncher to a halt, 'I've just had a tip-off about the Sithney gang.'

'Oh, ye-es,' Woodstock purred, with maddening slowness, 'a tip-off about the Sithney gang, eh?'

'It's a chance to catch 'em red-handed.'

'Oh, ye-es,' Woodstock produced a silver flask from his coat pocket. 'Up to their old tricks again, eh?' He slowly unscrewed the cap and put the spout to his lips.

'We'll have to move fast if we're to catch 'em,' Ashley urged, 'They'll be down at Gunwalloe already, I expect – working some devilish trick with their lamp.'

'Down at Gunwalloe, eh,' Woodstock murmured comfortably. 'Ah, ye-es.' He took another long swig before adding, with irritating deliberation, 'And what would their interest be down there, then?'

'A Portugese brig with a rich cargo. In trouble somewhere out in the Bay – trying to make Falmouth. But those devils'll have her on the Halsferran rocks unless we hurry.'

'Ah, ye-es.' Woodstock smoothed, 'I daresay they will. But there'll be time for a nip before we go, I 'spec.' He proferred the flask, hospitably.

'We really haven't a moment to lose, Nat,' Ashley replied, declining the offer, 'we may already be too late.'

Even Puncher seemed to sense his master's impatience; he began pawing the flinty track and prancing.

But nothing had ever been known to hurry Nathaniel Woodstock. He took another sip from the flask before adding yet one more long-drawn-out, 'Ye-es.' Then he tipped the tricorn on to the back of his head, saying, 'And what shall we two be doing agin a gang of murderers, I wonder?'

'Well, at least we can have a try,' Ashley parried, indignantly. 'We can't just sit here doing nothing.'

Woodstock shifted in the saddle, making himself more comfortable. 'Hmm. . . . Ye-es,' he temporised, 'ye-es.'

298

Ashley could stand it no longer. The long-awaited chance to avenge the butchery which, as a boy, he had witnessed up on the Trebarwith coast was slipping away in a stream of procrastination. With or without Woodstock's assistance he must act at once.

'Listen, Nat,' he blurted impatiently, 'are you willing to help? – or am I to tackle them alone?'

'Oh, I'll help ee, lad. You may be sure o' that,' came the warm, cosy, unhurried reply. 'Oh, ye-es, I'd not leave ee to face 'em on your own. Oh, no.' He took another swig, making up his mind, before declaring, 'I'll tell ee what I'll do. I'll go up round the top side o' Loe Pool and then come at 'em from the far side – up there by the Halzephron Inn. Know where I mean? I'll be there to cut 'em off if they try to escape that way.'

It was not the help Ashley hoped for. But it was better than nothing – always assuming his fellow Riding Officer got beyond the *Halzephron Inn*!

Thankful to be free at last from this unprofitable encounter, Ashley set off at speed along the rough, flinty track bordering the Loe Pool. He had been going no more than a few minutes when he heard hoof-beats following. Assuming that Nat Woodstock, having changed his plan, had decided to join him now, Ashley pulled Puncher to a halt, and twisting round in the saddle he expected the familiar lolling, sack-like figure beneath a lop-sided tricorn hat to emerge from the darkness. Instead, a small hooded figure astride a fast-moving little mare came galloping up.

From within the folds of her hood, Rose's voice was unmistakeable. 'Oh, my!' she exclaimed breathlessly, reining up alongside Ashley, 'but I'm mighty glad I caught up with you.'

Ashley held the rein of her mare while she caught her breath. He was glad to see her – in spite of himself.

'What is it?' he asked. 'Have you heard something?'

'No – I haven't heard anythin' new', she panted. 'But you didn't ought to be goin' after they on your own. They'm mighty dangerous.'

299

'It's all right. Woodstock, a fellow Riding Officer has joined me.'

Rose looked round. 'But where's he to, then? I don't see un.'

'He's off up round by Berepper to Halzephron. He'll cut 'em off if they try to escape that way.'

'But that still leaves you on your own, though. That's what I thought. That's why I'm comin' too.'

'You'll do no such thing!' Ashley growled, 'It's far too dangerous. You know, yourself, what a bloodthirsty gang of criminals they are!'

'But I have my little Muley flintlock,' she countered, 'I never ride without un. I can take care of myself, I'm sure of that. Besides. . . .'

Ashley fumed inwardly. Having just endured, with rapidly diminishing patience, the profoundly irritating slowness of Nathaniel Woodstock, he was in no mood for further delay. Every moment lost could be crucial. And it was so like a woman, he thought, to imagine that a little pocket pistol would be of the slightest use against a hell-bent gang of wreckers.

'Besides what?' he asked, irritably.

'Well, what I really come to say is . . . what about the Dragoons down here at Penrose? I thought they was supposed to be helpin' you.'

'They are!' Ashley retorted, 'And that's exactly where I'm going!' He dug his heels into Puncher's flanks, thankful to be on the move again at last. Over his shoulder he flung the grudging invitation, 'Come on, then – if you must. Let's see if we can flush them out.'

Relief, mingled with fear as well as excitement flooded through Rose as she set the willing little Belle in pursuit of Puncher's flying hooves. Riding Officer Penberth – her Riding Officer – had agreed to let her come with him. They were in a dangerous undertaking together; emotionally, perhaps, it might prove a watershed for them both. She wondered.

Racing along the track through the Loe Valley, with

Puncher's iron-shod hooves flashing trail-blazing sparks from the flinty surface, Rose began counting the cost of her involvement in this enterprise. From hearsay only did she know the activities of wreckers. That they were desperate men, greed-ridden, pitiless, and living forever within the grim shadow of the hangman's noose, she could well believe; that some of them became rich from their murderous trade she had heard. But to her knowledge she had never before come face to face with any of them. Now, it seemed, she was about to do so. She might even be killed! They would certainly show no mercy to an interfering woman!

Or would they? Might they not prefer to spare her; keep her for themselves, as a sexual plaything with whom to slake their filthy lust. A chilling prospect indeed!

But it was too late to dwell on such possibilities now. Ever since the debacle at *The Three Tuns Inn*, St. Keverne, she had sought a means of restoring the natural pride of her Riding Officer – of reinstating him, as she thought in the eyes of his superiors after that fall from grace. At least, that's what she had persuaded herself – and no matter what other successes he might have achieved, or might lie in the future, this she regarded as her great chance to prove to him that she was more than just a smuggler's decoy.

As they emerged from the dense woodland bordering the Loe Pool, the lights of Penrose Manor came into view, and having leapt the narrow stream bisecting the parkland, they rode up to the imposing main entrance.

Throwing Puncher's reins to Rose as he dismounted, Ashley hurried to the front door and rapped loudly.

Presently – but too tardily to satisfy Ashley's impatience – a shaft of light streamed out across the forecourt as the great oak door was swung open by an orderly.

After a few moments parley, Ashley disappeared inside.

CHAPTER TWENTY FOUR

Retribution

Cornet Rushford bounded into the room to which Ashley had been shown by the orderly. He looked even younger than at the Lanteague Ball. His boyish cheeks shone like burnished apples; his clear blue eyes positively sparkled with enthusiasm. Clearly, he was enormously proud of being commissioned in His Majesty's Light Dragoons.

Yes, he confirmed, Lieutenant Liggett-Fanshawe was the officer-in-command of the detachment, but unfortunately, just at the moment, the Lieutenant was not available. He did not say 'Off Duty' – just 'not available' – and when a crescendo of lewd girlish giggles wafted down from an upstairs direction, Cornet Rushford covered his confusion by blushingly offering his own services in the Lieutenant's stead.

'Actually,' he volunteered, with engaging eagerness, 'I'm second-in-command, you see, and whenever the Lieutenant is – er – otherwise engaged, I automatically take charge.'

Why, yes, most certainly – he would be only too pleased to support His Majesty's Riding Officer in dealing with a gang of wreckers. After all, what were his troopers there for if not to help in this way. Indeed, after months of inactivity, Cornet Rushford was absolutely itching for action of any kind. Within a very short time, he assured Ashley, he could have a party of dragoons mustered, and he would readily lead them in a sweep along the whole of the Porthleven Sands – and further, if necessary. They would be available for action whenever and wherever the Riding Officer required.

'Excellent,' Ashley applauded. 'As quickly as possible, please.'

It was a profound stroke of luck, Ashley concluded, as he rejoined Rose in the forecourt of the Manor, that Liggett-Fanshawe was so audibly absorbed with a local trollop. It would keep him well out of the way during the hazardous task ahead. Schoolboy impressions die hard and, ever since that first torrid encounter in the dormitory of Lydford College, the mere mention of the name Fanshawe had tolled in Ashley's mind a bell or warning. He not only disliked the man, he also held him in deep-seated distrust.

With Cornet Rushford, it was quite different; instinctively he trusted him. His youthful enthusiasm was infectious; he was the kind of young man who, no matter how many times you pushed his head under water, would invariably come up smiling.

'Yes, they're coming,' Ashley reported to Rose, as he climbed back into the saddle, 'but it'll take time. You know what the army are; turn up in perfect order, but half an hour too late!'

Gathering the reins into his hands, and with a muttered, 'Can't hang around till they're ready – must get on and see what's happening,' he urged the already prancing Puncher straight into a gallop.

Renewed contact with Liggett-Fanshawe – even though only by proxy – had brought Alethea back into Ashley's mind. True she was seldom far from his thoughts over the years, but especially just recently. During the lonely hours of riding the coast he had got into the habit of communing with her; every romantic poem, every love-song he had ever learned he would sing or recite to her as he and Puncher kept nightly vigil along the coastal paths. For as long as he could remember, she had been at the very core of his existence.

But ever since that night of the fire at *The Three Tuns Inn*, which had provided the scandal-mongers with such delightfully incandescent fuel, there had descended between them a seemingly impenetrable mist. He had tried to get through to her, but she had seen to it that they were never alone together.

At first, she had made it clear that she was not averse to

the increasing attentiveness of Lieutenant Liggett-Fanshawe – and it had hurt. If that had been her intention, then Ashley had to admit she had succeeded. How can you stand by and watch childhood affection, which has grown into adult love, disappear before your very eyes without feeling the mangle-twist in your heart.

And then, in defiance of everyone – including Liggett-Fanshawe – she had gone over to Brittany, to stay with her cousins near Morlaix.

But, as he thundered along the flinty path skirting the western shore of Loe Pool, Ashley wondered just what Alethea would think of her Lieutenant of Dragoons at this moment. Those girlish giggles from an upstairs room at Penrose would hardly be music to her ears, he guessed.

No sooner the thought, however, than it was banished. Matters far sterner than a harlot's giggles lay ahead. He must concentrate.

The wind, little more than a zephyr during the early part of the day, had been increasing strongly throughout the evening, and by the time Ashley and Rose reached the sands of Loe Bar, massive breakers were already pounding the shelving beach. At first, in the gloom of a moonless night and against the gusts of spindrift swept on-shore by a rising Sou'westerly, he could see nothing of particular consequence. Then he spotted her – the tall masts and spars of a brig, darkly outlined against the dull grey of the western sky. She did not appear to be in any great difficulty, and yet the course she was steering could not possibly take her clear of the Lizard. She was heading, as Rosie had correctly surmised, straight for the rocks below Halzephron – or 'Hell's Cliff', as it was more generally known.

'And I think I know why,' Ashley growled, '– and not a moment to lose.' Spurring Puncher straight into a gallop, and with Rose following bravely in his wake, he set off along the top edge of the beach. After a few hundred yards, he pulled up again.

'There it is, look!' he shouted, as Rose came up abreast, 'Just as I expected. Can you see it?'

Following the direction of his outstretched arm, Rose spotted it at once. There, on the faraway cliff-top, a light gleamed out into the darkness. For several moments Ashley sat slouched in the saddle, staring at the light. Then, half turning to Rose, he said, 'Do you see what I see?'

'Yes,' she replied slowly, 'I think I do.' Her voice was trembling slightly – a mixture of excitement and fear. 'It's moving, isn't it?'

'Exactly! And it's got to be stopped! And,' he went on, restraining an equally excited Puncher, 'this I'm afraid is where we must part company. Stay here, Rose,' he commanded. 'Keep well out of range. This could be quite nasty.'

Urging Puncher into a gallop once more, he sped off in the direction of the moving lamp. If the in-coming ship was to be saved, that deadly, misguiding beacon must be extinguished at once. It might be too late. But he must try.

Racing along the beach, he eventually came to a slight cleft in the cliffside where Puncher, exerting every ounce of strength in his powerful hindquarters, was able to scramble up on to the track running along the clifftop. It was the track, Ashley knew, which would bring him face to face with the ruthless criminal moving that lamp. As he rode he eased a pistol from its holster.

He had got within fifty yards of the lamp before the villain heard him. He was a short, wiry little man leading a donkey with a heavy lantern strapped to the pack-saddle, and as soon as he saw a uniformed Riding Officer bearing down on him he abandoned the donkey and raced back along the cliff-top path, uttering a long-drawn-out bloodcurdling scream of warning to the gang on the rocks below.

Sensing that at long last a real chase was on, Puncher responded by almost flying over the sandy turf in pursuit. As horse and rider came abreast of the fleeing lamp-man, Ashley threw himself out of the saddle, straight on to the man's back, bearing him to the ground. He knew he must collar the fugitive at the first attempt; a limping Riding Officer would be no match for a speedy little villain running for his life.

Ashley caught him round the neck, and as they rolled on

305

the ground, struggling and fighting perilously near to the cliff's edge, he saw that the man had extracted a vicious-looking butcher's knife from his belt. Even now it was poised above Ashley's left shoulder, seconds away from being plunged deep into his back. Just in time Ashley caught the man's wrist; and drawing on every reserve of strength in his arm he dug his finger nails into the flesh. For what seemed a long time they lay writhing, panting, struggling – the knife only inches away from its target; one care-less move, one unfortunate roll in the wrong direction, and the deed would be accomplished. But then, gradually, Ashley felt resistance waning until, eventually, the knife fell from the would-be murderer's grasp.

Puncher meanwhile, having obediently pulled up when Ashley left the saddle, was plunging and whinnying in an effort to help his master. He grew even more excited as his sharp ears picked up the sound of other hoof-beats approaching. Throwing up his head, he bounded off, only to return a few moments later, bucking and prancing in front of an almost equally excited Belle and Ashley saw that Rose, with great presence of mind, had captured the fright-ened donkey with its iniquitous pack-saddle lamp.

By now Ashley had the squirming, foul-smelling body of the lamp-man firmly under his knee, and he was just consid-ering how best to restrain this member of the gang when he saw Rose slip from her saddle and unhook the length of rope which Ashley always carried beneath his off-side saddle-flap.

'Good girl!' he breathed appreciatively, forcing the man's wrists together behind his back, 'Now tie him up good and tight.'

With remarkable speed and facility, and without saying a word, Rose proceeded to truss the man up like a roast-ready chicken. So thorough was her work that Ashley, rising at last from the inert but still blaspheming figure, chuckled with undisguised relief.

'Well done, my lovely,' he praised, brushing his hands together to rid them of sand and soil. 'We'll have no more

306

trouble from that little monkey, I fancy.' The chase, and subsequent desperate fight had stimulated the adrenalin; he felt supremely alive, ready to tackle the rest of the gang.

'Put out the lamp,' he shouted, one foot in the stirrup.

'I can't,' Rose replied, 'I've tried. I can't open the lantern.'

Ashley moved quickly across to the donkey, wrenched the lantern from the pack-saddle and smashed it on the ground, grinding it into the sand with the heel of his boot.

'There!' he grunted, 'that piece of vile equipment will never be used again.' He returned to Puncher's side once more.

'But look!' Rose shouted, pointing seawards, 'She's bein' driven on. We're too late.'

From the trussed-up, malodorous bundle at her feet came an echoing cackle. 'Hee, hee. You'm too late. I thought ee would be. 'Twas us that did un.' His voice rose to a triumphant scream. 'You'm too late!'

As if to underline the horrible truth of his words, maniacal shouts of delight could be heard coming up from the rocks below. Truly, irreversibly, the noble ship was being driven to her death – and the vultures were screeching for their pickings.

'Too late to save the ship,' Ashley growled, swinging back up into the saddle, 'but maybe not too late to save the crew.'

Before Rose could even try to deter him, Ashley had thundered off in the direction of the now inevitable wreck; and even as he rode, the ship was seen to give an ominous lurch. Moments later, it was clear she had struck.

Like a reverse migration of rats, from shore to sinking ship, the wreckers were already crawling over rocks, vying with each other to be first at the stricken vessel. It was a sickening sight – so sickening, in fact, that it had Ashley out of the saddle and scrambling down the cliffside in a cold, implacable fury. He was limping across the sand in pursuit when he heard Rose's voice screaming above the wind. 'Come back, Ashley. Come back! You'll be killed. You can do nothing on your own. Oh, for God's sake – come back!'

He knew she was right. The sensible thing was to await the arrival of the Dragoons. But the sight of those vicious wreckers swarming over the rail of that innocent vessel, the subsequent cries of pain and pathetic appeals for mercy blown on the wind from ship to shore – it was all more than he could abide. Once before, with Johnny Innes at his side, he had been forced to accept the prudent course and stand idly by. But not this time.

Brandishing a pistol in one hand he slithered across the seaweed-strewn rocks and grabbed a grapnel line left dangling over the ship's side by the wreckers. They were far too absorbed in their work of destruction to notice him clambering aboard, but when, in accordance with official procedure and in an attempt to prevent unnecessary bloodshed, he jumped on to a wooden crate, firing his pistol in the air and shouting, 'In the name of the King! I arrest you!', he was greeted by those who heard him with a gale of cynical laughter. It was neither more nor less than he expected; at least it gave the devils a chance to save their necks. Henceforward, any fatalities would go down in the records as 'Shot or killed while resisting arrest.'

But the ruffians had no thoughts for such legal niceties. Like snarling wolves they prowled the decks, pillaging the stranded brig from stem to stern – hacking at crates, filling their pockets with spilled doubloons, broaching casks and swilling the liquor – plundering anything and everything of value, and ruthlessly clubbing down any man fearless enough to stand in their way.

Although few of the crew would have understood Ashley's rallying shout of 'Keep at it, lads! Help's on the way!' the mere sight of a uniformed Customs Officer brandishing pistol and cutlass seemed to put fresh heart in them. From then on they began to make a fight of it.

The ship's Master, a swarthy Portugese, seemed to be holding his own fairly well until an horrific blow from a bearded giant wielding a nail-spiked cudgel dashed the sword from the skipper's hand. The wrecker's features curled into a devilish grin as he moved in for the kill.

Like a flash of lightning, and flailing his cutlass with a terrifying ferocity, Ashley leapt to the skipper's defence. 'Fight on, my friend!' he bellowed above the roar of the sea, 'There's . . . (slash). . . more help . . .(lunge). . . . Soldiers . . . (parry) . . . are on . . . (thrust) . . . the way!'

Taken by surprise, the bearded wrecker momentarily backed away – time enough for the skipper to regain his sword, time enough also for a grizzled crewman to join in the defence of his Master.

Using every fencing skill he had ever learned, and with an increasingly determined skipper and crewman at his side, Ashley succeeded in manoevring the three of them to a position with their backs to the starboard rail. At least they were now safe from attack in the rear.

But the wreckers began massing in a hideously threatening half-circle in front of them – cursing, swearing, flailing their spiked bludgeons, lunging with swords. One of them, recognising Ashley from a previous encounter, shouted, 'It's the lame bastard from Falmouth. Kill 'im, Jabe! Kill the bloody whelp!'

Another voice, further off, bellowed, 'Never mind 'bout they, you slimey shits! Get that stuff overboard!'

Someone else shouted, 'Hurry! They'm a' comin'.'

The warning had no effect on the gang half-circling Ashley. They surged forward, intent on one thing only – murder. The blood of a Customs man, a King's officer, a hated 'sarcher'; they were not to be deprived! And in the ensuing melee a flailing cudgel, with a sickening thud, found its mark. The grey-haired crewman crumpled like a sack. The murderer, eyes blazing with fury at having missed his intended victim, swung again; at the very last moment, Ashley dodged sideways; the bludgeon, its rusted spikes aimed at Ashley's head, crashed into the woodwork of the ship's side, embedding itself in the rail. The ruffian came on, knife drawn, gibbering with rage. Denied his victim at the first attempt, he was determined now to plunge the blade of his weapon deep into the Riding Officer's throat – to finish him off once and for all.

But as the murderous villain surged forward he tripped over the prostrate body of the crewman – and stumbled – right on to the point of Ashley's cutlass. Blood spurted – and gripping his belly, the man staggered; collapsed in a heap on the deck.

The sight of their confederate writhing at their feet so inflamed the rest of the gang that they came at Ashley and the ship's Master with such incensed fury, whirling their spiked bludgeons, thrusting and smashing with swords and staves, that Ashley knew he could not last much longer. Already his arms were feeling like lead, his knees sagging, his spirit slowly, remorselessly being drained. Another sickening thud beside him, and the ship's captain slumped.

Now he was alone. In a moment all those snarling faces would converge; in one headlong rush they would come at him; their concerted power must prevail. He would be battered to death where he stood – fighting, kicking, flailing to the end, but finally overcome – just like that innocent skipper up at Trebarwith Strand.

Convinced that his life could now be measured in seconds rather than minutes, he decided to make one last supreme effort to break out of the encircling gang. He would fight on till he dropped; he would *never* give in to these criminals.

And then, as he summoned the last dregs of resistance, there fell upon his ears a sound far sweeter than the softest melody – the single note of a bugle. The Dragoons! At last!

'Fight on, Ashley Penberth,' a voice said inside his head, 'Fight on!' – and the last drop of adrenalin flowed. Power from on High!

But the gang went berserk; their booty threatened, their very lives at risk. And as the Troopers, led by Cornet Rushford, began swarming over the side, a maddened wrecker came at Ashley like a fiend out of Hell. Nothing would deprive him of his victim now, and he managed to sink the rusty spike of his cudgel deep into Ashley's shoulder.

It must be the end, Ashley thought; he had no strength remaining. Slowly, his knees gave way, he slithered to the deck; and lying in a pool of his own blood, he watched his assailant spitted on Cornet Rushford's sword.

When he came to again, he found himself lying in the soft sand of Gunwalloe Cove, his head cradled in Rose's lap. Cornet Rushford was kneeling beside him, smiling.

'Well, sir,' the Cornet observed, his smile broadening ever wider, 'it seems we just got here in time. A few more minutes, and we'd have been hanging up those riding boots of yours for good!' He pulled a silver flask from his coat pocket and put it to Ashley's lips. 'Here, sir. Try a sip of this. Finest French brandy, sir,' he assured, before adding with an enormous, boyish wink, 'Duty Paid, of course!'

Ashley thankfully sipped the proferred cognac – duty paid or not he was far too exhausted to care – and as he returned the flask to the solicitous Rushford, his eyes focussed on a pair of black leather riding boots just beyond the Cornet's smiling face. Above them, the white kerseymere breeches, the silver-braided blue uniform jacket, and then the handsome face with its supercilious expression.

'Egad, Penberth;' the Lieutenant drawled, 'but you really mustn't go puttin' yourself at risk like that. Why, I do declare, these rascally fellas damned nearly had you!'

Typical Liggett-Fanshawe, Ashley reflected ruefully; fashioning a miraculous appearance to lead his troops – when all the danger had been removed by his subordinate, but just in time to take the credit.

'Good huntin', Rushford,' the Lieutenant patronised. 'You had a good run for your money, I do aver, but you bagged your fox in the end. Good huntin', Rushford; good huntin', I say.'

The Lieutenant leisurely surveyed the group of surly wreckers now rounded up by the Dragoons and about to be marched off to captivity while awaiting trial. 'I tell you, Rushford,' he continued, 'these fellas are gettin' too damned revolutionary for my approval. Pickin' up ideas from those accursed Frenchies, I wouldn't wonder.' He glanced down at the wounded Ashley. 'Positively uncivil, those Frenchies, eh Penberth? Dashed uncivil, what? – choppin' off the heads of all those aristos. Wouldn't care to be in Paris, meself, just now. Distinctly unsociable, I do declare. Moreover. . . .' He fixed Ashley with a quizzical look, 'none too healthy for the MacKenzie filly, I'd wager, what!'

Ashley struggled to raise himself on to one elbow, the spectre of Alethea in France – in danger – flashing across his mind. 'Why . . .? What's been happening?'

'Egad, but have you not heard?' The Lieutenant's voice was affectedly casual, 'Thousands of aristocrats, priests and royalists – including some English people, so they say – dragged from filthy prisons all over Paris, and butchered in the streets – and all because they refused to sign some rotten oath, or something. Rather a grisly business, don't y'know. I understand they're already calling it 'The September Massacres'. Positively uncivil, I'd call it.'

He scuffed the sand with one elegant boot. Then he turned on his heel, and stalked away.

CHAPTER TWENTY FIVE

Though the Mills of God grind slowly

The Assize building looked cold and forbidding. Even in the winter sunshine it glowered.

Inside the entrance hall small groups of litigants, shifting uneasily from one foot to the other, tried to make seemingly carefree conversation. Court officials went about their business with an air of lofty disdain. Prosecuting and defending Counsel, resplendent in wig and gown, majestically held court among anxious clients. Summoned jurors circulated aimlessly, not knowing what was expected of them but determined to conceal their ignorance.

Over in the corner by the window, Ashley stood between a remarkably calm Rose Roskruge and a fidgeting Captain Breward. A few paces away, in haughty isolation and with a shaft of sunshine glinting on their silver-laced uniforms, stood Lieutenant Liggett-Fanshawe and Cornet Rushford. While Rushford's face bore its usual ruddy, enthusiastic expression, Liggett-Fanshawe's was totally drained of colour. It was abundantly clear that the Lieutenant was deeply apprehensive. Ironic, to say the least, Ashley thought, that both the hero of Brandywine Creek and the dashing Lieutenant of Dragoons were clearly frightened by an English court of law.

And it was no idle thought, either, because when Mr Neville Muncaster, Counsel briefed by the Crown to conduct the case against the wreckers, came across to discuss procedure with his principal witnesses, both Captain Breward and Lieutenant Liggett-Fanshawe hastened to make it absolutely clear that although they were the senior officers, they were merely present as observers. Most emphatically, they were not available to be put in the witness box – indeed, they both had most pressing 'other official commitments' during the day which would render full-time court attendance quite out of the question. Moreover, Captain Breward contrived to convey – without actually saying so – that it would really be most inappropriate, on the grounds of rank and importance, for a Collector of Customs to give evidence in a sordid little case of wrecking.

Crown Counsel listened, but with an increasingly acid expression staining his rubicund features. During the ensuing silence he treated Captain Breward to a long, penetrating appraisal. He liked not what he beheld. The man was probably an upstart, he decided; quite brave with a weapon in his hand and a well-defined objective, but expose him to the rapier thrusts of cross-examination, and almost certainly he would crumble.

No, he would be useless as a witness – paralytically nervous – more a liability than an asset. Neville Muncaster dismissed Captain Breward with the merest flick of his little finger.

Then he turned to Liggett-Fanshawe. 'Similar,' he concluded; except that the Dragoon officer was undoubtedly of better breeding, and certainly more personable. But, so far as the case was concerned, they were both quite useless. Defence Counsel, Box-Johnson, would tie them up in knots. Far better to be without them altogether. He bestowed a withering glance upon Liggett-Fanshawe while dismissing him with equivalent disdain.

Thankful to be relieved of the frightening prospect of the witness box, the two senior officers lost no time in taking their departure. They had fulfilled the minimum requirements of their office – to attend the court with their juniors, and to be on hand in case prosecuting counsel should seek guidance on Customs regulations or military procedures – but now that they had both been so succinctly dismissed, neither felt in the least bit inclined to risk being recalled. They could not put too great a distance between themselves and the Assize court.

Prosecuting counsel, Mr Neville Muncaster, flicked the tyes of his wig free from the collar of his frock and then focussed his attention on the three witnesses left standing in front of him. He liked what he saw. Long years of professional experience at the bar had given him a sixth sense where witnesses were concerned. 'Can smell 'em a mile off,' he liked to boast to his juniors in chambers. 'Good, bad or indifferent – can smell 'em a mile off!'

But in this particular instance the use of his prominent, up-tilted nose was not necessary. His eyes told him all he needed to know. The square-set jaw, the rugged features tanned by constant exposure to sea wind, the powerful arms and shoulders of the Riding Officer, his principal witness, reassured him. A countryman, through and through, he would say – unlikely to be rattled in the 'box'. And the young Cornet of Dragoons; fresh-faced, bounding with enthusiasm – you could tell that just from the movement of his eyes – possibly a little too exuberant, perhaps, might have to be kept in check, but sound enough.

And as for the girl! Those eyes! That springy black hair popping out so prettily from beneath her 'Milkmaid' style hat worn over an undercap and tied beneath her dimpled chin! That milk-white complexion; those soft cheeks now showing just the faintest flush of anxiety! That figure!

Mr Muncaster, barrister-at-law, ran his tongue appreciatively over his full-fleshed lower lip. What wouldn't he give to be defending the lass on a capital charge! More pertinent still – what wouldn't he give to be *successfully* defending her. . . . Might not then her gratitude be truly *overwhelming*! – and how *little* would he mind being *overwhelmed*!

Counsel for the defence checked his thoughts, peremptorily. They were running away with him! But it *was* proving extremely difficult to drag his eyes away from his female witness. It was hard to believe she really was only a barmaid in an out-of-the-way Cornish tavern. But then, life was full of surprises these days.

One of them was undoubtedly the fact that the six

shabbily-clothed prisoners now arraigned had been able to retain a King's Counsel to defend them. It was well known that some gangs of wreckers occasionally made sizeable fortunes out of their pickings, but Mr Henry Box-Johnson, K.C., leading for the defence, could hardly be expected to accept a brief at only a modest fee. Or, could he? Was there not a rumour that this highly successful 'silk' had recently acquired a small estate near Fowey – in order to be near his paramour, so they said – and as a result was particularly interested in creating a legal reputation for himself in this remote corner of the circuit. The more briefs he could obtain in the West Country, the more often he could be away from his chambers in London. . . .

Whatever the motive, the fact remained that one of the most debonair and successful advocates in criminal law had agreed to defend a bunch of illiterate Cornish villains against charges of wrecking and murder. Perhaps he just welcomed the challenge – or was there some other, more sinister reason. Was he acting out of sympathy with the wreckers? – or was he beholden to someone richer and more powerful who pulled the puppet-strings!?

No matter what the answer, Neville George Muncaster, barrister-at-law, and now retained by the Crown, recognised that he would have a first class fight on his hands.

It was while outlining to Ashley, Rose and Cornet Rushford the probable course of the trial that Mr Muncaster became aware of a bow-legged figure, with tricorn tipped drunkenly over one eye, lurching in their direction.

Sampson Woodstock had been as good as his word. On the night of the wrecking he had ridden off along the Degibna side of Loe Pool, up through Higher Pentire, crossed the top end of Carminowe Creek, and then on to Chyanvounder. He had been making for the inn above Halzephron when he came upon a couple of wreckers fleeing from the Dragoons. Now Sampson, brought up on a Kynance farm where cattle and ponies freely roamed the cliff land, was handy with a rope. As a boy he had spent hour after hour out there on the cliffs perfecting his technique with a lasso. Very few calves or ponies escaped Sampson's noose, once he had them within range of his rope. It was a skill once learned never forgotten, and it had come in useful in later life. Many a farmer, trying to capture a reluctant animal, had been grateful to Sampson and his rope – and many a nip of best cognac had slipped easily down Sampson's throat by way of reward.

There had been no such reward, unfortunately – apart from a few words of grudging praise from the Collector – when Sampson had put his roping skill to such excellent use in nobbling one of the escaping wreckers. With a broad grin on his face, and his hat tilted at a precarious angle, he had brought his struggling captive down to the Gunwalloe sands where the Dragoons had taken him into custody. In reply to the injured Ashley's 'Good work, Sampson. A fair night's hunting, eh?' his fellow Riding Officer had given his usual, long drawn out rendering of 'Ye-e-es,' adding after a pregnant pause, 'I told ee I wouldn't let ee down.'

The only official recognition of Sampson's skill with his lasso on that particular night had been an order from Captain Breward that the lasso-ist himself must attend the subsequent trial as a material witness.

Sampson Woodstock had never made any attempt to disguise his dislike for Captain Breward. He liked him even less after receiving that order. Like many others he had a deeply felt horror of all courts of law. They conjured in his mind nothing but the nightmarish vision of rat-infested dungeons and grisly public hangings in front of jeering crowds. Only dire warnings from Breward about the penalties for non-attendance, coupled with the comforting assistance of the brandy bottle, had overcome his natural, deep-seated reluctance to become involved in anything contentious.

But he'd finally made his way to the Assize court; and punctuated by several contemplative observations of the 'Ye-e-s' variety, together with a few involuntary hiccups, he now made his presence known. Mr Muncaster took one look at the man – and decided to use him as a witness only in '*ultimum auxillium*'. Any suggestion of drunkenness by one of His Majesty's officials could easily damage the case for the prosecution.

The jury were in the process of being sworn in when Ashley, Rose, Cornet Rushford and the stertorously-breathing, copiously-perspiring Sampson Woodstock took their seats at the front of the court room. Leaving them there in the spider-like hands of H.M. Customs' solicitor, Mr Scrimgeour – of Messrs Scrimgeour, Hacket & Scrimgeour, Falmouth – Mr Muncaster joined his fellow barristers at the table below the judgment-seat where he and Counsel for the Defence were soon in the friendliest of conversations.

Every so often they would desist from their effusions of bonhomie while first one and then the other took part in the charade of 'objections'.

For no reason that Ashley could divine a summoned juror, Bible in hand and about to swear before Almighty God that he would do his utmost to judge the case fairly, would be stopped in mid-sentence and told by the clerk of the court to stand down. No reason would be given. On each such occasion the face of the man rejected, Ashley noticed, registered a mixture of bewilderment, relief – and, yes, injured pride. Although Counsel were merely exercising their legal rights, Ashley wondered how he would have felt if, having steeled himself to the nerve-tautening prospect of jury service, he found himself being rejected in a similar manner. He thought he would feel slightly besmirched.

Eventually a full jury was successfully empanelled, and an expectant hush seemed to fall upon the spectators at the back of the court and up in the gallery. Not so upon the barristers and court officials, shuffling papers and exchanging legal banter around their table. How strange, Ashley mused, that the two protagonists, Mr Henry Box-Johnson, K.C. and Mr Neville Muncaster, shortly to be locked in litigious combat, should be so openly chatting together like a couple of long lost friends. Just how much collusion was there between them, Ashley wondered. Was it all fixed up in the robing room beforehand – over a handshake and an invitation to a week-end in the country?

Ashley smiled ruefully; he thought it probably was. But that was none of his business; every man to his own devices – to his own deviousness; better keep out of it.

Sitting next to him, Cornet Rushford, though perspiring freely, was making a very creditable attempt not to appear nervous. But he was suffering. This first appearance in a court of law had found a chink in his armour of exuberance. He was not enjoying the experience.

Sampson Woodstock, on the other hand, had the carefree expression of a man peacefully inhaling his own alcoholic fumes. Seated on the far side of Rushford, his chin sunk deep into his chest, he was rapidly approaching the merciful oblivion of sleep. Something to be said for a drop of 'cousin jacky', Ashley concluded – something to lessen the oppresive gloom of the court room.

High up above the tall-backed judge's chair a brilliantly painted wooden replica of the royal arms was suspended. No other decoration relieved the drabness of the sombre, brooding walls. The court usher was dressed in black; so, too, were all the lawyers; a congregation of carrion crows about to dispute possession of a tasty morsel. The public seats were filled to overflowing. Mr Justice Grindley, before whom the case would be tried, was known to be a 'hanging judge'; and all the public were confidently expecting satisfaction.

Rose, sitting on Ashley's right – Mr Muncaster had deliberately placed her there so that the jury might enjoy an uninterrupted view of her – outwardly seemed unaffected by her first appearance in a court of law. She looked remarkably calm. But Ashley noticed that every now and then she gave an involuntary shiver. Also her knuckles showed white as she gripped the edge of the bench.

Seeking to reassure her and to give her courage, he placed one hand on hers – and as at *The Three Tuns Inn* on that hot summer's night, the mere contact with her, flesh upon flesh, sent an extraordinary thrill tingling through his body.

Reluctantly he withdrew his hand as the court usher, thumping the floor of the dais with his staff, cried 'Court rise!'; and to the accompaniment of scraping chairs and benches the court got to its feet.

Then, like a 'Mr Punch' emerging from the wings of a 'Punch and Judy' booth, the stooping, scarlet robed figure of Mr Justice Grindley appeared through a doorway in the side wall and, after bowing to the court, majestically assumed the judgment-seat. The court was in session.

Legal preliminaries – that pantomime when, above the heads of lesser mortals, lawyers seem to glory in the profundity of their legal acumen – are nearly always long and exceptionally tedious to the layman. Although Ashley tried to take an interest in the welter of verbiage flying between judge and advocate, his thoughts very soon wandered elsewhere.

During recent months public opinion in England had been perceptibly hardening against France. When, in the summer of '89 the Paris mob had stormed and captured the Bastille, the Whig leader, Charles James Fox, joyfully proclaimed, 'How much is this the greatest event that ever happened in the world, and how much the best!' At that time, and for much of the following three years, there had been a considerable undertow of public support for Fox's revolutionary enthusiasm – indeed, even the Prime Minister had declared his sympathy with the constitutional government of France.

But then, on the 21st January – less than a fortnight ago – the French had murdered their King!

Ever since leaving for St. Pol de Leon, to stay with her cousins at the Château Fontanelle, Alethea had stubbornly refused to acknowledge any danger to herself. Her letters had been full of the tranquillity of the Breton countryside, of the beauty of the Morlaix estuary, and of exciting parties and balls at the neighbouring Manoir de Kerlan, at the Château Kerouzere, and at the Manoir de Traonjoly.

In short, she was having a wonderful time, and she had no intention of being frightened into an early return to England.

And indeed it seemed she was not alone in her feeling of security. Fishermen – and others of more doubtful occupation – were returning from Roscoff saying that all was well; everything exactly as it had always been, and no talk of war.

But when the news came through that the King had been beheaded in the Place Louis Quinze, Sir Andrew MacKenzie – never one to be jostled into precipitate action – made up his mind. He was going over in his schooner and, no matter how strong her objections, he was going to bring his daughter home.

And had it not been for the impending trial of the wreckers now arraigned before Mr Justice Grindley, Ashley would have gone with him. Not that Sir Andrew was in need of pilotage or assistance of any kind – having developed extensive tobacco interests in Morlaix over the years he was well acquainted with the navigational hazards of the Baie de Morlaix – but Ashley wanted to share with him any dangers that might arise in bringing Alethea back.

Sir Andrew had set sail from his Helford berth just two days before the opening of the trial, and Ashley's thoughts had been with him almost ever since.

It was, therefore, hardly surprising that Riding Officer Penberth, principal witness in the case of the Crown versus Jabez Smollett and others should be less than fully attentive to the lengthy submissions now being put forward by Counsel.

It was tedious, but it was justice: English justice. So different from that now being dispensed by the courts of revolutionary France – like Monsieur Maillard's mockery of a trial of the priests at the Convent of the Carmelites, for instance.

'You are a priest, Monsieur, and you refuse to take the oath to our glorious Republic?'

'My allegiance is to God. I have committed no crime.' A reply greeted only by cynical laughter.

'Citizen, you must go from here and stand your trial.' The victim was then forced along a passage, and out on to

321

a platform overlooking a garden. The trial? – a group of assassins waiting to cut him down, bludgeon him to death.

Rumour had it – and rumour can sometimes strike with a palsy of fear – rumour had it that you only needed to be of gentle birth to attract the interest of the Paris Commune; to be dragged from your home and cast into one of the many rat-infested dungeons, as an enemy of the Republic; into the *'Souricière'* – the Mousetrap – from which the only escape was by way of the guillotine.

But that was in Paris, Ashley had been assured; not in the countryside, not in Brittany. Even so, he wished Sir Andrew had gone sooner.

Ashley's thoughts were abruptly brought back to the matter in hand when Mr Muncaster, turning in his chair, brandished a slip of paper in Ashley's direction. Ashley tip-toed forward, across the gangway separating witnesses from their illustrious legal representative, and took the note. In Neville Muncaster's scribbled handwriting the note merely said, 'Defence will try to shake you on question of 'identification' – so be prepared.'

Despite having convinced himself that to face judge and jury from the witness box was infinitely less alarming than confronting a band of smugglers, Ashley nevertheless felt a twisting of stomach muscles as he listened to the concluding cadences of Counsel's submissions. In a moment he would, he knew, be called upon to enter that lonely witness box; at best to become the centre of curiosity, at worst the object of hatred and vilification by the many up in the gallery who had come to enjoy the misfortunes of others. He would be giving evidence which would almost certainly lead to the death by hanging of at least one man.

Mr Muncaster, having done his polished best to create a favourable impression with the jury, now swivelled on his heel and addressed the judge. 'And now, m'lud, with your permission, I will call my first witness.' With an exaggerated sweep of his gown, he turned towards Ashley. 'Mr Penberth, please. . . .'

Taking a deep breath, Ashley rose awkwardly and stepped out into the gangway. Although no more than a few paces, the walk to the witness box seemed more like a furlong. The enforced lengthy sitting had made his knee go stiff, rendering his limp more pronounced than usual. He felt certain everyone was staring at him; he could almost hear the whispers.

Nothwithstanding his predetermination to appear cool and unflustered – to set an example and give encouragement to those coming after him – he could feel the colour flooding into his cheeks. For the first time in his life, he stepped into the witness box in an Assize court. Feeling the eyes of the judge as well as the jury boring into him, he took the proffered Bible and, prompted by the court usher, he swore by Almighty God to tell the truth, the whole truth, and nothing but the truth. Then he turned and faced Mr Muncaster.

Presecuting Counsel, endeavouring to put his witness at ease, flashed him a wintry smile.

'You are Mr Ashley Penberth, are you not?' he began.

'Yes, sir,' Ashley gripped the front of the box, seeking to give himself confidence.

'And you are employed as a Riding Officer in the Service of His Majesty, King George the Third. Is that so?'

Before the witness could reply, a low but nonetheless distinct sound of boo-ing came from the back of the court and gallery. Mr Muncaster swung round on his heel and glared at the offenders. Mr Justice Grindley was furious. At very great inconvenience and discomfort to himself he had agreed to hold the Assizes in the midst of these semi-illiterate savages, and if they thought he would tolerate the merest semblance of disrespect towards His Majesty and the authority of the court, then, by Heaven! he would teach them a lesson they would never forget.

He thumped the desk so vehemently with his fist that the inkwell in front of him leapt into an involuntary fandango, before depositing an unsightly spatter of ink drops on the tooled leather inlay.

'Silence!' he thundered 'If I hear so much as another squeak from you, I'll send you all to prison for contempt!'

But the murmuring and jesting continued, only slightly abated. The sturdy, independent Cornish folk were in no mood to be spoken to like that by anyone – least of all by someone from beyond the Tamar.

'Silence!' Mr Justice Grindley roared again, his face turning from peppery red to outraged purple, 'Silence! Do you hear me!'

This time, like the gradual fading of an echo, the grumbled protests died away. The stillness of the court became almost oppressive. His Majesty's justice was about to be dispensed – unhurriedly and without interference.

'Pray continue, Mr Muncaster,' the judge commanded, crumbling beneath his nose the herb leaves placed on his desk to neutralise the smells of the prisoners at the bar and to ward off their infective risks of gaol fever, 'Continue to examine your witness.'

Counsel for the Prosecution bowed deferentially to his Lordship. 'Thank you, m'lud. I will endeavour to do so.' Sweeping the tail-ends of his gown around his ample midriff, he turned once more towards the witness box.

'I repeat, Mr Penberth. . . . You are a Riding Officer in the service of His most excellent Majesty, King George the Third, are you not?'

'I am, sir. Yes.'

'And on the night of . . . er . . . er, on the evening of . . . er. . . .' Mr Muncaster shuffled his papers. Finding what he was looking for, he continued, 'Ah, yes, I have it. On the evening of Tuesday, 10th September last, you were riding the coast between Porhtleven and Mullion in the normal course of your duty. Is that correct, Mr Penberth?'

Momentarily Ashley hesitated. Strictly speaking it was not the 'normal course of his duty' because that part of the coast did not fall within his district. But after a moment's reflection he decided it was a very minor point, and it would only complicate matters if he attempted to explain, so he said, 'Er, . . . yes, sir.'

'And during that ride on your official business you witnessed something unusual, did you not, Mr Penberth?'

'That is correct, sir.'

Mr Muncaster smiled, thinly. 'Tell the members of the jury exactly what you saw, Mr Penberth, will you.'

Slowly, deliberately, step by step, Counsel for the Prosecution took Ashley through his evidence – the sighting of the moving lamp, the overtaking of the fleeing lamp-man, the terrible crunching of the stricken ship as she struck the rocks beneath Hell's Cliff, and finally the desperate battle with the infuriated wreckers as, cutlass in hand, he had done his best to save captain and crew. With masterly forensic skill, Mr Muncaster drew drom his witness a vivid picture of the noblest endeavour, against frightening odds, and in the devoted service of His Majesty, King George the Third. It sounded most impressive; it seemed as though the case was already convincingly won.

With a smile of the greatest satisfaction, Mr Muncaster bowed to the judge, and sat down.

Then, Mr Henry Box-Johnson, K.C. appearing on behalf of the defendants, slowly, almost languidly got to his feet.

He bowed low to Mr Justice Grindley. After carefully arranging and re-arranging his papers with the utmost deliberation, thereby extracting the maximum impact from the extended pause, he finally straightened up to his full height, and slowly turned his patrician head towards the witness box.

'Mr Penberth,' he began, bestowing upon the witness a paternal smile. 'In answer to my learned friend, you stated that on the night of . . . er . . . of . . .' he casually glanced at the document in his hand, 'Yes, on the night of September the 10th last you were riding a certain section of the coast 'in the normal course of your duty', did you not?'

'Yes, sir. I did.'

'Ah, yes. I thought as much.' Box-Johnson glanced pointedly at the jury. ' "In the normal course of your duty" ' he repeated slowly. Then, gently caressing the lobe of his left ear, he continued blandly, 'I may have been mistaken, Mr Penberth, but I thought I detected a slight hesitation in your reply. Was there any particular reason for that? Something you thought you ought to tell the jury, perhaps? An unusual feature of your duty that evening. . . .?'

Mr Muncaster was quickly on his feet – as quickly, that is, as his portly figure would allow. He could not quite see what his adversary was up to, but he felt certain some kind of trap was being laid.

'Really, m'lud!' he broke in, pink cheeked and ebullient, 'I must object to my learned friend's frivolous questioning. What possible significance could be attached to a mere hesitation of speech? Indeed, I am sure Your Lordship would not wish the court's time to be wasted on such trivialities.'

Mr Justice Grindley picked up a leaf of sweet basil, crushed it between finger and thumb, and sniffed it. 'I will decide whether or not the court's time is being wasted, Mr Muncaster, thank you.' He nodded towards Defence Counsel. 'Pray continue, Mr Box-Johnson.'

Question and answer, verbal thrust and parry, eventually drew from the witness that he had taken it upon himself to operate outside his normal area of responsibility. It was a small point, but it served to suggest to the jury that the witness, far from acting with commendable zeal, had been guilty of grossly exceeding his duty.

Counsel for the Defence decided to rub in a little more salt. 'Is it usual, Mr Penberth, for an officer of your . . . er . . . forgive me for saying so, but of your . . . er . . . somewhat lowly rank to usurp the responsibilities of a senior colleague?'

The old devil! Ashley thought to himself. Not for nothing is he nicknamed Fox-Johnson. The merest chink in the evidence, and he's spotted it. Now he's going to prize it right open.

And he did. By the time Counsel for the Defence had finished with the prosecution's first witness, Mr Muncaster's carefully drawn picture had been completely transformed. Instead of the brave, loyal member of His Majesty's Customs fearlessly attacking, single-handed, a murderous gang of wreckers, Riding Officer Ashley Penberth had become the vindictive scourge of humble, starving Cornishmen who, through age-old tradition, had come to regard a wreck upon their coasts as nothing more nor less than a visitation of 'God's Providence'.

Moreover, so determined was this Riding Officer to deprive his penurious fellow-countrymen of such small luxuries as might alleviate the treadmill of their existence – and the very barest existence at that, Counsel reminded the jury – so vindictively determined was this man that he was prepared to initiate punitive action in another officer's sphere of responsibility, and had taken it upon himself to call out a detachment of His Majesty's Dragoons – a very costly and time-consuming exercise paid for, as members of the jury would be well aware, out of taxation levied upon civilians like themselves. Moreover he had taken this precipitate action without any reference whatsoever to higher authority.

Mopping his brow with a folded silk handkerchief, Counsel for the Defence had then sat down, exhausted by his own eloquence.

Mr Justice Grindley had seemed exhausted, too. He had not slept very well in the judge's lodgings during the previous night, and to-day had seemed rather long and tedious.

He crumbled a piece of tarragon leaf beneath his nose – and then adjourned until tomorrow.

Overnight the news came through that war had been declared. Ever since the September Massacres when, for one whole day, and half into the night, a demented rabble had dragged from prisons and dungeons all over Paris more than two thousand aristocrats, royalists and priests, and butchered them in cold blood, the clamour for war with France had been growing. Alone, Prime Minister Pitt had resisted the cry, clinging to the hope that peace could be preserved. As late as December, he had made a last desperate

327

attempt, promising France that he would abstain from war if she would stop invading her neighbours. But in that country his gesture was interpreted as weakness, while in England the news of the French King's execution sparked a fresh outcry for revenge. And when Pitt's final initiative was rebuffed, diplomatic relations were broken off. War then became inevitable.

Throughout the remaining sessions of the court, Ashley found it impossible to concentrate on the proceedings. Declaration of war between France and England would almost certainly mean an embargo being placed on all English ships in French ports – and, unless he had got away in time, this would include Sir Andrew MacKenzie's schooner at Morlaix.

And what of Sir Andrew, himself? In the confusion of the hour, reliable news was hard to come by; rumour held sway – and rumour had it that all over France the châteaux and the manor houses of the wealthy were being taken over by the French government and turned into prisons for yet more royalists and aristocrats. Worse still, it was not only the French that were being imprisoned; foreign nationalities were being subjected to the same treatment.

So preoccupied was Ashley with thoughts of Alethea and Sir Andrew caught up in the maelstrom of revolutionary French politics that he scarcely heard the grilling meted out by Box-Johnson to the perspiring Cornet Rushford. And even though he managed to concentrate while Rose was so fearlessly, and so prettily giving her evidence – with special reference to the lamp-man – when she returned to his side, and he once again placed his hand over hers in appreciation of her performance, the former thrill was scarcely discernible. It had been dowsed by the cold reality of the danger threatening the girl he had loved since childhood and the man who, all his life, had been to him as a father.

By the time the judge had finished his summing-up, Ashley had formed a plan; by the time the jury had returned their verdict of 'Guilty' – despite the adroit manoeuvres of Mr Box-Johnson – and Mr Justice Grindley, donning the black cap, had pronounced sentence; the plan had taken positive shape.

But it was not until they were on their way home, huddled together on the outside seats of the Falmouth Mail coach, that Ashley unfolded the plan to Rose.

Above the howl of the wind, as they rattled and jolted along the deeply rutted turnpike, Rose shouted, 'I'm comin' with you.'

'Impossible!' Ashley shouted back, 'Far too dangerous!'

'That's what you said down by the Loe Pool – before us captured they criminals as has just got their deserts, remember?'

'That was different.'

'I didn't get in your way, then – did I?' she said, plaintively. 'I could be a help to ee, this time, as well.'

Ashley sank his chin further into the capes of his heavy cloth *surtout*. The wind whistling across the moor had the edge of a razor.

'You did well, Rosie – really well,' he growled. 'But let that be enough. And take good care of yourself,' he added, as an afterthought.

He was thinking at that moment of the one that got away. Sampson Woodstock had done well with his lasso to capture one of the two fleeing wreckers. But the other one had given him the slip. He was still free – free to mingle, in disguise, with the onlookers at the Assize court, to make mental notes – free to tell the tale where it mattered that it was Rose Roskruge, barmaid at *The Three Tuns Inn*, St Keverne, who had tipped off the Riding Officer that night at Helston.

Not everyone at St Keverne was a churchgoer and an angel!

As the Mail Coach finally rattled into the *The Royal Hotel* at Falmouth, punctually at 7 o'clock on a frosty February morning, Ashley was still thinking of Rose's safety. She had risked her life for him, and now he was planning to leave her to her fate. He liked it not at all.

But in response to her repeated request, he said gruffly, 'No, no, Rosie. It's out of the question. It's too dangerous.'

CHAPTER TWENTY SIX

Je t'adore!

There was no Alethea, no Liggett-Fanshawe, no Pruddy, and no Sir Andrew.

Ashley and Jeannie were alone.

Until a few moments ago, Pruddy had been with them, presiding over the dinner table in Sir Andrew's absence. More and more, since the two girls had become fully grown-up and no longer in need of her services, she had been doing this; more and more had Sir Andrew come to rely on her to take charge of the household whenever he was away from home.

But this evening, taking her cue from Jeannie whom she readily recognised as being the true mistress of the house, she had left the table at the end of the meal saying that she had household accounts to attend to as well as some letters to write. She knew that Jeannie had much to say to Ashley.

Bit by bit the news had been filtering through from France. It was worse than Ashley had feared. No sooner had *Highland Mist* tied up alongside the quay at Morlaix than a pair of musket-bearing soldiers of the newly formed citizen's army had seized the schooner and, relishing their unaccustomed authority, had arrested Sir Andrew and his crew, marching them all off to a prison in the nearby Place des Jacobins.

Using every persuasive device in his not inconsiderable repertoire, Sir Andrew had secured the release and homeward transportation of his crew, but he had only been able to do so by pledging his own imprisonment as security. With this the local Commune had agreed, not being interested in restraining their exploited, under-priviledged brethren of whatever nationality. In return for a substantial *ex gratia* payment to an official at the *Hôtel de Ville*, Sir Andrew had arranged for his own incarceration at his brother's castle, the Château Fontanelle.

As both Jeannie and Ashley had feared, this country residence of the MacKenzie cousins had been taken over by the authorities and turned into a well-guarded prison for St Pol de Leon and the surrounding district. Among the first to be herded into the confines of the château were a group of Carmelite sisters from a nearby convent.

'And it could be well guarded,' Jeannie was saying. 'It would make an excellent country prison. Look,' she left the table, highly polished and glittering beneath the candelabra, walked across to the Chippendale side table and from one of the shallow drawers extracted a stick of charcoal. Returning to the table she unfolded her white napkin and began to sketch the ground plan of the Château Fontanelle and its walled garden.

'In the first place,' she explained, illustrating her remarks with characteristically bold strokes of the charcoal stick, 'the whole château is surrounded by a high wall. That's obviously why they think of it as a secure prison.'

'How high is the wall?' Ashley asked.

'Oh, Ashley! You know how poor I am at guessing measurements. I don't know. . . . How tall are you?'

Ashley shrugged. 'Six foot standing on my right leg, five foot none on my left.'

Ignoring the sly joke Jeannie went on sketching. 'Well, it's about twice your height, I should think.'

Ashley nodded, taking mental note. 'Rough surfaced, or smooth?' he asked.

'Oh, *Ashley*! How should I know?'

'It's important.'

'Why?'

'Getting a foothold – climbing over.'

Jeannie stopped sketching; brushed the dark ringlets off her forehead, thinking. 'Smooth, I should imagine – but I honestly can't remember. In any case, I've never tried to climb it. Why should I?'

'As a child, perhaps; playing in the garden? You remember how we used to climb the wall round the orchard, here at Trevadne?'

'It's higher than our orchard wall, I think. Everything in France seems larger.'

'Never mind. It doesn't matter. I'll find a way over, somehow.'

'But there are *trees*,' Jeannie said suddenly, 'and some of them are quite close to the wall! Here . . . and here . . . and here . . .' She rapidly sketched them in on the napkin. 'In fact, if I remember correctly, some of their branches may even hang over the wall.'

'That'd be very convenient!'

'Oh, Ashley!' she burst out impulsively, 'Do please take care.' Her liquid eyes seemed suddenly on the verge of tears; her hand felt for his. 'You will, won't you?'

'Oh, I'll be all right,' he replied, rather too curtly, rather too gruffly. 'You needn't worry about me.'

'But I shall . . . of course I shall. The place is guarded . . . . . there are soldiers. . . .'

'All the better,' he said with false cheerfulness. 'Make it more exciting.'

Her eyes embraced him with a tenderness he'd not seen before. Her broad, clear brow puckered into a frown.

He cleared his throat noisily, suppressing a rising emotion. 'Tell me about the way in. You say there's a quay somewhere near. . . .'

Reluctantly she withdrew her hand; picked up the charcoal stick; began sketching again.

'Here,' she indicated, 'right beside the wall. There's a gate there, but it's bound to be locked – and there's a gate-keeper's lodge close beside it . . . here.' She drew the outline of a cottage.

'And how much water?'

Jeannie frowned for a moment, thinking deeply. 'Five or six feet I should say – perhaps a bit more.'

'For how long?'

'About an hour on either side of the top of the tide.'

Ashley grunted. 'None too much, eh. We'll have to time it right.' He pulled the fob watch from his breeches waistband; consulted it. It had belonged to his father – almost the only thing of his he possessed. The vision of his father, wrecked on the Manacles, flashed into his mind.

But he said, 'We haven't too much time.'

'We?. . . . Who else is. . . .?'

'Zeph Curnow,' he replied quickly. 'He'll be with me. He knows the navigation . . .' he glanced at her, beetle-browed, '. . . . . from the 'old days', I'm afraid.'

He felt guilty; he hadn't told her all.

Once more she took his hand; gazed at him, searching his face. 'Oh, Ashley,' she sighed, 'you *will* be careful, won't you!'

He was touched by the depth of her concern, more than he cared to admit. To smother his feelings he very carefully and very deliberately folded the napkin; and put it in his pocket. 'That'll be a tremendous help, Jeannie,' he said, clearing his throat again rather noisily, 'I'm most grateful to you.'

He got to his feet, drawing her up with him; taking her hands in his.

'Grateful!. . . . *You*, grateful to *me*!' she almost sobbed. 'Oh, no, Ashley, it is I who should be grateful to you! Just look what you're doing . . . for me . . . for us, as a family.'

Impulsively she threw her arms around him, pulled his face down to hers, kissed him . . . at first, no more than an expression of gratitude, a kiss of true thanksgiving to the man who, in her imagination, was about to snatch from the very shadow of the guillotine not only her sister but her beloved father as well.

Burying her face in the folds of his muslin cravat, she murmured, 'Oh, Ashley. . . . I feel so . . . so. . . . Oh, what is the word . . . I have for you such a feeling of . . . the French would say of *tendresse* . . .'

He made no reply. But when she drew away, looking up

at him, searching his eyes for the response she longed for, she saw in them the smouldering fire of deep physical passion. As he drew her ever closer she felt the great power of his arms encircling her, crushing her against his hard masculine body; and when his lips again brushed hers, softly at first, caressingly – but then harder, harder, harder – searching, exploring, devouring – they told her in the language of raw sensuality that deeply within him he wanted her with all the unleashed power of his manhood.

Instinctively she knew that in this fleeting moment he was hers: that by surrendering utterly to the rising crescendo of his passion she could make him her own. As a man of honour he would never thereafter forsake her.

It was so tempting; no one else in the house except Pruddy, and the servants. The secrecy of the night . . . the never recurring moment. . . . Should she . . . should she? . . . and would it really make him hers . . . or would the chill of the dawning morrow bring reaction revulsion, hatred even – so deep and so strong as to destroy forever that which she most wished to preserve?

But just when she felt her last remaining shreds of resistance melting beneath the heat of his overpowering passion – when like swansdown drifting towards the edge of a whirlpool she no longer had control of her emotional destiny – she felt him wrenching himself from her with an almost lacerating suddenness.

Breathing heavily, he said, 'I must go, Jeannie. God knows if I don't go now, I may never go at all. Don't hold me.'

But she did; she clung to him; would not let him go.

Looking up at him, her large dark eyes like fathomless pools of desire, she whispered, 'Oh, Ashley! *Je t'adore!*'

Gently, reluctantly, he removed her arms from around his neck, kissed her lightly on the forehead – and was gone.

CHAPTER TWENTY SEVEN

A La France!
(– et une ancienne connaissance)

The wind was dropping steadily as *Heatherbelle II*, helped by the flooding tide, quietly nosed her way eastwards between the Ile de Batz and the rock-strewn entrance to Roscoff harbour. Astern, the last segment of the setting sun, blood-red like a ball of fire, was sinking below the western horizon. Even so, there was still enough light for Ashley to observe with wry amusement the beatific smile on Zeph Curnow's face. It was almost as though he had seen a vision.

As soon as they had picked up the low outline of the Brittany coast, Ashley had handed the tiller over to Zeph, saying, 'You know the navigation, Zeph. Take her in, will you.'

Willingly, Zeph had taken over. Now, leaning lightly on the tiller, his eyes half-closed in seeming ecstacy, he lovingly coaxed the lugger round the Pointe de Bloscon and into the Baie de Morlaix.

Occasionally, his lips were seen moving, as if in prayer, but no sound could be heard. He was talking, yes – but only to himself. He was remembering, with the vividness that comes only with increasing age, that last fatal trip with his 'Mester', Amos Penberth, more than twenty years ago, when the beautiful *Percuel Rose*, loaded to the gunwales with valuable contraband, had been smashed into splinters on the merciless jaggedness of the Manacle rocks.

Twenty years! – twenty four, to be exact. And where had they gone, those twenty four years! How had they all managed to survive without the head of the family, the bread-winner, the one who took all the important decisions?

Well, they *had* survived – with a fair bit of help from Sir Andrew MacKenzie, and a lot of goodwill from the neighbours – and that baby son, born into the world at almost the very moment when his father had been torn from it, that little mite that Zeph had drooled over as he lay kicking his frog-like legs in the circular tin bath in front of the kitchen range – that same little baby boy had grown into the immensely strong young Master of the vessel which he, Zephanaiah Curnow, was now steering through the rock-infested waters of the Penzé estuary.

How had they done it – when after the sudden tragedy of that shipwreck the future had looked so bleak? Zeph's face screwed itself into a very fair imitation of a sun-dried prune as the memories came flooding back. A single tear, angrily dashed away almost before it had time to emerge, began a short-lived trickle down his cheek. It had been hard going at times; hard to make ends meet on the farm, even though he'd tried not to let the Mistress know it. But somehow – and with that invaluable help from Sir Andrew – they'd managed to keep afloat. And the money they'd eventually made out of the wreck – with no loss on account of 'stinkibus' tubs – had certainly provided Mester Ashley with a good education, him as having been at that there Lydford College. Not that it had been all that much of a benefit, Zeph reflected ruefully, what with him being unable to find anything better than this yere terrible job with the Preventives – enough to make the boy's father, Mester Amos, turn in his watery grave, Zeph wouldn't wonder – but at least it had enabled them all to keep going. Above all, it had meant that Zeph and his Missus could stay on in their cottage; he'd always be grateful to the young Mester for that.

And although he supposed he would have to admit to being what the Rector of Mawnan, the Reverend William Peter, would probably have described as 'well stricken in years', he certainly didn't feel old, and there was just about nothing he wouldn't do for Mester Ashley and his mother.

Like this trip over to Brittany, for instance. The Mistress

hadn't liked the idea one bit, at first; remembering all too well, no doubt, that it was one of those fishing trips over to Rusco' in the old days that had snatched her husband from her in the very prime of his life. And no wonder! But when she came to think of all the help Sir Andrew had given over the years – well, then she'd relented. She knew it would be an extremely dangerous undertaking, but she'd grown accustomed to her son living close to danger, and she realised he'd never be able to forgive himself if anything terrible should happen to Alethea and Sir Andrew.

But Zeph didn't think Mester Ashley had said anything to his mother about taking with him this young chit of a girl from St Keverne. The Mistress, Zeph thought, might not approve; the MacKenzie girl was one thing, a country barmaid was quite another!

'There do be two gert rocks us must keep well to starboard,' Zeph was saying to his skipper. 'They'm seaward o' what they Frenchies call the Isle Sainte Anne, I do mind. An' then, after they, 'tis a purty straight run in to th' inlet where we'm aimin' to be.'

For Rose, standing in the bows, dressed in the long brown tunic and white overmantle of a Carmelite nun, the low outline of the Brittany coast ahead held a special magic. It was the first time she had set eyes on a foreign land; and it was France! Involuntarily she fingered the gold-enamelled locket around her neck. Her Riding Officer, Ashley Penberth, had said it was a *Toutin*, 17th Century, made in Paris probably, and the little miniatures inside he thought looked like a pair of French aristocrats. Her ancestors? . . . perhaps she would never know . . . but ever since that thought had been planted in her mind by the man she was now accompanying on this perilous enterprise, scarcely a day had gone by without her wondering whether it might not be true.

And now she was actually looking at France. Could it be the country of her ancestors?. . . . Might it not hold the key – the very special key – that would one day unlock the mystery of her birth?

She had reminded him about the locket while hungrily devouring breakfast at The Royal Hotel, Falmouth, after the freezing journey homeward from the Assize Court. She had introduced the subject casually – without any particular reference to France, and without relating it in any way to his repeated refusals to allow her to come with him on this exciting adventure. He had looked at the locket again; examined it closely during the exasperatingly long interval between the porridge and the fried eggs; and once again expressed his opinion that the two miniature portraits inside, with their aquiline features, highly coloured cheeks and powdered wigs, were the likenesses of two members – probably man and wife – of the French aristocracy.

He had also told her that Henri Toutin had become quite famous for enamelled jewellery; that he had started in Blois, and eventually had a workshop in Paris as well, and had flourished during the middle of the last century.

Had it been her reminding him in this way of her obvious interest in France, she wondered, which had finally overcome his objections – or had it been her suggestion that she might be especially useful to him in the disguise of a Carmelite nun? Because it *had* been her suggestion, and it *was* rather a clever idea – even though perhaps she ought not to be thinking so.

Or could it have been that, having found her useful as well as brave while tackling the wreckers, he just wanted to have her with him?

No sooner the thought came than she suppressed it. Whatever her feelings for him, the unpalatable fact remained that he was embarking on this hazardous task in order to bring home the girl he loved – had always loved, or so she understood – the high-born daughter of the squire of Trevadne. What possible part could she, Rose Roskruge, humble barmaid of unknown pedigree, ever hope to play in his life – other than perhaps as the transitory plaything with whom to while away the tedious hours of official duty. And *that* she most certainly was *not* prepared to be!

But, as always when faced with the imponderables and

uncertainties of life, the natural gaiety of Rose's personality lifted her spirits. Of her own free will she had got herself into this situation, and she would cheerfully accept whatever consequences might befall. After all, as a child of nature, what had she got to lose; and besides, you never knew – something really dramatic might come out of it.

She ducked under the foresail, clambered over some fishing tackle amidships, bent low beneath the foot of the mainsail and then joined Ashley and Zeph in the stern. Away over the port bow, and beyond the Ile de Callot, loomed the threatening outline of the island fortress, the Château du Taureau.

'We'm in enemy waters now, I s'pose,' Zeph said darkly. 'Us'd betterway run up a Frenchie bit o' rag, eh, skipper? Just in case there do be any busybodies ashore wi' a spyglass havin' a look at we.'

Ashley nodded. 'Carry on, then, Zeph,' he said, taking over the helm once more. 'See what you can find.'

After rummaging around in the stern locker for several moments, Zeph finally produced a faded, rather dirty-looking pennant wrapped round what appeared to be short slats of timber.

Having put the pennant at the masthead he then resumed his former position beside Ashley at the tiller. ' 'Tis one I kep' from the days when your father, Mester Amos, an' me were doin' a bit o' tradin', see – but I shouldn't really oughta be mentionin' it, 'cause I promised the Mistress I'd never tell ee anythin' 'bout they tradin' days, like – but the Mester – Mester Amos that be – ee allus wanted the pennant to be a bit dirty-like, so's they Frenchies wouldn' be too sure just what us was.'

In response to a reassuring nod from his skipper, Zeph continued, 'An' I put these yere in the locker afore us left, as well. I thought un might be useful.'

Rose was fascinated to see Zeph showing Ashley the three slats of timber formerly wrapped in the pennant. They measured about seven or eight inches wide and were between two and three feet long. Moving closer, Rose could see that they were name plates bearing the word *C Y G N E* in large capitals above the word *Douarnenez* in smaller letters on each plate. The lettering on all three was none too clear – for the same reason that the pennant was kept faded and grubby, Rose supposed.

'Us used to carry these along wi' us, too,' Zeph grinned, clearly relishing the memory. 'That was wi' Mester Amos, like – an' us never had no trouble while us were wearin' they.'

Rose watched with unconcealed amusement as Zeph first fixed one name plate to the stern, completely obscuring the lugger's real name, then went for'ard and did the same thing on each side of the bow. Thus in a matter of minutes, *Heatherbelle II* of Porth Navas, became *Cygne* of Douarnenez – for the benefit of any prying eyes.

This simple act of transformation alerted Rose, as perhaps nothing else could, to the dangerous nature of their undertaking. They were in enemy waters, under false colours, and with a false name. Should they be discovered, unmasked, what then might be their fate? The rattle of the descending guillotine suddenly became a hideous possibility.

But she would not, dared not, think of that now. She had embarked upon this enterprise because she wanted to be with Ashley – to share with him yet another unifying moment of danger – and because, with *The Three Tuns Inn* reduced to a burnt-out shell, there was very little left for her to do in St Keverne. Besides, she was in the mood for some new adventure, a yearning for fresh fields – and who could tell, the green pastures of Brittany and France might yield for her the intriguing secret of the Toutin locket.

She had never really stopped to think precisely what it was she was doing. Helping Ashley to rescue the girl he loved – so that they could marry and live happily ever after! Her rival! The girl with everything – wealth, beauty, social position – and Ashley! Everything – almost – that she, Rose, did not possess. Just what *did* she think she was doing?

But it was too late to think of that now. Already

Heatherbelle II, alias *Cygne* of Douarnenez, was gliding silently past the Ile Ste Anne, and even in the fast fading light the houses of Pempoul were clearly discernible.

'Aah! I thought 'twas so,' Zeph was saying, 'Tedn hardly changed at all from how I mind un.' His keen, weather-tanned old face screwed itself into a replica of creased leather as he peered shorewards through the darkness. 'Unless I be much mistaken, we'm gettin' purty close to where us wants to be. In among they trees there, that's where I reckon 'tis to.'

'It's a good thing you know your way around so well,' Rose ventured, admiringly.

Ashley nodded agreement. 'We couldn't even have attempted it without Zeph.'

But Zeph, at that moment, was impervious to compliments. He was remembering 'the old days' – as if they were only yesterday. 'Aw, ais,' he chuckled to himself, 'I mind un well. There be a handy little cottage place – just beyond they trees there – where my old friend Jack Duboyes used to live.'

This reference to Monsieur Jacques Dubois evoked in Zeph the most delightful memories. His shoulders shook with silent laughter. Eventually, still chuckling reminiscently, he conceded, 'Aw, ais. A very funny fellow, were Jack. Very funny indeed, he were. Allus in the very best o' good spirits, you unnerstand me . . . the best o' good *spirits*.' He stroked his chin speculatively, saying, 'I just be a-wonderin' if th' old chap's still alive, like, an' if that be so, whether he'm still livin' in that thur little old cottage-ey place o' his.'

But that was as much as Zeph was permitted to speculate aloud because, now that they were nearing land, Ashley ordered silence on board. Voices carry so clearly over water, and the sound of English voices at this stage could well spell disaster.

Slowly, silently – except for the rhythmical lip-lap of wavelet against wooden hull – Zeph was coaxing the lugger nearer and nearer to the shore. Ahead of them lay an extensive area of dense woodland, some of the trees over-hanging the water's edge, just as they do along the shoreline of the Helford River. The similarity of terrain, Ashley thought, was quite remarkable.

He could now make out the rock-guarded inlet to which Zeph was obviously steering, and signalling Rose to follow he went for'ard, ready to down sails. All he could see at the moment was an apparently impenetrable forest all along three sides of the inlet, but as his eyesight gradually adjusted to the deep shadows cast by the trees, he could just discern a small jetty thrusting out from the land.

At the awaited signal, Rose let go the main halyard, allowing it to slide slowly through her hands while Ashley, as quietly as possible, gathered the crumpling sail. Then they repeated the operation at the foremast, leaving the lugger with just enough way on her to reach the jetty.

Quietly, skilfully, Zeph Curnow brought the lugger alongside, and as he did so the great mass of trees seemed momentarily to divide – like the parting of theatrical curtains on some massive stage – and there, at the far end of a long avenue, gaunt chimneys and pepperpot turrets could be seen piercing the blue-black of the western sky.

The Château Fontanelle, in all its challenging impene-trability, stood before them.

CHAPTER TWENTY EIGHT

Le Château Fontanelle

To his boundless delight, Zeph Curnow found his old smuggling friend, Jacques Dubois, alive and well, and still living in his cottage close by the Château Fontanelle.

They fell upon each other's neck, overjoyed at the reunion.

Jacques had no time for the Revolution. He spat contemptuously at the mention of Robespierre. A powdered pip-squeak! Had he not tried to wipe the name of 'Brittany' off the map of France? – the little pinch-faced poodle from Arras!

No, no, Jacques had no patience with the new-fangled ideas about liberty, fraternity and equality. He liked the 'old days', when a man was allowed unmolested to till his plot, fish his own waters – and carry on a little bit of lucrative 'trading' with 'les Anglais', like his most excellent friend, Zeph Curnow, yes?

But of course he would be only too pleased to help his old friend, in any way possible – but first of all, they must have a little drink together, just to celebrate the occasion and to remember old times.

Sensing Ashley's impatience at the delay, Zeph asked his friend – in that extraordinary mixture of Anglo-French and sign language which serves two members of the same 'trading' fraternity so well – to give as much information as he could about the present state of the Château Fontanelle.

Yes, Jacques confirmed, the castle had been turned into a prison for political suspects and *émigrés* trying to escape to England, and it was guarded by soldiers billeted in the coach house who, every so often patrolled the grounds.

There was, as they could see, a high stone wall all the way round the gardens and woodlands – about eight feet high, he would say, maybe more, maybe less – and although there was an entrance gate not far from his cottage, it was always kept locked and was guarded by soldiers billeted with the lodge-keeper.

And yes, it was very clever of Mam'selle to think of the Carmelite habit. It would make it much easier to gain entrance to the château because there were nuns similarly dressed going in and out all the time.

Jacques regarded the English girl as only a Frenchman can. Not even the inflationary pressures of artichokes and the repellant odours or raw garlic could strip the old man of his natural Gallic charm, and Ashley noticed with some amusement how prettily Rose responded.

But first, Jacques agreed, recognising Ashley's impatience but reluctantly dragging his attention from *la belle mignonne*, he would tell Monsieur how to get over the wall. Although it might not be as much as eight feet high in some places, and Jacques would tell him where, it would still present a problem.

It was then that Rose, shyly, half-apologetically, revealed that the belt encircling her habit was no ordinary nun's girdle.

'Aah! Mam'selle!' Jacques exclaimed delightedly, '*La cordelière! C'est merveilleuse!*'

He clapped his hands expressively as Rose began unwinding the stout, knotted rope from around her waist. It was another of her own ideas – another way to make herself useful, she hoped. She had thought of it while she had been making up the habit from a couple of old blankets – faded brown for the tunic, grey-white for the overmantle – and she couldn't help feeling pleased at the look of astonished admiration in Ashley's eyes.

At the same time, she could see how impatient he was to be off. They had only a very limited time before the tide would begin to ebb, and it would be absolutely disastrous if they were to be left high and dry on the mud.

344

Leaving Zeph in the exuberant embrace of his long-lost smuggling friend – and with strict instructions to be ready to cast off the lugger at a moment's notice – Ashley set off, with Rose following, to find the part of the wall which Jacques had indicated might be the least difficult to scale.

After groping their way for some distance along a rough path at the foot of the high wall, they came to a Lodge beside a pair of ornamental iron gates. A light streamed out from a downstairs window, and the unmistakeable sounds of revelry within suggested that the guards were happily carousing.

Arching above the tall, spike-topped gates, an elaborate design of scrolls and French curves supporting an iron-worked monogram caught Rose's attention. What exactly were the letters forming that monogram? Was it just the whimsy of a foolish heart forever seeking to discover the secret of a lifetime – or was it, could it really be, that those letters corresponded with the initials distinguishing her Toutin locket? Had she, Rose wondered, by some extraordinary co-incidence – or by some celestial intervention – stumbled upon a vital clue to her identity?

She tugged at Ashley's sleeve. 'Wait a minute,' she whispered. 'Take a look at that fancy work at the top o' they gates, for me, will you. That letterin'. What do you make those letters out to be?'

Somewhat impatiently Ashley glanced up. Etched against the pale light of the crescent moon, the monogram was sharply visible. But the letters were so artistically intertwined that it was impossible to determine exactly what they were.

'Sorry,' Ashley grunted, 'but I can't decipher them. In any case,' he went on, urging her forward, 'we haven't time to go ancestor-hunting. We must hurry!'

With a lingering backward glance at the massive gates and the intricate monogram, Rose allowed herself to be hustled along. She recognised now the inappropriateness of the moment. Perhaps it had been foolish of her to enquire. And yet, in her heart she longed to know. . . .

Presently, the rough path merged with the shingle of a

beach, and the sound of the gently lapping water confirmed that they were still close to the sea. Ashley paused; ran one hand over the surface of the wall; found it to be as smooth as a lily leaf; not the semblance of a foothold anywhere; and it was still at least eight feet high.

Keeping his voice down, but seeking to encourage his companion, he murmured, 'Brilliant idea of yours, that rope, Rosie. All we need now is something to hook it on to.'

They continued along the shingle, treading as quietly as they could but even so making heavy crunching sounds, until Ashley suddenly stopped, gripped Rose's arm and pointed ahead to a section of the wall in deep shadow. Overhead were the branches of a large tree. 'Just what we're looking for!' he breathed urgently. 'And the wall's a bit lower, too, I think.'

Selecting the strongest branch, he threw one end of the rope over it, jumped to catch the dangling end, quickly made a slip-knot, and pulled. It held perfectly.

'I'll go first,' he grunted, 'then you follow, pulling the rope up after you.'

Using the chunky knots on the rope to give extra leverage, Ashley was up and on top of the wall within seconds. He paused, searching this way and that. Then he disappeared, and Rose heard the slight thud as he landed on the far side. She began scrambling up the rope to join him.

The voluminous skirt of the home-made Carmelite habit made climbing difficult, but eventually, breathless with exertion and excitement, she sat triumphantly astride the cold, rough coping of the wall. She pulled the rope up beside her; threw it down on the other side.

Ashley stood beneath her, arms outstretched, motioning her to jump.

As she slithered off the top of the wall the hem of her brown tunic got caught up on a projecting flint, and when she landed in Ashley's arms her skirt was up round her waist.

In catching her, his hands inevitably slid up the back of her legs, and momentarily he found himself clutching the soft warmth of her bare thighs. For fractionally longer than he needed to, he held her tightly against his body – and in that fleeting moment he felt once again the rising power-surge of desire in his loins.

But with a suddenness that was self-condemnatory, he put her from him. There was work to be done, dangerous work – and this was no time to be weakened by sexual desire and divided loyalties. He had come to rescue Alethea and her father; nothing must be allowed to divert him.

Between the surrounding wall and the château itself lay a closely planted belt of trees. Gripping Rose's hand once more, Ashley began threading his way through the wood-land towards a clearing dimly visible ahead. As they crept nearer, the lights of the castle flickered eerily through the branches.

'There it is,' Ashley murmured grimly. 'There stands our objective.'

They had emerged from the broad, flat overhang of an ancient cedar and were standing on the open side of a ha-ha! Away to their left the grim outline of the château brooded menacingly.

'It looks like a gert fortress to me,' Rose shuddered. 'An' how are we ever goin' to get into that?' She had never seen anything like it before. All the noble houses and mansions on the Lizard peninsula – Trelowarren, Mudgeon, Merthen Manor, Bonython and Bochym – and not forgetting, of course, the Lanteague of such unhappy memory – all of these sizeable properties seemed, in her mind, but as doll's houses by comparison with the château now confronting her.

'We'll manage it somehow,' Ashley replied, through clenched teeth. 'Having come all this way, we're not going to be thwarted now.' The line of his jaw was set hard; his eyes glinted in the moonlight. He was actually enjoying it, Rose thought. The scent of danger was concentrating his mind, tautening every muscle in his body. He was like a panther ready to spring.

Once again he took her hand. It gave her no comfort. It merely heightened her sudden longing to be back in her own country, in her own village, in her own bed. The insaneness of her part in this whole enterprise struck her afresh. What on God's earth did she think she was doing? Risking her freedom, her life even, to help this man save the girl who, in truth, was her rival!

But she was being pulled towards the ha-ha, leaping to the soft turf below, then scrambling up to the balustraded terrace in front of the château. There was no going back now. She had thrown in her lot, for better, for worse, with this man to whom, without perhaps fully realising it, she had long ago surrendered her heart. A feeling of inevitability suffused her whole being – a sense of destiny taking over.

Stealthily they moved through the maze of flower beds towards a divided stone stairway curving down from the terrace. Pausing at the foot of the steps to observe the château more closely they noticed that while most of the windows were in darkness, all three on the first floor immediately to the left of the right-hand end turret were ablaze with light. One of the windows had been left slightly ajar, and through the opening there now flowed the sound of singing – female voices in such perfect harmony and purity of tone that both Ashley and Rose stood, transfixed – listening. It was an inexpressibly beautiful moment – like an interlude of prayer before battle. Involuntarily, Ashley felt for Rose's hand, held it; drew her closer.

Rudely disturbing this precious moment, a different sound grated on their ears.

Footsteps were crunching on the gravelled terrace.

Peering between the uprights of the stone balustrade, they watched two soldiers emerge round the far corner of the château. Not marching smartly, as professional guards should but slopping along casually; doing a final round of the castle grounds, supposedly, before turning in for the night.

They were making straight for the stone stairway beneath which Ashley and Rose were standing.

Flight was unthinkable; they would be spotted immediately. The alarm would be raised, more guards called out; the fugitives trapped. The whole daring enterprise would subside into dismal failure, snuffed out before it had even started. Two more English heads would drop into the basket below the guillotine!

To hide – immediately – was their only chance. But where . . . where?

Projecting from the base of the stone stairway was a semi-circular lily pool, and sheltering within the arch formed by the steps was a marble statuette of the Madonna and Child. It was mounted on a small platform, supported at each corner by a rotund little cherub, and it overlooked the pool. In front of the statuette, just above water level, a much larger cherub straddled a dolphin. Out of the dolphin's mouth spurted a jet of water.

Pushing Rose quickly beneath the arch on one side of the Madonna, Ashley then crossed the pool, using the dolphin's back as a stepping stone, and crouched backwards into the other half of the arch. He stretched his right arm across, behind the Madonna, and gripped Rose's shoulder – as much to increase the sense of companionship as to secure their cramped position.

Together, in silence, they waited.

Crunch . . . crunch . . . crunch . . . crunch. The leisurely foot-falls got louder . . . came nearer. At the top of the stone stairway, they halted for a moment – immediately above the crouching Rose and Ashley – and then very slowly, step by step, they began to descend, one down each flight of steps.

Perhaps they had separated so that each could go his own way . . . right round the gravelled path bordering the *parterre*. . . . 'Oh, please God,' Rose prayed, 'let them go away . . . right away. . . .'

But at the bottom of the steps the soldiers turned towards each other, casually strolling around the perimeter of the pool until they met in the middle, no more than a few yards from where Rose and Ashley were hiding.

Glancing across at Rose, Ashley put a cautionary finger to his lips; it was unnecessary; neither of them dared even to breathe.

As though from habit, each soldier now unshouldered his musket, eased the top button of his tunic, and stretched. In the growing light of the moon their crude, floppy caps looked like bedsocks soaked in blood, their tunics resembled tattered corn sacks, while their red, blue and white striped trousers were too short and frayed round the bottoms. Uncouth, low-grade soldiers, dredged from the gutters and sleazy wine bars of Brest, no doubt – but each man's musket had a viciously sharp-looking bayonet fixed at the end of the barrel.

One man sat down on the stone rim of the pool, while the other began relieving himself into it.

'*Esprit de vin,*' joked the urinater.

'*Pour les poissons, ha,*' rejoined his friend, adding to the pollution of the water with a huge gob of tobacco-fouled spittle, '*et pour les aristos!*'

Ashley glanced across at Rose again, sharing with her, even in this moment of danger, the comically uninhibited genital display and the use of the lily pool as a *pissotière*.

'*Ah!, Deuce!*' the already seated soldier was muttering, '*Cette allumette! Aah! c'est 'phuttt!!. . . .*' He fumbled ineffectually with tinder box and flints, but eventually produced a flame which he applied to an evil-looking clay pipe. Fortunately both men were now sitting with their backs to the grotto, the brazen performer having at last pouched his *pisseur*, so neither of them observed the two crouching figures momentarily illuminated by the flaring tinder.

But they sat, and they sat, and they sat – smoking and spitting – their companionable silence broken only by obscene expletives and periodic imprecations to the deity to rain down fire and brimstone on the heads of all kings and Austrian whores, but especially on all those in authority who order humble soldiers to mount guard in a God-forsaken, out-of-the-way place like St Pol de Leon!

At last, after much asthmatic coughings and many contemptuous expectorations into the blameless but now polluted lily pool, they shouldered muskets once more and moved off along the gravel path in the general direction of the perimeter wall.

It was several minutes before Ashley and Rose felt able to breathe again freely. Then, easing themselves thankfully from the constriction of the grotto, they stood at the foot of the terrace steps, listening to the reassuring sounds of the retreating soldiers.

'Now's our chance,' Ashley whispered. 'Almost certainly they'll stop for a night-cap with their cronies at the Lodge, and that'll give us a fair bit of time before the trouble starts.'

'And when it does?' Rose queried.

Ashley tapped his cutlass. 'This!' he growled, 'And these!' After patting the holstered pistols at his waist, Rose noticed that he drew from his jacket a much smaller pocket pistol. 'Handy little guns, these Richards flintlocks,' he said. 'Made specially for Revenue officers caught in a tight corner. Brought along a couple just in case we get reinforcements from within.'

Clinging to the shadows cast by the terrace balustrade, and using the grass verges to muffle footfalls, they skirted round the side of the château until they reached the forecourt. There they paused for a moment, confronted for the first time by the imposing façade of the Château Fontanelle, and viewing with mounting misgivings the seemingly impregnable front entrance.

'Well,' Ashley said at last, grimly – and with a sudden, sharp intake of breath – 'There it is! That's it. The only question now is – how do we get in?'

CHAPTER TWENTY NINE

Getting In

He drew her into the shadow of a tall tree; put his arms around her; brushed her cheek with his lips.

'And, Rosie,' he murmured, his voice losing its urgency, softening . . . tender, as she had never heard it before, 'whatever happens, I want you to know how grateful, and how glad I am that you came with us. You've been a wonderful help. I couldn't have managed without you.'

It sounded so formal, Rose thought; little more than perfunctory thanks. She felt gratified, of course – pleased to have been of assistance – but had she come all this way with him, not only on this day but at St Keverne, at Helston and Halzephron beach as well, to receive only his gratitude.

And then she felt his arms – both arms – encircling her, drawing her close against his body; felt his lips on hers . . . at first, only tenderly . . . caressingly . . . tracing the outlines . . . but then, with a sudden deep sigh of unleashed passion, he buried his mouth in the yielding softness of her own.

For several, indescribably beautiful moments they remained, locked . . . ethereally at one with the moon, the stars, and the poetic stillness of the night . . . until, at last, with an agonised groan, he tore his lips from hers.

In a strangulated voice, close to her ear, he sighed, 'Oh, Rosie! What are we doing . . . why are we here?' With the tip of his chin he caressed her cheek. 'Why don't we just . . . .,' he faltered.

She longed to reply, 'Oh, yes . . . yes! Why don't we! Why don't we race back to the lugger – even now – before

the tide runs out on us, to sail back to the land we both love
. . . to live happily ever after . . . *together*! Why don't we!
Yes, why don't we!'

Oh, how she longed to say just that.

Instead, she heard her voice, uncharacteristically lack-
lustre, saying, 'Because . . . because you'd never forgive
yourself. It would haunt you for the rest of your life.'

He remained silent for a long while, gently caressing her
forehead with his lips, staring across the forecourt at the
forbidding outline of the château. She was right, of course;
there could be no going back now. They had come to rescue
– and rescue they must.

'We'll try the front door first,' he said curtly, back in his
old matter-of-fact mood. 'We may as well . . . See what
happens. . . . Decide accordingly.'

He took her hand; skirted the forecourt in the shadow of
the trees; sidled along the château wall, up to the portico
above the front door. It occurred to him, as they went, that
he might be holding her hand, sensing that extraordinary
thrill of flesh upon flesh, for the last time. It set up an
uncomfortably poignant ache around his heart.

Reaching the massive pair of oak doors, they tried the
ringed latch. It moved . . . unfastened . . . with an ear-
splitting screech! Ashley's hand flew to his cutlass. They
waited; held their breath. Nothing happened.

Speaking low, and very close to her ear, he said, 'You're
a nun, returning from an evening stroll. If anyone speaks to
you, pretend to be deaf and dumb. If there's any trouble,
I'll be right beside you. If not, make for the room where
they're singing. I'll be watching, and if the coast's clear,
give me a signal.' He lifted her hand to his lips; kissed it
lovingly. 'And, Rosie,' he added, a slight croak in his voice,
'. . . . God Bless you!'

They pushed the heavy door; it yielded; and quietly she
stepped inside.

A typical flagstoned château entrance hall confronted
her. Straight ahead, a divided stone staircase swept
upwards to the first floor landing. Around the walls, various

353

trophies of the chase looked down accusingly. In each of the four corners stood a suit of small armour. But not a living soul was in sight.

Receiving a 'coast clear' signal from Rose, Ashley immediately entered, closing the door quietly behind him. The first thing that struck him as odd was the heavy *Louis Quatorze* kneehole table just inside the doorway, and the matching tapestry-covered *fauteuil* behind it. Both items of furniture looked incongruous in the otherwise austere surroundings of the hall. Presumably, Ashley thought, they had been dragged from their natural setting for use by a *concièrge*.

On the table a lamp burned brightly, and the debris around it suggested that someone had recently been eating supper. Crumbs littered the table and floor; crumpled news sheets lay scattered untidily. But whoever had been eating so indecorously had now gone elsewhere.

Upstairs, the singing voices sounded clearer, more beautiful – more celestial – than ever. In a sudden, inconsequential flash of memory, Rose was reminded of Charles Incledon's rendering of *Let my complaint come before Thee, Oh Lord* – a most beautifully sung solo part of a Sunday morning anthem in St Keverne Church. The memory merely aggravated in Rose's heart a great yearning for home and village.

Ashley's voice broke in on her reverie. 'Make for that sound, Rosie. See if the room's guarded, then signal me. We'll not disturb the hornets yet, unless we have to.'

No sooner had Rose started to mount the stairs than a door near the head of the staircase opened and a rough, formidable-looking woman emerged. The sleeves of her sack-like dress were rolled up, revealing forearms like small tree trunks. On her head was a soiled white cap. She glowered over the balusters at Rose. Silently, Ashley dodged behind the nearest suit of armour, easing the cutlass at his belt.

For the fraction of a second, Rose hesitated – swept by panic – her immediate instinct to turn and run.

But instantaneously she checked the impulse; to do that would mean certain discovery; at all costs she must continue in the disguise.

Pretending to have caught her foot in the folds of her long brown habit, she hitched the hem slightly higher and continued to mount the stairs. The woman was waiting, stolidly, menacingly, at the top. Rose, drawing her hood forward and keeping her head down as though in devotional contemplation, steadfastly walked past the threatening figure. At any moment, she expected to feel herself grabbed by those muscular forearms with their prize-fighter fists, to have her hood thrown back, her disguise uncovered.

Instead, the only attention she received was a surprisingly polite, '*Bon soir, citoyenne*', as she passed, and she was immensely relieved to hear the woman moving off along the passage in the opposite direction.

Realising that the guards might be returning at any moment, and that time was therefore infinitely precious, Rose picked up her skirts and ran. A door at the end of the passage was half open, and inside a long room a group of Carmelite nuns, dressed similarly to herself, were standing around a rotund, benign-looking figure who was conducting their singing. There seemed such an air of spiritual reverence surrounding them that Rose felt reluctant to investigate further. Having satisfied herself that the room was in no way guarded, she returned to the head of the stairs to give the anxiously waiting Ashley the 'All clear'.

Bounding up the stairs and following Rose along the passage, Ashley was shocked to find the room to which she led him had been stripped of all furniture. Only bedding straw lay on the once highly polished floor, with a few pathetic little personal belongings beside each pile. Men and women of all ages sat or stood, either singly or in small groups, trying to occupy themselves as best they could – with nothing to do, little to hope for. Except the nuns. They stood and sang in a circle – an inextinguishable beacon of faith.

Alethea was among them; the only one in secular clothes but singing with a fervour to match even the most ardent.

But she was changed, Ashley realised; subtly changed. It had nothing to do with her crumpled dress, her dusty shoes, her totally ungroomed appearance. No, the lovely corn-coloured hair was still the same; the eyes remained as blue and softly appealing as ever; the unassailable air of refinement had not been altered. Outwardly, although in fearsomely different circumstances, she was still the girl he once rode with, danced with, chaffed and teased – the girl he had fallen in love with during the tender years of childhood. Outwardly, yes – she was the same girl. But now, as she joined those Carmelite sisters in tuneful praise of the deity, her face uplifted, her hands together as though in prayer, there was a radiance in her expression which, Ashley could see, was not of this world.

Rose saw it as well. She had no difficulty in recognising the classic beauty she had once envied so much being whirled in Ashley's arms around the ballroom at Lanteague. No difficulty at all.

But when Ashley, impatient at the loss of time, and totally unmindful of the abruptness of the interruption, now strode into the room and clasped Alethea in his arms, she felt she could no longer play the eavesdropper.

She wandered off along the corridor – deliberately out of earshot . . . almost. She found a wooden carving above the lintel of a door. It was a monogram – not the same as the ironwork one above the gates – but a monogram. She looked at the other doors. Each one had a carved monogram above the lintel. But it was frustrating; she could not make out the letters – at least, not clearly. She felt drawn back to the doorway of the long room which she and Ashley had entered. The nuns had stopped singing; had dispersed. She tried to decipher the monogram; tried to make the letters into 'L de V'.

And then she heard Alethea crying – sobbing, sobbing, sobbing; repeating the words, 'I can't, Ashley. I can't!' – and sobbing. Then the deep murmur of Ashley's voice – coaxing, reasoning . . . pleading. Another voice – a Scottish accent, joining the pleas . . . trying to persuade.

Other voices . . . French accents . . . words unknown to Rose . . . but occasionally intelligible . . . 'Take us with you,

Monsieur . . . take us, *Monsieur, j'implore*!' Harrowing words, desperate pleas. Rose could stand it no longer, she knew how relatively few the lugger could carry.

She moved away; back to the carved monogram; she tried to concentrate on the letters. But still the hubbub in the room, a crescendo of noise; more desperate pleading to pierce her heart; more sobbing, but fainter now.

Only then did she realise the muscular woman *concièrge* had emerged on to the landing once more and was staring at her; she felt the pig-like eyes boring into her.

The woman was coming towards her – rapidly increasing her pace. She was going to hit Rose with those tree-trunk arms, tie her up, throw her into some horrible dungeon. Warn Ashley! . . . at all costs, warn Ashley! But she stood, rooted to the polished floor, paralysed with indicision . . . should she run, or should she try to act normally, brazen it out.

To her absolute astonishment, she saw the woman turn right at the top of the stairs, run down into the hall and out through the front door.

'She's gone for help,' Rose said to herself. 'Now I really must warn Ashley!.

She had scarcely done so when, above the clamour in the room, a deep-throated bell could be heard clanging in the distance.

'The alarm!' someone shouted. 'They're sounding the alarm. It's too late! The place'll be swarming with soldiers.'

'It's *NOT* too late!' Ashley shouted, momentarily quelling the uproar, 'Make for the quay! I'll hold the soldiers off for as long as possible – but you must *RUN* . . . run like fiends out of *Hell*!'

For the next few minutes, bedlam reigned – except, that is, among the nuns. They remained calm, resigned – with no thoughts of anything so undignified as a hurried escape. If, momentarily, any among them had doubts about her predetermined future, no outwards signs of it were permitted to show.

Alethea, though still tearful, continued steadfastly in

357

their midst. She had made up her mind, she had at last found inner peace; she would stay.

Among the rest, there were several who regarded themselves as too old to seek a fresh life in a foreign land. They, also, would stay and take their chance. But Ashley and Rose, after frequent urgings to their charges to 'hurry', found themselves shepherding a party of some ten or twelve fugitives down the stone staircase and out into the night.

From the stable block came the unmistakeable sounds of soldiers being flushed from the warmth of their night quarters – clattering boots on cobbles, jingling musket slings, cursings, swearings, spitting and coughing.

'Show them the way, Rosie – and make 'em hurry,' Ashley commanded. 'I'll stay here and delay the pursuit.'

'An' I'll stay alongside ye,' said a familiar Scottish voice in Ashley's ear. 'Just hand me one o' your flintlocks, an' we'll gie 'em a wight response to their haivers.'

'No, no, Sir Andrew. You cut along with the rest, down to the quay.'

'Och, no. Ye've been a richt guid laddie. I wadna want to leave ye on your ane,' Sir Andrew replied, the emergency seeming to invoke the vernacular. 'Gie me a gun, then, laddie, an' we'll mak' a bonnie fecht o' it.'

Ashley gladly handed over a holster pistol, also one of the Barnell 'Man Stopper' pistols from his jacket pocket. It was just the kind of support he'd been hoping for.

'Follow me, then,' he said, after handing the weapons to Sir Andrew, 'I know where we can get a bit of cover.'

He sprinted across the terrace, down the flight of stone steps, and once more found himself peering through the gaps in the balustrade. Puffing and blowing from the unaccustomed exercise, Sir Andrew soon joined him.

They had scarcely taken up position and cocked the flintlocks before a small group of soldiers could be heard marching in their direction.

'Give them a volley from here,' Ashley growled, 'then move along and give them another, eh.'

Both flintlocks blazed out into the night. Immediately,

the marching ceased, expletives rent the air, orders were shouted, confused, contradictory. The unexpected had caught the soldiery unprepared. The little volley had done its work – temporarily halted the advance, created confusion.

Ashley, with Sir Andrew close behind, raced along the grass verge to the far end of the terrace, halted.

'Give them another . . . from here. They'll think we're more than just the two of us.'

This time the little 'Man Stoppers' blazed. It mattered not that the aim was ineffectual; it created a false illusion of fire power.

But it also created further confusion. While Ashley and Sir Andrew were retiring to the shelter of the encircling woodlands to reload, it seemed that all hell was breaking loose between the château and the perimeter wall.

The continuous clanging of the bell had obviously alerted the guards billeted in the Lodge beside the iron gates, and they too were now adding to the mounting confusion; shots being fired indiscriminately in all directions, some disastrously finding targets among fellow soldiers advancing from the opposite direction – crunching footsteps, hither and thither; voices shouting – Rose's voice clearly heard shouting above the rest, 'Here . . . this way . . . this way . . .' followed by an ugly scream, then a silence that had Ashley's blood running cold . . . more screams, more running footsteps . . . more crackling, blazing muskets . . . more shouting of orders . . . pandemonium!

Another volley from Ashley and Sir Andrew drew the soldiers, now reforming into some order, in their direction – towards the woodlands, away from the wall by the jetty.

'Time to cut and run for it,' Ashley growled again, 'Can't leave it any longer . . . tide's running out.'

They didn't bother about finding Rose's rope. A leg-up from Sir Andrew, and Ashley was athwart the top of the wall, leaning down, hauling Sir Andrew after him, the urgency of the moment lending hitherto untapped power to their limbs.

At the jetty, Zeph was faithfully waiting, ready to cast off. 'Only just in time, zur,' he greeted. 'Water be runnin' out fast.'

Ashley's eyes swept the lugger. It looked alarmingly full of people. The extra weight would be lowering the hull, increasing the draft, needing more water to keep her afloat. *Heatherbelle II* was over-full – but it would be heartless to turn anyone off. They must just take the risk.

He peered more closely at the passengers. Something was wrong – very wrong! 'Where's Rosie!' he barked at Zeph, 'Where is she?'

'The little maid, you'm meanin',' Zeph replied obtusely, his voice a little slurred, 'Her don't seem to have returned yet, Mester.'

'*But where is she*?' Ashley flared, turning to the people already in the lugger. 'Was she not with you?'

Ranald Mackenzie, Sir Andrew's brother, volunteered, 'She was with us to begin with – right down to the wall. I was the last over. I felt sure she was right behind me. But when I looked back from the top of the wall, she'd disappeared.'

'That settles it!' Ashley growled. 'I'm going back for her.'

'But, Mester . . .' Zeph warned, '. . . the tide! Unless we'm away pretty smartly, we'm stuck!'

'I can't help that,' Ashley roared. 'I can't *possibly* leave without Rose!'

'Then we're all as good as dead,' Sir Andrew snapped. 'Caught like a lot o' rats in a trap!'

'Certain death for all of us,' wailed someone.

'They'll torture us for trying to escape!' came from another quarter.

'I'm sorry,' Ashley retorted, 'but I *cannot* leave Rose!'

Immediately, he set off along the path, calling over his shoulder, 'If I'm not back in time, then sail without me! D'you hear that, Zeph?' he shouted. 'That's an order!'

He disappeared into the semi-darkness.

Zeph looked again at the depth of the water. So did Sir Andrew. They looked at each other. Simultaneously, without a word being spoken, both men clambered on to the jetty, and started in pursuit. Zeph carried the blunderbuss; Sir Andrew held Ashley's holster pistol by the barrel. The butt-end was hard enough to knock a man senseless – and if it became necessary Sir Andrew was prepared to use it that way.

Ashley by this time had almost reached the great iron gates. He flattened himself against the wall, listening. The lodge-keeper, jostled by a group of cursing soldiers, was fumbling with a large bunch of keys . . . deliberately; too deliberately; for the soldiers' liking. They were in an ugly mood, prodding with their bayonets.

Any moment now, Ashley thought, the gate would burst open. The soldiers would pour forth on to the footpath leading to the jetty.

Out of the darkness came running footsteps behind him. Trapped! he concluded. Soldiers ahead – soldiers, presumably, at the rear. Only hope now – to make a dash for it; past the gate, then up over the wall by the over-hanging tree – somehow! Footsteps in the rear getting closer – too close! 'If I'm going it must be – *NOW*!'

He had taken no more than a few strides when a long-barrelled musket was pointed through the bars of the iron gate – and *FIRED*!

A searing pain shot through Ashley's right thigh. He staggered; crumpled; hit the flinty pathway with his cheek bone, his head crashing into a jagged boulder.

Then . . . complete darkness . . . Nothing.

CHAPTER THIRTY

Getting Out

The lodge-keeper continued to fumble; deliberately trying the wrong keys. Jacques Dubois, Zeph's old comrade was a friend of his as well. Their back gardens adjoined. He liked Monsieur MacKenzie. He was a good employer; looked after his staff. He hated the Revolution; hated soldiers. He tried another wrong key; he knew it wouldn't fit because it was from the wrong bunch – but he hated soldiers.

He liked the quiet life – and Monsieur MacKenzie had always treated him well. So had Madame; and he had grown fond of *les enfants*, the young Monsieur Hamish, and his sister, Mam'selle Fiona. They helped him in the vinery when the grapes were ripe; picked apples in the orchard for the cider press; admired his garden; and sometimes brought his wife a bunch of roses which they'd smuggled from the *parterre*. He hated the Revolution; hated soldiers.

He glanced through the bars of the great iron gates; saw that Zeph Curnow and the Monsieur's brother had dragged an inert body back to the lugger, and decided he could procrastinate no longer. For the good of his own health and the preservation of his body, he must now insert the right key. He still fumbled; but he knew that in a few moments the great iron gate would be swung open and the hated soldiery would swarm on to the footpath. He offered a silent prayer to Our Lady and St Thegonnec, hoping that he had kept the wolves at bay for long enough, and then he turned the key.

Zeph and Sir Andrew, having laid the still lifeless Ashley on a bundle of sailcloth, were now frantically trying to get the lugger under way. Sir Andrew had already cast off the bow-rope, and the nose of the ship was slowly swinging away from the quay. But not enough. Something was wrong.

Quick as a flash, Zeph had one of the sweeps over the side – shoving for all he was worth.

'She'm stickin' in the stern,' he panted. 'Git 'em for'arder, zur. Git 'em for'ard!'

Sir Andrew hastily jostled a few passengers into the bows, thereby shifting the weight off the sternpost.

But still she stuck.

Both he and Zeph realised that only seconds now separated them all from total disaster – re-capture and death as fugitives – so rapidly will a boat become stranded by a falling tide. Hurling an oar to his brother, Ranald, with a strident exhortation to 'Heave, man . . . Heave!', he picked up another and quickly joined Zeph in the stern.

Together, using oars like punt poles, and rocking the hull as much as they could, they heaved and shoved to the absolute limit of their strength.

Still she would not move. *Heatherbelle II* and her boatload of anxious fugitives, it seemed, was stuck on the mud for the next eight hours at least. At their leisure, the soldiers would now arrest the escaping *émigrés* and march them back to their grisly fate.

In desperation rather than in hope, Sir Andrew called for one more supreme effort. 'All together, now. . . . *Heave!*'

A grating sound . . . a slight shudder . . . and, suddenly, she was free!

Instantly, a little cheer burst forth from the small group of passengers. Simultaneously, a shot rang out from the shore.

'Up sails, then!' Zeph urged. 'Quick as ee can!'

Sir Andrew and his brother were already at the mainmast, hauling on the halyard, hoisting the sail. Leaving his brother to make fast, Sir Andrew went for'ard and hoisted the foresail.

The lodge-keeper, hearing the muffled crackle of the canvas as the sails caught the off-shore breeze, allowed the great iron gate to be pulled open. He had done his best for his friend, Jacques Dubois, but he could hold back the flood no longer.

Immediately, the soldiers were pouring through the gateway, on to the footpath – some kneeling, others standing – muskets cocked, taking aim – then the order. . . . '*TIREZ*!'

Bullets whistled through the lugger's shrouds, pierced canvas, thudded into masts.

'Daown! everyone,' Zeph shouted, 'Daown!'

'Heads *DOWN*!' Sir Andrew echoed, 'Keep well down! Don't give the devils anything to shoot at.'

Gladly the passengers obeyed, thankful for the protection of solid, clinker-built shipsides.

In the dim light, shadowy figures could be seen running towards the point forming the northern half of the pincer of land enclosing the inlet. To reach the safety of the massive Baie de Morlaix, the lugger must first slip through the narrow outlet, and the soldiers had been quick to appreciate the strategic value of the promontory as a firing platform. The rocks themselves would provide cover against retaliatory fire, and the very narrowness of the inlet mouth would force the escaping craft to come well within range. From such a vantage point, they could pepper the fugitives unmercifully.

Very slowly – painfully – Ashley opened his eyes. His head ached, his right temple was throbbing alarmingly, and the cheek bone below it felt horribly sore.

Through the swirling mists of returning consciousness, he realised that he was stretched out on a piece of rumpled sailcloth, with his head propped up on someone's lap. A ministering hand was dabbing at his cheek and his temple with a wad of sea-soaked muslin.

The top of his right leg felt as though held in a vice; there was very little feeling below it. He tried to raise himself on one elbow to investigate the cause, but the effort so exacerbated the pain in his head that immediately he fell back again. For the moment he could do no more than lie where he was, trying to bring into some kind of focus the blurred events of the immediate past. At first, in the confusion of his thoughts, he imagined himself to be back at Halzephron beach, recovering from the affray with the wreckers. But the sailcloth bed he was lying on was much harder than soft sand; and the gentle movement, the familiar sounds – the pungent smells of tarred rope, fish scales and pitch all around him – all that could mean only one thing, that for some extraordinary reason he was being taken somewhere by boat. But where? . . . and what on earth was happening?

He glanced upwards – seeking explanation, reassurance – confidently expecting to find Rose's sympathetic eyes smiling down at him.

Sympathy there was – even an attempt at reassurance – but it wasn't Rosie. The outline of the hair, shape of face, eyes – soulfully beautiful though they were – belonged to someone else. A stranger; and yet someone he'd seen before – quite recently – very recently. But not Rose.

Immediately, alarm bells rang through the confusion of his mind. Again he tried to sit up. Again the devastating pains threw him down again. Oh, God! – but let it not all be true!

As memory began its sinuous return, he deliberately closed his eyes . . . tried to shut it out. But it wouldn't go away. The Château Fontanelle . . . Alethea . . . her vocation found at last . . . resolutely determined to take the veil, and declining the chance to be rescued. The other MacKenzies . . . father and mother and two children, a boy and a girl . . . the other fugitives, some English, some French . . . fleeing from the château, across the *parterre*, down to the wall . . . all in the darkness . . . . . shots being fired . . . soldiers running . . . and Rosie! Where was she! . . . . . Why wasn't she. . . .

He forced himself to sit up . . . despite the pain. 'Rosie!' he shouted. 'Zeph! – Where's Rosie!' And receiving no answer, he repeated, '*Where is Rosie!*'

The only reply was a fresh explosion of musketry from the shore. This time it was more accurately directed. Splinters flew from the gunwales, from the masts, and even from the down-curving tiller, narrowly missing Zeph's guiding hand.

Ashley tried to raise himself higher; to manoeuvre legs and arms into a crawling position. In doing so he not only felt the pain but also saw the damage to his right thigh, – the blood-soaked breeches, and the strip of linen underskirt wound round his leg and twisted tight by a sliver of timber.

Full consciousness brought memory flooding back . . . the running battle with the soldiers in the château grounds, . . . hauling Sir Andrew up over the wall . . . the dash along the path to the lugger . . . the rapidly falling tide . . . the sudden, awful realisation that Rose was not there . . . the return dash along the rough path . . . the musket being pointed through the iron gate . . . the shot . . . the searing pain in his right thigh. . . .

It all came racing back.

Ignoring Sir Andrew's terse injunction to 'Keep your head down, man. Keep *D O W N*!' Ashley managed to raise himself high enough to see above the gunwale. The situation was clear. Away over the port bow the soldiers could be discerned, re-grouping on the very edge of the promontory – taking up close-range firing positions. It was equally clear that although Zeph was hugging the starboard shore, as closely as he dare, thus distancing *Heatherbelle II* as far as possible from the soldiers' fire, he could not ignore the constant danger of the ebbing tide. To run aground now, with freedom beckoning just beyond the mouth of the inlet, would be unforgiveable, and even though it meant taking the mid-channel, and sailing perilously close to the battery of muskets now forming among the rocks on the point, he must take that chance. Far better to risk a hull-full of shot and a tattered sail while running the gauntlet of bullets than to be stranded on the starboard shore like a paralysed duck.

Zeph knew what he was doing. He must be allowed, unhampered, uninstructed, to get on with it.

With a sigh of frustration, Ashley lay back again, resting his head once more among the rustling silks of a supportive lap. As though in answer to his thoughts, a voice, speaking with an attractive French-English accent, said softly, 'It is no use, Monsieur. You cannot do anything to assist. You must wait until we are free – and then we shall try to make you more comfortable.'

'But I *must*, Dammit!' Ashley blurted, trying to struggle up again, 'I must do something. What about the girl! Where is she? Why isn't she on board?'

Once more the attractively accented voice restrained him, saying 'Monsieur, you must be patient. The situation – as you have just seen – it is critical. Very critical. You cannot do anything now – not until we are all really free. Then . . . perhaps . . . after that . . . We shall see. . . .'

She was right, of course – this charmingly spoken fugitive from the Château Fontanelle. There was nothing he could do now in his present state of immobility. Even supposing he were to dive overboard, swim ashore in a dramatic attempt to rescue Rose, just how far would he get before a soldier put a bullet through his head. Besides, it would put Zeph in a terrible quandary. . . .

And Zeph was doing well. Nothing must be allowed to divert him from his task.

By now, *Heatherbelle II* was beginning to feel the wind; sails tauntening, burton, bowline and jump-stay taking the strain; and the steadily increasing 'slish' of her bow-wave – like music in the ears of a fugitive – confirming that the vessel was gathering speed. They were nearly there! Trouble ahead, perhaps, – as they sped through the gap – but they were so nearly free!

Closer and closer they came to the rock-strewn point. No sound yet from the shore; uncanny stillness, broken only by the ripple of sail edge, the creak of masts and spars, the 'slish-slish-slish' of hull through water.

Among the seaweed-covered rocks, musket barrels and bayonets glinted in the eerie moonlight.

'Heads down!' Sir Andrew ordered, assuming command in Ashleys' stead, '. . . and hold your fire.'

They were nearly there . . . nearly out through the mouth of the creek . . . out into the broad expanse of the Baie . . . and safety.

But the stillness; the suspense; the waiting for the inevitable. . . .

Then it came – with a suddenness that was almost a relief – a staccato voice, shattering the night, – '*T I R E Z!*' – and instantly every rock, every boulder seemed to be blazing defiance. Once again, like some elusive bird in a wildfowling competition, *Heatherbelle II* was caught in a hail of bullets – thudding into her hull, splintering her washstrake, tearing at her sails.

But still she kept going – Zeph keeping his head well down, but somehow seeing enough over the starboard bow to keep her on course. Nearly through the gap now – well within sight of freedom.

A second wave of soldiers were moving forward; scrambling over the rocks to be at the very edge of the point – to be nearer the fleeing lugger, to be able to pick off each individual member of the boatload, one by one.

This was the moment Sir Andrew had been waiting for.

Having relieved Ashley of his loaded holster pistol and his 'Man Stopper' flintlock, and handed them to his brother, Ranald, Sir Andrew had taken charge of the Ferguson, 'four-shots-a-minute' breech-loading rifle. Together the two brothers were forming a small broadside battery amidships.

Lying beside Zeph in the stern was the Waters, brass-barrelled blunderbuss – primed, loaded, and ready to fire:

Ashley glanced at it; glanced at Zeph. But Zeph must concentrate on navigation and seamanship, not marksmanship – and inactivity was gnawing at Ashley almost as much as the pain in his thigh.

He jerked himself on to hands and knees; crawled over to the blunderbuss; cocked it, and pointed it over the gunwale – at the very moment Sir Andrew shouted *F I R E*! First, the flintlocks and the Ferguson blazed – then, after a second's pause, the deafening roar of Ashley's blunderbuss.

As a damaging blast of fire it was insignificant. But it took the soldiers by surprise – stopped them in their tracks; gained precious time.

Time enough for Zeph to slip through the gap? Unbelievably, yes!

Spasmodic shooting only from the shore, now; bullets dropping short, hissing into the water.

Magical sound of tiller handle creaking on rudder head as Zeph brought the helm up. Ship now feeling the full power of the wind; joyfully bearing away to starboard . . . out into the Baie de Morlaix.

Freedom . . . Safety . . . at last!

CHAPTER THIRTY ONE

Cocking a Snook

Madame Michelle de Levoisier looked across at Sir Andrew. She had pretty eyes, Ashley thought; even in the pale light of dawn it was clear she had once been *une jeune fille, très jolie.* The passing years had done nothing to strip her of her charm; as with good wine, they had merely matured it.

'It would be good for it to come out, Andrew,' she said attractively. 'To leave it where it is would not be good, you understand. I think it might become *gangreneux* – gangrenous, is that how you say?'

They were discussing, of course, the bullet in Ashley's thigh, but in her voice, with its inflections, even a grisly subject like a gaping wound sounded almost exciting.

Sir Andrew nodded agreement. 'You know best, my dear. I must leave it to you.'

Gesticulating with that delicate finesse which only French women seem able to portray, she protested, 'But, no. I do not know what is best. I only know what Philippe, my 'usband tell me. He say it is better not to allow it to . . . er . . . *suppurer.* How you say, to *festerre*, no?'

'What do *you* say, Ashley?' Sir Andrew asked. 'Madame de Levoisier's late husband was a physician.'

Again the expressive hands – this time disclaiming. 'But everybody seems to think that because my 'usband was a *docteur*, then I also, will know . . . you understand, yes. But, of course, it is not so. I take an interest . . . yes, of course. But I do not know, really. . . .'

Sir Andrew took one of Madame de Levoisier's hands in

370

his; looked at it, admiringly. 'You have very pretty hands, Madame, but they are strong, the fingers look very skilful. Would you be prepared to try. . . . ?'

Once more those hands, pushing away an unpalatable situation, and unwanted decision. 'No, no, M'sieur. I could not. I have not the skill . . . or the knowledge. You must not ask me.'

Sir Andrew's bristling, sandy eyebrows rose questioningly, puckering his forehead. '*Wad ye not do't for the braw wee laddie*?' he asked, knowing full well she'd not understand the dialect but counting on the soft charm of the accent, 'He's come all the way from Cornwall to fetch us home . . . to save us all from . . .' He gave a horribly realistic imitation of the guillotine's chop.

'Ugh!' Madame almost screamed, 'Don't be so *descriptif*, Andrew. *Vous etes une bête*!' She bathed Ashley with her lovely, romantic-looking eyes. 'But of course I will try . . . that is if the . . . how do you call 'im, 'the vee laddie', yes? . . . if M'sieur wish me to.'

'Well?' Sir Andrew quizzed, 'What d'you say, Ashley, m'boy? Shall we ask Madame de Levoisier to get that damned bit o' lead out of your thigh . . . or shall we leave it there to fester?'

By now, *Heatherbelle II* was well clear of the Ile de Batz, and even in the growing light of dawn the Brittany coastline was rapidly fading into the distance. With a fair wind, Ashley reckoned, it would take at least another eight hours before the welcome outline of the Lizard peninsula loomed out of the Cornish sea. And even then it would be some time before he could get proper attention from his own doctor. During those intervening hours the wound, as Sir Andrew had suggested, would begin to fester; after that, gangrene might set in – and as every sailor in His Majesty's ships was well aware, the only known cure for *that* was amputation.

It would be painful, of course; but then, he had experienced pain before – on the cobbled courtyard at Lydford, for instance; fighting for his life on board that Portuguese brig at Halzephron; and even under the professional skill of Degory Logan. He had survived them all; it would be nothing new.

And after all, if you had to suffer, what better way than by surrendering yourself into such exquisite hands.

Ashley smiled somewhat ruefully at Sir Andrew. 'The left leg took a battering some years ago, so I suppose we may as well even things up a bit on the right.' He turned to Madame de Levoisier, saying, 'Yes. Please try. I know you'll do your best.'

The fact that Zeph had been able to supply everyone on board with copious swigs of brandy as soon as *Heatherbelle II* was well clear of the French coast had not surprised Ashley at all. What more natural that that his old smuggling friend Jacques Dubois, should have sealed their reunion with a commemorative gift of best quality white cognac. And Zeph was, by nature, a generous character. Everyone, it seemed, had been given more than enough just to keep out the early morning cold. Indeed, some of those unaccustomed to imbibing such heady liquid were already showing signs of over-indulgence. And that was no bad thing; with a long sea trip ahead of them they could well afford to drift off into a deep alcoholic slumber. It would keep them out of the way.

But it was when Ashley saw Zeph, having drained the keg at his side, lurch unsteadily for'ard to the foredeck, returning a few moments later with a fresh, unbroached cask – it was then that he began to wonder just what the two old smuggling friends had been up to during his absence in the Château Fontanelle.

Not that he gave the matter much penetrative thought. He felt immeasurably grateful to Zeph for the frequently proffered cup of pain-subduing liquid – all the more so when he saw Sir Andrew hand to Madame Levoisier a fearsome-looking marlin spike.

The pain was excrutiating while she was actually using it – so extreme, in fact, that Ashley knew he was on the point of fainting. The brandy made little difference. But just when he thought he could stand the agony no longer, the bullet rolled out of his thigh, and dropped into the sailcloth. It was all over.

But not for Madame de Levoisier. So intense had been her concentration, so steeled were her nerves – and so close had she come to the point of giving up – that when at last the gruesome task was completed, she fainted right away. Fortunately, Sir Andrew's arms were there to catch her. Willingly he soothed her, cosseted her – and when at length she returned to consciousness, Zeph was readily on hand with a sip of cognac.

Brandy, too, was her demand when, after several restorative sips from Zeph's beaker, she tore further bands from her underskirt, soaked one of them in the precious liquid, and swabbed the wound. The remainder she used as bandages, tying the top one especially tight in order to staunch the bleeding.

'My 'usband, Philippe, 'e tell me this is *le tourniquet*,' she enlightened, twisting the top bandage with the same sliver of timber she had used before, ' 'e say it was . . . ur . . . it was made . . . no, it was *invented* . . . yes, by a Frenchman, Monsieur Petit, you know. 'E was *inventeur*, you understand. It is very good because you can . . . ur . . . make it tight, yes, . . . but you can also make it loose again when the bleeding stop, you know, yes?'

'*Le tourniquet*,' Sir Andrew nodded sagely. '*Il est très bien, oui?*'

'*Oui, oui, M'sieur*,' Madame de Levoisier sparkled. 'You speak in French ver' well, mon ami.'

Having made Ashley as comfortable as possible on a fresh, less blood-stained piece of sailcloth, Madame de Levoisier, exhausted by her impromptu display of surgical skill, availed herself of the hospitable crook of Sir Andrew's arm, and dozed.

Ashley, exhausted also by his efforts to withstand the pain, gratefully accepted another swig of brandy, and then he, too, tried to doze.

But, for a while, the merciful arms of sleep eluded him.

Instead, the corrosion of doubt began eating away at his conviction, tenuously held but strengthened by the sympathetic opionion of Madame de Levoisier, that he had done all he could for Rose. But, had he? Might he not, despite his wounds, have made a further attempt to reach her – plunged overboard and struck out for the bank opposite – the one held by the soldiers? And even if he had been captured, might it not have been more honourable to share with Rose whatever fate might decree . . . even if it meant death for both of them? Might it not have been at least some comfort to her to know that he was with her to the end – she who had thrown in her lot with him in this perilous adventure, stood by him in his hour of need?

And yet, what of the other side of the coin? What about Zeph – who had also stood by him, not only in his hours of need but throughout his life; who had nurtured him from childhood and nobly sustained his mother throughout her long and lonely widowhood. What about him? How far could you strain the loyalty of a man like Zeph, a loyal servant if ever there was one? Which was it to be – to save the lives of a boatload of comparative strangers by sailing on, leaving his master to face almost certain death? – or to try to effect a rescue later on, thereby jeopardising the lives of all his passengers?

And among those passengers was Sir Andrew MacKenzie – another who had valiantly supported his mother since that disastrous homecoming of her husband from Roscoff which had ended on the rocks below Manacle Point.

How could you place Zeph in such a dilemma? Or, indeed, Sir Andrew – who probably would have assumed responsibility and command. Would not both of them have decided there could be no return home without the master of *Heatherbelle II*? Would they not have felt bound to turn back. . . .?

Had they done so, the whole venture would almost certainly have been lost; lives forfeited; no one would have gained. Whereas, as things now stood, a boatload of fugitives were safely on their way to freedom.

Perhaps, after all, Madame de Levoisier had been right. . . .

And yet . . . and yet . . . and yet. . . .

At last, sheer exhaustion came as a ministering angel, soothing pain, attenuating doubt, and suffusing blame, . . . and he slept.

When he awoke, sombre night was already merging into radiant dawn. Away over the port bow the dim outline of the Lizard could be faintly discerned, snaking its way out into the English Channel. Home in sight again at last.

Ashley thought of declaring the good news to his boatload of passengers – that their anxieties and privations were nearly at and end – but on reflection he decided to leave them undisturbed. They had all made themselves as comfortable as possible, some in the primitive sleeping quarters below the foredeck, others lying in the beam on whatever available boat tackle might bring them comfort.

Only Sir Andrew appeared to be awake. With Madame de Levoisier apparently asleep in the crook of his arm, he was quietly luxuriating in the aroma, and the swirling smoke clouds, of a long, fat cigar. Ashley wondered how on earth he had come by it. Surely he could never have concealed it from his so-recent captors; the starkness of the living conditions in the Château Fontanelle had suggested that the prisoners would certainly have been deprived of any such luxuries. Sir Andrew, it was known, had considerable financial interest in a tobacco factory further down the river at Morlaix, but he could hardly have received supplies from it during his captivity in the château.

Then the thought struck him . . . and he looked at Zeph. As so often in the past, Zeph had been watching his 'Mester', reading his thoughts.

'I was just wonderin', Mester Ashley,' he began, shyly, 'seein' as you'm feeling a little bit better, like, whether you'm in the mind to enjoy a cigar, zur?' He produced a flat wooden box from the stern locker, and proffered it to his skipper.

Ashley smiled. 'I didn't know you were in the habit of carrying cigars with you, Zeph.'

'Oh, no, zur. Not usual, like. But my friend, Jack Dub-oyes, he give me a few . . . just for old time's sake, if you unnerstan' me zur.'

'More than just a few, it seems,' Ashley chaffed, peering past Zeph into the open stern locker, 'and a little bit of liquid refreshment to go with it, too, I see.'

'Aw, that, zur,' Zeph replied with some confusion, and rather too hurriedly pulling closed the sliding locker door, 'That be a little keepsake from my old friend, as well, zur. Very generous fellow, is Jack Duboyes, very friendly, generous fellow, zur.'

Ashley nodded. 'It seems like it.' he mused, taking one of the proffered cigars, 'Very generous indeed. And how many kegs of that excellent cognac were included in his generosity, would you say, Zeph?'

Zeph fumbled with the tinder box; eventually produced a light, saying, 'Aw, 'tis only a few, zur. Nothin' much, if you know what I mean, like. 'Tis only a few.'

Cupping his hand around the burning taper, shielding it from the wind, he waited until satisfied that his Master's cigar was well alight before continuing: ' 'Twas while you an' . . .' he checked, sensing the indelicacy of mentioning Rose, then hurried on, ' 'Twas while you was in the castle, zur, my friend Jack, he were very determined, like, that his old smugg . . . that his ole friend o' many years ago should not go home without a bit o' . . . well, without a few keepsakes, if you understand me, zur.'

Ashley nodded sagely. 'Yes, I quite understand, Zeph,' he said solemnly – before adding, with a twinkle, 'and you, of course, did nothing very strenuous to prevent him, eh.'

Zeph smiled back. 'No, zur, nothin' extra special in that partikler; nothin' extra strong, like.'

They lapsed into silence; that companionable silence possible only between friends of long standing. Master and man, now, yes – but a relationship founded upon that unique affection which sometimes exists between servant and Master's son, and which knows no artificial barriers.

Ashley wondered just how much tobacco and spirits Zeph and his friend, Jacques Dubois, had found time to store aboard *Heatherbelle II*. A not inconsiderable quantity, he wouldn't wonder.

He shifted his position, easing the pain in his thigh; settled back to enjoy the fragrance of his cigar. All seemed very peaceful on board.

Madame de Levoisier, emerging from fitful slumber within Sir Andrew's protecting arms, yawned prettily, stretched, and sat up. Rubbing the sleep out of her eyes, she looked around. Already the dark outline of the Cornish coast was becoming increasingly visible.

'Aha!' she exclaimed with a sweeping gesture, 'England, *n'est pas*? It seem a ver' long time since I go in England.'

She gazed around, sleepily, before adding, 'And what is more, I see we have company, yes?'

Sir Andrew, stirring at the sound of her voice, also sat up and rubbed his eyes. 'Company? What d'yo mean – where?'

'Over there,' she said, pointing astern. 'Do you not see? It seem almost like a . . . ur . . . how you say . . . like a ghost ship, yes?'

Following the direction of her finger, Sir Andrew murmured, 'Och, yes. I see her. A cutter . . . with white sails. But I see what you mean, Madame. In the half light, she does look a wee bit ghostly. And she looks as though she's bearing down on us. *Excusez moi, un moment, Madame. Je consulter avec le maitre de bateau.*'

Madame de Levoisier clapped her hands approvingly. 'Mais oui, M'sieur. You speak so well. You shall do as you say.'

Clambering aft over fishing gear and recumbet passengers, Sir Andrew eventually knelt down at Ashley's side. 'D'ye see what I see?' he asked, pointing over Zeph's shoulder. 'As Madame says, I think we have company.'

Ashley raised himself on one arm; looked astern. 'Oho!' he exclaimed, a resilience returning to his voice for the first

377

time since leaving Brittany, 'We are not only being followed, but unless I'm very much mistaken, we're actually being chased.'

Zeph had followed Ashley's gaze. 'Aw, ais,' he purred, 'I believe you'm right, Mester. I do believe 'tis one o' they God-damned . . . aw, er . . . beggin' your pardon, zur . . . but I do reckon 'tis one o' they Revenue cruisers.'

'I know it is!' Ashley replied emphatically, 'And again, unless I'm mistaken, she's the *Vixen*, returning from her routine nightly sweep along the coast.'

Zeph, unable to suppress the old excitement stirring once more in his veins, edged closer to Ashley, saying; 'And what be plannin' to do, then, Mester?'

'Nothing,' Ashley replied evasively, 'why should I be?'

Zeph flashed an anxious glance at Sir Andrew – seeking help.

'After all,' Ashley went on, an enigmatic smile playing around his lips, 'what possible interest could a boatload of fugitives from revolutionary France be to one of His Majesty's revenue cruisers, eh?'

Sir Andrew inhaled noisily through the red whiskers of his moustache; regarded Zeph quizzically from beneath his bushy eyebrows; cleared his throat, and said, 'We can do without those beggars crawling all over the ship, eh, laddie? No reason to disturb the passengers unnecessarily, don't you agree?'

Ashley appeared not to be taking a great deal of notice. He had hauled himself upright against the ship's gunwale and was gingerly trying his weight on his bandaged right leg. At first, the pain was acute – almost unbearable – but after a few moments it gradually began to lessen, and he hopped rather than walked aft to the tiller.

For several minutes he stared at the cruiser. 'Hum,' he said at last, 'she really does seem to be interested in us. She's right on our tail . . . and she seems to be gaining on us steadily. Hmm!'

'Had us better not make sail a bit, then, zur,' Zeph enquired eagerly, '*Heatherbelle* can outsail any o' they darned revenue cutters, I reckon, and 'twouldn seem right to let un overhaul we.'

'You sound a bit nervous, Zeph,' Ashley remarked, tantalizingly. 'Is there something on your mind?'

Zeph shifted from one foot to the other. He was about to reply when Sir Andrew intervened. 'As you already know, laddie, there's a keg or two o' brandy on board – and right glad we've all been to have it – especially yourself, I'll aver, while the Madame de Levoisier was relieving you of a certain unwanted object. . . .'

'Very glad indeed,' Ashley interposed.

'. . . . and that cigar you're enjoying; rolled from best quality tobacco leaf, wouldn't you agree?'

'Unhesitatingly,' Ashley nodded.

'And . . . eh, . . . correct me if I'm wrong, laddie, but it would hardly be desirable for an officer of His Majesty's Customs Service to be found with contraband on board his own ship, would it?'

'Oh, I don't know,' Ashley responded wickedly, – teasingly, 'the odd keg or two – kept strictly for medicinal purposes, of course – would hardly interest the commander of a revenue cutter.'

'And if there were more than just a keg or two . . .?' Sir Andrew persisted.

'You sound, squire, like Abraham bargaining with the Lord over the destruction of Sodom and Gomorrah,' Ashley chaffed, ' "Peradventure there be fifty righteous within the city . . .?" '

Sir Andrew laughed. He was pleased to hear a lighter note in Ashley's voice; the laddie had been through a rough passage, and he was obviously still feeling extremely upset about the loss of that girl. Who did Zeph say she was; a barmaid from St. Keverne, was it? Well, the laddie had done all he could to save her: no doubt about that. Any further attempts would have resulted in disaster for all of them – and alsmost certianly the laddie would have got himself killed. Even so, it was only natural he should be feeling mighty uncomfortable about the whole episode.

Good thing, perhaps, to have this revenue cutter on their tail; might take his mind off recent unhappy events.

'She seems to be altering course,' he observed, 'heading inland a bit. Perhaps she's not chasing us after all.'

Ashley shook his head. 'She's on to us all right. She's going inland to cut us off from entering the Helford.'

'And what be goin' to do, then, Mester?' Zeph asked again, anxiously. 'Crowd on a bit more sail I 'spec.'

'No, no,' Ashley replied, non-committally. 'No need for that. *Heatherbelle*'s sailing very nicely as she is – and we're in no great hurry. Tide's on the make again now, and the longer we take, the more water there'll be at Porth Navas.'

Zeph felt bound to agree. 'Ais,' he said thoughtfully, 'an' if us leaves un go awhile, us'll be able to bring 'er alongside so's the ladies an' gent'lmen can step ashore, like.' Then he added, 'But, 'twad be a pile better not to have they revenue fellas comin' aboard we, don' ee think so, Mester?'

Ashley suppressed a smile. As Sir Andrew had accurately assumed, he was glad to be playing out this little charade; it took his mind off the painfully recurring thought of Rose, and anything that did that was to be welcomed.

After a pause, he said, 'Yes, it would be rather a nuisance to have to heave-to while they come scrambling all over us – especially as we're sailing so sweetly. So, we'll lead 'em a bit of a dance, shall we . . . give 'em a good run for their money, eh?'

Zeph did not like the sound of this; although it was good to see the Mester in more cheerful spirits – back in his old fighting mood, in fact – the words brought back echoes of the past, desperate actions, hideous memories. 'Give 'em the slip,' the old Mester had said; Zeph remembered the words as though said only yesterday – a feature of growing old, it seemed. Yes, 'Give 'em the slip,' he'd said – and then came disaster!

Even less did Zeph like the sound of Ashley's words when he observed the adjustment to the tiller which brought *Heatherbelle II* round on to a more westerly course.

Straight ahead, Zeph knew without even looking, lay the dreaded Manacles!

How it all came flooding back! The eerie spectre of grey-white sails looming out of the darkness; Tom Pengelly's bonfire blazing out its warning from Rosemullion Head; the old Mester's decision to 'Give 'em the slip' by risking a passage through the Manacles channel; the unbounded joy of apparent success – and then, suddenly, the awful realisation that the rudder had gone and the ship was at the mercy of the raging seas around her.

The intervening years slipped away like the diffusion of a cloud. In Zeph's mind he was back once more with the old Mester, Amos Penberth, in the fast-sailing lugger *Percuel Rose* . . . and being chased by the same God-damned Revenue ship.

The two situations were so uncomfortably similar. Away over the starboard quarter the Revenue cutter could be seen also to have altered course – but in the opposite direction. She was rapidly narrowing the gap, and it was clear she would now be able to intercept the lugger before they could reach the entrance to the Helford River.

'She'm aimin' to block us out of Falmouth, that's for certain,' Zeph observed sourly. 'She'm goin' to take us on the landward side.'

'And she'll keep us out of Helford, as well,' Sir Andrew added dryly. 'She's determined to seal off every bolt-hole.' He thoughtfully rubbed the pepper-and-salt beard which had grown during captivity. 'Had ye better not set ye'r topsails, laddie?' he queried with some diffidence. 'She seems to be gaining on us a wee bit fast, don't ye think?'

Still the enigmatic smile played around Ashley's mouth. 'Can't expect otherwise,' he replied, almost carelessly, '*Heatherbelle II* was built for speed, it's true – and normally she'd outstrip one of those revenue cutters – but we've got a fair bit of extra weight aboard, remember.'

Having long since taken over the tiller from Zeph, he kept on steering – straight for the Manacles.

Eventually, it became too much for Zeph. He could remain silent no longer.

'Mester Ashley,' he began, tentatively, 'I knows you'm doin' this for I – and 'tis no use me pertendin' Jack an' me didn't put a fair pile o' goods aboard – but I must beg ee not to try it, Mester. I knows I shouldn't ought to be tellin' ee now – because I promised the Mestress long ago that I wouldn't ever tell ee – but 'twas the tryin' o' what I believe you'm goin' to do that killed Mester Amos, your own father, all they years gone by.'

The admission, and the memory, had touched Zeph deeply. He was shaking. And seeing this, Ashley put an arm round the faithful old friend, saying, 'It's all right, Zeph, I knew you'd stowed a few 'mementoes' of days gone by – and I've known for a long time what happened to my father. So you needn't worry about that.'

'An' then you'll alter course, Mester . . . make for the Helford, just like if we had no trouble. An' if we get cotched, Mester, I'll take the whip. . . .'

Ashley shook his head. 'Not yet, Zeph. Not just yet.' He gave Zeph's lean, craggy shoulder a companionable squeeze. 'And if you'll take a look at the cutter now, Zeph, I think you'll see something interesting.'

Both Zeph and Sir Andrew followed Ashley's glance. Sure enough, Revenue cruiser *Vixen* had altered direction again and was making out to sea.

'See what I mean,' Ashley murmured. 'She daren't follow me through the Manacles – no commander would ever dare hazard one of His Majesty's ships like that – so he's giving himself plenty of sea room, expecting to be able to pick me up as I come through the channel.'

Zeph sadly shook his head. 'That be just what Mester Amos, your father, was aimin' to do when the keelson struck a rock an' the rudder sheared. So I beg of ee, Mester, don't ee go makin' the same mistake, or there'll be another terrible accident, an' you'll never forgive yersel'.'

'Things are different now, though, Zeph,' Ashley countered with a grim smile, 'the weather's not so bad, for one thing. You must admit that.'

'No, zur, the weather ted'n so bad, I'll grant ee that, but

382

there be nothin' different about they Manacles. They rocks is just the same as ever they was – an' you'm only needin' one mistake, an' you'm wrecked. I tell ee, Mester.'

By now the Revenue cruiser had made enough sea room so that she could go about and then come sou'-sou' west on a port tack, taking the lugger as she came through the Manacle group, and running her into Coverack.

It was exactly as it had been all those years ago, Zeph ruefully reflected – except that then it was Mester Amos Penberth at the helm, while this time it was his son.

And that son was still doggedly holding his course – heading straight for the narrow, treacherous channel through the Manacles – and, mystifyingly, being in no hurry. No order had been given to hoist the topsails. Puzzling, Zeph thought. If the Mester was planning to make a run for it, then surely *Heatherbelle II* needed every stitch of canvas she could carry. And why was the Revenue ship being allowed to get into such an advantageous position, like a cat sitting outside a mousehole, well south of the Manacles and ready to pounce on the lugger as she came out through the channel?

In a matter of minutes, Zeph had his answer.

'Stand by to go about,' came Ashley's voice – urgent, excited – forgetting the past, concentrating on the present. Thankful for the chance of positive action, Zeph scrambled for'ard, followed by Sir Andrew and his brother, to man the dipping lugsails.

'Ready about,' came the follow up order; then '*LEE-O!*'

With a lovely, smooth movement, round came the bows of *Heatherbelle II* – reassuringly, until they pointed directly at the entrance to the Helford River.

'Stand by to hoist topsails!' Ashley's voice rang out, . . . then, 'Up topsails!'

At last Zeph knew what the Mester was about. He'd waited until the Revenue cruiser was fully committed to her course, well south of the Manacles, before doubling back on his tracks. By now, *Heatherbelle II* was dancing along before the wind, heading for the Helford and safety, while the

Revenue ship *Vixen* was out there, on the far side of the Manacles, cumbrously swinging round on to the opposite tack – duped and infuriated – but determined to continue the chase.

But, for once, the cat had been too clever; the mouse had got back into its hole.

CHAPTER THIRTY TWO

The secrets of all hearts

Soon after half-past four on a peerless June afternoon, the Plymouth coach thundered into Falmouth. It had been travelling since seven o'clock that morning, and the passengers, especially those riding on the outside, were hot, dusty and tired.

Inside the Royal Hotel, Ashley was waiting. He had arrived early because he always enjoyed the ceaseless bustle and stir of the place whenever a Mail coach or a Packet ship was about to arrive or leave. Everyone was in a great hurry. With the outbreak of war the Packet Service had been extended; Falmouth was being linked with the Americas, the Mediterranean, India and the East Indies, and not only was the Royal a constant beehive of activity – porters and sailors hauling luggage in and out; boot boys running hither and thither; the washerwoman exchanging freshly laundered linen with that left by departing guests; the barber's boy armed with a 'cut throat' razor, hot water and shaving mug hurrying to the relief of some tired, unshaven traveller, while the barber himself, carelessly spilling the contents of his powder-bag, hastens upstairs in answer to some irascible dignitary's demand – the Hotel was also the most up-to-date source of news from around the world. Everyone talked; everyone had some story to relate.

Thus it was that Ashley, tankard in hand, awaited the arrival of his friend.

Johnny Innes climbed down off the exposed seats of the Mail coach and brushed a cloud of dust from his handsomely tailored frock and double-breasted waistcoat. Before he even had time to adjust his cravat, Ashley was pumping his hand.

'Good to see you, Johnny!' he beamed, 'It's been a long time. . . .'

'Too long,' Johnny retorted vehemently, 'Altogether too ruddy long, old son. But all the more delightful to see you now, you old rascal!'

One of the porters, already weighed down with other travellers' luggage, was mutely seeking instructions concerning Johnny's portmanteau. 'Leave it in the hall of the hotel, will you,' Ashley directed, 'my friend is not staying overnight.'

Then, gripping Johnny by the arm, Ashley propelled him into the hotel, saying, 'First of all you must have a long draught to wash the dust out of your gullet. What's it to be?'

'Just about anything that's wet and cool,' Johnny replied, miming the exhausted panting of an overworked dog, 'But first of all, old man, I really must pump the bilges. Although I duly anointed the bog-house at Truro, I also had a very copious thirst-quencher there in *The Red Lion*, and ever since then the old bladder's been threatening to burst!'

Ashley hurriedly led the way to the bowels of the hotel.

Standing companionably side by side at the primitive urinal, the years in between, like the excess liquid, streamed effortlessly away.

'Remember the old bog-house at Lydford?' Johnny quipped.

'Just like old times,' Ashley suggested.

'Same old stench . . . but different surroundings, eh?' Johnny laughed. 'God, but how I hated that place.'

Ashley nodded. 'Me, too. Especially that first year.'

'When you broke your leg, you mean. Don't blame you. How is it, by the way?'

'Oh, not too bad, thanks. Degory Logan did a fine job. Nearly did the other one in not so long ago, though.'

'You did . . .? What . . . broke it?'

'No. Stopped a bullet.'

'Good God! What sort of bullet?'

'A French bullet.'

Johnny stared . . . buttoning up the small falls of his nankeen breeches. 'A bloody French bullet! Don't tell me you've been out there already when we haven't even got into the scrap!'

'Tell you later,' Ashley agreed. 'We've got plenty of time to talk. That's the best of it. But first of all, let's get a drink.'

'Not till I've got rid of some of this Cornish grime, old son. Where's the wash room? I suppose you *have* heard of soap and water in this barbaric outpost!' Johnny mocked.

'You'll be on the next coach out of Cornwall,' Ashley threatened, gesturing pugilistically, 'unless you can produce something better than that!'

Since leaving Lydford College, eight years ago, Ashley had been able to link up with Johnny only at infrequent intervals – but they had always kept in touch. Like Ashley, after first leaving school Johnny had stayed at home leading the fairly idle life of a country gentleman's son and helping his father run the Goff's Hall estate, simply because he had not by then been able to make up his mind about what exactly he wanted to do with his life. His father had wished his son to follow him into the Army but Johnny had demurred. From his mother he had inherited artistic talents, and the prospect of a purely military existence seemed unacceptably stultifying. But when it became increasingly clear that, despite efforts to remain aloof from the conflict in Europe, Pitt would inevitably be drawn into war with France, Colonel Innes had purchased a commission for five hundred pounds and Johnny had joined his father's old regiment as a Lieutenant. It had been what his father had wanted all along, Johnny knew, and because he was very fond of the old man, son was happy enough to discuss with father interminable anecdotes about 'the regiment.'

Washed and brushed – and seated comfortably in the Royal Hotel with a tankard of refreshing best porter – Johnny subjected Ashley to a long, quizzical inspection, 'Now then,' he smiled suspiciously, 'just what *have* you been up to, eh. When I got your letter saying you were engaged to marry Jeannie MacKenzie and would I be your groomsman,

387

I thought you must have made a slip o' the pen. I always thought it was the younger sister, Alethea, you were fond of.'

Ashley knew that Johnny was watching him closely. Without meeting his eyes, he said, 'Yes, I was – but that was quite a long time ago. In any case, Alethea's decided to take the veil.'

'To take the v. . . .' Johnny almost exploded, 'To become a nun, you mean. Oh, my godfathers!'

Ashley smiled at Johnny's horror. 'Not quite your line of country, eh, Johnny. And not mine, either. But evidently it suits some people – and Alethea's one of them. She's been searching for it all her life. It's transformed her. I think it has something to do with the fact that her mother died giving birth to her – or very soon afterwards, I understand. It seems that Alethea's been searching for a maternal figure ever since – and in 'mother church', as it were, she seems to have found it.'

'Good God!' Johnny murmured uncomprehendingly, 'That *is* bad luck. And where is she now – in a convent somewhere, I suppose.'

'No. As a matter of fact, she is – or was, anyway, – a prisoner in a château in France.'

'Godstrewth! but that's terrible!'

Ashley nodded. 'I thought so too – so I went over to bring her back.'

'What – with a war on!'

Again Ashley nodded. 'We went in at night, mind. Had to wait for the tide to be right, of course. Her father had already been over to try and bring her back, but the very day he got there, war was declared.'

'Oh, my Lordy! What happened to him?'

'They seized his schooner and shut him up in the same prison.'

'The two of them. So you felt in honour bound to go over and bring 'em back?'

'That's it,' Ashley agreed, inhaling deeply, 'but Alethea wouldn't come. Refused to leave the Carmelite sisters who

388

were in the same prison; said she'd found what she'd been looking for all her life.'

'Hell's bells! What on earth did you do?'

'Had to leave her behind. There was nothing else. Her father tried – and I tried – but there was absolutely no persuading her. She was adamant; determined to stay.'

Johnny sounded genuinely distressed. 'So you had to leave her then – among all those bloodthirsty cut-throats! Egad! but I don't care for the sound of that!' He frowned deeply. 'And what about her father then?'

'Oh, we got him away, all right – and his brother and family – and several others as well, including, I may say, a very attractive French widow who seems to be coming up on the rails pretty fast alongside Sir Andrew!'

Johnny flexed his eyebrows meaningfully. 'June in Cornwall – gorse in bloom – romance filling the air, eh?' he chaffed. And then, returning to a subject more appropriate to his social ambience, he went on, 'But what about the bullet in your leg? How did that happen?'

'I went back to try and . . .' Ashley checked, quickly brushing the memory aside. 'Oh, it happened in the general turmoil,' he covered. 'You know . . . soldiers dashing about, firing muskets . . . that sort of thing.'

Johnny noticed the hesitation; made no comment. Instead, 'Quite a scramble, in fact,' he said admiringly, 'Which leg? Not the one you broke at Lydford!'

'No, the other one,' Ashley grinned, '. . . just to even things up.'

Johnny grimaced – the same old Johnny, Ashley mused, hardly changed at all; the good-hearted fellow who, with Braund and Courtier, had carried him back to the school and into the kindly hands of Mistress Chisholm. Funny how schoolboy memories remained so sharply etched; funny, too, that then it had been Mistress Chisholm whereas this time, so recently, the hands had been those of the alluring Madame de Levoisier.

'Ever go back there?' Johnny asked, as though reading Ashley's thoughts, 'to Lydford, I mean.'

Ashley shook his head. 'Never. I don't think I could stomach the Reverend Doctor Chaunter. . . .'

'With his smooth, woolly voice. . . .'

'And his 'Come here, boy, and look at my *Nemeobius lucina*,' Ashley mimicked. 'D' you remember. . . .?'

'Do I not!' Johnny retorted with disgust. 'The stupid old fart!'

Simultaneously they both raised their tankards. 'To Lydford!' they toasted – and then each made a very rude noise.

They laughed – as overgrown schoolboys sometimes will – and then Ashley said, 'Well, now, the mater's expecting us for supper, so we mustn't keep her waiting. She's greatly looking forward to seeing you again after all this time.'

'That's good of her,' Johnny smiled. 'Such a delightful person, your mater.'

But before leaving the Royal, Johnny insisted on calling for a refill of their tankards so that he might drink a toast – the first of many, as it turned out, – to tomorrow's bridegroom. This he did with due solemnity, spiced, of course, with much ribaldry, and then Ashley took him down to the hotel carriage park and introduced him to his new vehicle.

'Egad! Ashley,' Johnny chortled, 'but it looks just like the sawn-off front half of a stage coach. What on earth do they call that!'

Poker-faced, Ashley informed, 'A high cocking cart, Johnny.'

'A high *cocking* cart!' Johnny exploded, doubling up with laughter. 'Oh, no, Ash . . . I just can't believe it. A high cocking cart for a man about to be married! It's too rich! It's just too good to be true!'

'It's the latest thing,' Ashley gurgled, 'it really is. It's real purpose in life is to carry fighting cocks in this boot under the high seat. Here,' he continued, opening the door at the rear and flinging Johnny's portmanteau into the unsoiled interior, 'your bag shall keep company with the cocks.'

On the way to Treworden – both groom and groomsman already in high spirits – Johnny turned to Ashley saying, 'But seriously, Ash, you haven't so far said a word about the blushing bride. I mean . . . does she blush as prettily as her sister?'

'Of course she does,' Ashley replied very firmly, 'just as prettily. The only difference is she blushes rather less often. She's more 'worldly' than Alethea – more sophisticated. Also, she's a couple of years or so older. But she's *very* beautiful.'

Johnny noticed the firmness with which he spoke; almost as though convincing himself, he thought.

But Ashley was speaking again. 'In any case, Johnny, you've met her; I introduced you to both of them the last time you were down staying with us. Don't you remember?'

'Yes, yes, of course I do. She's the one with those lovely dark curls; the Meissen complexion; the dancing, vivacious eyes. Oh, yes, I remember her well – very attractive.' Then, turning to face Ashley squarely, Johnny added, 'In fact, you're a very lucky man, old son.'

Without returning his gaze, but concentrating on keeping the high-flying cocking cart on the track leading up to the smithy at Mawnan, Ashley replied simply, 'Yes, I know I am, Johnny.'

They drove on – rather recklessly fast, Johnny thought, – until the low-windowed, thatch roofed outline of *The Red Lion Inn* came into view, when Ashley hauled on the reins, saying, 'This is my last night of bachelorhood, my friend. What say you – we paint the *Red Lion* even redder, eh!'

Leaping down from the high seat of the cocking cart, then ducking low to avoid the lintel of an entrance doorway not constructed to admit men of their height, they strode into the front parlour of the ancient inn.

The room was empty – and there was no one behind the bar.

Not for the first time was Ashley struck by the similarity between *The Red Lion* at Mawnan and *The Three Tuns Inn* at St Keverne. Both inside and out, the resemblance was remarkable; and in a breath-catching moment of transitory aberration, he found himself half expecting Rose to emerge from the shadows. The sensation – the memory – stabbed like a knife, twisted painfully in a wound only partially healed.

But Johnny was speaking; breaking in on the fleeting reverie, dragging him back to the present. 'A bit like that inn up at Pendoggett, remember,' he was saying. 'That day when the mist rolled out of the sea; and when we stumbled upon those bloody wreckers. D' you remember?'

Determinedly brushing the other memory from his mind, Ashley nodded. 'Shall I ever forget.'

'And I remember you saying,' Johnny went on, 'that if ever you got the chance to have a go at those buggers. . . .'

Again Ashley nodded. 'Yes, I remember that, too.'

'And did you ever get a chance?'

Ashley took a deep breath. 'Yes, I did,' he agreed, a note of sadness creeping into his voice, 'thanks to some very courageous help from a young . . . er, from a young . . . er, person,' he cleared his throat noisily, then continued rather too hurriedly, 'and with timely assistance from a detachment of dragoons stationed out at Helston, we caught the devils red-handed, in *flagrante delicto*, as it were.'

'Good for you!' Johnny admired. 'I knew you would, eventually. And you brought 'em to book, of course.'

'Oh yes. They were convicted on the very day we declared war on France. But let's not talk about that,' Ashley said, brushing the subject out of his mind, 'Let us drink, eat and be merry – and in that order – because tomorrow we . . . we . . .'

Johnny grimaced – pretending tears streaming down his cheeks – put one arm around the groom, and in dirge-like tones, lamented, 'we lose the noblest 'high cocker' of 'em all!'

Simultaneously, they thumped the bar, shouting, 'Ale, wench! Bring us ale!' and from the nether regions of *The Red Lion Inn* emerged the more than ample figure of Melwyn Trevease.

'Evenin', Mister Penberth,' she sniggered, 'you'm quite a stranger, these days. An' what be your fancy tonight, sir?'

'Set 'em up, Melly,' Ashley demanded, with unusual harshness, 'Set 'em up! Two large tankards of best porter, Melly, and a chaser of spirits to go with each.'

'But, sir,' Melly protested, 'we'm only an ale house, as you well know, an' we'm not licenced to sell spirits.'

'Yes, yes, I'm well aware of that,' Ashley conceded, 'but I also know, Melly, that down in the cellar beneath this very room there's always been plenty of space for 'cousin jacky' and the rest of his family. So set 'em up, Mistress Melly, if you please, and look sharp about it!'

Melly blushed; it almost added a seductive charm to her plump, rough-moulded features, Johnny thought. The strong liquor recently quaffed at *The Royal Hotel* must be having its effect, he concluded; no one in their right, uninebriated mind could possibly see Melly as an object of sexual pleasure. But, with a few drinks inside a man, well. . . .

But Melly had disappeared; gone to fetch the landlord, Ashley guessed. And in a few moments, the impressive bulk of 'Tub' Richards – sinewy blacksmith by day but filler of bombards and tankards by night – loomed in the doorway from the kitchen.

'Oh-ho! So, it be you, Mester Ashley,' he boomed genially. 'My Melly she do say you'm askin' for a bit o' the strong stuff, but as you know, zur, we'm not licenced. . . .'

Ashley waved him down. 'It's quite all right, Tub,' he assured, 'I'm no longer one of His Majesty's Customs Officers, so you can go down into that cellar and bring up the best. My friend and I are celebrating a very auspicious occasion – a very auspicious occasion, indeed – so, for auld lang syne, Tub, let it be good!'

'An' what be that, then?' the landlord asked, puzzled. 'The auspicious occasion, you mean?'

'No, zur. The old lang whatever t'were.'

'Oh, that! That's an expression my future father-in-law uses. It means 'for old time's sake', Tub, – comes from a drinking song written by a young Scottish poet – ' Ashley quotes, ' "And surely ye'll be your pint-stoup, And surely I'll be mine; And we'll tak' a cup o' kindness yet, For Auld lang syne'. . . . So, bring us up a flowing pint-stoup, Tub, and let us be merry, for tomorrow the ram lamb goeth to the slaughter!'

'Just listen to him!' Johnny protested. 'The ram lamb indeed! What about the poor little ewe lamb, might I ask! Loss of maidenhead, and all that!'

Ashley feinted to give Johnny a punch in the lower abdomen; Johnny pretended to respond with a vicious uppercut; they struggled – foolishly laughing – just as they had done many years before, in the junior common room of Lydford College; grown men behaving, as they are some-times wont to do, like mindless schoolboys.

'An' how be that, then!' Tub Richards declared, placing two brimming tankards and two beakers of cognac on the bar, 'Them ought to send ee off to the slaughterhouse in good spirits, I reckon.' The effort involved in descending the narrow stairs to the cellar, then returning with filled drinking vessels had quite exhausted the blacksmith, and he stood there, enormous fists on hips, panting.

Ashley grinned wickedly. 'That's splendid, Tub. Now go down again and bring up a couple more – one for yourself and one for Melly – and then you can drink my health.'

Later, as the four of them sat carousing in the low-ceilinged homeliness of the timbered bar parlour of *The Red Lion Inn*, Tub Richards ventured, 'Ais, I yeard you was givin' up that there Customs business, Mester, – an' a good thing, too, I reckon.'

Ashley regarded an old friend with a look of mock severity. 'You were lucky, *Mister* Richards! For no more than a couple of thatcher's sways I'd have had you in Launceston goal, and you know it.'

The blacksmith smiled mischievously. 'Aw, 'twas that there splint I made for ee, wadn un. 'Twas so good, it kept ee lookin' up into the skies wi' thanksgivin' so's ee wouldn' see what was goin' on all around ee, like.'

394

Nods, winks and nudges all round, and then Tub continued, 'Aw, but 'tis a fine thing, Mester Ashley, – you gettin' away from they Customs folk. 'Tweren't quite the right colourin' for ee, were it. An' you'm actin' pertikler sensible, I reckon, by takin' on the managerin' o' Sir Andrew's farms, like.' He flashed a prodigious wink at his two customers before adding, 'Pertikler shrewd, I'd say. . . . Ais, pertikler shrewd.'

'Hear, hear!' applauded Johnny, 'Very shrewd, indeed. Managing the master's estates, and – like the biblical Jacob – marrying the master's elder daughter.'

' 'Tis ever so excitin',' put in the starry-eyed Melly. 'Us'll all be down at the church tomorrow to see ee get wed, sir. All of us.'

'Aw, ais,' agreed Tub, beaming, 'Us'll be there, all right. Ted'n every day o' the week that one o' us, like, gets wed to one o' they. One o' the 'quality', I'm meanin',' he added, just in case anyone was in doubt. 'An' I'm right pleased,' he went on, raising his tankard to Ashley, 'to be wishin' you, zur, an' Miss Jeannie up at the big house, there, good health and lasting happiness together in the future, zur, I'm sure.' He up-ended his tankard, draining it at a gulp.

Further Burnsian 'pint-stoups' . . . increasingly glowing bonhomie . . . deteriorating bawdiness . . . and, at last, merry groom and groomsman staggered from *The Red Lion Inn*, climbed with some difficulty aboard the mountainous cocking cart, and set out for Treworden.

On the way, they passed the entrance drive to Boscraddoc, and with an airy wave of the hand, Ashley indicated, 'Manager's farm house, Johnny. That's where Jeannie and I'll be staying tomorrow night, and then that'll be our home after we come back from the honeymoon.'

'Very pleasant I should say, old stick,' Johnny replied, his mind full of lascivious thoughts about that first night, 'You should be very comfortable there, both tomorrow night *and* afterwards. Good of Sir Andrew to provide such an excellent love-nest, eh what?'

'Handsome, indeed,' Ashley responded with genuine warmth. 'No man could wish for a better father-in-law. Ever since we brought him home from France, he's been kindness itself. In fact,' he added, trying to prevent the countryside from swaying so much, 'he's been so lavish with his offers of help that sometimes it's been quite difficult to refuse.'

Marianne Penberth was waiting – patiently, but with impatience – as nearly all mothers will. Her son and his groomsman were late arriving; she half expected that. But not so late as this. At the same time she kept reminding herself it was his last night as a bachelor. By this time tomorrow he would be married to a MacKenzie girl – and that, after all, was what she had hoped and prayed for most fervently through the years. So she mustn't complain – even if he was rather late coming home.

Wisely, she had prepared a cold supper – ham, tongue and cold roast beef; eggs in their shells; a large bowl of mixed salads; apricot tart and apple pie with cream – all laid out on the large dining room table. But she also had a skillet of soup being kept warm on the kitchen range for when 'the two boys', as she thought of them, eventually arrived.

Wisely, too, having warmly greeted her guest and remained chatting for half an hour or so, she prepared to take herself off to bed, saying, 'Now don't you two boys be sitting up late; you've a very busy and important day ahead of you, don't forget.'

She kissed her son 'Good-night', – for the very last time as 'hers', she reflected rather sadly – then formally, if somewhat awkwardly, presented her hand to her guest, expressing the sincerest hope that he would sleep well, and then left the room.

'What a truly charming person your mater is,' Johnny remarked, returning once more to the demolishment of the apricot tart. 'She's going to miss you, I'm afraid.'

'I shan't be far away,' Ashley assured. 'No more than a couple of gun shots, really. You saw the house.'

The meat, the bread, the potato salad and the pastry tart were all now having their much-needed absorbent effect, and after a visit to the newly-installed Bramah valve closet – the envy of the neighbourhood – groom and groomsman settled down, each with a glass of best white cognac, for a final nightcap. The chairs on either side of the fireplace, were comfortable rather than ornate, the good food had filled the vacant spaces, and the strong wine now infused the whole of life's prospect with a feeling of well-being. It was the hour for reverie, for the loosening of tongues, for the exchange of confidences.

Gently swilling the brandy around and around in his glass, Johnny said, 'Tell me about that rescue effort, Ash, that must have been quite a fracas.'

Ashley stared down into his balloon-shaped glass, also slowly swirling the liquid, deep in thought. 'It was,' he said at length, 'as you say, quite a fracas. I took Zeph Curnow – you remember Zeph, I expect –'

Johnny nodded. 'Yes, I remember Zeph – he's your man who runs the farm, isn't he.'

'Yes, that's right. I took Zeph with me, and . . . and . . .' He paused: took a long swig of brandy; swallowed hard, and continued . . . 'I took Zeph with me . . . We went over . . . arrived in darkness, of course . . . found the inlet . . . convenient little jetty . . . Zeph was with me, and . . . and. . . .'

Johnny was watching closely. He had never seen Ashley quite like this before; never known him show such emotion. At Lydford they'd learnt to bottle it up, keep it under. Never show emotion of any kind. 'Hard as nails, old stick. Tough as leather!' That's what they'd been taught – those were the watchwords. And Ashley was a *man*! . . . But he was having difficulty now.

'Yes, Zeph was with me,' he was continuing, trying hard to control his voice, 'And we tied up alongside all right . . . in the darkness, you understand. . . .' He drained his glass, put it on the small table beside him, leant forward, elbows on knees, stared at the floor. 'It was a castle, you understand

'. . . a typical French château . . . surrounded by a wall . . . a high wall . . . about eight or nine feet high. . . .'

'Good God!' Johnny murmured, 'How in hell did you get over that!'

'She'd brought a rope, Johnny,' Ashley continued in a strained voice, '. . . a knotted rope . . . wore it like a girdle round her habit . . . damned clever idea. . . .'

'Hold on, old son,' Johnny interrupted, 'What's this about a 'She'? Was there a girl involved as well?'

Afterwards he wished he'd never asked.

There can be few more heart-rending sights for a man than to see another man in deep, inconsolable distress. Oh, *how* are the mighty fallen! At the last part of Johnny's question, Ashley had suddenly buried his head in his hands and was now racked with uncontrollable sobbing. So quickly can revelry be turned to sorrow.

Johnny got up; stood beside Ashley's chair; gently laid a hand on his shoulder; said nothing.

Eventually, through his tears – tears that he angrily tried to dash away – Ashley was able to say, 'I loved her, Johnny . . . I loved her. She stood by me . . . and I had to leave her behind. I loved her . . . and that's the truth of it, Johnny . . . I loved her and I had to leave her behind, not knowing what had happened to her . . . not even knowing whether she's alive or dead.'

Once more he buried his head deeply in his hands, his powerful shoulders shaking as though they belonged to a small, desolate child.

'I loved her, Johnny . . . I loved her,' was all he seemed able to say . . . except to add, very softly, 'Her name was Rose.'

CHAPTER THIRTY THREE

Lawfully Joined Together

Dust-particled shafts of sunlight slant steeply through the stained glass East window, throwing a soft mosaic of colours – reds, blues, greens and yellows – onto the tiled chancel floor.

At the foot of the pulpit, and in front of the lectern, large stoneware urns, supported by sturdy oak stools, display a dramatic arrangement of white lilac, white irises, pink roses and pink carnations.

On the altar, on either side of the silver crucifix, two smaller urns of mixed sweet peas fill the chancel with their own inimitable fragrance.

The view through the clear, uncoloured South window is immaculate – the majestic Dennis Headland standing guard over the entrance to the Helford River, while the lower, more sinuous Nare Point snakes its way into the shimmering sea.

In the front pew, on the right of the centre aisle facing the altar, Ashley sits, composed and deeply thoughtful, with a much more nervous Johnny beside him. They speak only occasionally; neither of them looks round. But the constant rustle of taffeta and silk behind them confirms that the church is rapidly filling.

Above the low murmur of voices, the soothing strains of Handel's Water Music floats out from the organ pipes high above the choir stalls.

An air of excited anticipation – at times almost tangible – is steadily building up; the long-awaited moment of the bride's arrival can not now be long delayed.

For the hundredth time, Johnny feels for the ring in his pocket – as though, in the short intervals between such fumblings, a malign gremlin might have wafted it away. But it is always reassuringly there – exactly where he put it, from its box on the dressing cabinet, while he and Ashley were dressing that morning.

It had been an unusually silent breakfast time, neither groom nor groomsman feeling able to face, let alone do justice to, the fare laid out for them, but by the time they went upstairs again to don their finery, the after effects of a night's insobriety had begun to wear off. The familiar chaff and bawdy exchanges were soon returning.

No mention was made of Ashley's previous evening's emotional watershed; so far as Johnny was concerned, it would never be referred to again. Ashley knew that; he felt sure – as far as any man can feel sure – that with Johnny his secret was safe, and although in the cheerless solitude of his own bedroom he had once again given way to an over-whelming grief at the thought of Rose's unknown fate, by morning he was dry-eyed and firmly resolved to put the past behind him, dwelling only on the future. He was exceed-ingly lucky – and he knew it. He would concentrate on that.

The clip-clop of horses' hooves, the crunch of carriage wheels in gravel beyond the lych-gate, the excited crescendo of village voices outside the church – 'Aw, but aint her lovely. . . . Ah, an' she'm wearin' a veil, see. Good luck to ee, Mistress Jeannie!' – these sounds and the general stir within the church itself announce as nothing else can the arrival of the bride.

At a signal from the West door, the organist moves almost imperceptibly from Handel into the matchless beauty of Bach's *Sheep May Safely Graze*, and then, with a sound strongly resembling that of 'a mighty rushing wind', the large congregation rises to its feet.

Heads turning . . . audible gasps of admiration . . . the Rector of Mawnan taking up position on the chancel step . . . and Ashley moving into the aisle, followed immediately by his groomsman, turns to greet his bride. . . .

. . . and there, gliding gracefully towards him, and looking unbelievably beautiful in a white satin gown with train,
its silver lace overlay dancing and shimmering in the shafts of
sunshine, moves a radiant Jeannie. Her glorious thick, dark,
ringleted hair, piled high and dressed at the nape into an
elegant chignon, shines through a diaphanous lace veil. In
her right hand she carries a small bouquet of pink roses, lilies
of the valley and maidenhair fern.

Still on the arm of her handsome father she turns her lustrous eyes to her bridegroom – and in so doing she sends a
quite extraordinary vibration of desire plunging down his
spine.

'Dearly beloved, we are gathered together here in the sight
of God. . . .'

Before the bridegroom has time to absorb fully the ravishing beauty of his bride, the soul-searching process of joining
'this Man and this Woman in holy Matrimony' has been
launched on its sea of uncertainty.

'an honourable estate, instituted of God in the time of
man's innocency . . . .'

Ashley feels his mother's eye upon him . . . he knows a few
tears will be welling in her eyes; tears for the innocency of the
babe, her son, born amid circumstances of such tragedy, and
now grown to the full stature of man's estate; tears for the
memory of that father whose gravestone was no more than a
jagged Manacle rock and who did not even live to see his baby
son; tears of joy and thankfulness that the babe-grown-man
now standing there in front of her is about to be joined in wed-
lock with the daughter of such a high-born, highly esteemed
country squire.

'I require and charge you both, as ye will answer at the
dreadful day of judgement when the secrets of all hearts shall
be disclosed. . . .'

An awkward moment. '. . . the secrets of all hearts. . . .'
Quickly, brush it aside. . . .

'. . . why ye may not be lawfully joined together. . . .' It's
all right; the secrets relate to the legality . . . therefore, nothing to hide . . . not even at that *dreadful* day of judgement.

'Wilt thou have this Woman to thy wedded wife, to live together after God's ordinance in the holy estate of Matrimony . . . and forsaking all other, keep thee only unto her, so long as ye both shall live?'

Yes, he would do that; he had made up his mind. His mother wanted it – almost above all else, it seemed; Sir Andrew wanted it; Zeph had expressed respectful but undeniable approval – indeed, the whole village had apparently long since made up its mind that it was ordained; but most important of all, Jeannie seemed confidently determined that it should take place.

Firmly, therefore – unhesitatingly, 'I will.'

In the vestry, and while the organist gently streams out the notes of Bach's *Jesu, Joy of Man's Desiring*, Jeannie throws back her veil, revealing for all to see the full radiance of her beauty – her lovely, dancing eyes, her full, sensuous mouth, and the slightly flushed creamy-whiteness of her skin. Bride and bridegroom kiss – demurely, discreetly, of course – before the small group of family and close friends – but it is a kiss which promises moré – oh so very much more – in the hours that lie ahead.

Trevadne – house and garden – at its immaculate best. Rhododendrons lining the entrance drive, like a canyon of purple; lilies of the valley casting their heady scent and their biblical magic – 'consider the lilies of the field . . . they toil not, neither do they spin' – around the entrance porch; the lawns, freshly scythed that morning, their broad stripes as straight as the barrel of a gun, yet still lush with midsummer greenness; and the roses! – glorious abundance, almost overpowering fragrance, opening their silky petals to the sun and praising their heavenly designer with their smiling faces. And they grow in that terraced garden overlooked by the 'schoolroom' library which holds so many, many childhood memories for Jeannie, Ashley and Alethea.

Smiling guests offering congratulations, making small talk; Jeannie, looking quite dazzling, circulating, talking, laughing. Tables groaning with food; champagne, red and white wine, cider and brandy flowing like the rivers of

Damascus; small talk, small talk, small talk; backs beginning to ache; thankful for somewhere to sit down.

Then the cake – towering above the linen-topped table; Ashley and Jeannie cutting the first slice together – with Ashley's much cleaned and polished naval cutlass.

Ranald MacKenzie proposing 'Bride and Bridegroom', eulogising about the beauty of the bride, praising bridegroom for his courage – undying gratitude, everlasting good wishes – and then the toast.

Ashley replying – not haltingly or self-effacingly, but clearly and with forthrightness; appreciation of Sir Andrew, not only for his daughter but for many other kindnesses; a tender reference to his own mother, and a much appreciated shaft of humour at Zeph's expense.

And then it was all over.

Although the party would continue until well into the evening – it was a rare opportunity for estate workers and villagers to enjoy Sir Andrew's bountiful largesse – bride and bridegroom decided long before nine o'clock that it was time to leave. Other, less noisy delights were beckoning strongly.

To a shower of rose petals and a hail of rice – kisses and handshakes all round, and a rude, *sotto voce* reference by Johnny to the 'high cocking cart' – they climbed into Sir Andrew's coach which was to take them the short distance to their new home at Boscraddoc. Tonight, they would stay there. After that they would leave at their leisure for Sandlands, the house put at their disposal by one of Sir Andrew's wealthy friends. There would be no hurry.

The few servants at Boscraddoc were waiting to welcome their new master and mistress. Having done so, they immediately returned to the servants' quarters, very firmly closing the door behind them.

Bride and bridegroom were alone together for the first time since becoming man and wife.

In the complete privacy of their own withdrawing room, they kissed – a long, lingering, passion-kindled embrace.

And when at last they drew apart, those large, lustrous eyes of Jeannie's spoke one word only. . . . 'Bed!'

Upstairs, beside the giant four poster, Ashley took her in his arms once more, pressing her to him, smothering her neck and shoulders with hot, hungry kisses. 'You'll have to undo me,' she whispered, the taste of champagne still on her breath, her lips smouldering with the warmth of passion, 'I can't do it myself.'

Rapidly his fingers found the buttons, undid them – no more than necessary – slid the silken fabric off her shoulders, down over her breasts, let it drop. Then the underskirts. She kicked off her shoes, her arms still around his neck, and stood only in her chemise, melting against the hard contours of his body. 'It may hurt a little,' he murmured, brushing the lobe of her ear with his lips, 'at first – just a little perhaps.' In answer, she gave the merest shake of her head, moved closer . . . closer . . . pressing her thighs against his, seeking and finding his lips, devouring his mouth. Swaying and shuffling, locked as though one body, they fell back on to the bed – he still fully dressed, she in her chemise and blue-gartered white stockings only – the hunger, the urgency, the immediacy becoming intolerable. But he could not allow her sinuating body out of his grasp, could not free his hands – and yet, somehow, she knew what to do . . . how to unbutton the falls of his breeches . . . how to guide . . . how to encourage . . . and at last, ecstatically, how to surrender! And in the following glorious seconds they climbed the mountain of desire . . . up, up, up, in a rising, leaping flame of passion, scaling the heights, reaching out for the uttermost peaks . . . until, finally, groaning with repletion, panting with satiety, they slithered back down the slope of receding ecstacy.

Only in the languid aftermath did the thought recur to him that, at the supreme moment, the physical resistance to his advance had been entirely unapparent. Immediately he dismissed the speculation from his mind. It was the fulfilment that mattered, not the breadth of experience leading up to it.

Slowly, lazily, garment by garment, he shed his own clothes, casting them from him, to lie crumpled on the bedroom floor. In a single movement she peeled her chemise over her tousled head . . . drew him to her once again, closer, closer, this time flesh upon flesh; her lips sought his and found them . . . warmly caressing at first . . . then fiercely, demandingly – satisfied, yet not satisfied – wanting him, devouring him, more and yet more. His hands explored the precious mysteries of her body – the small of her back, her breasts, the exquisite contours of her soft, rounded hips – the silky smoothness of her thighs . . . she, thrilling to his touch, he, feeling once more the mounting demand of sexual hunger. Again they scaled the heights, wrestling and struggling in an ecstacy of erotic fulfilment; again they slithered slowly downwards to exhaustion and quiescence. He buried his face in those lovely soft curls; she fondling the lean strengths of his back, the muscles in his massive shoulders. Again she desired him. . . .

Three times they scaled the heights together; three times they reached the peak.

But for Ashley there was no heaven, there were no stars.

From long habit, he woke early next morning. The birds were greeting a peerless June day with their usual frenzy of joy. On the pillow beside him her face framed by a scattered mass of dark curls, Jeannie lay sleeping peacefully. He would not disturb her – but, again, from long habit, he could not lie abed. He always had to get up.

All round the giant four-poster, the bedroom floor bore comic evidence of last night's hurried 'deshabillement'; and gathering up Jeannie's excitingly feminine garments, now looking so lifeless and folorn, Ashley placed them as neatly as he could on one of the bedroom chairs. Then he picked up his own clothes and tip-toed into his dressing room.

Half an hour later, washed and shaved, and dressed in his ordinary day clothes, he descended to that haven of early morning risers, the farm kitchen. There the household staff were performing the daily rite; they were sipping a steaming hot cup of tea.

Nothing unusual about that. But what did surprise Ashley was the sight of Zeph sitting comfortably among the servants – also nursing a cup of tea.

On the well-scrubbed kitchen table in front of him lay a rectangular-shaped wooden box.

'Tiz for ee, sir,' Zeph said, handing the box to Ashley, 'her come last evenin', sir, – by boat, if ee unnerstands,' he added with an accompanying wink, 'but there weren't no chance to give it to ee, then, like.'

'Why, thank you, Zeph. But what is it? Do you know?'

'Tiz a present from France, sir . . . from my old friend, Jack Duboyes, if you remember. Him what did help we when us went over. . . .'

'Yes, yes, I remember,' Ashley replied sharply, cutting him off in anticipation of a reference to the rescue, and not wishing to be reminded of it, 'But what on earth could he be sending me, d'you think?'

'Aw, I dunno, sir; couldn' say.'

'A wedding present?. . . . Surely not.'

'Aw, no, sir, couldn' hardly be that. Jack, he do be a very generous fellow – but there be no way Jack could know ee was gettin' wed, sir.'

Ashley was prizing off the lid. 'Well, how did this come over, then, Zeph?'

'By one o' the boats, sir,' Zeph replied enigmatically, adding, 'An' as you'm well aware, Mester Ashley, in spite of the war, there do still be some that go a-smugglin'.'

Ashley smiled; as if he didn't know! Removing the lid, he saw that the box contained a bottle packed in straw – a bottle of cognac, no doubt. How kind of Jacques. But why was he sending a present to someone he scarcely knew!

He lifted the bottle carefully from the box – and as he did so his eye lighted on something which, in a moment of sudden premonition, made him catch his breath.

Lying in the straw, wrapped in what looked like a strip torn from an underskirt, was a small round object.

Unwrapping it gently, he saw that the piece of cloth contained, as the premonition had warned him, a small, gold enamelled locket bearing the initials 'L de V'.

Without doubt it was the locket that had belonged to Rose – the locket thrust into Sampson Roskruge's hand when, having plucked the child from the raging seas around him, he then tried to save the drowning mother – the locket which Rose had always felt must hold the key to her true identity.

But why had it been sent to him? Did it mean, as he now feared, that Rose was dead – that it was the only thing of value she had to bequeath – and somehow, by some miracle of divine intervention, it had found its way to the only man she had loved.

Or was it meant to convey some message – some positive indication that she was still alive!

He opened the locket. There was nothing inside; no message of any kind; only those exquisitely painted miniatures of the two French aristocrats with their haughty expressions.

And then he saw it! . . . on the strip of cotton scrawled in what could have been blood, the words 'PRISON at BREST'.

It was well known there was a guillotine at Brest.

He had been riding for the best part of an hour; it mattered little where he went. He needed to ride. It was something he had been doing for most of his life, and it was familiar things he needed now; the pungent smells of horse and saddle leather; the sight in front of him of Puncher's head with those pricked, intelligent ears, pumping up and down in sturdy, characteristic manner; the familiar clip-clop of hooves against flinted track. Above all, he needed time – time to think.

Without fully realising – or even caring very much – where they were going, he found that Puncher had climbed to the top of Rosemullion Head – a beauty spot which, over the years, had become a favourite place for quiet meditation.

Away to his left, Pendennis Castle rose above the swirling early morning mist; down to his right, gentle wavelets teased the rocks of Mawnan Shear.

He pulled Puncher to a halt; sat slumped in the saddle – gazing out to sea. Behind him, still sleeping peacefully in the four-poster at Boscraddoc, was the woman who, only yesterday, had become his wife . . . 'to have and to hold from this day forward, ...'

Ahead of him, across the formidable waters of the English Channel, and languishing in the foul stench of a revolutionary prison, was the girl he loved . . . and she was in mortal danger.

Must this be the end of his love for her, he wondered, . . . or was it really only the beginning!

Author's Note

THE RIDING OFFICER is fiction; any resemblance which the main characters may have to persons either living or dead is entirely accidental.

In making the background as authentic as possible, the following books have been consulted:-

1. The Autobiography of a Cornish Smuggler – Captain Harry Carter 1749–1809
2. Smuggling in Cornwall – by Cyril Noall
3. Coastguard – by William Webb
4. The Smugglers – by Lord Teignmouth and C.G. Harper
5. The Wesleys in Cornwall – by JohnPearce
6. A History of Cornish Mail & Stage Coaches – by Cyril Noall
7. Sailing Drifters – by E.J. March
8. A History of Cornwall – by F.E. Halliday
9. Davidson's History of Truro Grammar and Cathedral School
10. Heart of Oak – by G.J. Marcus
11. The British Army in North America 1775–1783 – by R. May
12. The Duke of Cornwall's Light Infantry – by R. Goldsmith
13. Clean and Decent – by Lawrence Wright
14. A History of Underclothes – by C. Willett & P. Cunnington

15. British Naval Dress – by Dudley Jarrett
16. Cornish Shipwrecks – by Richard Larn & Clive Carter
17. Brittany and Normandy – by Mary Elsy
18. Portrait of Brittany – by Marion Deschamps
19. Brittany & Channel Islands Cruising Guide – by D. Jefferson
20. A History of Light Houses – by Patrick Beaver
21. The French Revolution 1788–1792 – by G. Salvemini
22. The French Pilot, Vol 2 – by Malcolm Robson

23. Dress in Eighteenth Century England – by Anne Buck
24. Eighteenth Century English Costume – by C. W. & P. Cunnington
25. Costume in Pictures – by Phillis Cunnington
26. The Englishman's Food – by J.C. Drummond & Anne Wilbraham
27. Around Helston in the Old Days – by A.S. Oates
28. The History of Falmouth – by Dr. James Whetter
29. Words from a Cornish Village – The Parish of St. Keverne
30. Discovering Horse-Drawn Carriages – by D.J. Smith
31. England in Modern Times 1714–1930 – by Robert Rayner
32. A Short History of the English People – by J.R. Green
33. The World's Great Guns – by Frederick Wilkinson
34. How to Collect Old Furniture – by F. Litchfield
35. The Packet Captains – by M.E. Philbrick
36. Old Falmouth – by Susan E. Gay
37. Encyclopaedia Britannica and other encyclopaedias

PROMISES AND LIES
by Susanne Jaffe

Hers was a Cinderella story in search of a happy ending. As a shy girl in a small Midwest town, Valerie Cardell longed to escape her hateful life – and the violent family who abused her with their tyrannical jealousies and bitterness. But she shocked them all when she rose from her nightmarish life to marry David Kinnelon, society's most eligible, most desired bachelor.

Now a ravishing New York socialite, Valerie revels in a glittering world of dreams come true. With David by her side, she discovers a wealth of happiness so long denied her. But soon her dream is threatened by those who seek to bring the glorious Kinnelon empire crashing down, whose blind hatred could destroy Valerie's dazzling world forever . . . her own family.

Here is a magnificent, emotionally gripping novel of a woman fighting for a life to match her most secret desires, for a love to fulfil her deepest passions . . . yet a woman haunted by a past she could never escape.

0 553 17165 8   £1.95

JEALOUSIES
by Justin Marlowe

Sweeping the globe from Ireland to the fabulous ranches of the Australian Outback, from the *haut monde* world of Paris to Maryland's lush horse country – a tumultuous novel of two sisters, torn apart by ambition, betrayal, and their consuming passion for the same man . . .

JEALOUSIES

SHANNON. Her face is her fortune. Her incandescent and exotic beauty have propelled her from the dreary life of a ranch hand's daughter to conquest of the high-fashion world of Paris, London, and New York – but she would always be seeking the affections of the one man it seemed she could never have.

KERRY. She always lived in the shadow of her older sister Shannon's success – until finally her own chance comes. A superbly talented horsewoman, she unscrupulously schemes her way into one of Maryland's wealthiest horse breeding families, where she hopes to marry into a new life of power and privilege. And love doesn't need to be part of the package.

Shannon and Kerry each had a first love – that love was the same man. He was a handsome aristocrat who had eyes only for Shannon – until Kerry's one, jealous, impulsive act drove him out of Shannon's life, seemingly forever. Now, the rebellious, feisty Kerry is forced to turn to her sister for help – and Shannon is about to learn the full truth of Kerry's terrible betrayal.

0 553 17205 0 £2.95

THIS CHERISHED DREAM
by Barbara Harrison

'It was a man's world,' young Mary Kilburne had been told, 'and a woman could only find a place in it.' And find a place in it she did! Making her way to America's golden shores with nothing except a few pennies and her pride, the ambitious, chestnut-haired beauty was unwilling to give in to despair or concede to defeat. She was determined to work hard, to become rich, to rise above the Lower East Side squalor-even to give up a once-in-a-lifetime passion if it meant that she would succeed.

From the black mists of the moors to the elegance and grandeur of Sutton Place, from an insecure scullery maid to a poised, prominent empire builder, through two world wars and the Great Depression, Mary Kilburne sacrificed happiness, betrayed her own heart, but always fought for

This Cherished Dream

0 553 17185 2   £2.95

A SELECTED LIST OF NOVELS
AVAILABLE FROM BANTAM BOOKS

The prices shown below were correct at the time of going to press. However Transworld Publishers reserve the right to show new retail prices on covers which may differ from those previously advertised in the text or elsewhere.

☐	17172 0	**WILD SWAN**	*Celeste de Blasis*	£2.95
☐	17252 2	**SWAN'S CHANCE**	*Celeste de Blasis*	£2.95
☐	17240 9	**THE ALCHEMIST**	*Kenneth Goddard*	£2.95
☐	17354 5	**BALEFIRE**	*Kenneth Goddard*	£2.95
☐	17205 0	**JEALOUSIES**	*Justine Harlowe*	£2.95
☐	17185 2	**THIS CHERISHED DREAM**	*Barbara Harrison*	£2.95
☐	17208 5	**PASSION'S PRICE**	*Barbara Harrison*	£2.95
☐	17165 8	**PROMISES AND LIES**	*Susanne Jaffe*	£1.95
☐	17151 8	**SCENTS**	*Johanna Kingsley*	£2.95
☐	17207 7	**FACES**	*Johanna Kingsley*	£2.95
☐	17174 7	**MISTRAL'S DAUGHTER**	*Judith Krantz*	£2.95
☐	17389 8	**PRINCESS DAISY**	*Judith Krantz*	£3.50
☐	17204 2	**THE SICILIAN**	*Mario Puzo*	£2.95
☐	17209 3	**THE CLASS**	*Erick Segal*	£2.95
☐	17192 5	**THE ENCHANTRESS**	*Han Suyin*	£2.95
☐	17150 X	**TILL MORNING COMES**	*Han Suyin*	£3.50

ORDER FORM

All these books are available at your book shop or newsagent, or can be ordered direct from the publisher. Just tick the titles you want and fill in the form below.

Transworld Publishers, Cash Sales Department,
61–63 Uxbridge Road, Ealing, London, W5 5SA

Please send cheque or postal order, not cash. All cheques and postal orders must be in £ sterling and made payable to Transworld Publishers Ltd.

Please allow cost of book(s) plus the following for postage and packing:

U.K./Republic of Ireland Customers:
Orders in excess of £5; no charge
Orders under £5; add 50p

Overseas Customers:
All orders; add £1.50

NAME (Block Letters) ....

ADDRESS ....